P9-DNX-703

THE NESTING DOLLS

Other Joanne Kilbourn Mysteries
by Gail Bowen

Deadly Appearances
Murder at the Mendel (U.S. ed., *Love and Murder*)
The Wandering Soul Murders
A Colder Kind of Death
A Killing Spring
Verdict in Blood
Burying Ariel
The Glass Coffin
The Last Good Day
The Endless Knot
The Brutal Heart

THE NESTING DOLLS

A JOANNE KILBOURN MYSTERY

GAIL
BOWEN

McCLELLAND & STEWART

Library and Archives Canada Cataloguing in Publication

Bowen, Gail, 1942–
The nesting dolls / Gail Bowen.

ISBN 978-0-7710-1275-4

I. Title.

PS8553.08995N47 2010   C813'.54   C2010-901466-9

We acknowledge the financial support of the Government of Canada through the Book Publishing Industry Development Program and that of the Government of Ontario through the Ontario Media Development Corporation's Ontario Book Initiative. We further acknowledge the support of the Canada Council for the Arts and the Ontario Arts Council for our publishing program.

Published simultaneously in the United States of America by McClelland & Stewart Ltd., P.O. Box 1030, Plattsburgh, New York 12901

Library of Congress Control Number: 2010923468

Typeset in Trump Mediaeval by M&S, Toronto
Printed and bound in the United States of America

This book is printed on acid-free paper that is 100% recycled, ancient-forest friendly (100% post-consumer recycled).

McClelland & Stewart Ltd.
75 Sherbourne Street
Toronto, Ontario
M5A 2P9
www.mcclelland.com

1 2 3 4 5   14 13 12 11 10

For our grandchildren, Kai, Madeleine,
Lena, Chesney, Ben, Peyton,
and Alexandra Kate Bowen,
with love and gratitude

CHAPTER

1

There is not much stillness in my husband's life. He is a trial lawyer and a paraplegic – two factors that don't contribute to longevity. So, that Saturday afternoon in December, when I walked into the family room and found Zack and our mastiff, Pantera, gazing at the ten-foot Nova Scotia fir we'd chosen the day before, I felt a frisson of joy. Outside, the wind howled, the trees swayed and creaked, and the sky was dark with the threat of snow; inside, a fire burned low in the grate, the air was pungent with the sharpness of evergreen, and the man I loved was at peace with his dog beside him. It was over three weeks until Christmas, but our fourteen-year-old daughter, Taylor, had jump-started the season by hanging her collection of crystal stars in the windows, where they sparkled, evoking memories of other Christmases, other lives. I placed my hands on Zack's shoulders and rested my chin on his head. "'The house and the hall were lit with happiness,'" I said. "'And lords and ladies were luminous with joy.'"

Zack covered my hands with his. "Now that *is* beautiful," he said.

"It's from *Sir Gawain and the Green Knight.* I bought a copy last year and tucked it in with the Christmas decorations, thinking we could read it to the granddaughters when they're older."

"We're older," Zack said. "We could read it now."

"You'd like it. A green knight with a green beard rides his green horse into King Arthur's court at Christmas. The green knight takes out his axe and offers it to whichever of Arthur's knights will cut off his head."

Zack turned his chair around to face me. "The green knight wants somebody to cut off *his* head?"

"There's a catch. Whoever wields the axe must agree to be struck in return."

"By the guy whose head he just lopped off?"

"That's the challenge."

Zack chortled. "Blood in, blood out – my kind of story."

"In that case, when we get back here after the concert, we'll warm up some soup, build a fire, and start reading."

Zack held out his arms. "Who has more fun than us?"

"Nobody," I said. "Nobody has more fun than us."

It's not easy for a man in a wheelchair and an able-bodied woman to embrace, but Zack and I had had practice. When my husband ran his hand up my leg, he groaned with pleasure. "You're wearing the black slip," he said. "God, I love this slip."

"I'm wearing it because we have a party to go to. 'Tis the season, remember?"

"The Wainbergs' party, then the choir thing," he said.

"Speaking of the choir thing," I said, "I have something for you." I handed him a manila envelope. Zack opened it and grinned. "Hey, that's the photo that was in the paper."

"It is indeed," I said. "And having a copy made and enlarged cost more than it should have."

Zack put on his glasses and assessed the photo. "Money well spent," he said, and he was right.

Taylor's high school, Luther College, had been rehearsing its yearly Christmas choral concert, and she and her two best friends were in the junior handbell choir. The local paper's photographer had caught them in mid-ring. It was a seasonal photograph on a slow news day, and the layout person had given the picture pride of place on the front page.

In their Luther sweatshirts, blue jeans, and spotless white cotton gloves, the girls were an appealing trio. Gracie Falconer, athletic, big-boned, red-haired and ruddily freckled, was beaming, transported, as she always was, by the sheer joy of action. Isobel Wainberg's springy black curls had escaped the silver headband with which she had tried to tame them, and her fine features were drawn in concentration. The standards Isobel set herself were high; she would not easily forgive herself a mistake in performance. Taylor's expression was rapturous. She was a girl who lived life more deeply than most – her pleasures were more keenly experienced; her pains, sharper-edged. The photographer had captured Taylor at a moment when her private wellspring of joy overflowed, and it was a lovely sight.

As Zack's eyes remained fixed on the photo, I marvelled at how completely he had metamorphosed into a family man in the two years we had been together. He was forty-eight when we met, and he'd spent a lifetime travelling fast and light. There were two passions in his life: the law, and his legal partners, whom he'd loved since they gravitated to one another midway through their first year of law school and committed themselves to share what they were certain would be a golden destiny. There had been many women in Zack's life, but few had been invited to stick around for breakfast.

When we met, I was a widow with three grown children: Mieka, who was newly divorced, the mother of two young daughters, and the owner-operator of UpSlideDown, a café/play centre for young families; Peter, who had just graduated from the School of Veterinary Medicine; and Angus, who was at the College of Law in Saskatoon. Taylor was the only one of my children still at home. When her mother, the artist Sally Love, who had been my friend since childhood, died suddenly, Taylor was four. There was no one to take Sally's daughter, so I adopted her. It was one of the best decisions I'd ever made.

I was content with my life and then Zack came along. As our relationship grew serious, everyone who cared for us felt compelled to wave a red flag. We ignored them. Six months to the day after we met, Zack and I stood at the altar of St. Paul's Cathedral and exchanged vows. When I'd leaned down to kiss my new husband, he'd whispered, "This is forever, Ms. Shreve. We made a promise, and a deal's a deal." Since that grey New Year's morning, we'd never looked back. Ours was not an easy marriage, but it was a good one.

As he propped the photo on the mantel, Zack's voice was wistful. "Think we're looking at the next generation of partners at Falconer Shreve and Wainberg?"

"Let's see," I said. "Gracie is planning to be a professional basketball player, so she's out, and we both know that Taylor wants to make art – the way her mother did."

Zack frowned. "You're Taylor's mother, Joanne. Blood ties are significant, especially when the birth mother is someone as extraordinary as Sally Love, but Taylor's your daughter, our daughter, and we have the papers to prove it."

"Spoken like a lawyer," I said.

"Spoken like a lawyer who knows that in these cases smart people make themselves bulletproof, and we are bulletproof."

I felt my nerves twang. For a man who'd spent forty-three years in a wheelchair because he'd been in the wrong place at the wrong time, Zack was remarkably sanguine about the vagaries of fate. I needed to return to safe ground. I took the photo from the mantel. "Isobel's your best hope. She's smart and focused – "

"And way, way, way too hard on herself," Zack finished. "Izzy's just like her mother who, incidentally, is driving me crazy these days."

"What's the matter?"

Zack extended his hands, palms up in a gesture of exasperation. "Beats me. Delia never – and I mean *never* – makes mistakes, but lately she's made some doozies – forgetting meetings, not returning phone calls, and last week she almost missed a critical filing deadline. Luckily, the associate she's working with picked up on it, but it was a close call, so I went to Dee's office and asked her what the hell was going on."

"Did she have an explanation?"

"Nope. She told me to back off and said that it wouldn't happen again."

I examined the jumbo box of Christmas-tree balls Zack had bought that morning to replace the ones Pantera had eaten the year before. They were all red – Zack's favourite colour. "Do you think Delia and Noah could be having problems?" I said.

Zack raised an eyebrow. "Apart from the fact that Noah worships Delia, and she treats him like a piece of furniture? It's been that way for twenty-seven years, and they're still together."

"Maybe Delia's met a man who's more than a piece of furniture to her."

Zack's snort was derisive. "Nah – Delia's not built that way."

"We're all built that way," I said.

"Not Delia. The only thing that makes her heart pound is a real red-meat case. What would make you think she's having an affair?"

"I didn't use the word 'affair,' but something's disturbing her. A couple of days ago when we were waiting for the girls to get out of rehearsal, Delia got a phone call. I was sitting beside her so I couldn't avoid hearing her end of the conversation."

"What did she say?"

"Not much – just 'Can't I at least see you? I've done everything you asked.' The person she was speaking to must have broken the connection. Delia tried to blow it off – told me she'd been talking to a dissatisfied client who was moving to another lawyer. I guess that's possible."

The furrows that bracketed Zack's mouth like parentheses deepened – a sure sign that he was troubled. "Delia's clients never leave her," he said. "They may be dunderheads but they're smart enough to realize they'll never get a better lawyer than Dee."

"She's that good?" I said.

"She's better than me," Zack said, "and that's saying a lot."

"Time to get ready for the party, my self-effacing love," I said. "It starts at 2:00. It's come and go, but we should be there early because we have to get the girls to Luther by 3:45, and I need time to make a good impression on the guest of honour."

"You've already made a good impression," Zack said, "Justice Theo Brokaw has agreed to appear on the show you're doing for NationTV and explain the workings of the Supreme Court to eager Canadians from coast to coast."

"Correction. Theo Brokaw's wife says he's agreed. I haven't dealt with the Justice himself. It was Myra Brokaw who wrote volunteering her husband's services."

"And I'll bet Theo was standing over her shoulder telling her exactly what to write. Stepping down from the bench must be tough for a guy who's accustomed to having people hyperventilate when he enters the room."

"So you think Theo Brokaw's looking for some ego-stroking?"

"You bet he is, and you're offering him exactly what he needs, Ms. Shreve. Explaining how the court works while modestly enumerating his many contributions to Canadian jurisprudence will keep Theo's opinion of himself robust while he writes his memoirs."

"You don't like him?"

"Not a lot," Zack said. "I realize this sounds hypocritical coming from me, but I find Theo's passion for public notice unseemly, and he's never got his hands dirty actually practising law. He's an academic."

"I'm an academic."

"Yes, but you actually went out and worked in political campaigns. You understand that politics is complex, dirty, and occasionally noble. And your career as an academic stalled because of your involvement in party politics. You paid a price for knowing what you know. Theo never paid the price. He thinks people like me are hired guns and that people like him are the conduits through which God dispenses justice to Canada." Zack made a gesture of disgust. "The hell with it. This is a stupid discussion."

"Actually, since you're the only one talking, it's more of a soliloquy," I said.

Zack flashed me a vulpine smile. "That's probably why I scored all the points. Fuck it. Nothing ever changes. It's Christmas. Let's go to the party."

The Wainbergs lived in a neighbourhood of carefully restored early-twentieth-century homes stylistically faithful to the classical rules of proportion, balance, and symmetry. Delia and Noah's house, designed by an adherent of the Late Modernist school of architecture, was a daringly cantilevered skin-and-bones affair that thumbed its nose at its genteel neighbours.

The house had a history of one-sided passions. According to my friend Ed Mariani, who was an intimate of the man who designed the house, the architect's dream had been to live in the house with his partner, a chef, until death did them part. Fate intervened. While preparing his signature lobster diablo for the housewarming, the chef gave himself a nasty cut. He cabbed to the nearest clinic, where a young doctor with eyes the colour of jade stitched the wound. The doctor's touch was gentle. When the wound was wrapped, the doctor's hand lingered, and in that instant, the chef knew he wanted the doctor's hand to linger forever.

The next morning the architect put his dream house on the market, where it remained for months before the newly wed Wainbergs bought it for a song, and Noah set about making it their own.

Noah was a talented woodcarver, and there were striking pieces of his work throughout the house and grounds. Among the most intriguing were three life-sized oak bears positioned on the lawn by the path leading to the entranceway. The bears were astonishingly realistic, with foreheads sloping back suddenly from behind their small eyes, broad, prominent muzzles, heavily muscled bodies, and claws that were sharp enough to defend or attack. All three bears were standing on their hind legs: the large male was in front; behind and flanking him were two smaller bears, one an adult female, one a cub. The placement of the bears conveyed a powerful truth about the Wainbergs: Delia was the legal star, with her high six-figure income, but it was Noah who was the family's protector.

As we arrived at the Wainbergs', the wind, already fierce, picked up and filled the air with dry, granular snow that swirled as it fell. We were in for a blizzard. "Shit," said Zack. "Sweet," said Taylor. On the drive over Taylor had been pensive, wrapped in her own thoughts, but the prospect of a storm was a catalyst for one of those quicksilver mood changes that mark adolescence. As soon as we stopped, Taylor leapt from the car. Arms outstretched, she ran to the centre of the Wainbergs' lawn, spun exuberantly, then sprinted to the house, anxious to see her friends.

Zack touched my hand. "A blizzard's a small price to pay to see her like that again."

"Taylor's fine," I said. "Her hormones are just kicking in."

"Henry Chan says that as long as Taylor's keeping the lines of communication open and taking an interest in life, the brooding is nothing to worry about."

"You talked to our doctor about Taylor?"

"He's a professional. I thought maybe there was something we should do."

"Zack, she's a perfectly normal fourteen-year-old, and we're doing what the parents of a perfectly normal fourteen-year-old are supposed to do: we're there, we're watchful, and we're letting our daughter figure out who she is."

Zack's lips twitched in amusement. "That's exactly what Henry said."

"You could have saved yourself a trip to his office."

"Actually, the consultation occurred just as I'd drawn to an inside straight. I figured I'd get his advice before I cleaned his clock."

"Ever the family man."

"Don't be dismissive. I won $400 from Henry that night. Now, if I'm going to get up to the house under my own steam, we'd better boogie."

In the course of an average week, Zack unfolded his wheelchair and transferred his weight from the driver's seat to the chair dozens of times. Most times the manoeuvre was smoothly executed, but the snow complicated everything. I knew enough not to offer help, but the visibility was poor, so I was quick to move to Zack's side of the car, and when he started up the pathway, I stayed close behind. My husband's upper body was powerful, so despite the snow his progress was steady. But as we reached the oak bears, the snow caught his wheels. Zack uttered his favourite expletive and I stepped in front of his chair to kick his wheels free. That's when I realized that we weren't alone.

A woman carrying a baby car seat was coming up behind us. I stepped onto the lawn.

"Play through," Zack said, but the woman didn't move.

"Is this the Margolis-Wainberg residence?" she asked.

"It is," I said. The lower half of the woman's face was covered by her scarf and the hood of her jacket was pulled up. I glanced down at the baby seat. The cover was zipped against the weather. "Is there actually a baby in there?" I said.

"Yes," she said.

"Better get him or her inside," I said. "It'll be fun to have a baby at the party."

"There's a party?" she said. She repeated the word 'party' as if it were a noun from a language she'd forgotten, then turned abruptly and started back down the path. I watched until she and her child disappeared into the swirling snow.

"What do you suppose that was about?" I said.

My husband didn't answer. His focus was elsewhere. The Wainbergs' home, like the homes of all of Zack's partners, was fully accessible, but snow had drifted onto the ramp leading up to the front door. "Look at that," Zack said. "Sorry, Ms. Shreve, but you're going to have to push me up."

I'd just pulled the chair back, so I could take a run at the incline, when Noah Wainberg appeared at the front door. "Since Taylor arrived, I've been watching for you," he said. He zipped his parka, picked up the shovel leaning against the house, and cleared the ramp. We were inside and warm within minutes. Zack removed his toque and glanced up at Noah. "I owe you one."

"No, you don't. You gave me a chance to get out of the house." Noah nodded in the direction of the party. "I hate these things, but Delia wanted a party . . . "

"And what Delia wants, Delia gets," Zack said.

Noah didn't smile. "If it's within my power – yes." He removed his coat, revealing an impeccably tailored two-button pinstripe and a claret Windsor-knotted tie. He was dressed for the part and he would handle his duties as host without complaint, just as he unquestioningly handled everything that came his way.

Few people realized that Noah was a lawyer who had been in the same year at the University of Saskatchewan College of Law as the members of the Winners' Circle. He had been an indifferent student, and after graduation he had spent a year articling with a lacklustre firm, waiting for Delia to come back from Ottawa where she was clerking for another outstanding graduate of the College of Law, Mr. Justice Theo Brokaw.

The partners of Falconer Shreve Altieri Wainberg and Hynd marked the day they opened their first office as the beginning of their real lives. Noah was not the Wainberg of the firm's name, but as someone who knew the law and could be trusted to be discreet, he played an invaluable role in managing sensitive information and sheltering clients who didn't want to advertise their need for legal advice.

His services to Falconer Shreve went beyond the professional. All the partners owned cottages on a horseshoe of lakefront property that was less than an hour's drive from Regina. The community on Lawyers' Bay was gated because the cottages were often used for meetings and, occasionally, as a safe haven for clients who needed time away from prying eyes. Noah made certain the properties were kept in running order. Quietly and efficiently, within the office and outside it, Noah took care of what needed to be taken care of and that included the Wainbergs' only child, Isobel.

Delia and I weren't close, but because of our girls' friendship, Noah and I were often together. He was quiet and easygoing, and I always welcomed his company. That night, after a young woman in a crisp white blouse, black mid-calf skirt, and sensible shoes appeared and took our coats upstairs, Noah gestured in the direction of the party. "Shall we join the others?"

"Not so fast," Zack said. "Joanne and I want to hear about the guest of honour. Stripped of his ceremonial red robes and ermine, is he as much of a preening turd as he was on the bench?"

Noah shrugged. "Beats me. He's not here."

Zack glanced at his watch. "Two-thirty. The party started at two, so the guest of honour is half an hour late. One of the perks of being on the Supreme Court is making everybody hang around awaiting your dramatic entrance. I guess Theo still savours the moment."

Noah made a fist and slapped it into his palm. "This isn't the Supreme Court," he said tightly. "It's Delia's party, and Theo Brokaw should have the decency to show up on time."

"Agreed. But by definition, egoists set all clocks to their own time." Zack patted Noah's arm. "Now if I remember correctly, you make a fine martini. I wouldn't mind testing my memory."

"Follow me," Noah said.

The Wainberg house was designed for entertaining, with expanses of glass that offered guests a panorama of the ever-changing prairie sky, and a large open-plan reception area where deep couches beckoned and servers with trays of food and drink could move with ease. The party had moved quickly to a rolling boil – voices were vibrant, laughter exploded percussively against the cool riffs of a jazz pianist, and the air was heady with the blend of perfume, cologne, and body heat.

Most of the guests were people Zack and I would see many times before the old year ended. By then, we would be able to finish one another's stories, but the Wainbergs' party was an early one. The season had not yet lost its shine, and there was still real pleasure in seeing old friends and hearing news. When the servers brought out Noah's signature mesquite-smoked turkeys, there was a round of spontaneous applause. It was a good party. Everyone was having fun except Delia.

Striking in black dress pants and a sleeveless white sequined shirt that showcased her admirably toned upper arms, Delia roamed, tense and distracted, seeking the guest of honour who was yet to arrive. Noah's eyes seldom left his wife. Finally, he came over to the fireplace where Zack and I were trapped by a Falconer Shreve client named Roddy Dewar, who was rich, litigious, crazier than a bag of hammers, and hence much prized by the firm.

As always, Noah was quick to read the situation, and he knew that Zack and I had wearied of Roddy's fulminations. Noah gave the man a conspiratorial wink. "They just brought in the smoked turkeys. Better move fast. Those birds have a way of vanishing."

Roddy's food lust was legendary. "A word to the wise is sufficient," he said. Then he snatched the last cheese blintz from a passing tray, popped it in his mouth, and bolted for the birds.

Zack watched his progress, then raised an eyebrow at Noah. "Did you know that the soul leaves the body four minutes and seventeen seconds after death? Roddy was just about to provide Joanne and me with scientific proof. Once again, we are in your debt."

Noah's smile was rueful. "And payback time is here already. The Brokaws still haven't shown up and Dee's making herself crazy. Could you talk to her, Zack? She'll listen to you."

"Sure." Zack's eyes scanned the room. "Where is she?"

"Outside on the deck, freezing and smoking and trying to track down the guest of honour on her cell."

Zack was clearly exasperated. "What's with her lately? People forget parties all the time, and the Brokaws aren't young. Theo didn't wait for mandatory retirement, but he's got to be past seventy."

"Seventy-two," Noah said.

"So it slipped his mind. Big deal. Now that he's moved back to Regina, he and Delia can sing 'Auld Lang Syne' any time they want."

Noah's expression was weary. "Tell Dee that, and remind her that she doesn't have to sneak outside because she wants a cigarette. This is her house and people are damn lucky to be in the same room with her."

Zack patted Noah's arm and headed for the deck. It wasn't long before he and Delia rejoined the party. I wasn't surprised. Communication was never a problem between them. Noah appeared with a plate of smoked turkey and a glass of wine for his wife, and when she rewarded him with her three-cornered, cat-like smile, his relief was palpable.

Fuelled by alcohol, the party followed the inevitable trajectory from good cheer to raucousness to the loss of inhibition that teeters on danger. The discreet appearance of servers with pots of coffee and trays of honey cake, cheese, and fruit saved us from our baser selves. Soon, restored to civility by caffeine and one last bite, people began brushing one another's cheeks with their lips and moving along. It was time for us to leave too. Gracie's father, Blake Falconer, and Noah and Delia would be attending the afternoon concert on Sunday, so this afternoon Zack and I were responsible for shepherding the three girls. The choirs were to be robed and ready fifteen minutes before the concert started. But I was currently mired in conversation with a sad-eyed wispy woman, expensively dressed in a leather blazer and slacks the exact shade of her stiffly lacquered platinum ponytail and her platinum cuff bracelet. She was weaving slightly, and her eyes seemed to be focused somewhere past my right ear. She was complaining about her only child who apparently brought her neither comfort nor joy.

"I've been trying to remember my last good Christmas, and I cannot." She shifted her eyes to meet mine. "Don't waste your time trying to think of something to say. I'm a solo act." When I saw Zack wheeling towards me, I exhaled. I had never learned how to extricate myself gracefully from a conversation that was heading towards a land mine, but Zack always seemed to know how to make a smooth exit. I was in the clear.

My solo act hadn't volunteered her name, but Zack knew it. He took her hand. "As always, you look lovely, Louise," he said.

She shook an admonishing finger at him. "You're the only remotely interesting person at this party and you let that little toad monopolize you." She cocked her head. "The toad's name eludes me, but you know who I mean – the one who looks like the fat boy on the Snakes and Ladders board."

Zack laughed. "Nothing wrong with your powers of description. His name is Roddy Dewar."

"Well, let Roddy Dewar find his own amusement," Louise said. "I long to talk to you."

"Unfortunately, my wife and I are just leaving," Zack said. "Our daughter, Taylor, and her friends are due at their Christmas concert."

"At Luther College. I am due at that too," Louise said, "but I'm too drunk to go."

"There's another performance tomorrow," Zack said. "Enjoy the party and hear the carols when you're more in the mood."

Louise leaned down and kissed Zack. She missed his face and hit his shirt. "You're worth every penny my ex-husband pays you," she said. She frowned. "There's a smear of lipstick on your collar, and I fear I put it there. Next time you send Leland a bill, add a couple of hundred for a new shirt."

Zack took her hand. "No payment necessary, Louise. I'm honoured to have your lipstick on my collar."

"Jesus, you're sweet," she said, and she swayed off towards the bar.

I squeezed Zack's shoulder. "You are sweet, you know," I said.

Zack raised an eyebrow. "Hang onto that thought the next time Pantera chews up one of your grandmother's Christmas-tree ornaments."

Taylor, Isobel, and the third member of their triumvirate, Gracie Falconer, breezed in, already dressed for outdoors. Gracie and Isobel had grown up together. They were the same age; both were only children and both had a parent who was a founding partner of Falconer Shreve. Their ties were close, but when Zack and I married, Gracie and Isobel had embraced Taylor. Now the three girls were inseparable. That afternoon at the Wainbergs', they had found the food and politely endured questions about school and holiday plans from their parents' friends, but as Gracie flung her scarf around her neck, she made it clear they were ready to move along. "Let's make tracks," she said.

Isobel frowned at her wristwatch. "We have to hurry," she said. "We're supposed be there in ten minutes, and the weather will slow us down."

I handed Taylor the car keys. "Why don't you girls go to the car? We still have to get our coats."

Delia and Noah walked with us to the door and waited while the young woman who'd taken our things retrieved them.

"I was surprised to see Louise Hunter here," Zack said. "Leland says she's become a recluse."

"How would Leland know?" Noah said. "He's never around."

Zack shrugged. "Leland's company is involved in some serious international deals."

"And that excuses everything," Noah said mildly. Our coats arrived, and Noah held out mine. "Anyway, I thought Louise might enjoy a party, so I added her name to the invitation list."

Delia cocked her head. "I didn't realize you and Louise Hunter knew one another."

"Life sometimes gets too much for Louise and she calls me."

"And you take care of her till she sobers up," Delia said.

"Peyben is one of the firm's biggest clients," Noah said quietly. "And Louise was once married to Peyben's owner."

Delia linked her arm through her husband's. "You take care of a lot that we don't know about, don't you?"

"Thanks for noticing," Noah murmured.

It was a nice moment, but like many nice moments, it was interrupted by the outside world. When the doorbell rang, Zack was closest to the door and he reached over and opened it.

Theo and Myra Brokaw were standing on the step. The storm was still in full force, and the Brokaws had linked their arms, presenting a united front against the elements. Zack pushed his chair back, and Theo and Myra stepped past him into the safety of the entrance hall, frowning in concentration as they stomped their boots and brushed the snow from their shoulders.

Like many couples in a long marriage the Brokaws had grown to look like one another. Both were tall and lean with thick eyebrows, deep-set dark eyes, and strong features. That afternoon, both were wearing ankle-length grey cashmere coats with festive red scarves knotted around their necks. For people who were late for a party in their honour, they were remarkably unperturbed, but they had an explanation for their tardiness. "I'd forgotten how challenging a Saskatchewan winter can be," Myra Brokaw said. "We had quite the adventure getting here."

Zack moved his chair aside, and extended his hand to her. "I'm glad you triumphed," he said. Then he turned to Myra's husband. "It's a pleasure to see you again, Judge Brokaw."

Theo Brokaw's chiselled features were transformed by a smile that was surprisingly winsome. "Do I know you?" he asked.

"I've appeared before you many times," Zack said. "Obviously, I didn't make much of an impression. I'm Zack Shreve."

"And you're a lawyer," Theo Brokaw said, and his tone was self-congratulatory.

"I am," Zack agreed.

"Well, so am I," Theo Brokaw said. "At least I used to be."

For once, my husband was flummoxed. Myra smoothed over the awkward moment. She touched Theo's elbow, and he moved smartly towards the Wainbergs. Delia opened her arms in greeting, but her eyes were anxious as she scanned Theo's face. "Welcome. I'm so glad you could come."

Theo Brokaw stared at her, his forehead creased in bafflement. "You've gotten old," he said. Before Delia could react, he bent towards her, buried his face in her neck, and breathed deeply. "Ah, but your fragrance is the same," he said.

Until she disentangled herself, Theo clung to Delia in a way that was both passionate and strangely youthful. The situation was awkward, but Delia handled it with grace. "I'll have to send Chanel No. 5 a thank-you note," she said. She turned to her husband. "Noah, why don't you pour the Brokaws a drink, so we can all celebrate their arrival in Regina."

Zack shot his partner an approving look. "I wish we could join you, but Joanne and I will have to take a rain check. We need to get the girls to their Christmas concert."

Myra's eyes widened in recognition. "You're Joanne Kilbourn," she said.

"I am," I said. "And I was looking forward to talking to you and Justice Brokaw, but we're already late."

"I understand," Myra said. She stepped closer to me and lowered her voice. "We've made an unfortunate first impression, but I would like to talk to you about our project. It has merit and I believe it's still feasible. May I call you?"

My heart sank. Theo was clearly no longer ready for prime time. "Of course," I said. "You have my number."

Theo Brokaw had been watching his wife and me with interest. "We live over a store," he said brightly.

Myra's voice was gentle. "It's one of the new condos in Scarth Street Mall. We wrote Ms. Kilbourn about it, Theo."

"Well, whatever you call it, it's still rooms over a store," Theo said. "And it's handy for me because it's close to the courthouse." He gave Zack a conspiratorial wink. "You know how important that is."

"I do," Zack said. "Have a pleasant evening." He opened the door and wheeled out into the wild weather.

With Noah's help we made it to our car, but the weather was growing increasingly ugly. It is a truth universally acknowledged that the first snowfall means that everybody in town forgets how to drive. When the first snowfall is a blizzard, the potential for skids, fishtails, and rear-end collisions rises exponentially. Our trip to the school was a white-knuckler. Zack was driving. Steering the car through the drifts on Leopold Crescent demanded strength and attention, and we didn't exchange a word until we hit Albert Street.

City crews were on the job there; Zack's shoulders relaxed and he shot me a quick glance. "Wouldn't want to do that every day," he said.

I reached over and rubbed the back of his neck. "Better?"

"Thanks. What do you think is going on with Theo Brokaw?"

"Whatever it is," I said, "it explains his sudden retirement from the bench."

"He's not exactly *compos mentis*," Zack agreed.

"Yet the e-mail exchanges we had were perfectly lucid," I said. "Myra must take care of their correspondence."

"Promise me something," Zack said.

"What?"

"If I ever get like Theo, tip me into the nearest snowbank."

By the time we pulled up in front of the school, we were late. Gracie and Taylor were sanguine but Isobel, whose standards for herself were high, bolted from our vehicle before Zack had come to a full stop.

The parking lots at Luther were chaos. Everybody was in a hurry, but nobody was getting anywhere. Seemingly every parking space but the one with thc handicapped sign was taken. We had a disabled persons' ID parking card, but unless a client's needs were urgent, Zack never used it. My husband and I glanced at the seductive space and then at one another. Handbells were waiting to be rung. I rummaged through the glove compartment, found the card, and propped it on the dashboard. Desperate times called for desperate measures.

Gracie and Taylor dashed through the snow towards the gym, and Zack and I followed behind. It was tough sledding, but we made it. As we stood inside, brushing off the snow and checking out seating possibilities, a good-looking boy with blond dreadlocks and a tentative smile approached us.

His manner was breezily confident, but his voice was uncertain. "Hey Zack. How's it going?"

"No complaints," Zack said. He gestured towards me. "This is my wife, Joanne. Jo, this is Declan Hunter."

The boy extended his hand. "I recognized you from the picture in Zack's office. Nice to meet you, Ms. Shreve." His eyes darted past us towards the door. "You didn't happen to see my mother in the parking lot, did you? She might need some help getting in."

Zack's voice was gentle. "She decided to come tomorrow, Declan. I guess she didn't have a chance to let you know."

Declan's face tightened. "The big news would have been if she showed up."

Zack wheeled his chair closer. "Your mother really did want to come today."

"Right." Declan gave us a small wave and turned away. "See you," he said and started towards the crowd.

"Wait." Zack didn't have to raise his voice to get a response. Declan pivoted and took a step towards my husband. "If you've got some free time during the holidays, how about an evening at the Broken Rack," Zack said. "When we went there on your birthday, I thought you showed definite promise."

This time, Declan's smile was open. "I beat you," he said.

"I had an off night," Zack said. "So are you in?"

"I'm in," Declan said.

"Good, I'll call you and we'll set up a time."

"Cool."

I watched Declan sprint down the hall towards the gym. "You will call him, won't you?" I said.

"You know me – can't stand to lose, and this time the evening will be on our dime."

"The last time wasn't?"

"Nope. The last time was strictly business. It was Declan's sixteenth birthday and his father, whom you have no doubt deduced is Leland Hunter, decided his son needed a man-to-man talk."

"Doesn't a father usually do that himself?"

"It wasn't that kind of talk. Leland thought Declan needed a clearer understanding of the Youth Criminal Justice Act. So we shot some pool. I told Declan that while Section 3 says the Act is to be liberally construed, it doesn't mean sixteen-year-olds get a free pass, and I sent his father the bill. Hell of a note for a kid's birthday, eh?"

"It is a hell of a note," I agreed. "So did Declan need reminding?"

"He did," Zack said. "Jo, you know the drill about confidentiality. That's all I can say about that."

Every effort had been made to transform the gym for the carol service. The shining wooden floor on which so many heart-stopping basketball championships had been played was safe under protective floor covers; giant sparkly snowflakes were suspended from the rafters by lengths of fishing line that would, in theory, cease to be discernible when the lights were extinguished; artificial trees twinkled in every available space, and silvery garlands werc looped and duct-taped along the sides of the bleachers.

My husband took in the decor. "You can't say they didn't try," he said, and began wheeling towards what quickly became the last spot in the room to be occupied.

"Shit," he said.

The expletive conjured up a student usher. "We have special seating at the front," he said. "Just follow me."

As he always did when he was singled out because of his paraplegia, Zack bristled. I touched his shoulder. "This place is already packed. We can stay here and stare at the back of people's heads, and I can stand for the whole concert, or you can swallow your pride and we'll have the best seats in the house." Zack gave me a sharp look but he wheeled off after the young man.

We had just reached our places when the lights dimmed and the processional began. As the student orchestra played the familiar opening of "Adeste Fideles," the audience rose and the choirs entered, wearing academic gowns with satin yokes in the school colours, black and gold. The choirs sang in Latin, and their young voices stirred memories of my own school days. The service of lessons and carols was a familiar one to me, but Luther College had a large number of international students and so the selections from the Gospels were read in the first languages of students from Germany, Poland, China, France, Japan, Nigeria, and Korea, and the carols sung were those that had been sung for generations by celebrators of Christmas in those countries. When the bell-ringers moved into place on stage, Zack took my hand.

Gracie rang with ebullient loose-limbed grace; Taylor was surprisingly focused; but Isobel, her mother's daughter, shook her bell with furrowed brow and tight lips, bent on a perfect performance. As they finished, Zack whipped out his camera and snapped three forbidden photographs before I batted down his arm.

"Against the rules," I said.

"I've only been a father for two years. I have to make up for lost time." He snapped a couple more pictures, then returned the camera to his pocket.

The service ended. Students began moving down the aisle with baskets of candles, which they asked the person at the end of each row to distribute. The students then lit the candles of the people with aisle seats and invited them to light the candle of the person next to them. Faces softened by candlelight, the audience joined the choirs in the recessional "Joy to the World." It was a transcendent moment but, as Robert Frost knew, nothing golden can stay. The last line of the carol was sung; the candles were extinguished; the gym lights were flicked back on, and we were, once again, fragmented into our separate selves.

Despite the blizzard, no one seemed in a rush to leave. The adults were chatting; students were clinging to one another with the desperation of those who knew it might be five minutes before they could start texting again. Finally, I spotted Isobel, Taylor, and Gracie. They'd changed back into their street clothes and were standing near an exit, laughing and surrounded by friends. I pointed them out to Zack. "Now there's the picture I want."

"Let me get a little closer," he said. He pushed his wheelchair forward and began snapping. He was just in time to capture a disturbing tableau. The woman we'd seen that afternoon on the Wainbergs' front path approached the girls. She had the baby seat with her; she appeared to say something to Isobel, then she handed her the baby seat and disappeared through the exit.

We were with the girls in seconds. "What's going on?" I said.

Gracie was the first to speak. "That woman just gave her baby to Isobel."

Isobel shook her head. "She didn't just 'give' the baby to me. She made sure she knew who I was first. She asked if my mother was Delia Margolis Wainberg, and when I said yes, she said, 'Tell her I couldn't do it. This child belongs with her.' That's when she handed me the baby seat."

I looked down at the child. He was dressed in a Thomas the Tank Engine snowsuit, and his toque was pulled down over his ears. He was perhaps six months old with the kind of intelligent gaze people tag as "alert." I squatted down beside him. "How are you doing, big guy?"

He raised his arms and kept his dark eyes focused on mine. I unbuckled him and picked him up.

Taylor came close. Her adolescent cool had deserted her.

"His mother *is* coming back, isn't she?" she said, and her voice was small and scared.

As Zack wheeled in for a closer look, he squeezed Taylor's arm, but he didn't answer her question. My husband was more charmed by children than many men I knew, but when he gazed at the baby, he wasn't smiling. His eyes moved to me. "Let me hold him, would you?" Zack took the child, removed his toque, and ran his hand over the baby's springy black curls. He held the child out in front of him and examined him closely. "Did you girls get a good look at the baby's mother?" he asked.

"Not me," Gracie said. "I was too busy watching Declan Hunter embrace Taylor with his eyes. Sooooo romantic."

Taylor shot Gracie a look that would have curdled milk, then turned back to us. "I saw the mother," she said. "She looked like Isobel."

Isobel's blue eyes were troubled, but as always, she was precise. "Not the way I look now – the way I'll probably look when I'm older."

Then, for the second time that night, the gym was plunged into darkness. This darkness didn't inspire awe – simply confusion. There was a moment of stunned silence, some sputterings of nervous laughter, and then, obeying a response that had become second nature to us all, we reached for our cells. Within seconds, the gym was dotted with rectangles of light that darted through the gloom, fireflies for our electronic age.

The baby began to cry and I reached down and took him from Zack. The child's hair smelled of Baby's Own soap.

"This certainly complicates matters," Zack said, and I could hear the edge in his voice.

"They'll get the power back," I said. "We'll just have to sit tight."

"Great advice," he said. "Except while we're sitting tight, that child's mother is going to disappear without a trace."

CHAPTER

2

Fifteen minutes later, the school, and reportedly most of the city, was still without light. A spirit of cheerful anarchy had seized the crowd. Plunged into darkness in the company of friends and cellphones, the students, their voices shakily arrogant, split the silence with what Walt Whitman described as the barbaric yawps of the young. The adults were resigned. Blizzards and blackouts are part of a Saskatchewan winter. Everyone knows that, sooner or later, blizzards stop; power returns; streets are lit; traffic lights function – and life goes on.

Enjoying the moment was a sensible option, but not for Zack and me. As we waited by the door through which the baby's mother vanished, we were isolated by a growing fear and frustration. Zack was accustomed to deciding on an outcome and making it happen, but that afternoon, nothing was breaking his way. He couldn't get either Delia or Noah on the phone and Police Inspector Debbie Haczkewicz's private voicemail told him she would call when time permitted.

The room was growing noticeably cooler. I zipped up the baby's snowsuit, put his toque back on him, then wrapped him in the blanket that had been in the baby seat. Swaddled and held close, he fell asleep on my shoulder.

"One possibility, and it's chilling, is postpartum psychosis." Zack spoke softly as if to protect the child in my arms from hearing what he was about to say. "I had a client who heard voices telling her she had to kill her baby. She tried to get help, but everyone told her the 'baby blues' were common, and the feelings would pass. The voices became more and more insistent, so finally she threw her baby off the Albert Street Bridge."

My heart clenched. "What happened to the mother?"

"She was arrested. Arrangements were made for her to undergo psychological assessment, and she was released. She walked out of court, drove home, and hanged herself."

"Do you think this baby's mother is suicidal? When she gave the baby to Isobel, all she said was 'I couldn't do it.' That might just mean she felt she couldn't raise her son, so she was giving him to someone who could."

"Possibly," Zack said, "but I don't buy it. Mothers who abandon their newborns in the bathroom at Walmart or leave them in hospitals or fire stations are usually young and poor. When I was taking pictures of the girls I caught a glimpse of this boy's mother. She wasn't a kid, and she didn't look poor."

The penny dropped. "Zack, take out your camera," I said. "She'll be in those pictures."

The first photo was a dud. With the breathtaking symbolism of the quotidian, the baby's mother was heading through the door marked EXIT, her back to the camera. Zack scrolled to the previous picture. In this one the mother was handing the baby seat to Isobel. Her coat collar was turned up, and her dark hair had fallen over her face. Zack pushed the zoom button, isolating the woman's profile. She'd been moving, and the photo was blurred. He flicked to the first picture he'd taken, and when he saw it, he breathed a single word: "Bingo." Then he handed the camera to me.

Isobel had been right. The woman in the picture was an uncanny projection of what she, herself, would look like as an adult.

Zack was on another track. "She looks like Dee when we were in law school." He slipped the camera back in his pocket, took out his BlackBerry, and tried three numbers in rapid succession. "Yet again, no Debbie. No Delia. No Noah. And I don't know if you've noticed, my love, but it is getting cold in here."

On cue, the baby in my arms began to cry lustily.

"Fuck it. I'm sick of waiting," Zack said. "I'm going to text Taylor and tell her to round up Izzy and Gracie. Then we're going to take this boy down to Regina General. They have auxiliary power so they'll be able to keep him warm and fed until somebody figures out what to do next."

I kissed the baby's head. "Sound good to you, bud?"

"You're liking that little guy, aren't you?" Zack said.

"Baby lust," I said. "Our littlest granddaughter is already four. It's been a while since we had a baby in the family."

"I don't believe this is the last we'll see of this one."

"Zack, what do you think is going on?"

He sighed. "I wish I knew. All I know is this was not a random act. The mother said her son belongs with Delia, and one look at that picture proves that she and Dee are related. When we ran into her at the Wainbergs' this afternoon, the mother was taking the baby to Delia. She backed off because of the party, but she took the first available opportunity to get the child into Isobel's hands."

"She must have seen the girls' picture in the paper and made the connection," I said. "Wainberg isn't a common name and there is that stunning resemblance."

"So the deed was done," Zack said. "And now we have to deal with the consequences."

When Zack's phone rang, I tensed. I waited for a howl, but the little guy had snuggled in. It appeared our luck was turning. Not only had the baby slept through the ringtone, but the person calling was Inspector Debbie Haczkewicz. Zack's account of the evening's events was factual and concise, but his concern about the missing woman's mental state was palpable. When he hung up, he sounded weary but satisfied. "Success," he said. "Apparently it's shit city out there. No power except on the east side. Traffic lights are out and the roads are godawful, so there are plenty of accidents. According to Debbie, some of our less principled fellow citizens are taking advantage of the blackout to smash windows and do a little Christmas shopping. It's a bad night to be a cop, but Debbie's going to send an officer to take the little guy to Regina General, and she's going to put out an all-points bulletin on the mother."

"Good," I said. "So we should just wait here for the girls and the police."

"Yep. Nothing to do but sit tight."

"I noticed that when you described the baby's mother to Debbie, you didn't mention the connection with Delia."

"Time enough for that," Zack said. "It'll be easier for Delia to hear the story from me."

"It'll be a shock," I said.

Zack's tone was pensive. "I wonder if it will be," he said. "Only one way to find out."

This time when he called Delia, Zack hit pay dirt. He gave her a brief account of the events of the evening, and apparently she didn't ask questions. When he was finished, he listened for a moment. "Okay, I'll call when we're getting close," he said.

I shifted the baby's weight in my arms. "That was short and sweet."

"Short, sweet, and only the beginning," Zack said. "Delia's going to meet us outside their house. Noah's been driving home the sobriety-challenged, so he hasn't ploughed their driveway, and Dee thinks we'd get stuck. Also she wants to make sure that before she and I talk, Isobel is out of earshot."

The girls joined us, and not long afterwards a police officer found us, shone a flashlight on her badge, and took the baby. Her actions were swift and professional, but the darkness made the action surreal and, for me, deeply unsettling.

All of my children had been students at Luther: the three oldest for four years each, and Taylor for one semester so far. The campus was as familiar to me as my own backyard, but that night I lost my bearings. The school and the residences seemed part of an alien landscape, and the students bent over their shovels in the snow-choked parking lot had the cool menace of figures in a Magritte painting. Zack offered to drive, and I was relieved. I was normally a confident driver, but that night I felt unmoored.

Gracie Falconer's house was the nearest, so we dropped her off first. It had been a silent drive, but Gracie was a girl who believed in happy endings, and as she opened the car door, her voice was plaintive. "This is going to be okay, isn't it?"

Zack and I exchanged glances, but neither of us offered any reassurance. After Gracie was safely in the house, Zack called Delia and told her we were on our way. When we pulled up in front of the Wainbergs', Delia was huddled in the doorway. As soon as she spotted our car, Delia turned on the flashlight in her hand and began plodding towards us. I handed Isobel our flashlight, and she started towards her house. Halfway up the path, she and her mother passed one another without either a greeting or an embrace.

There was a puff of cold air when Delia climbed into the back seat. Delia's husky mezzo cracked as she asked Taylor to keep what she was about to hear private until Delia had had a chance to talk to Isobel. Then she leaned forward to get as close as she could to Zack. "What's the situation?"

"The police took the child to the General for the night and they're out looking for his mother."

"I didn't know there was a baby," Delia said.

"But you do know the woman," Zack said.

"We exchanged a few e-mails, and I spoke to her on the phone that day you were in the car with me, Joanne. I never met her face to face."

Zack took out his camera, pulled up the photo of the woman, and handed the camera to Delia. "There's her picture."

Delia's intake of breath was sharp. "I always wondered . . . " she said.

Zack's voice was low. "Dee, what's going on?"

She ignored Zack's question. "When can I get the child?"

"The child *is* related to you, then," Zack said.

"The child's mother is my daughter," Delia said tightly. "And that's as much as I can say tonight."

Zack didn't push it. "All right," he said. "Tomorrow, we'll see what can be done about getting the little boy."

"The child is a boy." Delia's voice was a whisper.

"Yes," Zack said. "And he looks just like Izzy did when she was a baby."

"Beautiful," Delia said.

"Very handsome," Zack agreed. "Dee, you do realize that you're going to have to tell the police everything. Inspector Debbie Haczkewicz is the officer I spoke to tonight. She's reasonable, but I have a feeling this is going to be a long haul. You'll want Debbie on your side, and if she finds out you've held back anything pertinent, she won't be."

"I'll be cooperative, but before I sit down with the Inspector, I have to talk to Noah and Isobel. And I'm going to need a lawyer. I know you hate family law, but if I'm going to be spending months dealing with this, I don't want to be stuck with a lawyer I don't know."

Zack shook his head. "Come on, Dee. You know the argument. A lawyer is supposed to give objective and dispassionate advice. That's impossible when people are as close as we are. You need someone from another firm."

"I don't want someone from another firm. The legal community here is tight, and not all lawyers are as discreet as you are. The last thing I need is every lawyer in town obsessing over my private life. If you won't take my case, I'll handle it myself, and you know what they say about lawyers who represent themselves."

Delia's tone made it clear that she was not to be dissuaded. Zack didn't even try. "Okay," he said. "I'm in. Give me a call when you're ready to talk."

Delia reached forward and squeezed Zack's shoulder. "Thanks." She climbed out of the car, slammed the door shut, and started trudging up the path. The snow swirled around the bears Noah had carved, softening the lines of their heavy bodies. As Delia passed them, Zack said, "She looks so small."

"Delia will be all right," I said. "She's one of the most capable people I know, and she has Noah. If the situation gets ugly, Papa Bear will step in."

As we turned the corner onto our street, the power came back on. The old safe world had returned. Even better, our neighbour Frank van Valzer had cleared our driveway with his snow blower.

Zack cheered. "Saved by the head lamp on the Toro Power Max 828."

"So you and Frank have been talking snow blowers," I said.

"It's a guy thing. Frank talks; I listen."

"That's pretty much the arrangement I have with Frank's wife. She tells me all I need are geraniums, and I keep planting perennials."

Zack drove into our garage and pulled the key out of the ignition. "Good to be home, eh?"

"Is it ever," Taylor said. "Does anybody have a clue about what's going on?"

"Why don't we make some tea and tell you what we know," Zack said.

Five minutes later, we were sitting at our kitchen table, waiting as the tea steeped. My old bouvier, Willie, was sprawled beside me; Pantera was in his customary place beside Zack's wheelchair, and Taylor's cats, Bruce and Benny, were curled up in their bed near the stove.

Zack poured the first cup and handed it to Taylor. "Okay, time for questions. Fire away."

Taylor met his gaze. "Is that woman who gave Isobel the baby her sister?"

"My guess is she is Isobel's half-sister," Zack said.

Taylor picked up Benny and began stroking him. Benny shot a triumphant look at Bruce and began to purr. "The woman and Isobel have different fathers," Taylor said. Her dark eyes darted from Zack to me. "Isobel always says her mother never makes mistakes. I guess she was wrong."

I slept fitfully. The baby's scent had clung to the material of the dress I'd been wearing, and when I hung it up, I remembered the weight of him in my arms, and the sharp and unexpected pain I'd felt when he'd been taken from me in the dark. Twice in the night I awoke, stabbed by a sense of loss, and lay in the dark, remembering, and listening to Zack's breathing. The next morning I awoke to the phantasmagoric landscape of a city after a blizzard. The storm was over, but powerful winds were lifting the snow that had accumulated overnight and whirling it into the air. The effect was vertiginous, like being suspended upside down in a snow globe. I pressed my forehead against the glass doors that looked out on the bank of Wascana Creek. The levee where the dogs and I usually began our morning run was barely visible. Seeing that I was in motion, Willie and Pantera sprang into action and ran up the hall towards the hooks where their leashes hung.

I listened to the click of their nails on the hardwood, then went to the closet where I kept the heavy sweater, jacket, and snow pants that I used for winter running. When I was dressed, I turned and was met by Zack's glare.

"You're not going out in this."

"The dogs are already at the door."

"One of the reasons we bought this house is because it has a double lot – plenty of room for them to chase each other."

"The dogs and I have an arrangement. I take them for a run, and they leave me alone for the rest of the morning."

"So I should stick a sock in it?"

"Pretty much," I said. I kissed him. "I'll be back before you know it."

"Carry your phone," he said.

My run was miserable. The wind whipping off the creek froze my hair and the icy strands snapped at my face as I ran. Blowing snow made it impossible to distinguish between the path and the creek bank, and when I stumbled over a rock I hadn't seen, only Willie's broad back kept me from falling flat. It was time to admit defeat.

"Okay, boys," I said. "We're heading home." Willie and Pantera didn't balk. When we got back, Zack was still in bed, thumbing his BlackBerry. I'd left my parka, snow pants, and boots in the mudroom, but my hair was still frozen; my face was scarlet and chapped and my nose was running.

Zack winced when he saw me. "You look like you could use a friend."

"Thanks for not saying 'I told you so.'"

"Get out of those wet clothes and come in here with me where it's warm."

"Said the Wolf to Little Red Riding Hood."

"You have nothing to fear from me, Little Red."

I stripped off my clothing and slid in. Zack leaned over and touched the button on the sound system beside the bed. Suddenly the room was filled Kiz Harp's soulful, smoky voice singing "Winter Warm" – a paean to making love while the winds whip.

"You planned this," I said.

Zack's smile was wicked. "You're a clever one, Little Red. I was planning to greet you in my smoking jacket, but you got back early."

"You don't own a smoking jacket."

"Then you must take me as I am," he said. And I did.

When we were through making love, Zack kissed the top of my head. "Better now?" he asked. "You were so sad last night."

"Just tired and worried," I said. "But I am once again ready to lick my weight in wild cats."

Zack gazed out the window. "You may be off the hook. Not a wild cat in sight. That's one lousy day out there."

I burrowed deeper. "Then let's stay in here."

"Fine with me. We can get started on *Sir Gawain*."

Zack was a skilful reader. Whenever our granddaughters, Madeleine and Lena, were with us overnight, he was always the storyteller of choice. He had an actor's voice, rich and sonorous, and he had an actor's ability to take his listeners to the heart of the tale.

The story was over five hundred years old, but it hadn't lost its power, and as I lay with my back against Zack's side and watched a snowdrift move incrementally up the glass patio door, I was content. The Green Knight had just challenged the gall, the gumption, and the guts of Arthur's court, when Taylor knocked on the door and, without waiting for an invitation, came in. I was grateful she hadn't wandered in fifteen minutes earlier. She was still in her pyjamas and, as she took in the scene, her mouth curled in a smile that was both affectionate and pitying. I had seen the smile a thousand times – it was her late mother's smile, and during the years when Sally and I had been best friends, it had often been directed at me.

Taylor sat on the corner of the bed. "Were you guys reading to each other?"

"Zack was reading to me."

"I'll bet you're the only parents in my entire school who do that," she said. She hugged her knees to herself. "I came in to see if you'd heard anything about the baby."

"Nothing yet," I said. "Delia's going to call Zack this morning."

"So we don't know why the baby's mother gave him to Izzy?"

"No. For the time being, I guess we'll just have be satisfied that the baby's fine."

"That's good," she said. "I woke up in the night wondering . . . " Taylor swung her legs off the bed and went to peer out the patio doors. "So are we going to church in this?"

"I think we'll stay put."

Taylor yawned and stretched. "Good, then I'm going to grab a bagel and go out to my studio. I've started this new piece, and I've been having a problem. This morning I figured out that if I . . . " She moved her hand in an arabesque of dismissal. "Well, never mind what I figured out." She gave us her new Sally smile. "You two probably want to get back to your reading."

After Taylor closed the door, Zack turned to me. "I sense that she no longer regards us as god-like."

"She's a teenager," I said. "We're starting to recede into the background."

Zack scowled. "Forever?"

"Not forever – but Taylor's trying to figure out who she is and what she wants out of life – those are pretty big questions."

"That's why she has us."

I took his hand. "She also has Sally."

"Sally's been dead for ten years."

"She still looms large for Taylor. The other day I went into her room and she was staring at a picture on her laptop. It was a self-portrait Sally had done when she was fourteen. Taylor said, 'I'll never be as good as she is,' then burst into tears."

"How did you handle it?"

"Badly. I gave her a hug and asked if she wanted to get two spoons and crack a carton of Häagen-Dazs Rocky Road with me.

"Sounds okay to me."

"It wasn't. I offered her comfort when she needed the truth."

"So what is the truth?"

"When Sally made that painting of herself, she was in a sexual relationship with a forty-one-year-old man."

"I thought you said she was fourteen."

"I did. The sex started when she was thirteen."

Zack placed *Gawain* face down on the bed. "That's statutory rape," he said.

"According to Sally it was a fair exchange. The man was an art critic named Izaak Levin. She needed what he could teach her and he needed –"

"To have sex with a prepubescent. Even if she consented, it's still statutory rape. But the law aside, what kind of prick would engage in sex with a kid?"

"An eminently respectable one – a trusted colleague of Sally's father. When Desmond Love died, Sally was lost. Desmond wasn't just Sally's father; he was her protector. He was an artist himself. Sally was, like Taylor, a prodigy. When Des recognized the talent Sally had, he created the conditions that would make it possible for her to do her best work."

"So her father was her teacher?"

I shook my head. "According to Sally, anyone could have taught her technique. She seemed to feel that Des's real gift was that he let her find out who she was as a painter. Des gave her space and he protected her against the people who Sally believed would cut off her air by talking to her about what she was doing. Sally and her mother had never been close. When Des died, Sally's mother withdrew into her own grief, and Sally was left alone.

"So Izaak took Des Love's place but extended the role." Zack's lip curled with disdain.

"Izaak and Sally went to the States and, to quote Sally, she spent a year seeing the U.S.A. in Izaak's Chevrolet, fucking and learning about how to make art. By the time she was out of her teens, she was an established artist and Izaak was her agent."

"He was having sex with her and taking her money." Zack ran his hand over his head. "In my line of work we call guys like that pimps."

"Sally didn't view it that way – at least not consciously – but I've seen the self-portrait that affected Taylor so much when she saw it on the Internet. Actually, Izaak showed it to me himself. The painting was in his private collection. It's the only piece of art Sally ever made that I can't bear to look at. She painted herself stretched over the hood of Izaak's convertible – the classic vintage pin-up pose. In the background is one of those no-tell motels that used to be along highways in the sixties. Even at fourteen, Sally was incredibly sensual, but there was so much more to her than that – she was smart and funny and thoughtful. None of that is in the self-portrait."

"If the painting stinks, why was Taylor so impressed?"

"Because the painting doesn't stink. Sally used acrylics in those saturated tones you see in old Technicolor movies, and the motel and Izaak's yellow convertible are so luridly seductive you can almost hear them panting. Sally herself is another story. She's absolutely lifeless – just a cut-out of a girl lying on the hood of a convertible waiting to be moved from motel to motel to serve a man."

"Jesus," Zack said. "And Taylor doesn't know any of this."

I shook my head. "No, and I don't want her to."

"You might revisit that decision, Jo. The truth has a way of coming out. Look at Delia's situation. Besides, if Taylor knew the price her mother paid to make that painting, she might realize that the cost is too high."

"She might," I said. "Or she might decide that being as good an artist as her mother is worth whatever price she has to pay."

"Over my dead body," Zack said.

"Mine too," I said. "Come on. Let's have a shower."

The phone rang just as I was handing Zack his towel. He squinted to see his watch through the steam. "Eight o'clock, straight up. It'll be Delia."

I picked up. Delia's husky adolescent-boy's voice cracked with urgency. "Jo, I need to talk to Zack."

"I'll get him."

"No. I'm outside your house. Can I come in?"

"Of course."

I hung up, wrapped a towel around my hair and picked up my robe. "It's Delia," I said. "She's outside, and she sounds tense."

"So much for starting our day sunny side up," Zack said.

Zack was right. Delia was not an ideal breakfast companion. She was a person who needed to have every detail under control, and that morning the world was conspiring against her. She'd been forced to drive through snow-clogged streets to deal with a problem whose magnitude and complexity I could only guess at, and for the first time in my memory, she had the wide-eyed gaze of someone whose life has just spun out of control.

No matter the season, Delia limited the colours in her wardrobe to black and white. That morning she was wearing a black ski jacket, a black wool cloche pulled down over her ears, and a black-and-white-striped wool scarf wound many times around her neck. She yanked off her hat, liberating her wiry salt-and-pepper hair. As always, several of Delia's curls, obeying their own law of kinetic energy, sprang over her forehead. She ignored them, unwound her scarf, and handed it to me.

I hung it over a hook inside the closet. "Nice scarf," I said.

"Check out the tension in the stitches. I made it while I was trying to quit smoking." She pulled a pack of Benson and Hedges from her bag. "Not that it worked, of course."

"You got a scarf out of it," I said.

Delia cocked an eyebrow. "Zack's been good for you – loosened you up. Where is he anyway?"

"Getting dressed. Come in and have some coffee while I get breakfast started."

Delia had the faint lines around her eyes and mouth most of us have after fifty, but her skin was taut and the cold air had made it glow. In her invariable weekend outfit of oversized turtleneck, chinos, and thick socks, she looked, at first glance, like a teenager who had added silver highlights to her hair on a whim.

When Zack came in, he wheeled his chair close to her. "Whatever it is, Dee, we can handle it. Have you eaten?"

Delia shook her head. Zack gestured to the table. "Then sit down and have some breakfast. We can talk afterwards."

I set a place for Delia, poured coffee and juice, and, when the porridge was ready, Zack spooned it into our bowls. Obedient as a well-schooled child, Delia ate what had been put in front of her. When she was through, she took her bowl to the sink, rinsed it, and returned to her chair. "The police called. The baby – his name, incidentally, is Jacob David Michaels – is fine. In fact he's more than fine. They've weighed him, measured him, and tested him, and he's healthy and responsive – perfect. There was an envelope addressed to me tucked under the lining of his baby seat. It contained Jacob's birth certificate: his mother's name is listed as Abigail Margaret Michaels; the name of the father is blank. There was a sheet with Jacob's medical history and a booklet with his vaccination record."

"Very thorough," Zack said.

Delia gave him a wan smile. "Very," she said. "There was also a note to me, stating that it was the mother's wish that I have full custody of Jacob, and that as a lawyer, I would know the procedures necessary to ensure that custody. The note was signed 'Abby Michaels.'"

"You two might find it easier to talk about this alone," I said. I picked up my coffee. "I haven't read the paper yet. I'll be in the family room if you need me."

Delia shook her head. "No, stay – please. This is going to come out anyway, and when it does, I'll need all the help I can get."

I sat back down.

Like all good trial lawyers, Delia knew how to create a gripping narrative, and her first sentence was dynamite.

"The year I clerked at the Supreme Court, I got pregnant." Her eyes darted between Zack and me. "I'll spare you the need to ask the burning question. I didn't get an abortion because by the time it dawned on me that I was pregnant, I was well into the second trimester." She shrugged. "I know it sounds like something out of a tabloid but there was a lot going on for me that year. I'd never lived outside Saskatchewan, and when I was at the College of Law I was cocooned with the Winners' Circle. Suddenly I was in Ottawa, passing powerful people in the corridors, and working for Theo Brokaw. Apart from you, Zack, he was the only person I'd ever met who was smarter than me."

When Zack smirked, Delia's glance was withering. "That's nothing to preen about," she said. "It's just a fact. Anyway, clerking at the Supreme Court was heady stuff – highly competitive. We were always working late – trying to out-dazzle one another." She smiled at the memory. "But we were also young and hormonal . . . "

"And you met somebody," Zack said.

Delia tilted her chin defiantly. "I met a lot of 'somebodies,'" she said.

The look Zack gave his partner was challenging. "That doesn't sound like you, Dee."

"Don't push it, Zack," Delia said, and her voice was steely. "I mean it. Let it go."

Zack shrugged. "You're the client."

She tried a smile and softened her tone. "Come on. Cast your mind back. You remember the syndrome. You're always at the office; you're not getting enough sleep; it occurs to you that you're missing out on life, so you decide to have a few drinks with the nearest warm body and you end up having sex. Usually it's just like scratching an itch – a relief with no permanent after-effects."

Zack's frown deepened. He wasn't buying Delia's story,

but he was willing to play along. "But this time there *was* something permanent," he said.

Delia's small chest heaved. "Yes, this time there were consequences, although it took me a long time to be aware of them. My menstrual cycle had always been erratic. I was running every morning, so I didn't put on much weight. And then one day I felt something inside me move. I went to an ob/gyn in Ottawa who told me I was five months' pregnant. She couldn't believe how stupid I'd been not to read the symptoms. Anyway, I had the baby in Ottawa, signed the appropriate papers, came home to Saskatchewan, and started studying for my bar exams. Being back with the Winners' Circle was like sliding into my old skin."

"Did you alert the men who might have fathered the child?" Zack said.

Delia shook her head. "There was no point. The doctor assured me the baby was healthy, and the agency said they had a long list of good families waiting for an infant. It was a closed chapter."

"But it's open now," Zack said.

"Yes," Delia said, "and not because I want it to be." Her fingers touched the pack of cigarettes in front of her as if for reassurance, then she opened her bag and removed the printout of an e-mail exchange. She handed it to Zack. "This arrived in my e-mail on November 22 – two weeks ago today," she said.

Zack slipped on his reading glasses and began to read. Delia fiddled with her cigarette package until I went to the cupboard, took down an ashtray, and put it in front of her. She mouthed the word "thanks" and lit up. Zack slid the printout to me.

Considering the subject of the note, the tone was cool.

On September 29, 1983, you, Delia Margolis Wainberg, gave birth to a female child in Ottawa Civic Hospital.

I have recently discovered that I am that child. My name is Abby Michaels. As an infant I was placed with a family, and until their recent deaths, I believed I was their natural child. My birth certificate, the adoption papers, and the genetic history you supplied to the adoption agency were appended to their wills.

A circumstance in my own life makes it imperative that I possess all data relevant to my genetic background. I would be grateful if you could supply me with the name and contact information of my biological father. You have my word that my only interest in communicating with him is to ascertain relevant medical information. Beyond that, I have no interest in communicating further either with him or with you.

Thank you for your attention to this matter.

I handed the paper back to Delia. "Did you get in touch with her?" I asked.

Delia nodded. "My doctor was on holidays for a few days. When he returned he gave me a précis of everything medically relevant that had come to light in the years since the baby was born. I sent the notes to Abby Michaels on November 30."

Zack leaned forward in his chair. "What did you tell Ms. Michaels about her biological father?"

"The same thing I told you," Delia said tightly. "I told her that during the period when I might have been impregnated I was sexually active, and I couldn't identify her biological father. I wished her well, and said that if she required any further information, she should feel free to get in touch."

"Did she?" Zack asked.

"She called that day I was in the car with Joanne. She identified herself. Then she said, 'You'll have to live with what you've done,' and hung up."

"Did that make sense to you?" Zack asked.

"No, because I'd done everything she asked me to do. Zack, none of this makes sense. You saw her e-mail to me. Two weeks ago, Abby Michaels was rational and in charge of her life. She wanted medical information, and I supplied it. Friday, she phones, pronounces judgment on me, and hangs up before I can ask her to explain; then yesterday she hands her child over to Isobel and says he belongs with me. What happened?"

"One possibility is postpartum psychosis," Zack said.

Remembering Zack's account of the woman who threw her baby from the bridge, my throat tightened, but Delia was cool. "I've had a couple of those cases," she said. "According to my reading, the onset of the disorder is usually quite soon after birth. Jacob is six months old, and the woman who wrote that e-mail didn't sound as if she was suffering from anything. She was absolutely lucid."

"But she wasn't lucid yesterday when she gave her baby to Isobel and said the child belonged with you," Zack said. "Whatever's going on, Dee, time is not our friend. The sooner you talk to the cops, the better. If anything happens to Abby Michaels because we screwed up, neither of us is going to be happy."

Delia inhaled deeply and blew a smoke ring. "Okay, call your friend the Inspector – and tell her I'm Abby Michaels's birth mother, and I want Jacob with me until they find her."

Zack shot her a hard look. "You're sure about this, Dee?"

Delia met his gaze. "I'm sure," she said. For the first time, her voice faltered. "Jacob is family, Zack."

Zack nodded. "In that case, I'll call Debbie Haczkewicz and get the ball rolling."

Zack was still on his cell with Debbie when the phone in the kitchen rang. The woman's voice was patrician and assured. "Joanne, this is Myra Brokaw. I know it's early to call, but I'm anxious to discuss Theo's participation in the Supreme Court special."

"Myra, I'm sorry. This isn't a good time," I said.

When she heard Myra Brokaw's name, Delia's attention shifted to me.

"Will there ever be a good time?" Myra said. Her words came rapidly. "I've given our situation a great deal of thought, and I believe I've come up with a plan that will work for us all. Will you at least come for tea and hear me out?"

"It's the end of term," I said. "And it's a busy time of year. Can I check my calendar and call you back?"

"I don't have a choice, do I?" Myra said. "I'll look forward to your call."

Zack and I hung up simultaneously. We exchanged glances. "You first," I said.

"The Inspector is on her way over," Zack said. "Your turn."

"I need your silver tongue," I said. "Myra Brokaw has invited me to tea so we can discuss Justice Brokaw's participation in our show."

Zack winced. "Ouch."

"What show?" Delia asked.

"NationTV is enamoured of those Issues for Dummies shows I've been working on. They're cheap, they're Canadian content, and they fill up airtime. The network's been talking about branching out – getting experts to explain some of the institutions that govern the lives of ordinary Canadians."

Delia frowned. "And Myra wants to involve Theo? My God, what's the matter with her? Why would she expose him that way?"

"I take it he didn't improve after we left yesterday."

"No, he couldn't seem to get past the fact that I wasn't the young woman who'd clerked for him," Delia said. "He and Myra stayed for about an hour yesterday afternoon. It was awkward. Theo kept staring at me and shaking his head. He seems to drift in and out." There was real sadness in Delia's voice. "He told me he was working on a book, but when I asked about the subject matter, he seemed confused. The next minute he was all excited because his papa was baking poppy seed bread and he'd promised him a slice before bed. He couldn't remember my name. He kept calling me 'that clever girl.' He'd turn to Myra and whisper, 'You remember her – that clever girl.' And she'd nod and smile and say, 'Of course.'"

"Had you met Myra before yesterday?" I asked.

"There was some kind of reception they had for the students the year I was clerking, but that was it."

"Do you think Myra brought Theo back to Regina to hide him away?" I asked.

The smoke from her cigarette drifted around Delia's face, obscuring her expression. "Probably. Revealing that her legal giant has feet of clay certainly wouldn't be in Myra's best interests. She's invested her life in him. My guess is she's just protecting her investment."

CHAPTER 3

Inspector Debbie Haczkewicz was a tall and powerfully built woman, with a smile that was as disarming as it was rare. Like most defence lawyers, Zack wasn't a big fan of the boys and girls in blue, but he and Debbie got along. When her eighteen-year-old son, Leo, was paralyzed in a motorcycle accident, Zack had, initially at Debbie's request, shown up at the rehabilitation hospital every day for a month, ducking Leo's punches, insults, and the business end of his catheter until Leo was ready to talk and to listen. Inspector Haczkewicz hadn't forgotten the favour.

When the Inspector arrived, we moved to the family room. I offered coffee, but Debbie waved me off. "Thanks, but I gather from what Zack says we should move quickly on this."

Delia handed the inspector the copy of Abby's e-mail and repeated the story she told us. When Delia said she was unable to remember the names of the men who might have fathered her child, Inspector Haczkewicz's eyes were questioning, but she didn't press the point. Twenty-seven years is a long time and, as Delia emphasized repeatedly, the sexual encounters had been casual. Having satisfied herself that Delia's memory on that point was a dry well, Inspector Haczkewicz moved along.

Zack had no difficulty convincing her to authorize a search for a missing person. Although there was no evidence of foul play, Abby Michaels's actions revealed a woman whose state of mind was fragile, and Debbie Haczkewicz had seen enough frozen bodies to know what a prairie winter can do to the vulnerable.

Zack had been concerned that Debbie might stick at the possibility of granting temporary custody of Jacob to the Wainbergs, but it was she who introduced the possibility. "Why not?" she said. "Abby Michaels made her intentions clear in the note she left in her son's car seat, and it's not as if Child Services is overrun by desirable foster homes."

Zack handed the Inspector his camera. The photos from the concert were on display. "Take a look at these," he said. "I've put them on a flash card for you in case you have to justify your decision later."

Debbie Haczkewicz's gaze moved from the images on Zack's camera to Delia. "The physical similarity between you and Abby Michaels is persuasive," she said. "But let's cover all the bases. If you and Zack agree, I'd like to take a DNA swab."

"Fine with me," Delia said.

Debbie nodded. "Good. Given the fact that you've been cooperative and relatively forthcoming, there shouldn't be a problem getting a court order granting you temporary custody." Zack handed her the flash card and she dropped it in her briefcase. "The fact that it's Sunday and the weather is godawful may slow us down, but I'll do my best."

Zack and I saw the inspector out. She reached for the doorknob, and then turned back to Zack. "Leo sends his regards. He loves Japan, he loves teaching English, and he loves his new girlfriend."

Zack grinned. "A happily-ever-after ending," he said.

"For Leo, yes, but not for me," Debbie said. "Sapporo is a long way from Regina. I want my son to be happy, but I want him to be happy closer to home."

When Zack and I came back into the kitchen, Delia was snaking her scarf around her neck. She stopped when she saw Zack. "So what are our chances?"

"Pretty good," Zack said. "Deb seems convinced that granting you and Noah temporary custody is the right course of action, and when she makes up her mind, she's a bulldog."

Delia gave the scarf a final toss. "Okay, I'll go back to the house and wait for the call."

"Are you still planning to take the girls to the concert this afternoon?" I asked.

Delia raised her eyebrows. "You don't think the school will cancel because of the weather?"

"Not a chance," I said. "Lutherans are a hardy bunch."

As she calculated her options, Delia was thoughtful. "Noah and I will drive the girls," she said finally. "We need to be there – especially now." With that, she headed for home, leaving behind the lingering scent of her signature Chanel No. 5 and many, many questions.

I asked Zack the big one first. "Is all of this really a surprise to you?"

"Believe it or not, it is," he said. "And ever since Delia dropped the bomb, I've been trying to figure why she didn't tell me at the time. As you've pointed out more than once, Delia and I are joined at the hip."

Zack began clearing the table, handing me the dishes to rinse and stack in the dishwasher.

"And you never suspected anything?" I said.

"No, and Delia was back that Christmas. She stayed with Noah. I remember thinking Ottawa must agree with her.

When we were in school, she was always kind of grubby, but that Christmas she looked great – new haircut, nice clothes, and her skin had cleared up."

"Delia has beautiful skin."

"She didn't when we were in school. She ate crap – well, we all ate crap – anyway, she was always kind of spotty, but that Christmas she was a knockout."

"Hmm."

"Why the 'hmm'?"

"That kind of physical change often means a woman's in a serious relationship."

"You don't believe Delia was sleeping around, do you?" Zack said.

"No," I said. "Neither do you and neither does Debbie Haczkewicz, but Delia made a decision about how she handles this part of her past, and she must have reasons."

Zack handed me a bowl. "Delia always has reasons. I just wonder why she didn't tell any of us. She must have felt isolated. Supreme Court clerkships begin in early September and end in September of the next year. Abby was born on September 29. Being pregnant, giving birth, and establishing a stellar legal reputation – that's a lot to handle on your own."

"Delia pulled it off," I said. "She deserves credit."

"She does. And to be honest, I don't know how much help any of the guys in the Winners' Circle would have been if Delia had told us she was pregnant. All we knew about pregnancies was to avoid them at all costs. Blake was the only one who was geographically close to Delia. He was in Toronto, but Kevin was in Calgary, Chris was in Vancouver, and I was here, slaving away for Fred L. Harney."

I wiped the countertop. "I always meant to ask you about that. How come you didn't article with one of the five-star firms? You graduated at the top of your class. You must have had offers."

"You bet I did." Zack poured the soap into the dishwasher and turned the dial. "Paraplegics are highly desirable. A lot of big firms like to have a cripple they can wheel out to show how enlightened they are. But I didn't have a year to waste being poster boy for the so-called differently abled. I knew how to research points of law, and I knew how to prepare memoranda of law, what I didn't know was how to actually *practise* law. When Fred Harney called, I knew I'd just discovered my yellow brick road.

"Fred was heavily into the sauce when I articled for him. But even drunk he was one hell of a lawyer. I learned more sitting with him in court than I learned in three years in law school. That year he was blacking out a lot, and my job was to go to court with him and remember what happened."

"People didn't notice he was drunk?"

Zack shook his head. "Nah. Fred was a pro. Never slurred; never stumbled; never lost his train of thought. Flawless performance. Couldn't ask for better representation, except for those huge gaps in his memory. That's where I came in. When court adjourned, we'd go back to the office, and when he sobered up, I'd tell him what the Crown said and what he'd said. And here's the wild part. Fred would critique the performances – both the Crown prosecutor's and his own. It might not have been a five-star law firm, but I was getting a master class in the law. Sometimes, when I'm facing a jury, I can still hear him. 'Don't stint on the smouldering rage,' he'd say. 'Convince the jury that only the utmost effort of will is keeping you from erupting at the vast injustice that has brought your client to this sorry pass.'"

Zack raised his hand, palm out. "Enough tripping down memory lane," he said. "Time for us to get to work. You have papers to grade, and I am not prepared for court tomorrow morning."

Willie and Pantera led the way to the office Zack and I share and took their places beside us as we settled in. I picked up an essay; Zack opened his laptop, found what he was looking for, and sighed. "This is worse than I thought. Ms. Shreve, if you've ever had a hankering to see your husband step on his joint, be in Courtroom B tomorrow morning."

I circled a misspelling of Afghanistan on the student's title page and kept on marking. "Smoulder with rage," I said. "If the jury's waiting for you to erupt, maybe they won't notice that you don't know what you're talking about."

It was the kind of morning I like best. We turned on the gas fireplace and moved methodically through the piles of work in front of us. When Debbie Haczkewicz called, Zack gave me the high sign. A judge had agreed to hear Delia and Noah's petition at noon. The news was good, but as Zack headed off to change, the glance we exchanged was tinged with regret. Once again, external events were intruding on our small and pleasant world.

After Zack left to meet with the Wainbergs, I put a pan of bacon in the oven, and the dogs and I hiked across the yard to let Taylor know that toasted BLTs were on the way.

Taylor's studio was a space for a serious artist and she spent hours there. On gloomy days, when I saw its lights and knew that Taylor was making the art that she loved and that she was safe, I realized that while nominally the studio had been a gift for Taylor, it had also been a gift for me.

I never entered her studio without knocking. Often she would invite me in and we'd talk about what she was doing, but if she was working on a piece she wasn't ready to show, she'd grab her jacket, jam her feet into her boots, and slip out the door. On those days, when her mind was still focused on the images she'd left in her studio, our walk back to the house would be silent. That blustery morning, the dogs swam through the snow, barking and chasing one another, exuberant with the sheer joy of being off leash, but Taylor was preoccupied.

While she was cleaning up before lunch, I made our sandwiches and placed a plastic zip-lock bag beside her plate. Every Christmas, when my oldest children were young, I bought them each an ornament to hold a photograph of themselves as they were that year. The tradition I'd started with Mieka, Angus, and Peter I continued with Taylor and the granddaughters, and every December Taylor took great pleasure in arranging these miniatures of her changing self. That day, she shook out the contents of the bag listlessly and picked up the ornament that held the most current picture – her first from high school. "I've been monitoring a couple of forums about Sally Love on the Internet," she said.

My nerves tightened. "There's that retrospective of her work coming up," I said. "I imagine the interest is pretty intense."

Taylor's gaze was steady. "Do you know what Sally was doing when she was my age?"

It was as if by telling Zack that morning about Izaak Levin and Sally's relationship I'd opened Pandora's box. "I know some of it," I said carefully.

Taylor dangled the ornament by the thin red ribbon that would loop it to the tree branch. "She was in New York City," my daughter said. "Experiencing life."

"You're experiencing life," I said.

Taylor's laugh was short and derisive. "Not the way she was. One of the people on the forum said Sally was . . . sexually active. She was my age, and she was sexually active." Taylor's dark eyes were accusing. "Did you know that?"

"I knew."

"But you never told me."

"No."

"Were you afraid that if I knew what my mother . . . what Sally did . . . I'd do it too?"

I pulled a chair close to her and picked up last year's ornament. Fittingly, it was an antique frame. In her photo, Taylor's glossy hair was still long and her smile was without shadow and a mile wide – a reminder that in a girl's rich and turbulent life, a year can be an eternity.

"Taylor, we've talked about this. Sex has consequences."

"To the way I feel about myself," she said.

"And to the way the boy feels about himself."

The mixture of resignation and defiance in her voice was pure Sally. "Being with me isn't going to make any boy feel worse about himself," Taylor said. She slammed the ornament on the table. "And for your information, this isn't about boys. This is about my work. There's nothing there." Taylor drew a breath. "On the forum, the man who's devoted his life to Sally Love says that artists have to live large to paint. He says that even when she was fourteen, Sally knew that she had to experience life to be a great artist."

"And this man equates experiencing life with having sex?"

"Sally did," Taylor said coldly. "If you'd seen that self-portrait she did when she was my age, you'd understand."

"I have seen it, Taylor. I saw it in the living room of the man who owned it."

Taylor's eyes were brimming. "Then you know how amazing it is."

"I do," I said. "I also know that by the time your mother was fourteen, she'd suffered more than any child should ever suffer."

"Because her father died and her mother didn't have a good relationship with her," Taylor said. "But she had Izaak Levin. You told me that when there was no one else, he took care of Sally. He gave her the chance to travel and the freedom to paint what she saw."

"That's true," I said. "But there was more. Taylor, Izaak used your mother. He used her beauty, and he used her talent."

"Whatever he did, it worked." Taylor's voice quivered, but her message was unequivocal. "When she was my age, Sally was making great art, and that's worth everything."

I picked up the ornament Taylor had slammed on the table. It was impossible to take a bad picture of Taylor, and this one wasn't unflattering, but it was revealing. In it, for the first time since she'd come to me, there was uncertainty in her eyes and her smile was guarded. I stared at the photograph for a second too long, and Taylor noticed. "Do you think I look geeky?"

"You don't look geeky," I said. "You look as if you have a lot on your mind, which, clearly, you do. Taylor, I can't even begin to imagine what it's like to make the kind of art that you and Sally make, but I do know that the life experience you bring to your work doesn't have to be harsh. Angela Cheng says that when she plays certain pieces, she thinks about the way the light shines on her child's hair."

"Angela Cheng is a pianist, not a painter."

"But she's found a way to live that feeds her art. If you're lucky and if you make the right choices, that can happen to you."

Taylor leapt out of her chair and bounded onto my knee. The leap was as unexpected as it was sweet. "Everything's changing," she said.

"I know," I said. "But you're going to be fine. Taylor, you *are* fine."

Taylor was as tall as I was. Sitting on my knee was no longer easy for her, but we held on, united by our awareness that while there were battles ahead, we had been granted a reprieve. As we watched the snow fall, it seemed we breathed in unison.

Zack's inability to do any but the most rudimentary jigsaw puzzle was a running joke between him and our granddaughters. That afternoon when Mieka and the girls arrived to help get our family dinner ready, both girls had puzzles jammed in their backpacks. Taylor was at the choral concert; Mieka and I had cooking to do; so, by process of elimination, Zack was on puzzle duty.

After the girls threw off their coats and boots, they descended on him. "The one I brought is so easy," Lena cooed. "It's a caterpillar, and even the littlest kids in junior kindergarten are bored with it." "Mine's a piano," Madeleine said. "The box says it's for ages five to eight, but you *play* the piano, Granddad, and there's a picture, so you should be able to do it. If you get stuck, I'll help you."

Zack wheeled his chair close to the table. "Thanks for the offer, Maddy," he said. "But a man's got to do what a man's got to do. I'm going to tackle these puzzles all by myself."

Maddy looked at her mother and me and rolled her eyes. Lena opened the caterpillar box and shook out the puzzle pieces. Zack groaned when he saw them. "There must be a hundred pieces there," he said.

"There are ten," Lena corrected, "and they're big."

Mieka and I went into the kitchen to put the finishing touches on what she called our duelling chilies: mine, *con carne*; hers, vegetarian. We stirred, grated, chopped, and listened to Zack trumpet his success with the puzzle as the girls chortled. When the caterpillar was complete, my husband called me in. "Ms. Shreve, I'd like a picture of this." The girls posed with him, and I snapped. "You're a madman," I said.

"Victors always look a little crazed," Zack said, then he slid the completed caterpillar into its box and turned to the girls. "We are now cooking with gas. Bring on the piano."

There had been plenty of groans and giggles from the dining room by the time Peter, our older son, and his girlfriend, Dacia, arrived. They said hello to Zack and the girls, then carried the plastic storage bins of lights and tree ornaments from the garage through to the family room. They popped off the containers' lids and began unwinding the lights from their newspaper cones, unwrapping the ornaments, and setting everything out on a trestle table by the tree. Mieka and I had just put Zack out of his agony by announcing that we were setting the dining room table so he had to either move his puzzle or scrap it, when Taylor and Isobel came bounding in, back from the concert. They were beaming, and the source of their pleasure was apparent. Delia and Noah were behind them, and Noah was holding the baby.

"The girls thought you'd like to see Jacob again," Noah said.

"You bet we would," I said. "May I take your coats?"

Noah and Delia exchanged glances. "I think we'll make this a quick visit," Delia said. "We should get Jacob home. The sooner he knows where he belongs, the better."

Noah unzipped Jacob's snowsuit, took off his toque, and carried him around so Jacob could inspect us as we inspected him. Isobel took Jacob's small hand in hers and followed her father. "He's a handsome baby, isn't he?" she said.

Indeed, Jacob was handsome, and in the natural light of the living room, his kinship with Delia and Isobel was even more obvious than it had been the night before in the gym. Jacob's eyes were brown, so dark they were almost black, but he shared the Wainberg women's milky white skin and their thick springy hair. Like Isobel and Delia, he was preternaturally alert, tense with the need to take in every detail and assign it a place.

Jacob gave Zack and me a solemn gaze then, apparently finding us satisfactory, he smiled. The dimple Jacob displayed was winning and my husband was easy prey. When Zack held out his arms and Noah handed him the baby, Jacob settled right in.

Noah held out a warning finger. "Hey, don't get too

comfortable there, Jacob," he said. "There's serious bonding to be done and it's supposed to be with Delia and me."

"Better get used to sharing him," I said. "He's a charmer." I turned to Taylor. "Your sister's in the kitchen. You know how she is about babies. If she doesn't get to hold Jacob, we won't hear the end of it. And Peter and Dacia will want to get acquainted too."

The girls came back, and Mieka was right behind them, drying her hands on a tea towel. "Peter and Dacia are walking the dogs," she said. "But I'm ready for this baby. Hand him over, Zack."

When she bent to take Jacob, Mieka's face clouded. She held him out, examining his face, then, still unsmiling, turned to Taylor and Isobel. "Would you two take Maddy and Lena into the kitchen and help them put some cookies on a plate for dessert?"

"We can do that ourselves," Lena said.

Isobel placed her hand on Lena's shoulder. "I think your mum has something to say that will be easier to say if we're not around."

The four girls disappeared into the kitchen and I caught my daughter's eye. "What's up?"

Mieka took Jacob and sat down in the wing chair by the fireplace. "Where's this child's mother?" she asked.

"You know her?" I said.

Mieka shook her head. "I don't know her, but I know who she is. She and this little guy have been at UpSlideDown every day this week."

Delia's face was strained. "Did you talk to her?"

"I tried," Mieka said. "But we've been crazy busy. A lot of parents promise their kids that if they behave while they're shopping, everybody gets to come to UpSlideDown for hot chocolate and a playtime afterward. Anyway, it's been hectic. The kids are wired, and the parents are wired, but everybody's in a good space. I guess that's why the woman who brought in this little guy was so noticeable."

"Her name is Abby Michaels," Delia said bleakly.

Mieka slid the baby out of his snowsuit. "So you're taking care of Jacob for her?"

"It's complicated," Noah said. "Yesterday afternoon, Abby Michaels went to the Luther Christmas concert. When the concert was over, she handed Jacob to Isobel and disappeared. It was just before the blackout, so there was a certain amount of confusion."

"Why did Abby give her baby to Isobel?" Mieka's eyes travelled across our faces, searching for an answer.

Noah glanced at Zack, and my husband picked up the thread. "We'll fill you in on the background later, Mieka. Right now, our concern – everybody's concern – is Abby Michaels. The police are looking for her, but they don't have much to go on. Do you know anything that could help?"

"Not really," Mieka said. "The woman – Abby – would come in around three and stay till we closed at five-thirty. She was so alone. She never connected with the other parents – and she never connected with her baby."

Delia tensed. "Abby Michaels neglected her child?"

Mieka smiled at the little boy. "He was never neglected – at least not physically. His mother – Abby – cared for him. When he whimpered, she gave him a bottle, and when he turned it down, she took him to the space where other mothers breast-feed."

"He was breast-fed?" I said. "It's pretty difficult for a woman not to connect with a child she's breast-feeding."

"His mother was trying to wean him, and Jacob obviously wasn't ready. He knew what he wanted, and it wasn't a bottle. A lot of women have had that experience, and I'm sure some of the other UpSlideDown regulars would have been only too willing to trade horror stories, but Abby didn't encourage conversation."

"So you left her alone," I said.

Mieka lowered her eyes. "Yes, and it was hard because she was clearly desperate – not just about the weaning, but about everything. I tried, Mum. I'd linger with the coffee pot when I refilled her cup, but Abby didn't let me in, and I didn't push."

Jacob grabbed at the necklace Mieka was wearing; she smiled at him and loosened his grip. "Once she asked me about the big holiday blast we were having before Christmas."

"Did she want to bring Jacob?" Noah said.

"No, she'd just noticed that people were stopping by with presents and leaving them under the tree, and she wondered what was going on. I told her parents were supposed to bring a gift for a child who might not be getting many presents."

"Did Abby bring a gift?" Noah asked.

"I don't know," Mieka said. "There's a mountain of presents, but we ask people to put the toys in gift bags, so that we can make sure the presents are new, safe, and age-appropriate."

The room was silent. Jacob had found Mieka's necklace again, and she began uncurling his fingers from the chain and play-biting his fingertips. The game made him chuckle.

Delia watched with a half-smile. "And that's all?" she said, finally.

Mieka coloured. "Not quite. There is something else, but it's embarrassing to talk about because it makes me sound like a stalker." She inhaled deeply. "On Friday evening when Jacob and his mother left, I tried to follow them."

Zack had often remarked on Mieka's solid common sense. He was genuinely gob-smacked. "Whatever made you do that?" he asked.

"Impulse? I don't know. I was just . . . uneasy," Mieka said. "It was closing time and Jacob and his mother were still there. Maddy and Lena had their jackets and boots on and were chomping at the bit to go home, so I went to Abby and said I was sorry but I had to close up. She got herself and the baby ready to leave and came over to pay her bill. She seemed very tired, but after she paid me, she didn't leave. She gave me this . . . penetrating look and asked me if I believed in God. When I said I did, she asked how I could reconcile my belief with the cruelties of the world."

"The unanswerable question," I said.

Mieka nodded. "Except Abby was so intense. It was as if she had really hoped I might provide an answer. When I didn't come up with anything, she thanked me and said that I shouldn't feel badly because there was nothing anyone could do to help her. Then she left."

Noah put his arm around his wife's slender shoulders.

"It was so sad, and so final," Mieka said. "I locked up. When the girls and I started towards our car, I saw that Abby was parked close to us. She was getting Jacob in his car seat and strapping him in. That always takes a while, so I hurried the girls and, when Abby left, I followed her."

"Where did she go?" Zack said.

"I don't know," Mieka said. "She drove down 13th, but when she got to Albert, she ran the light and turned left. There was a car coming across, so I had to stop. By the time the light changed, there must have been twenty cars between us, so I went home. All I know is that she was driving a Volvo – same vintage as yours, Mum, but black. I did manage to get her licence. It was an Ontario vanity plate that spelled out the word LECTOR – easy to remember because of Hannibal Lecter in *Silence of the Lambs*." Mieka's eyes were both sad and puzzled. "She didn't seem like the kind of person who would pay money to have the name of a cannibalistic serial killer on her licence."

"How was it spelled?" Noah asked.

"L-e-c-t-o-r," my daughter said.

"Lector is Latin for 'reader' or 'lecturer,'" Noah said. "That might be significant."

Zack nodded. "If somebody's willing to pay money to have a word put on their plate, that word has significance for them." He took out his BlackBerry and called police headquarters. "Debbie . . . we may have a break."

As Mieka gave her information to the Inspector, the Wainbergs zipped Jacob into his snowsuit and snapped him into his car seat. They both looked worried. No one offered words of comfort.

After we closed the door on the Wainbergs, Zack went to change for supper, and I made a last pass through the dining room to see if we'd forgotten anything. Taylor was there, adding a place setting. The slacks and shirt she'd been wearing under her choir robes had been replaced by a deep red jersey dress with a wide black patent-leather belt and a gently flowing skirt.

"Did I miscount?" I said.

Taylor folded a napkin and placed it on the bread and butter plate. "No. I invited somebody. Is that okay?"

"Sure. Anyone I know?"

"You met him last night at the concert. Zack knows him." She straightened a fork without looking up. "It's Declan Hunter."

"Hmm," I said.

Taylor's gaze was level. "Is that all you're going to say?"

"Your friends are always welcome. You know that."

"Has Zack said anything about Declan?"

"Zack never talks about his clients."

"But Declan's not Zack's client. His dad is. Declan's just . . . " Taylor shrugged and smiled her old open smile. "He's just Declan."

"Well, I'm glad 'just Declan' is coming for supper," I said. "Is he into tree decorating?"

The tension drained from Taylor's face. "He's really stoked about this whole evening," she said.

"You look pretty stoked yourself."

Her expression was impish. "You're the one who said I have to feed my art."

I went to our room to clean up for dinner and found Zack struggling with the price tag on a turtleneck the shade of a eucalyptus leaf. I handed him my manicure scissors so he could snip off the tag, and fingered the material. "Cashmere," I said. "Very nice."

"I ordered one for you, too," he said, pulling on his sweater. "It's in that box on your dresser."

I picked up my gift and touched it to my cheek. The material was sinfully soft. "Thank you," I said. "It's gorgeous."

He raised an eyebrow. "But you're not going to put it on."

"Mieka says that the day you and I start wearing matching outfits is the day she puts us into Golden Memories."

"I've got pull at Golden Memories. I kept the owner out of the hoosegow. I could get us adjoining rooms."

I unbuttoned my blouse. "So what did the owner do?"

"He was alleged to have encouraged some of his female guests to give him power of attorney."

"Did he?"

"All my clients are innocent, Ms. Shreve. Now come on, let's see the sweater."

I pulled it over my head and held out my arms.

"Looks better on you than it does on me," Zack said.

"Thanks," I said. "For the sweater and for the compliment. Hey, guess who's coming to dinner?"

"The Green Knight."

"Close. Declan Hunter."

Zack's smile vanished. "How come?"

"Taylor invited him." I sat down on the bed, so Zack and I could face one another. "She isn't aware that Declan's your client," I said.

"He's under no legal obligation to tell her."

"But there are legal issues in his life," I said.

Zack wheeled closer. "Jo, you know I can't give you any specifics, but if I thought for a moment that Taylor was in danger, Declan wouldn't get past the front door."

"His transgressions are minor?" I asked.

"So far, but they're the kinds of dumb-ass things that can put a kid on the glide path to disaster, so I worry."

"You like him, don't you?"

"I do. We had a great time that night we went to the Broken Rack, so in the spirit of camaraderie I asked Declan why he's so determined to make trouble for himself. He said that it's easy to get lost when you live in your father's shadow."

Our family had endured tree-decorating nights when our tempers were as snarled as the strings of lights. The mood the year before had been close to perfect until we hung the last ornament, flicked on the lights, and Pantera, responding to some dark atavistic impulse buried deep in his mastiff psyche, took a run at the tree, knocked it to the ground, attacked it, then streaked to the basement and refused to come upstairs for three days. This Christmas the tree-trimming was without incident, and there were some Hallmark moments: Declan, his dreads tied back with hemp twine, carefully examining each of the ornaments that held a picture of Taylor before he handed it to her so she could place it on the tree; Lena and Maddy suspending all the sparkliest ornaments from branches at their level, so that the lower third of the tree glittered as bright as a showgirl's fan and the upper two-thirds were bare; Zack, his chair at a safe distance from the tree, his fingers looped through Pantera's collar, murmuring reassurances to his dog.

The one moment of real tension was short-lived. When Madeleine and Lena reached a noisy standoff about whose toilet-paper-roll angel would have pride of place as the tree-topper, Peter jammed the angels together on the top branch, where they perched, listing slightly, their silver doily wings mashed and their twin maniacal smiles reminding us all that Christmas is a time of sisterhood and lunacy.

Zack led Pantera to our bedroom and shut him in, safe from human folly, before we lit the tree. After we turned on the lights, Zack took photos of the tree on his BlackBerry and sent them to Angus who was studying for exams in Saskatoon. Angus texted back a one-word sentence: "Cooooooooool." After handing around Angus's text of praise for our handiwork, Zack pushed his chair to the piano and played "Round Midnight" – not because the Thelonius Monk standard was seasonal, but because I loved it. After that, it was request time. Lena asked for "Puff, the Magic Dragon," and when Puff had slipped into his cave for the last time, Mieka and her daughters sang along as Zack played "Girls Just Want to Have Fun." Peter's girlfriend, Dacia, the self-described daughter of old hippies, did what the daughter of old hippies do. She pulled out her guitar and sang "Scarborough Fair" in a voice that was as powerful as it was sweet.

"Hard act to follow, but I'm convinced there's yet more talent in the audience," Zack said. "If there are no volunteers, I'm doing my Barry Manilow medley."

Taylor touched Declan's arm. The touch was enough. Declan went to Dacia, whispered a word in her ear, and she handed him her guitar. Without prelude, he began to play Green Day's "Time of Your Life," first with poignant resignation, then with a fierce snarling anger. It was a riveting performance, but it also revealed Declan's pain, and as he handed the guitar back to Dacia, there was an awkward silence in the room.

Pete's girlfriend smoothed the raw edges. "You do realize how good you are?" she said.

Declan's smile was heartbreaking. "I realize exactly how good I am," he said. "And I know I'm not good enough." He held out his hand to Taylor. "Time for me to take off," he said.

Taylor's hand was in Declan's as he thanked us and said good night. Except for Peter, we were a family of talkers, but after Taylor walked Declan to the front door, it seemed that none of us had anything to say.

Lena saved the moment. Out of nowhere she snagged some lines from her favourite story and began reciting in her fluty little-girl voice. "'Today is gone. Today was fun. Tomorrow is another one.'" She turned to her sister. "There's more, but I can't remember."

Maddy sighed. "'Every day, from here to there, funny things are everywhere.'"

Soothed by Dr. Seuss, we began packing the empty ornament boxes in the storage bins and carrying them out to the garage. Ready or not, another Christmas was underway.

CHAPTER 4

Like all people in a deep and passionate relationship, my life was shadowed by five words that Zack and I had uttered on our wedding day without a second thought: "Till death do us part." When Zack was seven, a drunk driver fumbling for his cigarette lighter had failed to see him crossing the street on his way to baseball practice. The drunk's momentary distraction meant that three thousand pounds of steel hit Zack's sinewy young body, ripping it apart and leaving him a paraplegic with a host of physical problems that worsened with age. My husband always said that he had chosen law because it was a sedentary profession, but it could also be a deadly one. Trial law was high stakes, and the hours and pressures were punishing. The average time between a lawyer's first court appearance and his or her first heart attack was twenty years. This was not a statistic that encouraged me.

During the early months of our marriage our most serious quarrels had centred on Zack's determination to shut me out when his body betrayed him and my determination not to be shut out. There were some compromises. I convinced him that caring for one another's bodies could be a sensual pleasure, so we swam together and rubbed one another down and massaged each other until the knots disappeared. Zack also worked at home as much as he could, but despite his promises to cut back, his hours were long, and there were mornings when after his customary five hours of sleep, he awoke grey and drawn.

This morning was one of them, but I had long since learned not to comment. By the time the dogs and I got back from our run, Zack had showered, made the porridge and coffee, poured the juice, and placed the local paper beside my plate. I put my arms around him. "You are a scarily handsome guy," I said. "Why don't we have breakfast and go back to bed after Taylor leaves for school?"

"Can't. Got to get my client ready for court. Besides, I have a feeling the phone will be ringing soon. Check out the paper."

The picture of Abby Michaels on the front page was the one Zack had taken at the concert Saturday afternoon, but it had been cropped and blown up, so that her broad expanse of forehead and piercing eyes dominated the page. The headline was stark: "MOTHER MISSING."

Zack sipped his coffee. "See what you think of the story."

I read it through. "Standard journalism," I said. "The five W's and one H with no answers to *why* and *how* and a deliberate obfuscation of *who*. Do you see something sinister there?"

Zack removed his reading glasses. "Nothing sinister. On the contrary, the press are cooperating with the police. Abby Michaels reads the paper. We know that because she showed up at Luther for the concert. You'll notice that all the references in the story are generic."

I skimmed the story again. "The baby was handed over to 'a student' and is now in the custody of 'an area family.'" I looked at Zack. "So you think this story is calculated to bring Abby Michaels out of hiding."

"I do."

"Do you think it will work?"

He pinched the bridge of his nose and rubbed. "We live in hope," he said. "If Abby comes forward, she can be hospitalized, and if they can find the right doctor and the right meds, she'll have a second chance."

"But you don't think it's going to happen."

Zack shook his head. "After twenty-four hours, the odds aren't great, and I've learned not to play long shots."

Zack's BlackBerry rang just as he was ladling out the porridge. I answered. It was Delia. "Can he call you back?" I said. "We're just about to eat."

"Nothing important," she said. "I'll talk to him later."

"Everyone make it through the night okay?"

"Jacob almost slept through. Noah wasn't able to find a baby monitor, so Isobel moved that inflatable mattress the kids use for sleepovers into Jacob's room. When Noah went in this morning, Jacob was curled up in Isobel's arms, and they were both sound asleep."

I glanced at the picture of Abby Michaels on the front page and felt my throat close. Wherever she was, her night must have been an agony.

Delia's voice was insistent. "Jo, are you there?"

"Sorry, just woolgathering."

"That's an odd expression," she said. "Anyway, would you mind telling Zack I'm going to work at home today?"

"I'll pass along the message," I said. "And, Delia, I'm glad things are going well."

After I rang off, Zack pulled his chair up to the table. "You don't look glad," he said.

"It's hard not to think about what Abby Michaels is going through," I said.

"Somebody always loses," Zack said, and his voice was heavy. "Should we call Taylor for breakfast?"

I looked at my watch. "Let her sleep. It's early, and the buses will be a nightmare. I'll drive her to school."

"And you're not quite ready to put on your game face."

"That too," I said. "By the way, Delia's working at home today."

"For the first time in living memory," he said. "Well, good for her."

"For wanting to be with Jacob?"

"Yes, and for being smart enough to establish that she stayed home with her grandson on his first day in her care."

When we'd finished eating, Zack turned down a second cup of coffee. "I have to get a move on," he said. "Why don't you keep me company while I get dressed?"

As always, Zack had laid out his clothes the night before. He picked up a pair of silk briefs. "So what's on your agenda?"

"I'm going up to the university," I said. "I told my first-year students I'd be in my office this morning in case they had any questions about the exam. I don't imagine I'll have many customers, but I'll be able to get some marking out of the way. And this afternoon I'm having tea with the Brokaws."

Zack grimaced. "Better you than me," he said. "Although I'm not going to be having much fun either. The sentencing decision in the road-racing case is at hand, so this morning my client and I will be in court listening to victims' impact statements."

I shuddered. "I can't imagine losing someone I loved and then standing up in court and telling everybody how much that person meant to me."

"You're not alone. Everyone sitting in that courtroom will be wishing they were somewhere else."

"Do the statements do any good?"

Zack shrugged. "Well, there are two schools of thought. Proponents say the statements give judges information they wouldn't normally have and keep victims from feeling they've been left out of the process. Theoretically, the statements also make offenders appreciate the pain they've caused."

"But you don't believe that?"

"No. I think the statements just cause everybody grief and raise false expectations for the victims. And defence lawyers share a dirty little secret. We know that 99 per cent of offenders just don't give a shit. They leave tire tracks on the backs of everyone who's ever been unlucky enough to care about them, and they never look back. The other 1 per cent, and I would include my client in this small group, are already filled with guilt about what they've done. They don't need to sit in court and have coals heaped upon their head. So my job this morning is to desensitize Jeremy to what he's going to hear in court."

"How do you do that?"

"By sitting him down and making him listen while one of our students or admin assistants reads the victim impact statements until Jeremy learns to react appropriately."

"With contrition and remorse."

"And without disintegrating."

"Granted everything I know about the case comes from the media," I said, "but the consensus seems to be that Jeremy Sawchuk is responsible for the death of another eighteen-year-old boy. Maybe a little suffering is in order."

Zack raised an eyebrow. "Lucky for me you're not the judge. You're the gentlest person I know – if you think Jeremy should get the thumbscrews for what he did, I'm in more trouble than I realized. All I have is the fact that the boy Jeremy killed was his best friend and that he's suffering."

"I guess the counter-argument would be that at least Jeremy is alive to suffer," I said.

"And I've got nothing to throw at that one," Zack said. "All I can do is hope that the judge handing down the sentence sees the whole picture. Jeremy has had a rough life but he's done his best to stay afloat. He attends school regularly, maintains a B-minus average – which for a kid like Jeremy is the equivalent of being in Phi Beta Kappa. He's worked his entire life to keep himself fed and clothed because his parents' interests run more to drugs than child care. Before the night of the accident, Jeremy had never been involved in anything that could be construed as risky behaviour. He made a mistake. My job is to see that one mistake doesn't ruin the rest of his life."

"Are you going to use that line from your speech at the wheelchair athletes' barbecue last fall?"

Zack moved his chair in front of the mirror and began knotting his tie. "There were a lot of lines in that speech – too many if I remember correctly. I cut it short when I noticed my audience's attention had drifted from me to the unopened cases of Molson's."

"The line I'm thinking of came before the attention drifted. It was something about all of us having to live larger than the pain that's been done to us or the pain that we've caused others."

Zack tightened the knot on his tie and caught my eye in the mirror. "Do you think that would work?"

"I think it's worth a shot," I said. "I also think it's true."

Usually, Taylor, Gracie, and Isobel met at the bus stop and travelled to school together, but when I called Blake Falconer and the Wainbergs, we agreed that this might not be the morning to rely on public transit. Taylor and I set out in the car, grateful that the wind had finally stopped howling. Shrouded in fresh snow, the city had the silence that comes after a winter storm. Our house was close to Albert Street, one of the city's main arteries, but the Falconers lived several blocks in, and Gracie, with the athlete's passion for challenge, had volunteered to hike down to Albert Street to meet us. While we waited, Taylor filled me in on the salient events of her life that morning. Declan had texted twice and phoned once. He'd had a great time last night and he'd invited Taylor to a party New Year's Eve. She'd also had a call from the Animal Friends Group she belonged to, asking if Taylor could feed the colonies of feral cats in the warehouse district and behind Scarth Street Mall, because the flu had knocked out the scheduled volunteers.

We'd just agreed that I'd buy some bags of cat food and pick her up after school when Gracie arrived, pink-cheeked and breathless. She jumped in, I pulled back into traffic, and my BlackBerry rang. Taylor answered. "It's Isobel's mum. She'd like to talk to you. She says it's important."

"Tell her I'm driving, but I'll run in when we stop by her house to pick up Isobel."

Taylor relayed the message and Isobel was waiting when we arrived. She and I waved at one another as we passed on the front walk. "I'll be right back," I said. "I just have to talk to your mum for a minute."

Delia had been watching from the window, and she met me at the door and motioned me inside. She was on edge, but Delia was always on edge.

"I know you haven't got much time, but you and Zack need to know the latest. The police have traced the licence plate of the car Abby Michaels was driving. The licence was issued to Hugh Fraser Michaels of Port Hope, Ontario. Mr. Michaels is deceased. The police have also discovered that Abby has been staying in a suite she rented at the Chelton Inn. She checked in last Tuesday. She and the baby seemed to have a routine. She took him out in the stroller in the morning and then, in mid-afternoon, she took him out in the baby carrier."

"And stayed at UpSlideDown till closing time," I said.

Delia nodded. "Abby and the baby always returned around six, but Saturday night they didn't come back."

"And there's no indication where Abby is?"

Delia half-turned from me. "None. According to Inspector Haczkewicz, the bed in the suite hadn't been slept in, and the bathroom was pristine."

"So, Abby left town?"

Delia slumped. "If she did, she travelled light. Her toiletry bag was in the bathroom, and her clothes were in the closet."

My stomach clenched. "What about the baby's things?"

"There was nothing to indicate that a baby had ever been in the room."

Noah came downstairs carrying Jacob wrapped in a thick white bath towel. "Dee, there's a phone call for you. It's a client, and he says it's important."

Delia was already moving down the hall. "I'll talk to you later, Joanne. Thanks for coming in."

I smiled at Noah and the baby. "The kids are waiting in the car," I said. "But I have to say hi to Jacob. Can you bring him over here? My boots are wet."

Noah came close enough for me to smell the sweet smell of a baby just out of the bath. He pushed the towel back, so I could see Jacob's face. The little boy's hair curled wetly – the way Isobel's did after she'd been swimming at the lake. As he took my measure, Jacob's dark eyes were solemn. "Do you ever smile?" I whispered, and he rewarded me with a gummy grin. "Now that was worth tromping through the snow for," I said.

Noah capped the baby's head with his palm as if to protect him. "I guess Dee told you about the room at the Chelton."

"She did."

"Do you think Abby Michaels is dead?"

"I hope not," I said.

Noah's face was troubled. "You want to hear something lousy?" he asked. "I don't know what I hope."

When I opened the car door, the girls were laughing and whispering, deeply engaged in exchanging the secrets of girl-land. I snapped on my seat belt. "With luck, we'll make it, just before the bell," I said. My announcement was greeted with a trio of groans.

"Look at that," Isobel said.

I did a shoulder check. "I don't see anything," I said.

Isobel leaned forward, tapped my shoulder, and pointed. "Not on the road. At my house," she said. I glanced towards the Wainbergs. Delia had joined her husband. She was holding Jacob, and Noah's powerful arm encircled them, drawing them close. Framed in the rectangle of light from the living room, they were a Norman Rockwell image of family.

After the last day of lectures, a university is a silent place. The students who come to campus are there to write exams or study for them. Most faculty members take advantage of their open calendars to work at home. Corridors and classrooms and coffee shops are virtually empty. It's my favourite time in the semester.

I walked into the political science office at the university and found Sheila Acoose-Gould, our administrative assistant, at her desk reading an old issue of *Maclean's*. Twinkling silently behind her was a musical Christmas tree that had played twelve seasonal tunes until, by one of our few unanimous decisions, our department voted to rip out its musical heart.

"Anything happening around here?" I said.

Sheila leaned back in her chair and sighed contentedly. "Not a thing. All is calm. All is bright."

"Let's keep it that way," I said.

I picked up my mail and headed for my office. The message light on my phone was blinking. I pressed the message retrieval button and heard Myra Brokaw's voice. "Good morning, Joanne. Just a gentle reminder that Theo and I are expecting you for tea today at two-thirty. There are no names on the security panel of our building, so I wanted to make sure you had our code. It's 201. We're very much looking forward to seeing you." I deleted the message, uttered Zack's second-favourite expletive, wrote down the Brokaws' apartment security code, and moved a stack of essays from the side of my desk to the middle. It was going to be a long day.

By eleven o'clock I'd made a large enough dent in the essay pile that I felt I could take a break and get something to eat. I went downstairs to the cafeteria, filled my mug with tea, and selected a Granny Smith apple. When I got back to my office, I stared at my essays and decided I needed a change of pace. I opened my laptop and found a file I'd started when I was considering Theo Brokaw as the audience's guide to the workings of the Supreme Court. There had been plenty of sources to mine for nuggets about Theo's philosophy of law, but very little biographical material, and most of what I'd found was without value. However, when I'd been seated at a dinner party with Nicholas Zaba, a man who'd grown up with Theo, I hit the mother lode. The two men had remained close, and my dinner companion had drunk just enough to make him an indiscreet and utterly charming raconteur.

The next morning when I'd written up Nick's memories of Mr. Justice Brokaw, I began as Nick had begun. "Theo owes everything he has to women," he'd said, refilling my glass with a very fine Shiraz. "His genius is that he makes the women in his life feel as if they owe everything to him."

In Nick's telling, Theo led a charmed life. He was the only son of hard-working, proud, first-generation Canadians who lived over the bakery they owned in Regina in the solid working-class area of Broders Annex. The Brokaws' dreams for their four daughters were modest: they wanted the girls to grow into industrious and pious women who would marry good men and give them grandchildren. The girls were clever, but they were also dutiful, and so after they graduated high school, they worked in Brokaw's Bakery, expanded to include delivery service, and in the butcher's shop that the family had purchased, renovated, and transformed into Brokaw's Market, a business with a generic name and an impressive ability to ferret out and supply the needs of the neighbourhood's Eastern European population. The shops prospered, but the family's most extravagant dreams were vested in their only son.

Theo not only complied with their expectations; he excelled. After graduating from the College of Law, he articled for a respected Saskatoon law firm, decided that his real passion was not practising law but research and teaching, completed an L.L.M., discovered a talent for critical legal theory and analytical jurisprudence, taught law at the University of Saskatchewan, married the daughter of a distinguished jurist, was appointed to the province's Court of Appeals, and found himself, at forty-five, appointed to the highest court in the land.

His rise had been meteoric, fuelled by his powerful father-in-law and by his wife who knew how the game was played. As Nick Zaba wryly noted, the equation was simple: Myra's father loved Myra, Myra loved Theo, and Theo loved Theo. The marriage was a happy one. Until they retired from the family business, Theo's sisters regularly wrapped and shipped his favourites from the bakery: the poppy seed cake; the thick black bread that his father credited with giving him the brains to become a judge; the special Christmas baking that Theo's sisters knew, without asking, Myra would never think to make him. But

Myra was, they hastened to add, the perfect wife for a professional man.

When I finished reading I packed up the unmarked essays, put on my coat and boots, told Sheila that if any students wanted to get in touch with me, they had my e-mail address, and drove to Broders Annex. It wasn't hard to justify my visit to Brokaw's. Loaves of the elaborately twisted and braided Ukrainian Christmas bread were always on the table at our family's Christmas Day open house and it was time to place my order. Besides, anything beat reading another paper on Canada's involvement in Afghanistan.

On a day in which all colour and warmth seemed to have been leached from the world, the bakery, bright, warm, and redolent of fresh baking, was a welcome destination. Except for Christmas and Easter and an occasional impulse buy if I was in the neighbourhood, I wasn't a regular customer, and so it was a surprise but not a shock when a young couple who introduced themselves as Tony and Rose Nguyen said they were the bakery's new owners.

I looked at the metal shelves of bread – whole wheat, multigrain, dense dark pumpernickel, sour rye, hearth loaves, and egg bread – and at the glass case of turnovers, doughnuts, strudel, poppy seed rolls, honey cake, sweet buns, and tarts. "Everything looks the same as it was," I said.

"Everything *is* the same," Tony Nguyen said. He spoke with the care of someone for whom English is a second language. "We bought the bakery lock, stock, and barrel and that included the recipes. We follow them to the letter."

"Good," I said. "I'll have a loaf of the dark pumpernickel, an apple strudel, and three gingerbread girls. And I'd like to place my Christmas order: four dozen cinnamon rolls, half without raisins, and three loaves of Ukrainian Christmas bread."

"Kolach," Tony Nguyen said, and he wrote my order in a small ringed notebook. "And your name?"

"Joanne Shreve," I said. I gave him my address and phone number and said I'd pick up the baking on December 24. "Are the Brokaws still in Regina?"

"They moved to Victoria," Tony Nguyen said. "They sought more pleasant winters."

His wife boxed the strudel. "They worked hard all their lives," she said softly. "Now this is our dream."

"I'm sure you'll have great success," I said. "You seem to be doing all the right things." I paid my bill; Rose Nguyen handed me my purchases, and I dropped them in my shopping bag.

"My brother, Phuoc Huu, bought the grocery store," Tony said. "His borscht is very good with pumpernickel."

I glanced outside. The grey was oppressive. "It looks like a perfect day for borscht," I said. "Thanks for the suggestion."

Like the Brokaw's Bakery, the Brokaw's Market was unchanged: the refrigerated display cases were filled with fresh and deli meats and an impressive variety of sausages. The freezers held cabbage rolls, perogies of every permutation or combination, and borscht – vegetarian and meat. Even the aisle that displayed Ukrainian gifts and cards was the same. I considered a pretty embroidered cloth, then, remembering that I had thirty-five years' worth of tablecloths at home, put it back. There was a glass shelf of Russian nesting dolls. They had fascinated my own children when they were little. Their dolls had long since gone the way of all toys with moveable parts, but looking at twin Natasha dolls, one with black painted hair, one blonde, I knew they'd be a hit in Madeleine's and Lena's stockings and I placed them in my basket. There was a larger matryoshka nesting doll, dark-haired, pink-cheeked, and very pretty. I wouldn't have minded finding her in my own stocking, but the price tag was $37.50, so I left her behind and went off in search of borscht and sausage.

Phuoc Huu Nguyen rang up my purchases. "Merry Christmas," he said.

"And to you," I said. I started for the door, but the lure of the pink-cheeked bright-eyed matryoshka doll was powerful. "I'll be right back," I said, and I went to the gift area, found my doll, and handed her and enough additional cash to Phuoc Huu Nguyen.

"Impulse buy," I said.

"Works for me," Phuoc Huu said, and he slipped the money into the register and handed me my purchase.

The Brokaws' condo was downtown over a vintage record shop in a pedestrian mall of upscale shops and bistros. Whatever the season, Scarth Street Mall was a good place to be. Twice a week from the May 24 long weekend till Thanksgiving, it was the site of an open-air farmers' market; in winter, the space became a skating rink. That afternoon the rink was all but deserted. The ice had been cleared, but there was only one skater, and he moved with a mechanical joylessness that seemed in tune with the grey and lowering sky.

The entrance to the condos was unprepossessing – just an ordinary door opening into a small vestibule with a panel of buzzers. I touched 201 and waited. There was no response. I tried again – and again. Finally, I gave up. As I turned to open the door to the street, I walked into Louise Hunter.

She was wearing a hot pink knitted cap with earflaps, a black leather jacket with matching pants, and knee-high black leather boots with knitted tops of hot pink – very chic and very youthful. She looked two decades younger than the world-weary, self-loathing woman I'd met at the Wainbergs' party, but it wasn't a question of clothes making the woman. That afternoon, Louise was sober, and that fact alone made all the difference.

"I just got here," she said. "But I think I understand your problem." Her voice was full of life. "You're trying to get through to the older couple who just moved in down the hall from me." She opened the inner door and we walked together to the elevator. "They haven't quite mastered the buzzer-door relationship," she said as we stepped into a lift the size of an old-fashioned phone booth. "They really do need to learn how to let guests in. I know of at least one potential visitor who simply left in frustration. God knows if she ever summoned up the fortitude to try again."

She laughed. "I should probably introduce myself. I'm Louise Hunter. I'm a pianist and I have a studio here."

She had no memory of meeting me. I extended my hand. "Joanne Shreve," I said.

The light faded from Louise's face. "You're Zack Shreve's wife," she said. "I've probably met you a dozen times. I apologize for not remembering."

"Don't apologize," I said. "A.S. Byatt calls it nominal amnesia – it's common enough at our age."

Louise's smile was wry. "Thanks, but I imagine my nominal amnesia was fuelled by Grey Goose vodka."

When we stepped off the elevator, Louise gestured towards an apartment with an open door. "That's their place," she said. "It was nice to meet you, Joanne. Sobriety has its advantages. Who knows? I might even remember who you are next time."

The door to the Brokaws' was open wide. I called inside, but there was no response. A chair and a boot rack had been placed against the wall by the door. I took off my boots and stepped over the threshold and called again. The condo had an open-plan living-dining-kitchen area. Three chairs had been drawn around a low table that held everything needed for tea. As in a fairy-tale, all was in readiness but no one was there. I turned to leave but then I heard voices in the hall.

The combination of relief and anger in Myra Brokaw's voice was familiar. I'd heard it in my own voice when one of my children had wandered off and my mind had been a blur of terrifying possibilities until I'd found them. "Theo, you can't just leave like that, without telling me," she said. "If you get lost, and I have to call the police, they'll take you from me."

Theo's tone was querulous. "I just went out to get a . . . a . . . a thing I needed. I would have come back." He paused, and when he spoke again, his voice lacked its previous assurance. "I do always come back, don't I?"

"Yes, Theo. You always come back," Myra said. "Sit down and let me take off your boots. Our guest will be here any minute."

I was trapped, but anything was better than letting them know I'd heard their conversation. I walked to the window and looked down at the mall. The solitary skater was still making his joyless rounds, but there was plenty of activity: shoppers, their heads bent against the snow, darted into stores. A man, big as a sumo wrestler, had set up a charitable donation box and was loudly ringing a bell.

"You're here," Myra said.

"The door was open," I said. "I thought you wanted me to come inside to wait."

"Of course," she said. "Theo and I just had to step out for a minute. Let me take your coat." She laughed. "Actually, I might have to ask you to help me off with mine." She held out her arm awkwardly. "Last night, coming back from the party, I slipped and sprained my wrist."

I helped Myra and Theo off with their jackets, removed my own, and hung the jackets on a clothes tree just inside the door.

"I apologize, Joanne," she said. "To say the least, this is an unconventional welcome."

"One of your neighbours let me in downstairs. I shouldn't have walked in, but I must admit I enjoyed looking out your window. You have a great view."

"Theo agrees with you," she said, and I could hear the assurance flowing back into her voice. "When I tell him we have front-row seats for the Human Comedy, he always concurs, don't you, love?"

His back ramrod-straight, his strong sculpted features still without an ounce of extra flesh, Theo was, as he had apparently always been, a handsome man, but his expression was blank. When Myra raised her arm to touch her husband's, she winced. At the Wainbergs' I'd been struck by her vitality and by the translucent glow of her skin. The woman leading Theo into the living room was pale and clearly tired but she did not allow her social mask to drop. "Remember my telling you that Joanne Kilbourn was coming for tea this afternoon?" she said brightly.

Theo's eyes darted anxiously towards his wife. "Did I invite her?"

"We both invited her," Myra said. "Now, why don't you and Joanne chat while I get things ready."

Theo waited until his wife was in the kitchen area, then he moved purposefully towards the chairs that had been set out for tea, picked up one, moved it in front of the window, and sat down. I picked up another chair and carried it to the place next to Theo's in front of the window.

For a beat we sat in silence: Theo staring at the street, me, staring at Theo. He was carefully dressed. His suede loafers were brushed, his grey slacks were knife-edged, and his black turtleneck made him seem both distinguished and rakish.

"It can't be easy coming back to a city you left almost thirty years ago," I said.

"Everything changes," he said; then he leaned so close to the window that his forehead almost pressed the glass.

A young woman and two little girls in snowsuits the colour of lime popsicles had joined the solitary skater. "I'm hoping to get skates for Christmas," Theo said. He lowered his voice. "Maybe you could tell the woman," he said, jerking his head in Myra's direction. After that, he and I retreated to our private thoughts. There didn't seem to be much left to say.

When Myra asked if I could come and help with the tea tray, I was relieved. Bringing in the tray, moving my chair back to the table, and exclaiming over the little feast Myra produced gave me something to do. The tray was festive with damask napkins, and pale green cups, saucers, and plates so thin I could see through them. The tea itself was excellent: Darjeeling and very strong. Myra had made bite-sized lemon tarts with pastry that I envied. There was fruit bread thinly sliced and lavishly buttered and a fine winter surprise – a bowl of strawberries. Theo popped a tart into his mouth; then, like the schoolboy he had apparently become again, loaded his plate. Myra laughingly shook a chastising finger at him, but wholly absorbed in contemplating his food, he ignored her. She shook her head fondly, and she and I exchanged smiles.

"We saw your husband in action this morning," she said. "We get gloomy staying in the apartment, so we put on our boots and tromped through the snow to the courthouse. Mr. Shreve puts on quite a show."

Theo was just about to pop another lemon tart in his mouth, but our conversation had captured his interest.

"The one in the chair?" he asked me.

"He's my husband," I said.

Theo's brown eyes were suddenly bright and shrewd – as if the veil had been lifted. "His argument was smart but not sound," he said.

"Lots of snap and dazzle, but no substance?" I said.

Theo stared at me without comprehension. The veil had dropped again.

"I disagree," Myra said, knitting the ragged pieces of our discussion into a coherent whole. "Not with Joanne's answer, but with your assessment, Theo. In my opinion, Mr. Shreve is right. No otherwise blameless person should have to pay for a moment of indiscretion with a lifetime of penance."

"So say you," Theo said, and he went back to his plate.

We moved to safer subjects: the changes that had taken place in the city in the past three decades; the effect sudden prosperity was having on the province; some interesting small galleries Myra and Theo might enjoy. Myra was a quick and intelligent conversationalist, but her slip on the ice had taken its toll, and she was flagging.

When Theo yawned, Myra stood quickly. The party was over, but she was gracious. "Joanne, I haven't given you a tour of the apartment." She had already begun to move, and I followed. The small kitchen was separated from the living room by a counter on which there were two martini glasses: the first held red jelly beans; the second, green. "That's a nice festive touch," I said.

"There were three," Theo volunteered, "but she broke one."

"Joanne doesn't need to hear about our domestic mishaps, Theo," Myra said sharply. "We'll get another." She turned to me. "My husband has a sweet tooth," she said.

I smiled. "So does mine, but he'd regard using his martini glasses for anything other than gin as sacrilege."

"I'll remember that when we entertain you," Myra said. "Now here's the master bedroom – sleek, no? I'm still getting accustomed to the new look of our lives. I decided it would be better to look forward, not back. Except for our clothing and Theo's papers, we didn't bring a thing with us from Ottawa. A fresh start was best. All my collections were . . . dispersed."

"It must have been difficult leaving all that behind," I said.

"It was a small death," she said flatly. "Now here's the bathroom – also sleek and soul-less. And," she said, moving down the hall, "here's my little warren." She gestured to a study with a cranberry-coloured reading chair, stacks of novels with glossy dust jackets, and six framed black-and-white photos arranged in rows of three on the wall. The photographs in the top row were of a woman's foot, its toes gnarled by arthritis, a graceful, liver-spotted hand, and a drooping breast. The photographs in the row beneath were of an eye with its lid slightly pouched, a mouth with thinning lips, and a buttock no longer firm. The pictures were oddly mesmerizing. As I turned to Myra, she read the question in my eyes. "My work," she said. "A portrait of me as I am now: fragmented and aging."

"Myra! Myra!" Theo's voice, youthful and excited, rang out from the other room. Myra sighed softly. "And there is Theo as he is now."

An odd scene greeted us. Theo was holding the matryoshka I'd purchased at Brokaw's. My purse lay open on the table in front of him, and he was beaming. "She brought the doll, Myra. Every year at Christmas, we get a new one, and here it is. I spied it in her purse when she opened it to get her glasses, but I didn't want to spoil the surprise."

"I'm so sorry, Joanne," Myra whispered. She looked at her husband with concern. "I don't think I can take it away from him."

"Keep it," I said. "Please. Let it be my gift."

"Thank you," Myra said.

"Come and look," Theo crowed. "This one is a real beauty." The wooden matryoshka with her brightly painted headscarf, her shiny black hair, rosebud lips, and rounded flower-painted body was traditional, and Theo was clearly delighted. He held the doll between his thumb and forefinger. "I have a secret," he said in a soft imitation of a feminine voice. He transferred the doll to the palm of his other hand, opened it, and removed a second doll. "I have a secret," he said in a voice that was slightly higher in pitch. He repeated the action and the phrase "I have a secret" until five identical dolls, each smaller than her predecessor, were lined up on the coffee table. When he opened the sixth and found the final doll – no larger than a child's fingernail but identical in every way to the others – he spoke the climactic line in a voice that was very small and very high. "And I am the secret," he said. Then his eyes darted between his wife and me, seeking our approval.

Myra smiled at him fondly. "That was splendid, Theo. Thank you." She put her fingers firmly under my elbow. "Joanne's leaving us now," she said.

Theo stood and bowed. "Thank you for coming," he said. "Not many do."

Myra led the way to the door and then came with me as I stepped outside. She pulled the door closed behind us. Because the door had been open when I arrived, I hadn't seen the wreath. It was fresh and eye-catching: a perfect circle of bay leaves, eucalyptus, and pomegranates dusted with gold mica powder.

"That's exquisite," I said.

"I made it," Myra said. "I suddenly find myself with ample time for the womanly arts." Her eyes met mine. "We're going to have to take a different approach to our television project, aren't we?" She began speaking quickly, cutting off the possibility of objection. "Perhaps we could arrange for an actor, someone really fine like Donald Sutherland, to read from Theo's judgments. The TV people could intersperse the readings with videos of Theo talking about the law – before – when he was himself. I have a box of home movies: Theo hiking, picnicking – the human side of the man – and excellent videos of him discussing the philosophy of law with his students. Joanne, there are endless ways this could be done."

"Is it Alzheimer's?" I asked.

Myra slumped. She hadn't convinced me, and she knew it. "No, but the effect is the same. He was shingling the roof of our cottage Labour Day weekend. We could have paid to have it done, but you know Theo." Her laugh was short. "But, of course, you don't know Theo. Not Theo as he was – as I believe he still is somewhere inside that shell you saw. The man I was married to for over four decades was the most capable human being I've ever known. He was also clever and charming and fascinating. And it was all over in a second."

"What happened?"

"He fell. One minute we were leading the lives we'd always led. I was in my garden picking beans for lunch, and Theo was on the roof shingling. He lost his footing, fell to the ground, and suffered what is characterized as a 'traumatic frontal lobe brain injury' – it was devastating. Parts of his long-term memory are intact, but he has no short-term memory to put daily life into context. He's confused; he's agitated; he's unpredictable. Drugs don't help, but I'm not giving up. I believe I still see flashes of the man he was."

"There was a spark when he described Zack's performance in court," I said.

"There was." She was ardent. "I live for those glimpses of the man he was. They're proof that the real Theo is still in there. My husband has always set himself goals and not only met but exceeded them. He's already made progress. At first, he didn't know where he was or whether it was night or day. Now, he's putting the pieces together." Myra's eyes glittered. "Theo needs a reason to get up in the morning. So do I. Don't take that away from us, Joanne."

It took Taylor and me an hour to feed the colonies of cats in the warehouse district and in the abandoned building across the alley from the condos on Scarth Street Mall. When we'd emptied our last bag of food on the snow, I looked across the alley and saw Louise Hunter getting into a Mercedes parked behind her building. She seemed to be in a hurry. She backed out, hit a garbage can, jerked forward, then backed out again and sped off. Angus, who had owned a series of clunkers but loved cars, would have said it was a shitty way to treat 200,000 dollars' worth of sweet driving machine, and he would have been right.

By the time we all got home, Zack and Taylor and I were hungry and tired, so we ate early. The borscht and thick slices of dark pumpernickel from the Brokaw family bakery made for a deeply satisfying meal. When he'd finished his second bowl of soup, Zack pushed his chair back and sighed with contentment. "You know, even the lousiest day has its moments," he said.

"And the evening has just begun," I said.

Right on cue, Zack's cell rang. As he listened, his face grew sombre. When the call ended, he turned to us. "That was Delia," he said. "The police just found Abby Michaels."

CHAPTER

5

Zack was a realist. If the truth was painful, he faced it, dealt with it, and moved along. That evening after he talked to Delia, he didn't waste time on any preamble when he spoke to Taylor and me. "Bad news," he said. His voice was low and his eyes were filled with concern as his gaze moved between us. "Abby Michaels is dead. An hour ago, two men digging out the parking lot behind the A-1 Jewellery and Pawn Shop on Toronto Street found a black Volvo with the licence plate LECTOR. Abby Michaels's body was in the front seat. It's early times yet but the police believe she was raped and strangled."

Taylor's body tensed at the news. I put my arm around her and rubbed her shoulder. "How could something like that happen?" she said.

The parentheses that bracketed Zack's lips deepened. "I ask myself that every time I see a case like this. It's hard to believe that human beings can treat one another so brutally. But it happens. All I can tell you is that the person who did this will be caught and punished."

Taylor's face was strained. "But will anyone ever know *why* he did it?"

Zack didn't lie. "The Crown will present theories. The man's lawyer will present other theories. But the only person who will ever really know what went through his mind before he attacked Abby Michaels is the man himself. Generally rapists are men who feel powerless and who feel a need to prove their power. Sometimes, the situation spins out of control, and they kill their victim. I know that's not a satisfactory answer, but those are the facts."

I could feel Taylor's muscles tighten again. When she spoke she couldn't hide her fear and frustration. "I understand that part of it, but with Abby, there are other facts. Before the rape happened, she gave away her baby. It's almost as if she knew something terrible was coming, and she wanted to make sure Jacob was safe."

Zack and I exchanged glances. "We're all in the dark here," I said. "But we'll know more soon. Your dad's friend, Inspector Haczkewicz, always says that a police investigation is like turning on the lights in a room where everything's in place. You just need to see what's already there."

"So you think the police will find out why she gave away her baby before that terrible thing happened to her?"

"I know they will," Zack said. "As your mother says, it's a matter of time."

Taylor's voice was tight. "I guess Izzy's parents have already told her."

"I'm sure they have," Zack said. He looked closely at Taylor's face. It was pale and pinched. "Are you all right?"

Without answering, she picked up her bowl and plate, walked to the sink and rinsed them. "Isobel was so excited about having a sister," she said.

"She could probably use someone to talk to," I said. "Why don't you give her a call?"

Taylor glanced at the dishes on the table. "Do you need me to help?"

"Your dad and I can handle it," I said.

After we'd finished cleaning up, Zack took two tulip-shaped Scotch glasses from the cupboard.

I looked at him questioningly. "You're not going over to the Wainbergs'?"

He shook his head. "There's nothing I can do except hold Delia's hand, and she has Noah for that. Besides, I'm tired. Tonight I need a hand to hold, and Delia's is not my hand of choice."

It was the first time I could remember Zack acknowledging that he was tired. "You're in luck," I said. "Mine is available."

"One of my clients gave me what he claims is a bottle of excellent single malt," Zack said. "It's called Old Pulteney. Interested in giving it a test run?"

"You bet," I said. "I'll bring the glasses; you get Old Pulteney, and I'll meet you in the family room. We can light the fire, turn on the tree lights, and try to remember that it's Christmas."

When we were together on the couch, I handed Zack his drink. He held the glass under his nose and inhaled deeply. "My client told me that to be fair to the single malt, I should allow myself a half-hour free of stress and distractions before I sip." He stared at the Scotch thoughtfully. "Screw that." He took a large swallow. "You know, this really is pretty good."

I sipped. "More than pretty good," I said. "Here's to a half-hour free of stress and distractions."

For a few minutes we sat in companionable silence, letting the warmth of the Scotch spread through our veins while we savoured the fire, the tree, and the closeness to one another. "I could get used to this," I said.

"So could I," Zack agreed, "but we're going to have to talk about Abby Michaels."

"Whenever you're ready."

"I'm as ready as I'm ever going to be," he said. "Taylor posed the right question. What happened? In a murder investigation, the police start with the body, then focus on the scene where the body was found and the victim's history. The old cops call it the golden triangle, and a lot of the time they can make an educated guess about why someone was murdered just by checking out where the body was found. If a body is left in a public place, as Abby's was, chances are they're looking at what the cops call 'a crime of opportunity.'"

"The victim is just in the wrong place at the wrong time," I said.

"Right, but this time, the formula doesn't work."

"Because of Abby's determination to get Jacob into the Wainbergs' hands before she was attacked," I said.

Zack nodded. "As Taylor says, it was almost as if Abby knew something was going to happen to her, and she wanted to make sure Jacob was safe."

"It does look that way," I said. "Except Abby couldn't have had any enemies in Regina. The only people she knew here were the Wainbergs."

"And she'd never met them," Zack said. "So Abby Michaels comes to a city where she knows no one, gives away her son, and is raped and murdered in the parking lot behind a pawn shop."

"Abby had an appointment in Samarra," I said.

"You think her death was fated?" Zack said.

I shrugged. "You know the old story. A man believes he sees Death threatening him in the market in Baghdad so he runs to Samarra to escape. When he goes to the market in Samarra, Death is waiting for him, because that's where the man was supposed to die all along."

Zack was pensive. "I wonder how eager Abby Michaels was to outwit death," he said finally.

I looked at him hard. "Surely you don't think Abby brought this on herself?"

"Of course not," Zack said. "But from what Mieka says, Abby was suffering from something that sounds very much like clinical depression. I was trying to imagine her state of mind the night she gave away her son."

"Do the police have any ideas about how Abby ended up in that parking lot?"

"Uh-uh. The A-l Jewellery and Pawn Shop is in the industrial area, so the cops can't count on information from residents, but they're checking out cab companies to see if any driver picked up a fare on Toronto Street the night of the blizzard. And now that the police have traced the licence plate, the answers about Abby Michaels's personal history will start coming."

"Delia said the car's owner was Hugh Michaels. Was he Abby's husband?"

"Could be. Could also be a brother, a father, an uncle, or a cousin. All they know for certain is that Hugh Michaels is from Port Hope."

"That's where Alwyn Henry lives."

"Your university friend who sent us our first Christmas card this year – the card with the picture of the cardinal at her bird feeder."

"Not much gets by you, does it?" I said.

"Nope. I'm ever vigilant. Port Hope is a small town. Maybe you should give Alwyn a call. See what you can find out."

"Maybe I should." I curled my feet under me. "But not now. I'm warm; I'm next to you, and I'm drinking some very good Scotch. Let's finish our drinks and go to bed and catch up with Gawain. We could use an escape from reality, and we're at a good part: the lord of the castle has just led everyone off on the hunt. Gawain stayed back at the castle, and the lady of the house has just tiptoed into his room."

The phone on the end table shrilled. "Let it ring," Zack said.

"Can't," I said. "We have kids and grandkids – we've given hostages to fortune."

I reached over, picked up the phone, and heard a voice I'd heard for the first time when I was a nineteen-year-old student at the University of Toronto. Alwyn Henry was a talker, and for thirty-seven years, I had revelled in my role as her listener. As a rule, her words tumbled over one another as if life was too short to say all she had to say about her many passions – teaching, bird watching, poetry, theatre, cooking, fine wines, travel, photography – but that night, the bounce was gone from her voice. "Joanne, I don't know where to start with this . . . "

"Is it about Abby Michaels?" I said.

"So you know that she's dead," Alwyn said. "Calling you was just a shot in the dark, but I thought with your media contacts you might have some information."

"I do," I said. "Can you hold for a minute?" I put my hand over the receiver. "It's Alwyn Henry. How much should I tell her?"

"Play it by ear," Zack said. "See what you can get in return. If Jacob's father is in the picture, we should know. You can certainly say that Jacob is with Abby's birth mother."

I took my hand off the receiver. "Sorry, Alwyn. There was something here I had to take care of. So, do you want to go first or shall I?"

Her laugh was ragged. "You know me. I rush in where angels fear to tread, but I should tell you this isn't just a matter of small-town curiosity. I'm calling on behalf of Abby's partner. Her name is Nadine Perrault. Two hours ago, she learned Abby had been murdered. The police apparently traced the licence on Abby's car, and they called

Abby's house. Nadine answered. The authorities won't tell her anything. Nadine is, understandably, beside herself. Her biggest concern of course is Jacob. She's planning to fly to Regina tomorrow to get him. She and I teach English together at Trinity College School. She came to my house tonight because she needs someone to cover her classes. I agreed of course."

Something inside me twisted and tightened. "Is she there now?"

"She went out to get some air. She'll be back."

"Alwyn, you'll have to talk her out of coming to Regina. I don't know what Nadine Perrault's understanding of the situation is, but Abby Michaels made it clear that she wants Jacob to be with her birth mother. She handed Jacob over to the family before she was attacked."

"Birth mother? This doesn't make any sense," Alwyn said. "Abby's mother was Peggy Michaels. I've known her for forty years. There must be some mistake."

"There's no mistake," I said. "We know the biological mother, and we know the circumstances of Abby's birth. The mother was at a point in her life where she didn't feel she could raise a child, so she arranged for her baby to be adopted."

"That's not possible," Alwyn said. "Hugh and I taught together for years at TCS, and I remember him and Peggy bringing Abby out to the school to show her off after she was born. She was a lovely little thing – all that curly black hair. Hugh made a joke about Peggy's ancestors obviously not spending all their time in the Highlands."

"Abby's birth date is September 29, 1983," I said. "Does that date fit with what you know?"

"It does." Alwyn's voice was heavy. "The new school year was just nicely underway when Abby was born. We were all thrilled for them. Peggy and Hugh had been trying for years to have a child."

"So they faked a pregnancy? How could they carry that off in a town the size of Port Hope?"

Alwyn paused before answering. "They weren't here," she said. "We were told that there were difficulties. Peggy was hospitalized for months at a hospital in Toronto that specialized in high-risk pregnancies. Hugh spent the summer there with her."

"And when they came back in September, they had Abby."

"They were ecstatic. Do you know what the name Abigail means? 'Father's joy.' From the day they brought that child home, she was a joy to them both."

"Alwyn, do you have any idea why Hugh and Peggy Michaels would go to such lengths to hide the truth? They must have realized that at some point Abby would find out that they weren't her biological parents."

"You don't think they told her?"

"Abby didn't contact her biological mother until two weeks ago."

"Hugh and Peggy were killed in a car accident Thanksgiving weekend," Alwyn said. "Abby must have discovered the truth about her birth when she went through her parents' papers."

"Coming so soon after losing both her parents, the news must have been a terrible blow."

"Especially for someone who'd been as protected as Abby was," said Alwyn. "At the funeral, I sat with Hugh's other colleagues. When Abby walked back down the aisle after the service, I couldn't bear to look at her face. The woman I was sitting next to said, 'This is the first time that child has ever seen that life can be cruel.'"

"You knew Abby," I said. "Would the shock of discovering she'd been adopted be enough to make her give up her child?"

Alwyn's tone was curt. "Of course not. Abby was an extraordinarily confident and capable woman. She would have been wounded, but she wouldn't have been irrational."

"Alwyn, she drove halfway across the country over winter roads. She was alone with her baby. Anything could have happened. When she arrived here, she was deeply depressed. She was also determined to give Jacob to her birth mother."

"Those are not the actions of the woman I knew," Alwyn said flatly. "Something else must have happened."

"Do you remember what Dr. Buitenhuis used to say? 'When speculation has done its worse, two and two still make four.'"

"He was quoting Samuel Johnson, but I concede the point. Facts are facts, but in this case, I don't think we know all the facts."

"Then I guess all anyone can do is deal with the situation as it stands. Jacob is here in Regina and he's being well cared for. We know the family he's with."

"And they're planning to keep him?"

"Yes."

"I'll tell Nadine." Her breath caught. "This is going to break her heart, Jo."

"It will be worse if she comes here. Believe me. Why don't you give me a call tomorrow morning? We'll know more then, but for the time being, please just keep Nadine away."

"I'll do my best."

Zack had been watching me intently. When I hung up, he frowned. "To quote one of your favourites, 'What fresh hell is this?'"

"It seems Abby had a partner. Her name is Nadine Perrault, and she was planning to fly here tomorrow to get Jacob."

"But she's not coming now?"

"You heard my end of the conversation," I said. "Your guess is as good as mine."

"Shit," Zack said. "More complications."

"You think Nadine Perrault has a legitimate claim on Jacob?"

"Hard to say – depends on the nature and duration of her relationship with Abby Michaels. Anyway, there's nothing we can do tonight."

"In that case," I said, "let's say good night to Taylor and hit the sack. I'll read you *Gawain* until you fall asleep."

Zack raised an eyebrow. "Gawain demands a man's deep and sonorous voice."

"You'll be amazed at how sonorous I can be with a couple of ounces of Old Pulteney under my belt."

The next morning, long before the first blue light of day began to seep through our bedroom windows, Zack's cell rang. It was Delia. I rolled over and listened as Zack presented his argument about how Delia could best handle the situation facing her. Zack's voice was low but urgent, and as he and Delia continued talking I could feel his concern. When the call was finally over, Zack turned to face me.

"So what's next?" I said.

"I don't know. Delia's in terrible shape, Joanne. I didn't know until she told me this morning that she spent half an hour alone in Abby's car with her body."

"My God. How did that happen?"

Zack pushed himself up to a seated position. "The men who found Abby's body were casual workers from the Wayfarers' Mission. They reasoned, correctly, that they were being paid to shovel snow, not deal with cops. To their credit, these guys tried to do the right thing. Having opened the car door and discovered a scene that, to say the least, must have been traumatic, they went through Abby's wallet, found Delia's address and phone number, and used Abby's cell to call her."

"What a nightmare. Poor Delia."

Zack's shifted his weight, an automatic gesture to protect his skin against pressure sores. "It gets worse," he said.

"Dee assumed the cops had been called, so she showed up at the parking lot alone."

"Where was Noah?"

"At home with the kids," Zack said, "confident that the police had everything under control."

"But nobody had called them." I moved closer to Zack. "Just the thought of Delia, down there alone with her daughter's body."

"As you probably heard, I told Dee to take some time off. We're having a partners' meeting this morning. I suggested that her admin assistant could bring in her priority files, and we could divvy them up."

"But Delia didn't agree to that?"

"Nope. She says the only thing that's going to get her through this is work. And to be honest, I understand that. I'm the same way. But she has agreed to let me act as her liaison with Debbie Haczkewicz, and that was a big concession. It was also a smart move. As next-of-kin, Dee has the right to be kept informed about developments in the case, and she figured she could handle it, but she's never practised criminal law. She didn't realize what she was letting herself in for."

"And you do."

"Yes, and I wouldn't wish the kind of reports that are going to be coming out of the medical examiner's office on my worst enemy. Right now the pathologist and his team will be waiting for Abby's body to thaw so they can start their examination. A uniformed cop will have put paper bags on Abby's hands to preserve any traces of DNA from her attacker that may be under her nails. And this is only the beginning. The M.E. always says that the answers don't leap out of the body; his team has to dig for them. As soon as Abby's body thaws, they'll be fingerprinting her, swabbing her genitals, taking blood, getting samples of her pubic hair, cutting her nails – well, you get the drift."

"I do," I said. "God, Zack, this is terrible. If it were one of our kids . . . " I closed my eyes against the image. "It's going to be hard enough for Delia. This story will be an early Christmas present for the media. A beautiful young woman comes to a strange city, gives away her baby, and is raped and murdered. That picture you took of Abby at the carol service will be everywhere."

Zack nodded. "And I have a feeling that picture will be with us for a long time. According to Dee, the police don't have any leads. People were dealing with the blizzard and the blackout. And of course, the snow obliterated everything around the crime scene."

"What about the men who found the body?"

"The police will check them out, but Dee says that after the men called her they apparently went straight back to the Wayfarers' Mission and told the pastor everything that had happened. At that point the pastor called the police. As you know too well, I'm a betting man, but I'm an informed bettor. Abby Michaels had close to $500 in her wallet and the Wayfarer shovellers didn't touch it. I'm betting they're clean."

Zack and I exchanged a glance. "I wish this problem had landed on someone else's plate," I said.

"Me too," Zack said. "But it's on our plate, Jo. So we'll have to deal with it."

I leaned over and kissed him. "Alwyn said she'd phone me this morning and tell me what she knew about Nadine Perrault's plans. She won't call this early, so I might as well take the dogs for their run."

"This is not an ideal way to start the day," Zack said.

"The day is young," I said. "Keep that Kiz Harp CD at the ready."

When I got back from my run, I put our tickets for *The Nutcracker* by Zack's plate – a not so subtle reminder that we were taking Madeleine and Lena out for dinner and the ballet and that he should be home from work early.

Surprisingly, Taylor beat him to the breakfast table. She was dressed for school. I looked at my watch. "Six o'clock," I said. "Did I forget about a practice or something?"

She cut a grapefruit and put half in my bowl and half in hers. "No, I thought I'd work in the studio for a while before I caught the bus." She picked up one of the tickets and read the information on its face. After several years of waning interest, she'd decided to give *The Nutcracker* a pass. She and Mieka were going to a restaurant where the rock was loud and the burgers were loaded and then to a chick flick. As Taylor placed the ticket back on the table, her face was wistful.

"Second thoughts?" I said.

Her brow furrowed. "Not really. Going to *The Nutcracker* together was just one of our ten million traditions."

I laughed. "Do you remember your first *Nutcracker*?"

She rolled her eyes. "I was so excited I threw up as soon as they raised the curtain."

"We had good seats too. Right near the orchestra. The ushers came and cleaned up, but you refused to go home."

"The people around us must have hated us."

"The musicians weren't too wild about us, either, but it was worth it. Watching you that night was one of the great thrills of my life."

Taylor chewed her lip. "Do you ever wish we could go back to the way it was?"

"Sometimes," I said. "But then I realize if we went back, we wouldn't have Zack or Maddy and Lena –"

"Or Bruce and Benny or Willie and Pantera." Taylor picked up her grapefruit spoon. "Or Declan," she said innocently.

"Or Declan," I agreed. "On the whole, I'd say we've gained more than we've lost. But going back is not an option.

To paraphrase Joni Mitchell, we're all captives on the carousel of time."

Taylor cocked her head. "Who's Joni Mitchell?"

Alwyn called just after Taylor left for school. Zack and I were in the office we shared at home. To me, the speakerphone violated everything conversation was supposed to be, but Zack had questions and it was possible Alwyn could answer them. When I explained that Zack was acting as the lawyer for Delia Wainberg, Abby's birth mother, and asked if he could take part in our call, Alwyn's response was characteristically pragmatic. "Whatever helps," she said.

Zack introduced himself and apologized. "This is a hell of a way to meet," he said. "But thank you for agreeing to talk to me. I know you're in a difficult position. It's never easy to be caught in the middle."

"Especially when the situation is so murky," Alwyn said.

"Well, let's see if we can un-muddy the waters – exchange a little information. Joanne tells me that you knew Abby from the time she was a baby. What was her life like?"

"Gilded," Alwyn said. "She was the only child of parents who adored her, and as an adult she found a partner who adored her and whom she adored. She had a child she loved. She was bright, attractive, focused, and accomplished."

"You say that Abby and her partner adored one another. Doesn't it strike you as odd that Nadine Perrault wouldn't have realized that her partner was planning to bring their child out here and leave him with another family?"

"It's inconceivable," Alwyn said flatly. "Nonetheless, Nadine says that's exactly what happened. According to her, she and Abby had grown even closer after Peggy and Hugh died. But after Abby examined the contents of her parents' safety-deposit box, everything changed. Abby withdrew from Nadine. She became secretive. Nadine pleaded with Abby to tell her what was wrong, but Abby remained silent. The last morning they were together, Nadine went off to teach as usual, but when she returned, the house was empty. Abby had taken her parents' old Volvo, so Nadine didn't think she'd gone far, but as the days went by she grew frantic. Understandably, she was terrified at the thought of Abby driving alone with that baby on winter roads."

"That's another thing that puzzles me," Zack said. "Why did Abby drive out here? It would have been so much simpler just to book a flight – especially when she was travelling with a baby."

"Plane tickets can be traced," Alwyn said. "Nadine's theory is that Abby didn't want anyone to interfere with her plans."

"So from the time she left Port Hope, Abby was determined to hand Jacob over to the Wainbergs," I said.

"Apparently so," Alwyn said.

I could tell by his voice that Zack was both baffled and exasperated. "Alwyn, I understand that you have to respect Ms. Perrault's confidence, but what the hell is going on here?"

My old friend's level of exasperation matched Zack's. "Your guess is as good as mine. It's not a question of confidentiality, Zack. Nadine and I aren't close. Until last night we were simply colleagues who taught English at the same school. I like and respect Nadine, but she and Abby were one of those couples who never seemed to need anyone else."

"And now Nadine has nobody," I said.

"It's even worse than that," Alwyn said. "It seems that before she left Port Hope, Abby took steps to cut Nadine out of her life."

"What kind of steps?" Zack asked.

"Legal steps. This morning Nadine went to the lawyer she and Abby used to draw up their wills," Alwyn said. "Nadine was hoping the fact that she and Abby named one another as their respective sole beneficiaries would strengthen her hand when she sought custody of Jacob."

"So Nadine knew that Abby hadn't named her as Jacob's guardian in her will?" Zack said.

"According to Nadine, they hadn't gotten around to it. They were both in good health, and then there was the tragedy with Abby's parents. Nadine said it was simply *understood* that if something happened to one of them, the other would raise Jacob."

"'Understandings' aren't worth the paper they're written on," Zack said caustically. "Although to be fair, Nadine would have had a persuasive case if Abby hadn't left that note with Jacob."

"Surely the will Abby had drawn up by her lawyer would have more legal force than a note she wrote when she was obviously in a very fragile state of mind," I said.

"One would think so," Alwyn said. "Except this morning Nadine learned that on November 22 Abby signed a new will. In it, the bulk of her estate still goes to Nadine, but in the event of Abby's death, Delia Margolis Wainberg is designated as Jacob's legal guardian."

Zack tensed. "Alwyn, tell Nadine Perrault to get a lawyer. Not the guy who drew up the wills. She needs her own lawyer – somebody smart and aggressive. Then she should have her lawyer call me." He turned his chair towards the door. "I'm leaving the room now," he said. "You and Joanne can talk freely."

I waited until the door had closed. "He's gone," I said. "Anything you want to talk about?"

Alwyn's voice was flat. "For probably the only time in my life, I have nothing to say."

"Neither do I," I said. "A double first."

Zack was putting on his jacket when I came down the hall. "The partners' meeting?" I said.

"Yep. You want to come?"

"No thanks. I'm going for a swim – which incidentally, you should be doing – and then I'm going to find last year's gift bags and wrap presents."

Zack held out his arms. "I wish I was spending the morning with you and Kiz Harp," he said.

I folded myself into him. "I wish you were too. Zack, is this going to be terrible?"

My husband rubbed my back. "Ms. Shreve, if you can show me a way out of this where no one suffers, King Solomon will have to move over."

Alwyn Henry and I first met in a half-course in early Canadian literature. Our instructor, a young Ph.D. from Cornell, made no attempt to hide his contempt for the subject matter. As we left class with our book lists the first day, Alwyn took me aside. "This course is going to kill us if we let it," she said. "So let's not let it," I said. And we didn't. We made a list of the writers: Haliburton, Lampman, Carman, Roberts, and Scott. Each of us read half the list and made concise and useful notes on what we'd read for the other. We wrote our major papers on the nineteenth-century settler-sisters, the Stricklands. Alwyn took Susanna Moodie; I took Catharine Parr Traill. Together, we drank coffee at Hart House and beer in Lundy's Lane, the ladies' and escorts' room at the Bay-Bloor Tavern, and checked out the men everywhere. We both received firsts in the course. Alywn went on to do her master's in English, and after graduation moved back home to Strickland country to teach. I majored in political science and economics, started a doctoral program, married and moved west. Not much stuck with me from that long-ago class, but Catharine Parr Traill's recipe for dealing with troubles had. "When disaster strikes," she wrote, "it's no good to wring one's hands, better to be up and doing."

And that's what I did. After my swim and shower, I dug out last year's gift bags, tissue, and ribbons, put on Bach's Brandenburgs, brewed myself some ginger tea, and tried not to think about lives full of promise that end in tragedy. By the end of the morning, my equilibrium was restored, and I had a stack of presents tree-ready in used but still festive gift bags. As I stowed the gifts in the laundry-room closet – well away from Pantera – I was grateful to Catharine Parr Traill for knowing that nothing answers vexing existential questions like mindless work, and to Bach for proving that, in the end, beauty trumps death.

Every Christmas time, I hand out candy canes with the exam papers and booklets. The students, even those in their graduating year, brighten at the reminder that there will be life after the misery of the next three hours, and the candy provides them with a necessary sugar boost when the first adrenalin rush subsides. That day, after the students had settled in and the rattle of candy paper and exam booklets ceased, calm fell over the room. For a few minutes, I watched the snow fall in fat lazy flakes outside the classroom window and let the peace wash over me. Then the Protestant work ethic kicked in, and I took out my laptop and set to work.

I was supervising a master's thesis by that rarest of rare birds in our graduate school: a genuine right-winger. Christian Luzny's thesis was that Canada's best hope for surviving in the post-9/11 world was a stronger alliance with the United States, and his first draft had been sharp, lively, opinionated, and wildly one-sided. His bibliography was extensive and revealing: it did not include the name of a single scholar whose opinion deviated from Christian's own. When he and I met to discuss his draft, I'd suggested that, at the very least, he should flush out a paper tiger to fight. Accordingly, the first thing I checked that afternoon was the bibliography.

It was lengthy, and Christian had chosen some formidable opponents. Most were the usual suspects, but there was a Ph.D. whose surname caught my eye: Michaels, A.M. It seemed a long shot, but I googled Michaels, A.M. and came up with the scholar's full name, Abigail Margaret Michaels, and the dates of her degrees and the universities from which she had received them. It all fit.

I googled her dissertation and found the abstract. Mercifully free of the bafflegab of academe, the abstract seemed frighteningly prescient: predicting that with a fragile economy, deep divisions about foreign and domestic policy and a spiralling debt load, America was a house of cards vulnerable to the slightest breeze. This dissertation argued that Canada offered a template that might be useful as America rebuilt after what Abby Michaels saw as its inevitable crash. On impulse, I ordered the dissertation through an interlibrary loan, then set to work on Christian's thesis.

Christian argued with passion and abandon. Attempting to track his thought processes was like trying to follow a talented but erratic dancer – exhausting but exciting. The time passed quickly, and I was surprised when students began handing in their papers. After the last laggard left the room, I closed my laptop with that pleasant buzz of excitement that came when I knew I was going to be working with a gifted student. Judging by her abstract, it was a feeling that Abby Michaels, too, must have inspired many times in the men and women who taught her.

Zack was better at compartmentalizing than anyone I'd ever met. He had spent the day defending an alleged stalker who was accused of pursuing a perky local TV anchorwoman. It was an unpopular case; the media had been critical of Zack's defence, and he had received some ugly calls at work and at home. More significantly, his case was going south. He'd put in a hard day, but that night we were taking our granddaughters to the ballet, and he greeted me at the door wearing his tux and a smile, martini in hand.

"Thank you for laying out my tux," he said. "I was feeling like homemade shit; now I feel like homemade shit on the way to the ball." He held out his martini to give me a sip.

"That is sublime," I said. "Is there one of those for me?"

"You bet," he said. "But I thought you might want to take off your boots first."

I took another sip of his drink. "I owe you, and I'll repay you by not asking you how your day was, and also by telling you that you look incredibly handsome."

Zack gave me a nod of appreciation. "It's a big night. Now fill me in on the time line again."

"Mieka's going to drop the girls here at 5:30 – then we're off to the Hotel Saskatchewan for a fashionably early dinner. It'll take us twenty minutes to get from the Hotel to the ballet; curtain's at 7:30; by 7:31 we'll be listening to Tchaikovsky and waiting for the mysterious Herr Drosselmeyer to appear at the Stahlbaums' Christmas Eve party." I hung my scarf and toque on top of my coat and aligned my boots. "I am now ready for my martini."

"Follow me," Zack said, and he turned his chair towards the kitchen. "So how was your day?"

"Productive." I studied his face. Under the direct light in the kitchen, I could see the lines of fatigue. The addition of Delia's case to his already heavy workload was taking its toll. "I spent the morning wrapping Christmas presents," I said. "We are now one step closer to being ready for the big day."

Zack extracted an olive from the jar on the counter. "What do you want for Christmas?" he said. "I've got a bunch of little stuff, but nothing with a wow factor."

"I have the solution," I said. "I called Stan Gardiner at the Point Store the other day. He says the ice on the lake is 'punky' – not good for skating. Since we're all going to be at the cottage between Christmas and New Year's, I thought we could get somebody to flood that space between the cottage and the hill. It's perfect for a rink: it's big, it's flat, and you and I can stay inside where it's warm and watch the kids."

Zack chewed his olive and offered me the jar. "I'll bet you're the only woman in Canada who wants a skating rink for Christmas." Suddenly his face split in a grin. "Do you remember Lee Sandison? The one with the much younger wife?"

"There seems to be an epidemic of much younger wives," I said. "But I remember Missy. She has the only Birkin bag I've ever seen in Regina."

"Well, she earned it," Zack said. "Lee told me he asked her for a blow job and she said she'd give him one if he bought her a Birkin bag."

"Isn't that a little high?" I said. "Birkins start at $7,000."

"According to Lee, Missy prides herself on being 'fastidious.'"

"Fastidious, but flexible," I said. "Well, good for them. Everyone deserves a special moment. I hope Lee knows that Birkin bags are reputed to last forever."

Zack grinned. "I'll be sure to point that out next time I see him."

I glanced at the clock. "Time to move along," I said. "Mieka's going to be here with the girls in twenty minutes, and I still have to get dressed."

"Can I watch?"

"Isn't that getting a little old?"

"Never."

"Okay, you can watch, but it's going to cost you a skating rink."

CHAPTER

6

The Hotel Saskatchewan is one of the grand hotels built by the nation-building Canadian Pacific Railway in the early part of the twentieth century. At the peak of construction, a thousand men were working shifts twenty-four hours a day, so that the young blades of Regina would have vaulted ceilings under which to waltz their belles and marble thresholds over which to carry them. The clientele today tends to be corporate, more interested in mergers than romance, and there are places in town where the food is cheaper and better. That said, for an evening of mid-winter enchantment, the Hotel Saskatchewan is the place to be, especially if you are six years old and four years old, as Madeleine and Lena were, respectively, on that starry December night.

From the moment the girls looked up at the towering wooden soldiers flanking the entrance and spied themselves in the floor-to-ceiling mirrors, they were captivated. The lobby held more charms: the frothy extravagances of the tree decorations were a reminder, if we needed one, that Christmas is the season when too much is not enough, and the chandeliers glittering in the dining rooms promised further delights. Best of all, there was the hotel's gingerbread display. This year's theme was an Alpine village with a real train that ran on a figure-eight track past candy-covered houses. Transcendent.

There had been secrecy about what Lena would be wearing that evening. New holiday dresses, along with dinner and *The Nutcracker*, were our present to the girls. When I had taken them shopping, Madeleine found a dress she liked within the first half-hour. It was classic: a simple, scoop-necked, long-sleeved black velvet bodice, with a pretty dark green shot taffeta skirt. Standing in front of the triple mirrors in her undershirt and panties, she handed the dress to me with a sigh of relief. "Now I don't have to try on any more," she said. Lena had proved harder to satisfy, and when finally we gave up and went for hot chocolate we weren't even close. In the end, Mieka had taken Lena dress shopping while Madeleine and I stayed at Mieka's and read. Lena was wrestling with a large box when they returned. She refused all offers of help and all requests for a preview, saying only that she wanted the dress to be a surprise. As I was leaving, I asked Mieka about the dress, but she just rolled her eyes and changed the subject.

When Lena took off her coat at the hotel, I understood Mieka's eye-roll. Lena's dress was a poufy explosion of satin, tulle, ribbons, and pearls, all the colour of grape Kool-Aid. Zack and I were both speechless. Maddy, who was always quick to pick up on nuance and was a loyal sister, gave us our cue. "Lena really looks nice, doesn't she?" she said, and there was an edge in her voice that suggested she would not brook contradiction.

"Unforgettable," Zack said.

"Absolutely," I said, and with that, the four of us swanned into dinner.

We decided on the buffet – mostly because of the dessert table – so our only order was for drinks. The girls ordered Shirley Temples, but when the server handed Zack the wine list, Madeleine frowned. "Wine is kind of plain for a party. Why don't you and Mimi get Shirley Temples too? They come with cherries on a crazy straw."

Zack looked at me. "I don't know about you, but that cherries-on-a-crazy-straw sounds tempting."

"I'm tempted, too," I said.

Zack handed the wine list back to the server. "Shirley Temples all around," he said, "and please don't stint on the cherries."

When the drinks came, Lena took her napkin and tucked it into her collar. "I don't want to spill on my dress," she said.

"Very prudent," Zack said. His gaze swept the faces at our table. "I'd like to propose a toast."

"I'll bet it's to us," Lena said.

"Only indirectly," Zack said. He raised his glass. "To Mimi's toothbrush, because without your grandmother's toothbrush, none of us would be here tonight."

Madeleine narrowed her eyes. "Is this one of your funny stories?"

"No, this is one of my true stories, but before I tell it, we have to drink a toast to Mimi's toothbrush."

Giggling, the girls raised their glasses. "To Mimi's toothbrush," they chorused.

"Now you have to tell the story," Madeleine said.

"It starts the morning after Mimi and I had our first date," he said.

I shot my husband a warning glance. Madeleine and Lena didn't need to know that their grandparents' first evening together had lasted all night.

"Did you have fun?" Lena asked.

"Yes," Zack said. "And that was the problem."

"How could fun be a problem?" Madeleine asked.

Zack's eyes met mine over our Shirley Temples. "Because I'd always been on my own – I'd always been able to do what I wanted to do when I wanted to do it. I never had to think about anybody other than myself."

"That doesn't sound so bad," Maddy said judiciously.

"It wasn't," Zack said. "In fact, it was pretty good, but when I met your grandmother, I knew that if I stayed with her, everything would be different, so I was scared."

Lena furrowed her brow in disbelief. "You're not scared of anything."

"Everybody's scared of something. Anyway, we were at the lake, but I had business in Regina, so when I was ready to go, I asked your Mimi if I could bring her anything and she said she'd like a toothbrush."

"Where was her toothbrush?" Madeleine asked.

"She must have lost it," Lena said.

"She didn't have it with her at the time," Zack said. "So she asked me to bring her one. And this is the scary part. This is the part where things almost didn't work out – where if I'd done one thing instead of another we wouldn't be sitting here tonight drinking Shirley Temples."

Struck by the solemnity of the possibility, the girls put down their drinks.

"As you well know, it's a long drive from the lake into Regina."

"Forty-five minutes," Madeleine said.

Zack nodded. "By the time I got to the city, I decided that I didn't want to change my life, and I wasn't going to see your Mimi any more."

Madeleine's eyes were anxious. "You were going to dump her?"

"I was going to send flowers and a note first. I called the florist, and when I started telling her what to write on the card, I thought of your grandmother . . . "

"Waiting for her toothbrush . . . " Lena said, and her voice was tragic.

"Waiting for her toothbrush," Zack agreed. "So I tore up the note, cancelled the flowers, bought the best toothbrush I could find, and drove back to the lake –"

Zack's cell rang. His eyes met mine. "Sorry," he said.

"I'll take the girls to the buffet," I said.

Zack was still on the phone when we got back with our food. When he rang off, he did not look happy. "I'll tell you later," he said.

"Better get something to eat," I said.

When we had finished our meal, the girls and I went into the ladies' room to freshen up. It was an elegant space with two chaise longues and many mirrors. Tearing Lena away from a space that offered endless reflections of herself was not easy, but the ballet beckoned. Zack was waiting for us at the gingerbread village. When the girls gravitated towards a chalet overlooking a surprisingly realistic waterfall, Zack motioned me to join him.

"What's up?" I said.

"I was going to save this particular sugarplum till later, but Debbie called this afternoon. The medical examiner's team have done a preliminary examination of Abby Michaels's body – just observing and gathering samples – no autopsy yet. In their opinion, Abby died of traumatic asphyxia caused by neck compression."

"She was strangled," I said.

Zack nodded. "There was seminal fluid in the vagina and on the perineum and inner thighs. There were no contusions in the genital area, so apparently the penetration was not forced."

"The sex was consensual?" I said.

Zack took a deep breath and exhaled. "No. The theory is that Abby was already dead when penetration took place."

For a moment I felt light-headed. I gripped the edge of the table that held the idyllic gingerbread village.

"You okay?" Zack said.

"Yes," I said. "Just overwhelmed."

"Do you want me to stop?"

"No. You know what they say: a burden shared is a burden halved."

"That works for me," Zack said, "because this particular burden isn't getting any lighter."

A hotel employee approached the girls, spoke to them for a moment, and Lena came running. "That man says we can work the controls for the train if it's okay with you. He says we can even make the train go backwards."

"Can't pass up an opportunity like that," Zack said.

"We'll watch from here," I said.

Lena ran back to the other side of the display. Zack nodded assent to the man from the hotel, and the man handed the controls to the girls and began explaining how to work them.

I turned to Zack. "You were saying . . . ?"

"That I'm glad you're around." He took my hand. "But that's old news. Today's news is not cheering. The M.E. thinks Abby was probably attacked somewhere else and then dragged to her car and driven to the parking lot. Apparently the contusion on the back of her head and body were consistent with some pretty rough treatment."

"When did she die?"

"The old dogs, which is what old cops call themselves, would say that Abby died at some point between the time we saw her walking out of the gym at Luther and the time the shovellers from the mission found her body in the parking lot."

"Old dog humour?" I said.

"Yeah, but right on the money. Despite what TV would have us believe, it's pretty difficult to pinpoint the time of a death. That's why the police spend a lot of time trying to find the second-last person who saw the victim alive."

Madeleine, who paid attention to instructions, had just navigated the train safely through the mountains with their icing snow peaks, past the village houses with their jelly fruit shingles, and back safely to the chalet. Zack and I both gave her the thumbs-up. Now it was Lena's turn, but for once, Zack and I weren't focused on our younger granddaughter's performance. Neither of us doubted that Lena would snarl the train somewhere on the tracks, but we both knew that her charm and her poufy grape Kool-Aid dress would win the day.

"Debbie's big push right now is finding someone who saw Abby after she left Luther," Zack said. "But so far, nada. The cameras downtown weren't working because of the power failure and people were too busy dealing with the blizzard to notice what their fellow citizens were up to."

"How much of this did you tell Delia?"

Zack's laugh was short and humourless. "As little as possible, but Dee isn't stupid. She knows what's happening, and it's driving her crazy. Which brings us to the second sugarplum. That was Dee on the phone just now. Nadine Perrault called to invite her to a memorial service Friday morning in the chapel at Trinity College School. Abby was a graduate and her father taught there all his life."

"But the police won't have released the body by then, will they?" I asked.

"It'll be weeks before that happens," Zack said. "When a woman is the victim of a seemingly random rape and murder, people get scared. The police don't want this to be a catch-and-release case; neither does the Crown. Everybody wants a conviction, and that means hanging onto the body until they're sure the forensic work, especially all the lab tests, are properly done."

"Why doesn't Nadine wait and have the service after the body's been cremated?"

"That would be logical, wouldn't it?" Zack said. "But grief isn't logical. And a violent death like Abby's brings its own horrors. It's not easy to live with the knowledge that the body of someone you loved is lying on a slab somewhere while pathologists run their tests. Apparently, Nadine is convinced the memorial service will help Abby's friends and colleagues get through the holidays."

"That makes sense," I said. "So did Delia accept Nadine's invitation?"

"Not to the memorial service," Zack said. "Delia's in court that morning. I could, of course, have asked for an adjournment of the hearing, but Delia doesn't want that. The time she spent with Abby's body in the parking lot has hit her hard. She says she's not ready to sit in a roomful of strangers and hear them talk about the daughter she never knew."

"But she is going to go to Port Hope?"

"Yes, she's taking the noon flight on Friday. She wants to meet Nadine and see where Abby grew up."

"I think that's a good idea," I said. "Delia needs to know what Abby was like – not just for herself, but for Jacob. He'll have questions about his mother, and Delia will have to be able to answer them."

Zack nodded. "And one good thing. I was able to convince Delia not to take Jacob – no use overloading the emotional circuits."

"I agree," I said. "So, is Noah staying here with the baby?"

"Yep, and that's where I come in. Dee may not be at the top of her game, but she still knows she should have her lawyer with her when she meets Nadine Perrault."

I felt a flicker of worry. Zack was a healthy man, but keeping a paraplegic's body in shape demanded attention and routine; both would be in short supply on a trip like this one.

"Isn't there anybody else who can go?" I said.

"No, Jo. I'm it." His voice was uncharacteristically weary.

We both watched as Lena slowed the little train for the curve and speeded it up again for its round of figure eights. Incredibly, the train stayed on the tracks.

"I'll come with you," I said.

Zack looked up at me. "Joanne, the flight from here to Toronto is over three hours. You go through hell if we have to fly to Saskatoon, and that's fifty minutes."

"I'll figure something out," I said. "Besides, you'll be there, and I'm always better when you're around."

"That works both ways, Jo. I appreciate this."

I bent down to kiss him. "Whither thou goest."

The Nutcracker was *The Nutcracker*. Madeleine was rapt; Lena was semi-rapt.

When the Mouse King appeared, Lena leapt out of her seat, clambered up onto Zack's lap, and buried her head in his chest. "Tell me when this part's over," she said.

I knew the feeling.

The next morning while Zack was dressing, I poured Taylor a glass of juice and went to her room. The door was closed. I knocked and waited until she invited me in. She was standing in front of her full-length mirror in her bra and panties, examining an aubergine turtleneck. She took the juice, thanked me, and drained the glass. Then she held the sweater against her body and gazed critically at her reflection. "What do you think?" she said.

"I think we'll send you to a convent," I said.

She gave me the Sally smile. "I'd sneak out."

"We'd hunt you down." I sat on the corner of her bed. "Taylor, something's come up. Zack and I have to go away this weekend. Pete and his girlfriend are coming over to take care of the dogs. Are you okay spending the weekend with them?"

"Sure. What's up?"

"Nothing fun. Delia wants to meet Abby's partner and see the house where Abby grew up. Noah's staying here with Jacob, so Zack and I are going with Delia."

Taylor's face clouded. "Every time I think of Izzy's sister I get this sick feeling in my stomach."

"We all do," I said. "That's why I'm going. It's going to be hard for Delia and that means it's going to be hard for Zack. I'm hoping I can make it easier."

Taylor turned to the mirror. "So where did Abby grow up?"

"In Port Hope. It's sixty miles east of Toronto."

My daughter whirled around to face me. "You'll have to fly there."

"That's the plan."

"But you hate everything about planes."

"Just boarding them and being in them," I said. "I'm fine with the idea of getting off."

Taylor's face was serious. "I'll make a deal with you. If you do this, I won't cry the next time I get a needle."

"Six hours of agony versus a split second of pain? That's not much of a deal, Taylor."

"It's the best one I can think of." She held out her hand. "Deal?"

I took her hand. "Deal," I said.

Taylor walked over to her sock drawer and began rummaging and pitching rejects onto her bed. "Why don't I stay with the Wainbergs while you're away? It'll be fun to help take care of Jacob, and Izzy could probably use some company."

"How's she doing?"

"Not great. You know Izzy. She's a control freak. She needs to know exactly how everything is going to be, and she needs to know it's going to be perfect."

"And none of this has been either predictable or perfect."

The pile of socks on the bed was growing. "Well, just think about it," Taylor said. "Izzy discovers that she has a sister, and before she even has a chance to get to know her, the sister is killed. Then, all of a sudden, there's a baby in the house. Isobel's crazy about Jacob but . . . "

"It is a lot to adjust to."

The sock drawer was empty. Taylor turned to me. "Do you know where those fuzzy purple socks are?"

"In my sock drawer," I said. "Do you want to borrow them?"

"Do you mind?"

"No," I said. "Do you mind if I extricate some of my socks from this pile on your bed?"

Taylor's face grew thoughtful. "Don't socks just kind of belong to everybody?"

"You mean like air?" I said.

"Good one," she said. Then she raced out of the room, returned with the fuzzy purple socks in hand, pulled them on, padded over to her cupboard, and emerged with a pair of grey slacks. She slipped them on, and then gave herself an assessing glance in the mirror. "I think the hardest part for Izzy is knowing that her mother's not perfect. It means she has to rethink everything."

"How so?" I asked.

Taylor smoothed her sweater and turned to face me. "Izzy's always thought she has to be as amazing as her mother, and now . . . "

"And now she's discovered that her mother is human," I said. "Maybe that's not such a bad thing."

Taylor raised an eyebrow. "Because now she can stop obsessing about measuring up?"

"That's a thought," I said.

"And this message is aimed at who?"

"At whomever finds it helpful," I said.

"You are *so* not subtle," my daughter said. She picked up her backpack. "Do we have any crumpets? I'm dying for a crumpet slathered in butter with a ton of brown sugar on top."

I looked at her body – not an ounce where it shouldn't be. Taylor had not only inherited her mother's talent, she'd inherited her metabolism. "Fridge door," I said. "Go for it."

Zack joined us in the kitchen, and while we ate, we chatted about the kinds of things families chat about two weeks before Christmas. Angus had called the night before. He was always a happy guy, but when I'd talked to him he'd been over the moon. He was pretty certain he'd aced his law school exams. His ex-girlfriend, Leah, had broken up with her boyfriend and she'd invited Angus to take the ex's place on a post-exam ski trip. Angus had accepted. That would leave Zack with an extra ticket for the Junior A game the following week. Zack said that the Regina Pats were looking good, so if Taylor wanted to take in a hockey game, she was in luck. Taylor said that she was washing her hair that night – whatever night it was – but that Declan was crazy about hockey, and that speaking of Declan, if we hadn't bought her a Christmas gift yet, we might consider giving her shopping money for a cool new dress for New Year's Eve. Zack suggested that Taylor ask Lena where she'd bought her grape Kool-Aid dress because it was beyond cool.

The exchange of information was as lazily pleasant as it was unremarkable, but Zack had noticed a persistent strand in the conversation. After Taylor left, he popped a crumpet in the toaster for himself. "Was it my imagination, or did Declan's name come up with some frequency?"

"It wasn't your imagination," I said.

"So what do we do?"

"Taylor's fourteen years old. She wants to be with Declan; we don't want her to be alone with Declan; so, I guess you and I prepare ourselves for plenty of double dates over the holidays."

Zack groaned.

"So what are you up to today?" I said.

"Getting the adoption underway, and there's some background stuff I'd like to check out."

"What kind of 'stuff'?"

Zack shrugged. "Just stuff." He wheeled off – his invariable move when he wanted to cut short the discussion.

After Zack left for work, I made myself a pot of tea and attacked my tower of first-year essays again. My plan was to mark till ten-thirty and reward myself with a mid-morning phone call to Alwyn Henry, but she beat me to it.

"There are five blue jays at my bird feeder," she said. "I put peanuts out on the feeding shelf after breakfast and the jays just swooped in. They make a racket and they make a mess, but they're fun."

"I'll bet they look spectacular against the snow," I said.

"When there's snow, they do, but no snow for us this year. The weatherman predicts a green Christmas."

I gazed out my window at the thigh-high drifts. "This weekend, I'll be able to see for myself. Zack and I are coming to Port Hope."

Alwyn whooped with joy. "This is the best news. How long has it been since you and I last saw one another?"

"Too long," I said.

"And I finally get to meet the new husband."

"And he finally gets to meet you," I said.

There was a pause. When Alwyn spoke again, her tone was tentative. "Jo, how are you getting here?"

"The way normal people do – we're flying, but Al, I don't want to talk about it. I don't even want to think about it."

"Sufficient unto the day is the evil thereof?"

"Something like that," I said.

"All right," she said, briskly. "Let's discuss a problem we can solve. Accommodation. My house is out because the bedrooms and bathroom are on the second floor, but tell me what you need, and I promise that by Friday night I will either find it or build it."

"No heroic measures necessary," I said. "All we need is something accessible with a double bed and enough space for Zack's chair to move around."

"The Lantern Inn would be perfect. It's on Mill Street, overlooking the river. They have a good dining room, an elevator, and very romantic suites – fireplaces and canopies over the beds."

"I can't imagine Zack sleeping under a canopy," I said.

"He's a manly man?" Alwyn said.

"In his law office, he has a picture of Mohammed Ali knocking out Sonny Liston, and you should see our house. It's sleek and functional."

"That doesn't sound like you."

"It's like me now. I like the simplicity. Zack is complication enough."

"I'll call and reserve a suite at the Lantern Inn for you."

"Thanks, and Alwyn, we'll need one for Delia Wainberg, too."

Alwyn's voice sagged. "That's right, this isn't just a Christmas visit, is it?"

"No," I said. "It isn't. Delia doesn't feel she can get through the memorial service on Friday morning, but she thinks seeing where Abby grew up and meeting the woman Abby loved might help both Nadine and her."

"Very praiseworthy," Alwyn said tightly, "except that Ms. Wainberg isn't playing by the rules. Nadine Perrault just called. Someone is going around town asking questions about her relationship with Abby."

I remembered Zack's overly casual dismissal of the 'background stuff' he needed to check out. "You think the man's a private investigator?" I said.

"The word is he's from a big agency in Toronto," Alwyn said.

I thought of Zack's first rule of practising law: prepare, prepare, prepare.

Before he'd even filed the papers, Zack had hired somebody to dig the dirt that would undermine any claims Nadine had to Jacob. "What kind of questions is this detective asking?"

"Nadine says he's focusing on whether Abby's relationship with her was stable."

"Was it?"

"Abby and Nadine didn't draw others into their private lives, but this morning she told me that when Abby became pregnant, there were problems."

"What kind of problems?"

Alwyn's voice was heavy. "Nadine was opposed to the idea of bringing a child into their relationship."

"And Abby still went through with it?"

"According to Nadine, she was determined."

"She also must have been persuasive," I said. "From what I've heard, donor insemination programs have a rigid screening process. Having a partner who was opposed to the pregnancy must have been an impediment."

Alwyn sighed. "It would have been, but Abby didn't go the donor insemination route. She got pregnant the old-fashioned way."

"So there is a biological father in the picture?"

"Well, the father's role certainly went beyond his contribution of a specimen in a test tube, but according to Nadine, he understood from the outset that he was simply accommodating a friend. She says Abby didn't communicate with the man during the pregnancy or when Jacob was born."

"That seems unlikely, doesn't it?" I said. "If the man and Abby were friends, surely she'd at least let him know that she'd given birth to a healthy child."

"One would think," Alwyn said, "but Nadine says not. She also says that when she finally accepted Abby's pregnancy, she and Abby were happier than they'd ever been."

"And yet two weeks before her death, Abby changed her will to give Delia custody of Jacob," I said. "There are still far too many blanks in this story."

"I guess that's why God gave us private detectives," Alwyn said. She didn't sound grateful.

I was making lunch when Noah arrived with Jacob. They were both pink-cheeked from the cold. "We walked over," Noah said. "Check out Jacob's new vehicle." I stepped past him and spied a bright yellow-and-red sled on our porch.

"Very slick." I lifted the sled into the front hall. "Also very tempting to sled thieves. This must be the deluxe model."

Noah's smile was boyish. "Nothing but the best," he said. "Ergonomically designed, and that shield protects Jacob from the wind."

I took Jacob in my arms. "What did you think, big guy?"

His dark eyes took my measure and then he gave me a gummy grin. "The sled's a keeper," I said. "And so are you. Now, let's get you out of that snowsuit." I unzipped him, and carried him into the kitchen. After Noah took off his boots and jacket, he followed. "I was just about to have lunch," I said. "Can I interest you in a tuna-fish sandwich?"

"Me, definitely," Noah said. "But Jacob brought his own lunch."

"What's on the menu?"

"Rice cereal mixed with formula. In the envelope Abby left with him, there was a list of suggested foods and of foods that were prohibited until he was older." Noah went to the sink, washed his hands, and prepared the cereal. Jacob was on my knee, but he strained to keep Noah in sight.

"Every time I think about Abby sitting down and making that list . . . " Noah's voice was tight, but when he turned to us, he managed a smile. "Lunch is served," he said. "Jo, there's a bib in his diaper bag. Would you mind . . . ? I'm a little out of practice with this."

I handed him the bib. "You're doing brilliantly," I said.

Noah's hands seemed huge against the baby's small body. "Open up, Jacob," he said. "There's no meat-lovers' option."

I brought our plate of sandwiches and two glasses of juice to the kitchen table. Noah played a game where he took a bite of his sandwich, then gave Jacob some cereal. The baby was an enthusiastic eater, but he never took his eyes off the man at the other end of the spoon. "You two seem to have a mutual admiration society," I said.

"So much depends on him," Noah said softly. The words invited explication, but none was forthcoming. Noah took a washcloth from the diaper bag, secured the baby in the crook of his arm, then wet the cloth at the sink and cleaned Jacob's face and hands. He was as gentle as he was efficient. "Now for the big job," he said, and still holding Jacob close, Noah dropped to his knees, rolled out a change pad, and put a fresh diaper and sleeper on the baby, all the while giving Jacob a running account of exactly what was going on. Jacob rewarded him by gurgling, snorting, and finally erupting in a real belly laugh. When Noah picked him up, he quickly fell asleep. It had been an exciting morning.

Noah shifted position so that he could see the baby's face. "Zack says you have an old university friend in Port Hope who knows Abby Michaels's partner."

"I do," I said. "Her name is Alwyn Henry. I was talking to her this morning."

Noah met my eyes. "And . . . ?"

"Nadine Perrault is convinced Abby wanted her to raise Jacob."

Noah's expression hardened. "Nothing Abby Michaels did in the last two weeks of her life supports that claim," he said. "Abby wanted Jacob to be with Delia and me. We're prepared to do whatever's necessary to make that happen."

"I understand you have a private detective looking into Nadine Perrault's background."

Noah's gaze was level. "I don't like it any more than you do, Joanne, but that's the way it's done." He drew the baby closer. "I imagine it's simply a matter of time before Nadine Perrault returns the favour and hires someone to start digging up the dirt on us."

"Is there dirt?"

"Everybody has dirt, and Ms. Perrault's investigators will do what our investigators are doing. They'll keep digging until they unearth something that will stick and do real damage."

"Is there anything in Delia's background that will stick?"

Noah's answer was careful. "Not in Delia's," he said.

For minutes, we sat in the quiet kitchen, listening to the tick of the grandmother clock in the hall and the baby's fizzy snore. I knew that Noah had reached what Zack called 'the confessional moment' – the moment when the need to reveal trumps the need to conceal.

When the phone shrilled, I lurched to grab it before it woke the baby. Zack was on the other end.

"Start your engines. I'm on my way."

"Noah and Jacob are here."

"Hmm. Well, that's good – there are a couple of things we should talk about. I'll be there in ten minutes. And, Ms. Shreve, I am home for the day."

"Hallelujah."

I hung up and turned to Noah. "That was Zack," I said. "He'll be in home in ten minutes, and he'd like you to stick around if you can."

"I'm not going anywhere," Noah said, and there was steel in his voice. In the time he and I had been sitting together, listening to the sounds of a quiet house and a baby sleeping, Noah had obviously made a decision. He had always struck me as a gentle giant, but as I looked at him again, I was reminded of his sheer physical power. Like the male bear he had carved as a totem for his lawn, Noah was heavily muscled, clear-eyed, and prepared to defend what was his. Jacob stirred in his arms and Noah's face softened. Abashed, he smiled and became himself again. "Sorry if I sounded like Neanderthal man," he said softly. "It's just that I have a family and my job is to take care of them."

Zack changes the energy in any room he enters. Once I had tried to explain the phenomenon to him, but since by the very act of entering the room he changes the energy, it was a hard sell. By the time Zack got home that day, Jacob had awakened and was lying on his stomach on a blanket in the living room, pushing himself up, rocking, rolling, and craning his neck to see what was happening. Noah and I were sitting at one end of the blanket offering him toys and interpreting his babble. The atmosphere in the room was calm and domestic but when Zack rolled in the air began to crackle.

He was amazed at Jacob's prowess. "Look at those shoulders," he said. "There's a football scholarship in that boy's future."

"So where do you think he should go?" I said. "One of the Big Ten or Notre Dame?"

"Notre Dame," Zack said. "Better academics." He raised an eyebrow. "You're mocking me, but you know I'm right."

I went over to his chair and began massaging the spot between the top of Zack's spine and his shoulders. "Have you had lunch?"

"I had cake. It was somebody's birthday."

"Why don't I get you an apple and a glass of milk?" I said.

"Thanks," he said. "I'll have something later. Right now, could you please just keep rubbing?"

"With pleasure," I said. I could feel the tension in his body, and I dug my fingers in more deeply.

Zack groaned. "You have no idea how good that feels," he said. "But I've earned it. I spoke to Nadine Perrault's lawyer in Port Hope. "

"And . . . ?" Noah said.

"And it may be smart to use somebody other than me to represent you."

Noah shook his head. "You and Dee have already discussed this. She won't even consider it."

"Okay," Zack said. "But forewarned is forearmed. When I introduced myself, Llewellyn Llewellyn-Smith said he knows me only by reputation, and what he's heard he doesn't like. He's got this high whiny little voice, so when he tries to be menacing he sounds like Elmer Fudd. He told me he's prepared to 'take me to the mat' on this one." Zack laughed. "Jesus, can you imagine anyone dumb enough to threaten a cripple with taking him to the mat?

"Anyway, apart from a few yuks, I didn't get much from him. My talk with our private investigator was more fruitful. He says the relationship between Abby and Nadine Perrault was not idyllic. A year and a half ago, Ms. Perrault moved out of the house she and Abby Michaels shared. They lived apart for five months. A colleague at the school where Nadine teaches described her as 'quixotic,' which the colleague defined for our guy as meaning impulsive, rash, and unpredictable. Apparently, Ms. Perrault also has a voice that carries. This colleague was able to describe in some detail Ms. Perrault's anguished and angry phone calls to Abby when they were estranged. Also, although they were together in the months before Abby left for Regina, there were tensions."

Noah rattled some bright plastic keys in front of Jacob. When Jacob reached for the keys and grasped them, he squealed with delight, and Noah's face creased with pleasure. "Did the colleague know why Abby and Nadine were having problems?" he asked.

"No, she just said that, given Ms. Perrault's rage and sense of betrayal, it was a surprise when she and Abby Michaels reconciled."

I gave Zack's neck a last squeeze and moved back to my place on the rug. "I know what caused the problem," I said. "Nadine Perrault didn't want a baby, but Abby did. She found a man who was willing to father her child and they had intercourse."

"Whoa," Zack said. "How did you find that out?"

"Nadine told Alwyn."

Noah winced. "So now we have a father to deal with."

"Not if Nadine's story is accurate. She says there was no contact between him and Abby after she conceived the child."

"And you don't believe her," Zack said.

"No," I said. "But that's just me thinking like me."

"Nothing wrong with your thought processes," Zack said.

"I agree," Noah said. "But whatever the relationship was between Abby and this man, we need to find him and get him on our side. That's not going to be easy. I'm sure Nadine Perrault has already pulled out all the stops."

"I don't think Nadine knows who he is," I said. "Abby had nothing to gain by telling her. Knowing the identity of the man who fathered Jacob would have made Nadine even more insecure about her relationship with Abby than she was, and it would have made the father vulnerable. Whoever he is, Abby trusted the father to honour their agreement; I think she would have protected his identity."

Zack nodded. "Let's hope you're right. I don't like the idea of Nadine having a head start. I guess our move now is to get our investigator to look into the identity of dear old dad. And I'd better call Deb and fill her in on what we've learned. It's always wise to spread the quid pro quo around."

"Jacob was born June 16," I said. "That means he was conceived a year ago last September."

"This can work for us," Zack said. "Asking people in Port Hope where Abby was a year ago last September is a nice straightforward question. It'll get the conversational ball rolling, and give us a chance to spread the word that we're looking for the father of Abby's baby."

I squeezed a fuzzy duck that was out of Jacob's range on the blanket. The duck emitted an oddly tortured sound, and Jacob clouded up. "That's the worst quack I've ever heard," I said. "Let's put that duck away." I dropped it in the diaper bag and looked up at Zack. "Isn't a private investigator supposed to operate under the radar?"

"Sometimes it's good to let people know you're out there, digging away," Zack said. "We have to keep Ms. Perrault off-base, make sure she knows the ground beneath her feet is shifting."

I felt a sting of anger. "Zack, for God's sake, Nadine Perrault has just lost her partner and the baby she thought they were going to raise together. The ground beneath her feet has already shifted."

I'd raised my voice, and Jacob craned his head and looked at me with solemn eyes. Noah moved quickly. He scooped the baby into his arms, protecting him – against me.

I was taken aback. "Noah, I'm sorry. I didn't mean to frighten Jacob, but I think you and Zack have lost perspective here. We don't know Nadine Perrault. She may not be an enemy."

Zack's voice was almost a whisper – a courtroom trick he used to calm overly excited witnesses. "We can't take that chance, Jo," he said. "The stakes are too high."

"I hate this," I said.

Zack shot me a weary look. "Jesus, Jo, do you think I like it? But the days of King Solomon are long past. Today people are prepared to rip the baby in two rather than give an inch."

After that, there wasn't much to say. I picked up Jacob's toys and rolled up the blanket. Playtime was over. I brought Jacob's snowsuit to Noah.

He slid the baby into the suit. "Thanks for the sandwich, Joanne. We'll get through this."

After Jacob was dressed, the three of us went into the front hall, and I held the baby while Noah pulled on his own boots and jacket. When the doorbell rang, Zack opened the door.

A cab driver stood there, holding a box. Beside him was Mr. Justice Theodore Brokaw.

CHAPTER

7

Discovering Theo Brokaw on our doorstep was a surprise, but Zack was poised. "Hello, Judge, it's good to see you again." He wheeled closer to the door. "Is Mrs. Brokaw with you?"

Theo winked. "She was napping, and I snuck out."

"Ah," Zack said.

The cab driver wasn't diverted by the deeds of others. "Somebody owes me $9.75," he said.

Theo Brokaw ignored him. Zack pulled out his wallet and gave the cabbie $15.00. "Where did you pick up Justice Brokaw?" he said. "I'm not questioning your rate. I'm just curious."

"He was on 11th Avenue just off Scarth Street Mall. He flagged me down. Gave me this box, pointed to the address, and said, 'Take me there.'"

Zack took the box from the driver, glanced at the address. "Well, that's where he is. Thanks."

"So I can leave?" said the driver.

"Yes," Zack said. "We can handle it now."

Jacob was still in my arms, and Theo Brokaw seemed mesmerized by him. "Is this your baby?" he asked me.

"No," I said.

He turned to Zack. "Is it your baby?"

"No," Zack said.

Theo Brokaw waggled a gloved finger at Jacob. "Are you my baby?" he asked. Jacob laughed, and Theo waggled his finger again. "Well, if you're nobody's baby, whose baby are you?"

Zack turned his chair towards the living room. "You may no longer be on the bench, Judge Brokaw, but you still know the right question to ask. Why don't you come in and make yourself comfortable while we call Mrs. Brokaw and let her know you're here."

"Tell her I brought the box." Theo took off his gloves and coat and placed them carefully on the cobbler's bench. I led him into the living room; he sat in the rocking chair by the fireplace and held out his arms. I looked over at Noah. He nodded, and I handed the baby to Theo. He held Jacob awkwardly, and I reached over and adjusted the angle of his arm. Theo didn't acknowledge my assistance. Instead, he began crooning a song in a language I took to be Ukrainian. His voice was surprisingly strong and young. As Theo sang, Jacob's eyes grow heavy and then closed.

"There. He's asleep," Theo said. When Noah took Jacob, Theo nodded sagely. "So he's yours," he said.

"Yes," Noah said. "He's mine, and it's time that he and I went home."

After Noah and Jacob left, I called Myra Brokaw. On the voice message for her home phone, Myra Brokaw offered her cell number to callers with "pressing business." As the minutes passed, our business became increasingly pressing. Theo Brokaw had grown agitated. He was an athletic man, and as he paced back and forth across our living room, his steps were long and powerful. He was cursing, but the source of his rage was unclear. Zack had positioned his chair at mid-point and was murmuring reassurances. At first, Theo ignored him, but suddenly he pivoted and raised a clenched fist at Zack. "Do you want me to punch you in the face?" he said.

Zack was matey. "Come on. Judges don't punch lawyers. You know that. We're not worth the effort."

Theo cocked his head. "Was I appointed to the bench?"

Zack enunciated each word slowly and distinctly. "Yes, Justice Brokaw," he said. "You were appointed to the bench."

After I reached her on her cell, Myra was at our front door within minutes. "Where is he?" she asked. I pointed towards the room where her husband strode desperately towards a destination only he could fathom. Myra slipped off her boots and walked towards the living room. She stopped on the threshold and took in the scene. "He doesn't know where he is," she murmured. Then she pasted on her social smile, glided towards her husband, and took his arm. "Thank you so much for delivering our gift to the Shreves," she said, drawing him towards the door. "It was clever of you to think of it. Now we must be on our way, sweetheart. The Shreves have plans, and so do we."

Myra's presence seemed to calm Theo. In a world that was suddenly senseless and menacing, she offered safe haven. "I got here with the box," he said.

The gift was on the sideboard. "So I see," she said. "Good work. You saved us the expense of the courier."

She helped him on with his coat and tied his bright holiday scarf. As he had on the two previous occasions when I'd met him, Theo Brokaw appeared natty and distinguished, but as he turned towards the door, I saw the expression in his eyes. He was desperate.

"Thank you for taking care of him," Myra said.

"May we drive you home?" I said.

"I brought my car," she said, knotting her own red scarf and pulling on the matching tam. "There's a note inside the gift box," she said. "I hope you'll take the words to heart, Joanne."

When we closed the door behind them, Zack and I exchanged glances. I opened the box on the sideboard. As I'd anticipated, the gift was a twin of the pomegranate wreath I'd admired on the Brokaws' door. Myra's handwriting was as strong and clear as her message. "The pomegranate is said to symbolize regeneration. May this wreath be a reminder that there are always new beginnings."

I handed the card to Zack. "Nice," he said. "Unfortunately, while people are working on new beginnings, the past has a way of jumping up and biting them in the ass."

I removed the wreath from the box and held it over the mirror on the sideboard. "What do you think?" I said.

Zack cocked his head. "Looks good. Want me to get a hammer and one of those little finishing nails?"

"In a minute," I said. "Zack, do you know of anything in Noah's past that might cause problems with Jacob's custody?"

Pantera plastered his body against the side of Zack's wheelchair, putting himself within easy reach if Zack felt the need to rub his head.

I had hoped for quick reassurance, but Zack was silent as he scratched behind Pantera's ears. I sat down on one of the dining room chairs. "There is something, isn't there?" I said.

"There is," he said. "But it was so long ago. I can't imagine anybody remembering it but us."

"Us, meaning . . . ?"

"Noah, Delia, me, and our late, sainted partner Chris Altieri."

"So what happened?"

Zack cocked his head. "Short and sweet: Noah got into a fight with a guy and the guy died."

"Noah killed a man?"

"No. The guy, an obnoxious prick named Murray Jeffreys, died of a heart attack."

"So Noah wasn't responsible?"

Zack raised an eyebrow. "You could argue that point either way. Murray died because his heart stopped, not because of the injuries Noah inflicted upon him. That said, if the fight hadn't happened, Murray would probably have lived to die another day."

I went to the sideboard and picked up the wreath. The mica from the pomegranates flaked onto my fingers. "So when did this happen?"

"Guess."

"The year you all articled."

Zack turned his chair towards the window. "It seems like another lifetime. It *was* another lifetime."

"But you do remember the fight."

"You bet. It's not every day you see a guy die. Since then I've had dozens of clients who've either caused or been present at the violent death of another human being and 90 per cent of them say the same thing: 'It was all over so fast. I didn't realize what had happened.'" Zack turned his chair to face me. "That's exactly the way it was that night. Murray's firm, which consisted of Murray and two associates, was having its Christmas party at some restaurant downtown. Dee had come back for Christmas, and that meant that Noah was walking around with this shit-eating grin."

"He loved her even then?"

Pantera nudged Zack's hand with his head and Zack rewarded him with a head scratch. "Noah's love for Delia is the kind people write songs about . . . "

"Or kill for?"

Zack winced. "Do me a favour, Jo. Don't make that connection again. Anyway, we were at the party. By our modest standards, it was stellar: free booze, free food, and a chance to suck up to people who could be useful to us when we opened our own firm. Putting up with a prick like Murray seemed a small price to pay, but putting up with isn't the same as putting out for, and that distinction was lost on Murray. Did I mention that Dee looked really primo that Christmas?"

"You did," I said.

Zack gave me a quick smile. "I knew your memory would be solid on that point. Anyway, Murray started pawing at Delia. She brushed him off, but he wouldn't stop. Then Murray made a really crude suggestion, and Noah started to hammer him. Murray was a little guy and he was twenty years older than Noah, plus he was paying for the party, so somebody intervened."

"It doesn't sound as if Murray's death was Noah's fault."

"That's not the end of the story. We were all pretty juiced. Delia was staying with Noah, and I didn't live far from his place, so Noah decided it would be a good idea if we walked – fresh air being a well-known antidote to a hangover. Chris, ever the good shepherd, decided he should see us safely to our beds. We took a shortcut through the alley back of the restaurant, and Murray came after us. He grabbed Delia and said maybe if she played ball, he could slide some cases her way. Noah went nuts. As I said, he was pretty drunk."

"I've never seen Noah take a drink."

"After that night, he never did. Anyway, Noah started swinging. He's a powerful guy, but luckily the booze had affected his ability to connect. He only landed one punch and it wasn't much, but Murray went down and stayed down. Chris was still sober. He checked and said he couldn't find a pulse. Then . . . " Zack shrugged. "Decisions were made."

"Passive voice," I said.

Zack's smile was ironic. "You hang around with cops, you learn a few tricks . . . Anyway, Chris went back inside the restaurant to call for an ambulance, and Noah told Dee to go to my place. She was staying with him, but he didn't want her involved in any trouble. Dee was always the decision-maker, but that night she was reeling. When she came to bed, she couldn't stop shaking, and she hung onto me all night. The next day she stayed in bed, eating cereal out of the box, and watching reruns of sitcoms until Noah came."

"The police didn't hold him?"

"The police didn't know he was involved in Round Two. Chris sent Noah home before the cops came. A dozen people had witnessed Round One of his fight with Murray, so of course he was on the cops' visiting list, but Noah had an ace up his sleeve. Chris Altieri, a young lawyer who went to mass every day of his life, was prepared to swear that by the time Murray dropped dead in the alley behind the hotel, Noah had left the scene."

"And Chris's word was enough?"

"The cops didn't have anything else," Zack said softly. "And none of us has ever talked about that evening since." He shrugged. "Now, I'm going to get the hammer and nails so you can put up our new wreath." His finger touched one of the pomegranates. As it had with me, the mica came off on his fingertip. He stared at it thoughtfully. "Did you know that the French word for grenade is pomegranate?"

"You think Myra's gift is a weapon?"

He shrugged. "We live in dangerous times."

We left for Port Hope on the morning of Friday, December 11 – six days after Abby Michaels had handed Jacob over to the Wainbergs and disappeared into the blizzard. Despite intensive media coverage and appeals from Inspector Debbie Haczkewicz, no one who had seen Abby that night came forward. Seemingly, the blizzard and the blackout had obliterated memories both human and electronic. People who might have seen her as she left the school and got into her car had been absorbed by their own efforts to deal with the storm and darkness. Security cameras at intersections that she might have driven through and in the area around the pawn shop parking lot where, presumably, she was attacked and killed, were not functioning. Zack's bleak prediction that the blackout would make it possible for Jacob's mother to disappear without a trace had been right on the money.

Debbie Haczkewicz stopped by our house the night before we left. Her son, Leo, had sent a Christmas gift from Japan for Zack. It was a laughing Buddha. Debbie was droll as she handed the Buddha to Zack. "This is supposed to bring you happiness and good luck. I told Leo I'd trade you my new peony kimono for twenty-four hours of good luck on the Michaels case."

Zack handed the laughing Buddha back to Debbie. "Why don't you hold onto our friend here while I get you a drink? Maybe some of that luck will rub off on you."

"Here's hoping," Debbie said.

"Still drinking Crown Royal on the rocks?" Zack asked.

"It's been my drink since I hit legal age," Debbie said. "Legal age is but a memory, but in my opinion, there's no reason to question a smart decision."

"Agreed," Zack said. "I'll pour, and you and Joanne can relax and enjoy the season."

In a fruitless effort to help me before the flight, Zack had built a fire and put on *The Messiah*. Debbie gazed at the tree and the fire and sighed. "I had a choice: the police college or law school."

"It's never too late," I said.

Debbie's smile was rueful. "It is if you have a pension you can't afford to walk away from."

Zack came in with the drinks on a tray balanced on his lap. He handed Debbie her rye. She raised her glass. "Happy holidays."

We toasted the season, then Zack got down to business. "Anything new?"

Debbie shot him a withering glance. "No. I'm still squandering time, personnel, and taxpayer dollars on dead ends." She took a sip of rye and her irritation melted. "Let's see. We ran a preliminary match of the semen. The VI-class data on the match came up negative, so that eliminates every man in Canada who's ever been convicted of a violent sexual assault. Abby Michaels was raped and murdered by an amateur or at least a rapist cunning enough not to get caught. The field is wide open, Zack, and you know what that means."

"You're hooped," my husband said.

Debbie nodded. "It gets worse. Considering that Ms. Michaels didn't know anyone in Regina, it seemed possible that a woman who'd just given away her child might have been sufficiently despondent to hit the clubs and pick up Mr. Wrong. We had officers checking the downtown bars to see if a bartender or server had spotted a woman meeting Abby Michaels's description the night of the blizzard, but no luck." Debbie looked at Zack. "Of course, when you told us that she was a lesbian, we checked the gay bars, but they were a wash too. Not surprising, I guess, considering that pesky presence of semen on the body."

"I'm assuming Abby had no visitors at the Chelton," Zack said.

Debbie shook her head. "No visitors and, as you know, an invariable routine. Incidentally, Joanne, thanks for suggesting we talk to your daughter. Mieka's the only person we've found who actually had a conversation with the victim. The people who worked at the hotel said she was polite but withdrawn. When they tried to engage with the baby, she did not encourage them. We've checked the calls she made on her cell. There were remarkably few. She called ahead to a couple of motels when she was driving out here – apparently to let them know she'd be late arriving – but apart from that, the only calls were made the early evening of the blizzard. The first two calls were made at 6:01 and 6:02 p.m."

"That would have been just after Abby left Luther," I said.

"The calls were to Nadine Perrault's cell, but Ms. Perrault's cell was turned off. The third was to Our Lady of Mercy Church in Port Hope. That call was made at 6:03. Father Rafael Quines answered, and he and the victim spoke for seven minutes and thirteen seconds."

"I take it you contacted Father Quines," Zack said.

"I did." The twist of Debbie's lip was sardonic. "My conversation with Father Quines was not lengthy."

"The Seal of the Confessional?" Zack said.

"He didn't say. He just said he couldn't discuss the conversation and that he was praying for Abby's soul."

"Maybe that's why she called a priest," I said. "Abby made a lot of serious decisions the day she died. Maybe she needed to clear the slate."

"Let's hope she did." Debbie's voice was sombre. She stood, then bent to embrace my husband. "Merry Christmas," she said.

Zack patted her back. "We'll figure this one out, Deb."

"I know," she said. "But if you want to speed the process along, before you go to Port Hope, give your laughing Buddha a pat."

Zack chuckled. "You've got it. Merry Christmas, Deb."

I awoke the next morning with Zack's arms around me. All week, he had done his best to reassure and distract me, but he knew me well. "So how bad is it?" he said.

"Can't you hear my heart pounding?"

"I have a suggestion. Why don't we fool around for a while? You always say that making love relaxes you."

"I'll try anything," I said.

"I'm prepared to take one for the team."

My husband did the team proud. When we were finished, I kissed his shoulder. "What did you say your name was again?"

"Planning to recommend me to your friends?

"No. I was thinking of using your services during take-off."

"I'm available, but you'd better bring a blanket."

Our flight left Regina at noon. Zack was due in court at ten to hear the judge's sentencing of his client in the road-racing case. The timing was going to be tight, but our bags were packed and we lived seven minutes from the airport. After we said goodbye to Taylor, Zack went to the office and I took the things Taylor needed for the weekend over to the Wainbergs'. Delia had already left for court, so Noah and Jacob met me at the door.

Jacob was curled in the crook of Noah's arm. It was difficult to reconcile the mental image of the gentle man in front of me, his face creased in a smile of welcome, with the scene of animal violence Zack's account had painted. My eyes stayed on Noah's face a beat too long, and he noticed.

"Is something the matter?" he said.

"Zack told me about Murray Jeffreys," I said.

"What did he tell you?"

"That the two of you were fighting and Murray Jeffreys died of a heart attack."

"I've spent a lot of years trying to make up for that night," Noah said simply. "Now come inside. You arrived just in time for a landmark in Jacob's life. Today we begin vegetables. First up – strained pureed peas."

Noah's voice, warm and ordinary, was deeply reassuring. "I don't think I could handle peas at eight-thirty in the morning," I said.

"You don't have to. You just have to watch."

Jacob was an eager eater. He gobbled the peas as if they were truffles. "Good man," Noah said. "So the plan is that you pick up Zack and Delia and leave your car at the airport?"

"That's the plan. Zack got a call last night that the sentence for that road-racing case is coming down this morning. He's a little tense about it."

"He shouldn't be. You know how compelling Zack is in the courtroom, and he has the Criminal Code on his side. It says an appropriate sentence is based half on the offence and half on the offender. What Jeremy Sawchuk did was horrific, but from what I hear, he's a decent kid who was guilty of a terrible lapse of judgment."

"A lapse that proved fatal for his best friend," I said.

"And Jeremy will live with that for the rest of his life. He'll also have a criminal record, but in my opinion, society will not be served by throwing him in the penitentiary for twenty years."

"Still . . ."

Noah wiped a smear of peas from Jacob's chin. "I don't have the answers, Jo. As a lawyer, I was pretty much of a bust. But at the risk of sounding self-serving, I don't see the justice in having fifteen minutes of stupidity wreck an otherwise fairly blameless life." He untied Jacob's bib. "The café is closing, bud. Time to turn off the deep fryer and clean you up." His eyes shifted to me. "Jo, there's a washcloth over there on the counter, would you mind?"

I walked over to the sink, dampened the cloth with warm water, and handed it to Noah.

"Have you ever wished you'd made a career of the law?" I said.

"No," he said. "Look at the Winners' Circle. They were the best, and their lives have not exactly been the stuff of dreams. Chris committed suicide; Kevin wandered around Tibet for a couple of years and came back to the firm with ideas that drive everybody nuts. Blake is one of the top-ten real-estate lawyers in Western Canada, but except for Gracie, his personal life has been a disaster. Zack and Dee are the only ones who remained true believers and didn't crack under the strain. But in my opinion, Zack came close to crashing before he met you."

"We're happy," I said. "That changes a lot."

"With Zack, there was a lot that needed changing," Noah said. "When we met in law school, there was something sweet in him, but success made him rapacious – no matter how much he had, it was never enough."

"He seems content now."

"He *is* content," Noah said. "I guess there's always hope." He wiped the washcloth around the whorl of Jacob's ear. "Look at that ear," he said. "Perfection."

"You're going to have to carve another bear for the front lawn," I said.

He nuzzled Jacob. "I already have the wood."

The news was on as I was loading the car. Noah had been right. The judge had taken Jeremy Sawchuk's exemplary record into account and been lenient. He had sentenced the teenager to two years less a day in the provincial jail.

I was relieved. One less burden for Zack.

I texted Zack telling him I was on my way, and when I pulled up in front of the courthouse, he and Delia came out immediately. Zack slid into the passenger seat, folded his wheelchair, and put it next to Delia in the back.

They were both in high spirits. "Zack won," Delia said. "A good day for the firm."

"Congratulations," I said.

Zack snapped his seat belt and turned to me. "How was your morning?"

"Eventful," I said. "I was there when Jacob was introduced to strained peas."

Delia leaned forward. "So how did he do?"

"He cleaned his plate," I said.

"Well, I'm going to be there when he graduates to squash," Delia said. "I sent a memo to the other partners this morning saying I'm cutting back on my caseload."

"Dee's given notice that she's only going to work twelve hours a day instead of sixteen," Zack said.

"Ignore him," Delia said. "I've missed out on too much."

The stab of fear I felt had nothing to do with the fact that within an hour I'd be 35,000 feet in the air. The Wainbergs were operating on the assumption that Jacob was now a permanent member of their family. I had a nagging sense that the matter of his custody was far from settled.

It was a little after six when Delia, Zack, and I arrived at the Lantern Inn & Suites. We'd arranged for a car and driver to meet us at Toronto Pearson International Airport and take us to Port Hope. Spending an hour inside a limo jammed between speeding semis on Highway 401 would normally have made me anxious, but I was preoccupied with my relief at being back on solid ground. That said, when we turned onto the exit that led into town, I think I exhaled for the first time since we left Regina.

It had been many years since I'd spent a Christmas in Port Hope but the town was much as I'd remembered. Now as then, the historic brick buildings that housed the shops on Walton Street were trimmed with evergreen boughs, fairy lights, and fresh holly, but there was something noteworthy about this particular December. I nudged my husband. "Look," I said. "No snow. We're meeting Alwyn in the hotel dining room at seven. After we eat, we'll be able to walk her home."

"She lives that close?"

"Everything's that close in Port Hope," I said.

As the hotel's Web site had promised, our room on the third floor was spacious and high-ceilinged, with a fireplace, large windows, a terrace overlooking the Ganaraska River, and, best of all, a queen-sized bed with a canopy.

While Zack checked out the new digs, I called the Wainbergs'. Noah reported that Taylor and Isobel had bundled up Jacob, tucked him into his ergonomically correct sled, and taken him to the park to watch the big kids toboggan. He promised to have Taylor call us when she got back. The news from our house was mixed. According to Pete, Willie was fine. However, Pantera was already pining for Zack, and in his grief he had eaten a dozen bran muffins Pete had left on the counter to cool.

"You *are* keeping Pantera outside?" I said.

Pete sounded exasperated, "You know, Mum, you'd be amazed the stuff they teach at the School of Vet Med."

"Sorry," I said. "Do you want Zack to talk to his dog?"

"Not much point," Pete said. "Pantera would just eat the phone."

"Are you finding this too much?" I said.

"Nope. You forget I live in a hovel. The big TV here is nice. So is the indoor pool. Hey, Pantera did laps with me this afternoon."

"There must be some sort of health regulation about that," I said.

"I'm sure there is," Pete said. "Say hi to Zack. See you Sunday night."

When I hung up, Zack was looking at me quizzically. "There must be some sort of health regulation about what?" he said.

"Pantera doing laps in the pool with Peter."

Zack made a gesture of dismissal. "When you're not around, Pantera does laps in the pool with me all the time. He and I believe in the buddy system."

As I hung up our clothes, Zack picked up the leather-bound folder explaining the Lantern Inn's services and history. He was gloomy as he read aloud from the insert describing the town's Olde Tyme Christmas. "We've already missed the Festival of Trees, the Jack and the Beanstalk Pantomime, the Candlelight Walk and Carol Singing, the Christmas Tree Lighting, the Santa Claus Parade, and the Kinette Christmas General Store." He dropped the insert in the wastepaper basket, then glanced at the folder and brightened. "But listen to this. 'The Great Farini, famous high-wire walker, world circus impresario, and native of Port Hope, made an exciting walk across the Ganaraska River from the roof of the Lantern Inn on May 16, 1861. He wore peach baskets on his feet in the day, and in the evening, he tossed fireworks high in the sky while crossing the river.' We're part of history, Ms. Shreve. Let's go out on our balcony and look at the river."

It was chilly outside, but it was also very lovely. Alwyn was right. Port Hope would have a green Christmas. The Ganaraska hadn't frozen, and listening to the rush of the water and looking at the lights across the river was a quiet thrill.

"Just think," Zack said, "the Great Farini walked across that river."

"With peach baskets on his feet," I said.

"I can't do the peach basket thing," Zack said. "But say the word and I'll toss fireworks into the sky for you, Jo. I'm very glad you're here."

I put my arms around him. "So am I."

We met Alwyn and Delia in the Lantern Inn's dining room at seven that evening. With its wood-burning fireplace, period art and decor, and cherry furniture, the room couldn't have been more welcoming, but five minutes into the evening, I knew it had been a mistake to invite both

Alwyn and Delia for dinner. Zack often starts cases by asking clients the outcome for which they are hoping. Had Alwyn and Delia been asked that question, their answers would have signalled trouble ahead. Alwyn wanted to share a convivial dinner with an old friend and the old friend's new husband; Delia wanted to unearth anything that would make her custody case invulnerable.

We ordered our food and a bottle of Ontario VQA Cabernet Sauvignon that Alwyn recommended. It was a pleasant choice to ease us into the evening, but as Zack and Alwyn and I chatted, Delia sizzled with impatience, drumming her fingers on the table, and answering every question with a monosyllabic response. Finally, Zack had enough. He glared at his law partner. "Dee, if you don't smarten up, you're paying for dinner."

"I thought I *was* paying for dinner," Delia said. "I apologize, Alwyn. I'm not good at small talk."

"Abby wasn't good at small talk either," Alwyn said quietly.

The words were clearly intended to comfort her, but their effect on Delia was devastating. She flinched as if from a blow, and when she spoke her voice was tentative. "Tell me about her," she said.

Alwyn's brow creased in concentration. "It's difficult to distil twenty-seven years of impressions into a few sentences. At the moment, what strikes me most is simply how much she was like you. Physically, the resemblance is startling. And something else . . . unless I'm mistaken, Abby wore the same perfume you're wearing tonight."

Delia bit her lip. "Chanel No. 5," she said. "It's the only perfume I've ever worn."

"That's remarkable, isn't it? That without ever knowing one another, you'd choose the same scent." Alwyn shook her head as if to regain her focus. "Let's see. Even as a child, Abby set goals for herself, and like you, she was impatient with anything that stood in the way of realizing them. Her parents – Peggy and Hugh – adored her, and they were wise enough to smooth her path, so Abby could achieve what she believed she had to achieve."

Delia leaned closer to Alwyn. "They spoiled her?"

Alwyn shook her head. "No. It was impossible to spoil that child. She never wanted *things* – she wanted to *know* things. Of course, that made her a perfect fit for Peggy and Hugh. She was the centre of their lives."

Delia leaned forward. "Yet they never told her she was adopted." Delia reached for her wineglass with trembling fingers. "Why would they do that?"

"I'm sure they thought they were protecting her, just as they'd protected her all her life. Abby was home-schooled until she was in Grade Five – that's when students begin at Trinity. Of course, her father taught there and Abby knew all the other teachers, so she was protected there, too. The faculty was like an extended family for her."

"And she did well?" The mother's inevitable question.

"Brilliantly. She had extraordinarily high standards, and she drove herself hard."

Delia placed her wine, untasted, back on the table. "Did she have friends?"

"Not many, but the friendships she had were intense. The year she started at TCS, she linked up with a group – both boys and girls – who were as bright as she was. Nadine Perrault was among them. The students in that group were inseparable till they graduated."

It was the Winners' Circle all over again. Zack's eyes moved to Delia, but her attention was still on Alwyn. "Was Abby's sexual orientation a problem?" Delia asked.

"It never appeared to be," Alwyn said. "Everybody, including Hugh and Peggy, seemed to know, but nobody ever made a big deal about it."

"Nadine was the only partner?" I said.

Alwyn shrugged. "She and Abby were seldom apart. The world isn't always hospitable to same-sex couples, but perhaps because they'd always been inseparable, Abby and Nadine were lucky. One of the memories I've been cherishing lately is of Hugh and Peggy walking down Walton Street with their daughter and Nadine last Thanksgiving. Jacob was in Abby's old pram. Hugh and Peggy had ordered it from Britain. They always made certain their daughter had the best."

Delia lowered her head and stared at her lap at the reference to Abby as the Michaelses' daughter; Alwyn noticed and hurried through the rest of her narrative. "My point," she said, "is that they were happy – all of them. It was one of those scarlet and gold early October days, and seeing Hugh and Margaret with Abby, Nadine, and the child they all loved seemed to affirm that the world can be a fine place." Alwyn's voice broke. "The next day Margaret and Hugh were killed on the 401, and you know the rest."

Delia stared at Alwyn wide-eyed. "But we don't know 'the rest.' We don't really know anything." She stood abruptly. "I'm sorry. I don't think I can take this tonight. You'll have to excuse me."

"Of course," Alwyn said. She touched Delia's arm. "One of Abby's friends recorded the memorial service this morning. She'll burn it to a DVD. I'll get a copy to you before you go back to Regina."

"Thank you."

"Nadine thought you might like to spend the morning quietly and come out to the country after lunch and see where Abby grew up and the home they shared."

"She wants me to know Abby better," Delia said bleakly.

Alwyn was clearly taken aback. "Don't you want to?"

"I don't know. Sitting here tonight, listening to you talk about Abby, made me realize how much I've missed out on." Then, her face pinched with misery, Delia turned and walked out of the dining room.

When our trout arrived, Zack ordered another bottle of wine, and the three of us tried to salvage the evening. By the time we were weighing the options on the dessert menu, we had covered all the conversational topics that mattered: books, movies, holiday plans, Pantera's exploits, and the exceptional intelligence of Alwyn's three-legged tuxedo cat, Wilson. Given the circumstances, the evening had been pleasant, and I welcomed Zack's suggestion that we walk Alwyn home.

The night was mild and starry – perfect for sky-gazing or river-watching. Zack stopped in the middle of the walkway on the bridge over the Ganaraska, and I thought he was giving himself over to the pleasures of the evening, but his mind was on his case. "What's Nadine Perrault like?" he said.

Alwyn moved closer to the railing and looked down at the inky, swirling water. "If you'd asked me two weeks ago, I could have given you an answer, but Nadine has been broken by this. I can't predict anything about the woman you're going to meet tomorrow."

"What was she like before?"

"Complex," Alwyn said. "As most interesting people are. She was a boarder at TCS from the time she was in Grade Five, and after university she came back and taught with us. I've been acquainted with her for much of her life, but Nadine doesn't encourage intimacy."

"Her attachment to the school must have been powerful to bring her back to teach," I said.

"It was – it is for a lot of our students. Our Web site trots out the usual stirring phrases about developing hearts and minds, offering academic challenges, and building leadership skills. That's for the parents; a lot of our students just want to find a place where they belong, and that's what

Nadine found with us. When she first arrived, she was like a skittish colt that would bolt if you extended a hand to it. The school calmed her. Whatever had happened in the past, being part of the school taught her to trust. Then when Peggy and Hugh realized how close she and Abby were, they welcomed her into their family."

"And they were aware that the girls' relationship went beyond friendship?" I said.

"The girls were discreet, but they made no secret of their feelings for one another," Alwyn said. "Hugh and Peggy accepted the situation. They loved Nadine because Abby loved her and that seemed to ease any problems the town might have had about the relationship."

"Their deaths must have been terrible for Nadine," I said.

"They were, but she and Abby were both practising Roman Catholics, and they seemed to find consolation in their faith."

"So Hugh and Peggy were Catholic, then," I said.

Alwyn hooted. "God no! Hugh was a staunch Darwinist. Every February 12th, he hosted a luncheon to commemorate Darwin's birth and celebrate science, reason, and humanity. Peggy had her own religion." Alwyn's lips twitched. "I believe it had something to do with wood nymphs. The Catholicism came from Nadine. Abby was a convert."

"If the conversion got them through the loss of Hugh and Peggy Michaels, it must have taken," I said.

"It did," Alwyn said. "Nadine and Abby were both devastated, but they seemed to feel they could survive, because they had their faith, one another, and Jacob." Alwyn gazed at the water. "I wonder what Nadine's position on God is now?" she said.

It had been a long day, and Zack and I slept well under our canopy. We awoke at eight – which for both of us was very late.

"Let's get room service," I said. "It's too cold to sit on the balcony, but we can pull back the curtains and watch Port Hope spring into action."

Zack sneezed. "Fair enough," he said. "But this is a holiday – no steel-cut oatmeal and 600-grain toast. I want a manly breakfast: bacon, sausage, eggs, and home fries."

"The defibrillator special." I picked up the phone. "I'll see what I can do."

Zack and Delia were meeting the Michaelses' family lawyer at nine-thirty to discuss the will; after that, they were meeting Nadine Perrault's lawyer. Alwyn and I had both finished our Christmas shopping, but the town's antique and specialty stores were seductive, and we were willing to be seduced.

When I found a leaf-shaped mercury-glass relish dish that I knew my friend Ed Mariani would treasure, I pulled out my credit card. "I hate shopping," I said. "But shopping here with you is actually fun."

"The stores are open year-round," Alwyn said. "And you appear to have conquered your fear of flying."

"Appearance is not reality," I said. "I'm already starting to count down the hours till we're in the air again."

"Does Zack mind that you don't fly?"

"No. Travel's not easy for him either."

"Because of the wheelchair?"

"That's an indignity – there's other stuff that's harder to manage."

"I like him," Alwyn said.

"So do I," I said.

The drive from Port Hope to the house in which Abby had grown up took fifteen minutes. The Michaels property was situated in a valley among gentle hills with ponds and ditches that filled with wildflowers in summer. The soil was rich and the water supply so abundant that legend had it a toddler with a stick could stumble and find water. For years, most of the houses in the area had been century homes – over a hundred years old, solid brick, built to last, quiet and unprepossessing, close to the road. But Toronto money had moved to the country. Now the hills were crested with new homes that boasted spectacular views, triple garages, winding driveways, and million-dollar price tags.

The Michaels' house had been built on thirty acres of land that was now considered prime real estate. One hour's commute from the city, the property was treed and private with a tributary of the Ganaraska running through it. The house was a solid red-brick Georgian with shuttered windows and an oak front door with a transom and side-lights. Mercifully, there was only one step, so Zack managed to manoeuvre his chair onto the porch area without help before Nadine Perrault opened the door to greet us.

She was a slender, fine-featured natural blonde with deep-set hazel eyes that were red from weeping. When she came face to face with Delia, her intake of breath was audible. "I'm sorry," she said, "It's just . . . the physical resemblance is overwhelming." She recovered quickly, inviting us in although she had trouble taking her eyes from Delia's face. "You probably should leave your coats on," she said. Her voice was low and commanding – a teacher's voice. "I don't live here," she said, "so I'm keeping the thermostat low. I should have thought about it this morning, but the memorial service yesterday was very difficult for me. I apologize." She threw her hands up in a gesture of impotence.

"We're fine," I said.

"We won't stay long here," Nadine said. Her hair was centre-parted in a good mid-length cut. She wore no makeup, but she didn't need any. She led us into the room on the left. "Don't worry about your boots," she said. "These rugs have endured a great deal over the years." She shrugged. "As you can see, this house has been well lived in."

The wood in the living room gleamed and the plants in the windows were thriving, but the fabric on the furniture was worn and faded. There were books everywhere. Over the fireplace was a family portrait. Delia was drawn to it immediately. Hugh Michaels was a bald, rumpled-looking man with grey eyes, heavy brows, and the quarter-smile of the ironist; his wife, tanned and blonde, had the sleepily content smile of a woman who revelled in the sensual. The eyes of both parents were on Abby, who stood in front of them, pale, intense, and impatient.

"I could look at that painting forever," Nadine said softly. "It is so like them. Abby was fourteen. The artist wanted her to put on a dress, but she refused. Peggy insisted on wearing her garden hat and having a cigarette in her hand because she was never without a cigarette. And Hugh, of course, wore his invariable four-in-hand tie and three-piece suit."

"Abby looks just like Isobel," Zack said. "Same hair. Same eyes. Same focus."

I turned to Nadine. "Isobel is Delia's daughter. She's the same age as Abby was in that painting."

Nadine's voice was dreamy. "Abby had a very happy life with them," she said. "I thought you'd like to see that."

Delia's lips tightened. "I've seen enough," she said.

Nadine raised an eyebrow. "You don't want to look at the rest of the house? Abby's old room is filled with things that were important to her – things that I know she wanted Jacob to cherish some day."

Delia's headshake was violent. "No."

Zack turned his chair to face Nadine. His voice was gentle. "Was there anything special you wanted to show us?"

Nadine nodded. "There's a spot by the river that Abby loved. We talked about taking Jacob there next summer and letting him paddle in the water. Abby and I spent hours there, swimming and doing homework and reading and dreaming." She smiled at the memory. "It's a magical place for a child."

Delia turned away sharply. "I forgot something in the car," she said, and she walked out. When we heard the door slam, Zack pointed his chair towards the hall. "I'll talk to her," he said.

I waited as Nadine put on her jacket and boots. "Delia's not easy with emotions," I said.

Nadine's voice was jagged. "Is she capable of love?"

"I don't know," I said.

Nadine knotted her scarf. "I never knew with Abby either," she said bleakly. "But I loved enough for both of us." She pulled her knitted cap down over her ears and headed for the door.

CHAPTER

8

When Nadine and I left the house, Zack and Delia were waiting by the car we'd rented from the agency in Port Hope. As soon as we joined them, Delia reached inside her purse and took out a ring. "You should have this," she said, handing the ring to Nadine. "It was in Abby's hotel room. The police agreed that there was no need to hold onto it."

Nadine's eyes were wide. "She wasn't wearing it when . . . "

"No," Delia said. "She wasn't."

Nadine removed her mitten and slid the ring onto the third finger of her left hand. The twin of the ring, a white-gold Celtic band, was already there. "Thank you," she said and then she turned towards the woods.

Despite her own pain, Nadine was solicitous of Zack. She dropped back to talk to him. "There's a path that's wide enough for your chair, but I can't guarantee its condition."

"I'll make it," Zack said, and then he coughed. "Allergic to country air," he muttered.

Nadine set off along the path and led us into the woods. The terrain was rough, but she moved confidently, with the muscular grace and power of a woman at home in her own body. "This is virgin land," she said. "The trees you're looking at have been here forever. In the spring the ferns grow so quickly it seems like a trick. On the hottest day, it's cool here because the trees block the sun."

The land sloped towards the river. It hadn't been cold enough for the forest floor to freeze and the ground under my feet was spongy. It was also strewn with fallen branches and exposed roots. Zack hated me to push his chair but there were places where we had no alternative. Finally, we arrived at the water. Downriver, partially hidden by trees, was a cabin. Nadine gestured towards it. "That's where we spent most of our time. It's simple, but we were happy there."

She moved towards the river, gathered some fallen cedar branches, and dropped to her knees. She turned to face us. "Would you like to join me? We don't have to say anything – just watch the water and think of her for a few minutes."

Delia and I joined Nadine, and Zack pushed his chair closer. Nadine rocked back on her heels. "So many people read poems at the memorial service. My mind was a blur, but I remember hearing a poem by Raymond Carver about feeling beloved on this earth." Nadine's eyes sought Delia's. "There wasn't a moment of Abby's life when she didn't feel beloved on this earth. It helps me to know that." She prayed silently for a minute, then made the sign of the cross and looked at Delia. "Would you like to say something?"

Delia's face was a mask. "What can I say? I never knew her."

Nadine stood and wiped her hands on her jeans. "In that case, would you like to join me at the cabin for a drink?"

Delia didn't answer. Zack eyed his partner anxiously, then turned to me. "You and Nadine go ahead. We'll be along."

I caught his eye. "That wind is raw."

"I'll be all right," he said.

The cabin was square and solidly built with large windows, and a glassed-in porch overlooking the river. The front door was unlocked and when Nadine opened it we were met with a wave of warmth from a Franklin stove in the corner. Nadine took my coat. "Do you like Scotch?" she asked.

I nodded. As a host, she was charmingly awkward – shakily splashing the Scotch into the glasses, discovering one glass had too much and the other too little and attempting to even out the levels by pouring from one glass to the other. Finally, she handed me the glass with the most and smiled ruefully. "Abby always took care of the drinks," she said. She motioned me to a chair by the stove, pulled her own chair close, and raised her glass. "To absent friends," she said.

"To absent friends," I repeated. I gazed around the room. The walls were bright with quilts, and abstracts. Two desks were placed side by side in front of a large window with a dramatic view of the river. A closed laptop and a bud vase with a single white rose were on one desk; on the other was a stack of essays.

"The marking never ends, does it?" I said.

Nadine glanced at me with interest. "You're a teacher?"

"I teach political science at the university."

Nadine's face brightened. "Political science was Abby's field. She just finished her Ph.D. dissertation last year."

"I happened upon Abby's name in a student's bibliography, so I Googled her dissertation," I said. "The abstract was excellent."

"Everything Abby did was 'excellent'," Nadine said. "She was exceptional in every way. She was also very easy to love."

"I gathered that from your reference to the poem by Raymond Carver," I said. "When I get home I'll look it up. That line about feeling beloved on this earth is beautiful."

"It is," Nadine agreed. "And perhaps that was all any of us needed to hear at the service for Abby. I didn't speak. There was so much I wanted to say, but my mind was blank." She smiled thinly. "Abby would have done better.

She would have delayed the ceremony until she found the perfect words."

"That sounds like Delia."

"They're very much alike, aren't they? Not just in their appearance, but in their guardedness. Do you think that's why they don't let anyone in?" Nadine said. "Because they can't risk revealing an imperfection?"

"Abby didn't let you in?"

Nadine met my gaze. "I wanted more. I was content with what I had."

"It's the same with Delia's husband," I said.

Nadine swirled the amber liquid in her glass. She and I had both ended up with stiff drinks; hers remained untouched. "In a perfect world, Delia's husband and I could commiserate. But this world is far from perfect." Nadine picked up her glass, knocked back her drink, and shuddered. "I'm not a Scotch drinker. We kept the Glenfiddich for Hugh, but if ever there was a time to begin drinking Scotch, this is it." Her eyes were watering, and I handed her a tissue. She gave me a small smile. "I wish you and I were on the same side."

"So do I," I said. I sipped my drink. "Nadine, you know this will get ugly. Your life will be exposed."

She shrugged. "The fact that I'm a lesbian? That's hardly a secret."

"Not that. I was thinking of what a lawyer will do with the fact that you left Abby when she became pregnant. That period in your life will have to be explained if this ends up in court."

"So you know about that," Nadine said. I nodded. She closed her eyes as if to erase the memory. "I made a mistake. Out of my own stupidity and insecurity and fear, I made a mistake. I thought if there was a child, she would love me less." Nadine stood abruptly, her hands balled into fists at her side. "But it didn't happen. The period after we were reconciled was the best time in our lives. The last months of the pregnancy, the birth, watching Jacob grow – it was so good – so very, very good."

"What went wrong?"

Nadine walked to the window overlooking the river and stared at the rushing water. The view appeared to bring her a measure of peace or at least of weary acceptance. "You know the facts," she said. "The accident. The deaths of Hugh and Peggy. The discovery that she was adopted. But we withstood those blows. We were grieving, but we were also looking forward, making plans; then everything fell apart because . . . " I could almost hear the click of self-censure. "Who knows why such things happen?" she said, then she picked up my empty glass. "May I refresh your drink?"

"Thanks," I said. "I should go."

Nadine picked up the two glasses she'd set out for Zack and Delia. "You don't think they're going to come?"

"Apparently not," I said. I made no attempt to disguise my irritation.

"I'll walk you back," Nadine said, but she didn't move towards the door. Instead she extended her forefinger to stroke the petals of the rose on Abby's desk. Her hand lingered.

Her reluctance to leave the room where she had been happy with the woman she loved touched me. I took a step towards her. "Nadine, I know my husband and Delia haven't been fair to you, but they're good people. Could you give them another chance?"

"To reject me?" She shrugged. "Well, it wouldn't be my first rejection."

She handed me my jacket, and took her own off the hook. As we walked towards the main house, she was silent. Zack and Delia were waiting in the car: Zack in the passenger seat in front, Delia in back. When Zack spotted us, he rolled down the window, but Delia stared straight ahead.

As we approached, the only sound was the crunch of our boots on the gravel. "Joanne has suggested a policy of détente," Nadine said. "Shall we try again? We all want what's best for Jacob."

Delia turned away.

"Perhaps the time isn't right," Zack said quickly.

Nadine's hazel eyes took their measure of her two adversaries. "What are you afraid of?" she said, and she seemed to be speaking as much to herself as to them.

She put her arms around me. The gesture was more than social. "Thank you for staying behind," she said softly.

The drive back to town was tense. When Zack touched my arm, I made no effort to control my anger. "What is the matter with you?" I said. "That woman just went through the most painful experience of her life. She invited us into her home because she thought she and Delia might be able to help one another through their grief. And don't even think about using your wheelchair as an excuse. We could have managed."

"I was the one who refused to go," Delia said. "In cases like these, emotions can muddy the waters. Zack and I understand that."

"Thank you for the lesson," I said. "Delia, exactly how many cases 'like this' have you handled? Cases where a woman, whom her mother gave up twenty-seven years earlier, leaves her lover, gives her baby to someone who for all intents and purposes is a stranger, and then is raped and murdered?"

Zack's voice was low but insistent. "Why don't we just park this discussion for a while? Things are being said that are best –"

Delia leaned forward. "Maybe some things need to be said. I was under the impression that I came to Port Hope to learn about my daughter, but Nadine Perrault has an agenda."

"Delia, you have an agenda too," I said.

"To get custody of Jacob," she said. "Which is exactly what his mother wanted. Sitting around grieving with Nadine Perrault wouldn't have advanced our case. In fact, it might well have undercut it."

I glared at my husband. "Is that the way you feel?"

He exhaled. "Jesus, Jo. Let it go."

I pulled into a parking spot in the lot behind the Lantern Inn, jumped out of the car, and slammed the door. "My pleasure," I said, then I ran from him.

Zack and I didn't quarrel often. Once, after an angry day in which every word was a weapon, and every silence a bludgeon, Zack said something that became a touchstone for us. The morning had started well. On my run, I'd spotted a pair of American avocets, and Zack and I agreed to return to the spot after dinner to see if the birds were still there. Life and tempers intervened, and by dusk, we were raw. Like all lovers, we knew where to stick the knife. Zack hated silence and throughout dinner I'd responded to his overtures with monosyllables. Finally – exasperated – he pounded the table. "If an actuary were here," he said, "she could produce a table that would give us an idea of how much time we have left together before we die. It's not long enough, Jo. Let's go see the fucking avocets."

When Zack followed me into our room at the Lantern Inn, he shrugged off his jacket, then headed straight for the bed, lifted himself out of his chair, and lay down. For a man who slept five hours a night whether he needed it or not, it was an uncharacteristic move, and it scared me. I went to him. "Time to remember the avocets?" I said.

He turned his head to face me. "Boy, is it ever. This has been a lousy day, and having you pissed off at me has been the cherry on the cheesecake." He started coughing.

"Can I get you anything?" I asked.

He shook his head.

I kicked off my shoes. "Well, at least I can keep you company," I said.

"I don't want to give you whatever it is I'm getting," he said.

"Our relationship is hardly platonic," I said. "If I'm going to get what you have, I've already got it."

I lay down beside him, and took his hand. It was warm. "You have a fever."

"It's just the nearness of you."

"Maybe so," I said. "But I'm still going to buy some Aspirin and juice before the stores close." I swung out of bed.

Zack groaned. "You can't leave now. You just got here."

"I'll be right back," I said. "Put on your pyjamas and get into bed where it's warm. We'll light a fire and have dinner in our room. See if we can head off that bug."

Watson's Guardian Drugs was crowded. It was the season for colds and flu, so everything I needed had been gathered into one convenient location. Humidifiers were on sale. Buying one for a single night was an extravagance, but Zack's paraplegia meant he was vulnerable to attack from secondary infections, so I didn't hesitate. As I made my way to the checkout counter, I spotted a rack of newspapers. The lead story of the *Northumberland News* was Abby Michaels's memorial service, so I added a copy to my shopping cart and headed for the checkout line.

I took my place behind two ladies with silver sausage curls, sparkly Christmas corsages, lips red as holly berries, and gossip to share.

"There's something so sad about the funeral of a young person, isn't there, Eileen?" the one closer to me said.

"It was a memorial service, Doris," her companion replied. "The body's still out west. So this was just a gathering of friends."

"Well, body or no body, it was very sad. I remember those girls walking down Walton Street together in their school uniforms. They were inseparable, Eileen. Whatever could have happened?"

"Doris, women like that are very emotional."

"You mean . . . sapphites?"

"No, Doris, I mean the French. That Nadine Perrault is French, you know. Still, they make good neighbours."

"The French?"

"No, Doris, sapphites. The two who moved in next to me have transformed that old rose garden." She paused. "I wonder how they do it."

"Hard pruning and organic food," answered Doris.

Eileen leaned in to her friend and whispered, "I was talking about how sapphites *have sex*."

Doris's chuckle was lusty. "I know you were."

When I got back to our room, the gas fireplace was on, and Zack was in his robe warming himself in front of it. I filled the humidifier, handed my husband the Aspirin, a glass of water, a bottle of orange juice, and a box of tissues, and told him what I'd learned about sapphite love, hard pruning, and organic food.

"You broaden my horizons," he said. He rubbed my arm. "I really am sorry about today."

"So am I," I said. "You were in a rotten position."

"You don't know the half of it. When I saw Nadine Perrault down by the river, all I could think about was how I would feel if I were in her place. Loving you is making me a lousy lawyer, Jo, and I can't afford to blow this one." He pinched the bridge of his nose wearily. "After you left, I called Dee to let her know you and I were in for the night. She understood, of course, but she sounded whipped."

"Nadine is the one who's whipped," I said. "Delia's holding all the cards."

Zack's eyes turned back to the flickering flames of the fireplace. "I'm not so sure about that. The Michaelses' family lawyer, Graham Exton, appears to know something I don't know, and that makes me uneasy."

"Was he hostile?"

"No. He's a nice enough guy. He said he wished we'd met under happier circumstances – that he'd known Abby all her life, and that she was a fine human being. He offered coffee and extended all the professional courtesies, but he wasn't exactly forthcoming."

"Did he show you the will?"

"Sure. No reason not to. There were no surprises. Jacob gets $250,000 when he turns twenty-five. The rest of Abby's effects, assets, and considerable property holdings go to Nadine Perrault. Delia Margolis Wainberg is designated as the person to raise Jacob in the event of Abby's death."

"Nothing personal for Jacob?" I asked. "No photographs or family heirlooms? I would have thought Abby would want him to have that painting of her with her parents that we saw at the house."

Zack shook his head. "All that goes to Nadine."

"I don't get it," I said. "Today Nadine told me that until three weeks ago she and Abby and Jacob were a family. They'd been through a nightmare, but they were doing what families do – they were pressing on. Why would Abby make a will that handed Jacob over to a woman who was a stranger and severed his connections with the only family she'd ever known?"

Zack sneezed percussively. He gazed at his box of tissues. "Man-size," he said. "I'm flattered. And to answer your question with a question: Why would Abby Michaels do any of the things she did in the last few weeks?"

"If Graham Exton knew Abby all her life, surely he would realize that she was in a fragile mental state. Didn't he have an obligation to keep her from changing her will?"

"You bet he did, and when I raised that point, he was ready for me. He said, 'I satisfied myself that, given the circumstances, Ms. Michaels was justified in asking me to draw up a new will and that she was of sound mind.' When I pointed out that two weeks after he had pronounced Ms. Michaels 'of sound mind' she walked away from her partner and gave away their baby, the situation got ugly."

"What happened?"

"Mr. Exton told me to advise my client that if she dug too deeply into the question of Abby Michaels's state of mind when she had him draft the second will, she'd regret it. Then he said, 'Delia Wainberg has reaped what she sowed.'"

"That's a little melodramatic, isn't it?"

Zack raised an eyebrow. "For a guy who wears both a belt and suspenders, it's way out there. And something else – Graham Exton can't say Delia's name without spitting it out. It's as if he hates her. And she's never met him. I asked. She'd never heard of him until she came to Port Hope."

"As long as he keeps what he knows to himself, I guess his feelings about Delia are irrelevant," I said.

Zack looked thoughtful. "I wonder. I hate secrets. They have a way of blowing up at a critical moment, and this adoption has to go through. My newfound empathy aside, I would hate to lose to that putz Nadine Perrault hired to represent her."

"You don't like Llewellyn Llewellyn-Smith?"

"We got off to a bad start," Zack said. "By the time I arrived at his office, after my meeting with Exton, I had to go to the can. There was only one men's room in the building. There were three regular stalls and one that was accessible. The three regular stalls were empty but the accessible stall was in use. So I waited – and waited. Whoever was in there was either reading the comics or whacking off. By this point, my need was great. So I rapped on the door, and said, 'There's a cripple out here who needs to be in there.'"

I laughed. "You didn't."

"I did, and the son of a bitch still didn't come out. So I banged the door, and yelled, 'Listen, fuck-wad, when you come out of there, you'd better be in a wheelchair or I'm going to sue your ass.' Finally, the toilet flushed, and guess who swaggered out?"

"Llewellyn Llewellyn-Smith?"

"The putz himself, zipping up, proud as hell for having kept the big-time lawyer waiting. So that's how we started."

"I take it the situation didn't improve."

"Nope. Llewellyn Llewellyn-Smith is a banty rooster – one of those strutting guys with a whiny high-pitched voice, and he yells all the time. He's determined to make this the case of his career. I tried to explain that I don't have a coterie of press people following me at all times – that the only time I'm on TV is when the case involves big names or big issues." Zack wheeled over to the waste-basket, picked it up, placed it on his knee, and wheeled back. "Hard to sink a tissue from across the room," he explained. "Anyway, in an ideal world, this shouldn't end up in a courtroom. Llewellyn-Smith and I should be able to sit down with our clients and come up with an arrangement that semi-satisfies everybody."

"But that's not what he wants."

"No," Zack said. "He wants a three-ring circus, and he wants to be the ringmaster. He told me that he has detectives out there looking for Jacob's father and that when Jacob's father finds out 'the truth,' he'll support Nadine's case."

"If he hasn't found the father, how can he predict what the father will do?"

"He can't," Zack said. "Good lawyers know enough not to show their hand until the time is right, but Putz isn't a good lawyer. He's a chest-pounder. He also wears a bow tie, and you know your theory about that."

"Wearing bow ties tells the world that you can no longer get an erection," I said. "It's actually David Sedaris's line. I just used it to get you to throw out your bow ties. So did you share the theory with Putz?"

"Hell, no," Zack said. "I know how to keep my cards close to my chest." He sneezed. "Shit, I *am* getting a cold. Airplanes!"

"I told you they're dangerous. Come on, let's order some dinner. I brought Gawain along. I'll read to you till our meal comes."

It didn't take long. By the time Gawain had met and made his fateful pact with the lord of the great manor, our meal had arrived. We'd both ordered the brome duck. It was excellent, but Zack picked at his food.

"Do you want me to order something else for you?" I asked.

Zack shook his head. "I'm not hungry. I'm just going to try to sleep."

I called room service to pick up our trays, made Zack as comfortable as possible, and settled by the fireplace with the *Northumberland News*. The account of the memorial service was detailed. More than seven hundred people had been in attendance. Anticipating an overflow crowd, two rooms had been set up with closed-circuit televisions. The event was still standing room only.

The article noted that while there had been readings and musical selections, the highlights of the gathering had been anecdotes about Abby Michaels. There were three pictures with the story: one was a studio portrait of Abby wearing her academic gown and Ph.D. hood; the second was of the crowd in the chapel; the third was of an unidentified young girl, her face tear-stained and knifed by grief. As I folded the paper, there was a lump in my throat, and I knew our decision not to attend the service had been a wise one.

The room contained a bookcase filled with paperbacks: a shelf of mysteries; what appeared to be the entire oeuvre of Zane Grey, and a small selection of worthy books about the history of Port Hope and Hope Township. I chose one of the history books and, seduced by the epigraph from Santayana, "History is a pack of lies about events that never happened told by people who weren't there," began reading.

The memories of the town's first newspaper editors were compelling, but the combination of the wine I had had with dinner and the warmth from the fireplace made my eyelids heavy. Zack was snoring peacefully, and I decided that oblivion was not without appeal.

I readied myself for bed, slid in beside my husband, and closed my eyes. After an hour, the painful images of the day were still sharp. When my restlessness threatened to waken Zack, I slipped out of bed, put on my jacket, and went out onto the balcony. The air was chilly, but the night was clear. Beneath me, the Ganaraska flowed inexorably towards Lake Ontario; above me the sky was filled with stars. Finally, my pulse slowed, and my mind grew calm. I went inside, and this time when I lay down under the canopy, I slept.

The next morning, we awakened to the sound of rain. Beside me, Zack stirred. "Bet it's not raining at home," he said.

"The forecast for Regina today is thirty-eight below," I said. "I checked last night. How are you feeling?"

"The same." Zack raised his arm to see his watch. "Too early to call home and see how everybody's doing?"

"Better hold off on calling Taylor, but Pete's a safe bet. He gets up earlier than I do."

Zack picked up his BlackBerry and called our house. After he'd chatted with Pete and spoken to Pantera, he handed the phone to me. As always, Pete was laconic. "Nothing much going on here," he said. "Noah brought the baby by last night to play with the dogs."

"How did that go?" I said.

"Willie herded Jacob for a while, but when he satisfied himself that Jacob was safe, we put Jacob down on the floor and Pantera pushed him along with his nose. Every time Jacob rolled over, he'd laugh, and every time Jacob laughed, Pantera pushed him again."

"You do realize that when Zack hears about this, he'll be arranging play dates."

"Jacob could do worse," Pete said. "Pantera plays well with others."

"Agreed," I said. "Thanks for taking care of everything, Pete."

"My pleasure. Have a good flight."

"Impossible," I said, "but I appreciate the thought." After I rang off, I called Alwyn, and we arranged to go to the ten-thirty service at St. Mark's Anglican Church. Zack was in the shower, and I was ironing slacks for church when Noah called.

"Nothing special," he said. "I just thought I'd let you know that everybody here is fine."

"That's always a relief to hear," I said. "May I talk to Taylor?"

"She and Izzy are still sleeping. Big night – the girls and I took Jacob over to your place; then we ordered in pizza. I had beer and a slice, Jacob had formula and pureed peas, then we gents went to bed and left the ladies to their stack of holiday DVDs."

"I hear your boy fell under Pantera's spell," I said.

Noah chuckled. "You've been talking to Peter. I wish Delia could have been here – not just to see Jacob, but to see Izzy having so much fun. She's always looking for the next mountain to climb. It was great to see her rolling around on the floor with her brother." Noah caught himself. "I guess 'nephew' is more accurate, but the term doesn't matter. Izzy loves that little boy. So do I."

"Jacob's pretty easy to love," I said. "Thanks for the update, Noah. I'll give Taylor a call when I'm back from church."

When Zack came out of the shower, I told him about Pantera and Jacob. His laughter turned into a coughing jag, so I pulled out the jar of Vicks and told him to open his robe so I could rub his chest.

"Does that stuff work?" he said.

"I have no idea," I said. "But it smells like it means business."

He extended his arms. "Have at me," he said, and then he started hacking again.

"That's quite the bark you've got," I said. "I wouldn't want to sit next to us in the dining room. Let's call room service again."

"Fine with me, but I'd appreciate it if you'd have breakfast with Dee. Do you think you could sit across the table from her without squashing a grapefruit in her face?"

"This is Loyalist country," I said. "People don't make scenes. I'll call her."

"If it's any consolation, Dee knows she behaved badly. She said she was going to send Nadine some flowers and a note this morning."

I slammed the jar of Vicks on the bedside table. "Flowers and a note," I said tightly. "Falconer Shreve's signature kiss-off when one of the partners wants to end an inconvenient relationship."

Zack picked up his pyjama top. "Can we give it a rest? I feel like shit. Delia feels like shit. If she can't control every detail, she goes up her ass, and from the minute we got here, she hasn't been able to control anything."

"What did she hope to accomplish?"

Zack shook his head. "Beats me. I don't think Dee knew herself. She never makes a move without considering every possible ramification, but she threw herself into this. If she'd been herself, Dee would have realized that Nadine Perrault was not a disinterested party and she would have finessed the situation. Dee works in a tricky field. Insurance litigation is high stakes. She gets paid the big bucks because she never makes a false move."

"But she's blowing this," I said.

"And she knows it," Zack said. "Yesterday in the car, Delia told me she was afraid. I've known her thirty years, and this is the first time I've heard her say she was afraid of anything."

I sat on the bed, so that Zack and I were at eye level. "Is she afraid of losing Jacob?"

"That, and everything else. Delia feels as if her life is unravelling. She thought when she signed the papers giving up her child, she'd closed the chapter."

"And now the child appears as a grown woman, hands Delia a baby, and is raped and murdered." I touched one of the lines that bracketed Zack's mouth like parentheses. "I guess that sequence of events is enough to overwhelm anyone."

Short of the Fezziwigs' Christmas party, there was no more festive scene than the Lantern Inn's dining room on that wet December morning. Instead of a fiddler striking up Sir Roger de Coverley, there was the silvery staccato of Vivaldi's "Winter," and the buffet didn't appear to feature cold boiled beef and mince pie, but the atmosphere of the room was one of Dickensian hopefulness and good cheer.

Delia had found a table for two near the fireplace. She stood to motion me over when I came in. In her black leather-trimmed sweater, white turtleneck, fitted jeans, and black Fluevog lace-up boots, she looked successful, fashionable, and utterly miserable.

"If this table is too close to the fireplace for you, I can ask them to move us," she said. Her face was pale and strained and her husky voice cracked into the odd little hiccup it made whenever she was on edge.

"It's good to be warm," I said.

"Thanks for coming. I know you're angry."

"I promised Zack I wouldn't smash a grapefruit in your face."

She flashed her three-point cat smile. "That's a start."

The server poured us coffee and asked if we needed menus. When we said we were going with the buffet, she nodded gravely and told us we'd made a very wise choice.

"First wise choice I've made since I got here," Delia said.

During breakfast Delia and I made a deliberate attempt to keep the conversation light. She and Noah had talked, so the story of Jacob and Pantera gave us one safe topic. The skating rink Zack and I were putting in at the lake gave us another. Delia was intrigued, and she had enough questions about exactly how a skating rink came into being to get us smoothly through to our second cup of coffee.

As the server cleared our plates, Delia held out her coffee cup in a mock toast. "Well, we made it. No grapefruit smashing. Not even a raised voice. So I'm going to push my luck and ask you whether Nadine won you over when you went back to her cabin."

"I like her very much," I said carefully.

"So you're on her side."

"No," I said. "I'm on your side, but I'm hoping you can extend an olive branch to Nadine."

"She doesn't want an olive branch," Delia said. "She wants the whole tree – full custody, and she's not going to get it. I'm prepared to offer Nadine access. She can visit Jacob in Regina when she has time off from teaching. She can even come out to the lake with us for a couple of weeks every summer. But Jacob will never be left alone with her."

"You think Nadine poses a threat to Jacob?" I said. "Where did that come from?"

"Abby's will," Delia said flatly. "Joanne, most wills have a subtext. A father bequeaths equal parts of his estate to each of his three sons, but he leaves the watch that has been passed down through the family to his youngest son. There's a message there."

"The youngest son is the father's favourite," I said.

Delia nodded. "In her revised will, Abby left Nadine Perrault money and property but she made certain that Jacob came to me. Clearly there's something in Nadine's background that makes it impossible for Jacob to be left in her care."

"Abby and Nadine were inseparable from the time they were ten," I said. "It's difficult to believe there was anything of significance that they didn't know about one another."

"There's no disputing the facts," Delia said. "Three weeks ago. Abby changed her will. Something convinced her that Nadine would not be a fit parent, and that Jacob belonged with us. We may not be able to see the logic, but it's there. Once we've figured out what caused Abby to leave the bulk of her estate to Nadine but grant custody of her son to us, we have our case."

"And winning the case is all that matters?" I said.

Delia's mouth twisted in an ironic half-smile. "We seem to be moving into dangerous territory. I'd better get the bill." She caught the server's eye and picked up her bag. "Is Zack up for our meeting with Nadine's lawyer this morning? He sounded terrible when I talked to him, but he minimized it."

"It's his decision," I said. "But I think he should stay in bed. The cold is worse. He has a fever and he's coughing."

Delia's face pinched with worry. "Has he seen a doctor?"

"I think he's better off just staying in bed until we go to the airport. Sitting in a waiting room filled with sick people doesn't strike me as a great idea. I'll call our family doctor as soon as we get back to Regina."

"But Zack is going to be all right?" Delia said.

"He's had his flu shot, and he's strong as an ox. You know that."

She looked at me hard. "No, I don't know that. I'm sure you've read all the same articles about paraplegia that I've read. I've worried about Zack's health from the moment I met him. He always says that when he became part of the Winners' Circle he felt like a drunk discovering Jesus – reborn. But for me it was like finding a family, and Zack has always been the one I was closest to."

"You're very much alike."

"Both damaged high achievers."

"I've never thought of you as damaged."

"I present well, and the law saved me – just as it saved Zack. Chris Altieri used to say that for Zack and me the law was redemptive." Delia's eyes welled. She wiped the tears away with the back of her hand. "Sorry. Tell Zack I can talk to Nadine's lawyer alone. And tell him please to take care of himself. I can't handle another loss."

Delia paid the bill, and we threaded our way through the laughter at the festively decorated tables. Anyone seeing us together, two middle-aged women, affluent and amiable, would have thought we didn't have a care in the world.

When I got back to the room, Zack's breakfast was on its tray uneaten, and he was lying down. I sat beside him on the bed and rubbed his shoulder. "Feeling lousy?" I said.

"Lousy would be an improvement," he said.

"I told Delia you were going to stay in the room until we left for the airport. I'll call Alwyn and let her know we're confined to quarters for the day."

"No reason for you to stay here," Zack said. "I'm just going to sleep. You and Alwyn only have a few hours. You were planning to go to church together, weren't you?"

"Yes, and then back to her house for tea."

"Well, do that," he said.

"Are you sure you'll be all right?"

"Yep. But just in case, say a prayer for me."

"I always pray for you."

"Well, keep up the good work, and leave your cell on vibrate."

It was the third Sunday in Advent and St. Mark's was full. The recessional hymn was "Let There Be Light," but the voices of a host of the faithful were unable to stave off the torrent that greeted us when we left the church. Alwyn squinted at the pewter sky. "What do you want to do?"

"Let me call and see how Zack's doing, and then we can decide."

Alwyn made a studious effort not to listen to my end of the conversation, but when I rang off, she looked at me inquiringly. "Well?"

"Zack says we should have fun."

Alwyn opened her umbrella. "In that case, let's get started."

Zack's mockery of Ye Olde Tyme Christmas aside, Port Hope knew how to be merry. The rain sharpened the scent of the evergreen boughs framing the storefronts, and the windows of the antique and specialty shops were tastefully seasonal. It was fun to be with Alwyn again, goofing and gossiping like the undergraduates we had once been.

Alwyn had just finished telling me about the donnybrook at St. Mark's after the vestry painted the church's two-hundred-year-old golden oak pews robin's egg blue when Nadine Perrault called out to us from across the street.

She was coming down the steps of Our Lady of Mercy Church, and her faith had obviously been kicked into high gear, because when she spotted us she ran across the street without checking for oncoming traffic. A black SUV swerved, missing her by inches. Nadine was oblivious. She was wearing the jacket she'd worn the day before, but she hadn't pulled the hood up, so her hair and face were rain-slicked. She was breathless but radiant.

"I'm so glad to see you," she said. "I've had wonderful news. I have to tell someone, and I know you've both been concerned about me." Her laugh was carefree. "I've been concerned about me, too, but this morning after mass, everything changed. Father Quines told me that Abby didn't leave because I failed her. He said she left because she wanted to spare me."

The day before, when she had knelt on the riverbank, I'd been struck by Nadine's self-control. Now, drenched by rain, she couldn't contain her joy and relief. "It wasn't my fault." Repeating the comforting words, her voice was soft with wonder. "I was so certain I'd failed her again, but it wasn't me at all."

Nadine's jacket was unzipped. The Celtic ring that had belonged to Abby was hanging from her neck on a chain so fine it was almost invisible. As she talked, her slender fingers found the ring. "I wasn't planning to go to mass, but the woman from the florist called saying someone had sent me flowers, and I thought since I was in town I might as well go to Our Lady's." Her smile was transforming. "Father Quines was very careful not to violate Abby's trust, but what he told me was enough."

Nadine gazed at the skies happily. "Look, the rain's easing off. It's going to be a pretty day after all." She was growing calm now. "You must think I'm insane. It's just – these last weeks – even the weeks before she left, Abby was lost to me. I could see her, but when I tried to talk to her, she didn't hear me. It was as if she was underwater. Now, it's almost as if she's with me again, and I can do what we'd planned to do all along."

"What had you planned?" I asked.

"To raise Jacob with love – in the house where Abby grew up, by the river that brought her such happiness." Nadine ran her fingers through her hair. "Thank you for listening. Now, I'd better pick up my flowers."

As she walked down Walton Street, Nadine's step was light. "So much for the Seal of the Confessional," Alwyn said. "Still, I'm glad Father Quines realized that compassion trumps doctrine. Let's go to my place, and dry off."

We had our tea in the sunroom, so we could watch the birds visit the feeder. Alwyn's Earl Grey was hot and strong and her fruitcake was studded with pecans, dates, and candied cherries and pineapple. "Every piece you eat brings a month of happiness in the new year," she said.

"That's only if you eat it in the week between Christmas and New Year," I said, "but this cake doesn't require justification. I wish Zack were here. He's the only man I've ever met who truly likes Christmas cake."

"Is that why you married him?"

"No." I sipped my tea. "I married Zack because I knew if I didn't, I'd regret it for the rest of my life. I wish you two had been able to spend more time together."

"Next time," Alwyn said. "Jo, what do you think is going to happen here?"

"Nothing good," I said. "Zack said he hates family law because somebody decent always gets hurt. When I think about Nadine and the Wainbergs, I feel sick."

"You think this is going to get ugly?"

"I know it is. Both sides are willing to risk everything to win Jacob, and that means the gloves are off. My husband and Delia are close and when it comes to his job, Zack has never been afraid to get blood on his hands."

Alwyn shuddered. "When I think about how Hugh and Peggy protected that girl, it's hard to believe all that love and all those good intentions could end up in such misery."

"Why do you think they never told Abby that she was adopted?"

Alwyn sipped her tea. "My guess is that they simply wanted to believe she was their own flesh and blood. In retrospect, the charade they played out about how much she was like them is poignant. They were always talking about how they could see one another in her, but she bore no resemblance to either of them. Peggy and Hugh were both strawberry blondes, grey-eyed with high colour. Abby had that tangle of wiry black curls; her skin was pale, like Delia's, and she had those same piercing blue eyes."

"Abby's father doesn't appear to have made much of a genetic contribution."

"Who is he?"

"No one knows."

Alwyn shot me a sharp look. "Including Delia Wainberg?"

"Her story is that she was articling in Ottawa – working crazy hours – and she had a series of casual liaisons."

"Is she the kind of woman to have casual sex?"

"No," I said. "She isn't. Delia's one of the most disciplined people I've ever met." A pair of black-capped chickadees landed on the bird feeder. "Even on a wet day, chickadees seem cheerful," I said.

"You'd be cheerful too if you'd hidden seeds all over the backyard. My bird books tell me that chickadees can remember literally thousands of hiding places." Alwyn peered out the window as if to test her observation. "I can't even remember where I left my glasses. May I warm your cup?"

"No, I should get going."

"Take your husband some Christmas cake – remember what our grandmothers used to say, 'Feed a cold; starve a fever.'"

"Zack has both, but he'll appreciate the thought."

Alwyn sliced and wrapped the cake. Then she reached into her knitting bag, pulled out a DVD and a greeting card, and handed both to me. "The DVD of the memorial service is for Delia, but the card is for Jacob," she said. "It was the Michaelses' holiday greeting last year." The red holiday frame was snowflake-spangled, but the photograph it surrounded was of a family enjoying a summer day: Nadine and Abby, wearing ball caps, shorts, and T-shirts, standing between Hugh and Peggy Michaels. Peggy's straw hat shaded her face and she was squinting against the smoke curling from her cigarette; Hugh was in his three-piece suit, his small self-mocking grin fixed as firmly as his four-in-hand tie.

Alwyn handed the card to me. "At some point, Jacob might want to know about his mother," she said.

I thought about Taylor. I dropped the card in my purse. "He will," I said. "And when the time comes, he'll be grateful for this. You're a good soul, Alwyn."

We embraced and promised to stay in touch, and then I started back to the hotel. When I passed Our Lady of Mercy, I remembered how Nadine's eyes had shone and how her face, washed clean of guilt and misery, had seemed suddenly young again.

A question flicked at my consciousness. It had to do with perspective.

Zack and Delia were working on the assumption that Abby's final irrational actions had been driven by a revelation about her life partner. But the comforting words Father

Quines offered to Nadine opened another possibility. Perhaps Abby had changed her will not because she believed that Nadine was unfit but because she had stumbled upon a fact that convinced her that Jacob was Delia's responsibility. That prospect carried a dark coda: whatever Abby discovered had been devastating enough to destroy not only Abby Michaels's faith in God but in herself.

CHAPTER 9

Howling winds and horizontally blowing snow met our plane when it landed in Regina Sunday night. Noah was there to pick up Delia, but he had parked their car at our house and driven ours to a waiting area outside to minimize the distance Zack had to push his chair. I was grateful for that and, as always, for the fact that we lived so close to the airport.

The kids had shovelled the driveway, so the pavement to the garage was clear. Declan Hunter's Acura was parked out front; so was Pete's old beater. When we walked into the kitchen, the phone was ringing, and jazz that was live, loud, and surprisingly solid was soaring in the family room. The dogs heard us and bounded into the kitchen. Pantera leaped on Zack, knocking over his wheelchair. Willie gave me a cursory sniff and slunk away, sulking because I'd abandoned him. In an hour he would forget my betrayal and assume his habitual place by my side. We were home.

Pete helped Zack back into his chair and went out to get our bags, and Zack and I headed to the family room. Taylor was sitting cross-legged on the couch with her sketchbook, Bruce and Benny curled up beside her, and Declan and his trio were wailing. When they spotted us, the music stopped, and Taylor jumped to her feet. "I didn't hear you," she said. "I'm sorry. We could have helped bring in your stuff." She hugged us both and waved towards the musicians. "Declan's band came over to jam. There was nobody here but Pete, and he didn't mind."

Declan put down his guitar and moved close to Taylor. His stance was protective. If she was in trouble with her parents, he was beside her – gold-star behaviour in my books. "I'm sorry if this is a problem," he said.

Zack grinned. "My only problem is that you're not inviting me to sit in."

"Consider yourself in," Declan said. He gestured towards the trumpet player, an intense young man with a shaved head. "This is Nigel Fleming."

"I recognize you from the symphony," Zack said. "Nice to meet you."

Declan pointed to the drummer. "And this is Nattybedhead." Natty greeted us with a lick on the drums and a dazzling smile. "You really want to sit in?" he asked Zack.

"One number," Zack said.

"Blues in F," Declan said, picking up his guitar.

Zack moved over to the Steinway. He had slept during most of the flight to Regina. He'd awakened feeling tired, but I could see the life come back into him as he began to play. After six or seven minutes, I could also see the flush in his cheeks and the sweat beading on his forehead. When the music faded, I stepped in.

"That was terrific," I said. "But the piano player needs to hit the sack. He came home with the flu."

Surprisingly, Zack didn't resist. He called out a casual "later" to the band and wheeled towards the hall that led to our bedroom. The boys took this as a cue to call it a day and had just begun packing up their instruments when Declan's cell rang. He waved as we left, but his face was grave.

Zack was undressing and I was turning down the bed when there was a knock on our bedroom door. Declan and Taylor were there, hands linked.

Our daughter spoke first. "Dad, I know you're feeling rotten, but we need help. Declan's mother's in trouble."

Declan and Taylor exchanged a quick look. It was clear they had decided beforehand on how they would present this problem, and it was Declan's turn to take the lead. His tone was matter-of-fact. "My mother thinks she hit someone with her car." Declan lowered his gaze. "She's been drinking, so who knows what really happened."

Zack started rebuttoning his shirt. "Is she at the police station?"

"She says she's at home."

"Jesus Christ," Zack said. "Not a hit-and-run?"

Declan's laugh was short and derisive. "No, she never does anything that normal. Apparently, my mother brought the man she hit home with her. I guess he's sitting in the living room. My dad's in Houston. I was going to call Noah Wainberg. He spends a lot of time with my mother, but Taylor thinks we need you."

"Taylor's right," Zack said, and he looked hard at me. The weather was wretched, he was sick, and our city was full of lawyers who, in that stunning phrase from Deuteronomy, would "circumcise their hearts" to handle a file for Leland Hunter. Zack knew all this, and none of it mattered. He wanted the case.

"At least let me drive you," I said.

Zack hacked. "Thank you, Ms. Shreve. I could use help tonight. Okay, Declan, why don't you go through your mother's story again? We don't want to be met with any surprises. The Boy Scouts are right about being prepared."

We were committed. Taylor ran down the hall and returned with Declan's jacket and her own. Declan took his jacket, but shook his head when Taylor started to put on hers.

"I should be there," she said.

"No," Declan said. "You shouldn't. My mother would never forgive you if you saw her when she was drunk."

The insight was both mature and poignant. Declan might have appeared to be fortune's favourite, but being the only child of Leland and Louise Hunter brought its own burdens. Declan touched Taylor's arm. "I'll call you," he said. He turned to Zack. "You know where we live. I'll meet you there."

The Hunters' house was a new and massive structure in a neighbourhood of other new and massive structures. The neighbourhood was a favourite of professionals and executives who were on second or third marriages to much younger women. With their elaborate topiary, lacquered doors, great rooms, and sparkling chandeliers, the houses had all the artful surgery, high gloss, and fragile beauty of their young mistresses. Like them, the houses seemed temporary – not places for the long haul.

The scene we walked in on was surreal. A knapsack and a battered sign with the words HOME FOR CHRISTMAS hand-lettered on cardboard had been tossed on the marble floor in the entranceway. In the great room, a man in an army surplus camouflage jacket, waterproof pants, and steel-toed boots slumped on a loveseat upholstered in silver silk. Louise sat facing him on the twin of the loveseat. Between them was a rectangular glass table that held a bucket of ice and a bottle of Grey Goose. Louise and the man both had drinks in hand. They looked like a couple on the world's most mismatched blind date.

When we came in, the man bolted up and shot an accusing look at Louise. "That's Zack Shreve. I've seen him on the news. You didn't say anything about a lawyer. You just said your kid was coming."

Zack took control. "Relax. Declan happened to be at our home visiting, so my wife and I decided to drop by to see Louise. Just obeying an impulse. Declan, why don't you sit with your mother's guest. Mr. . . . ?"

"Usher. Paul Usher." Louise's visitor was surly but he wasn't stupid. Zack hadn't thrown him out. Paul Usher resumed his seat, no longer looking like a man on the defensive. He had sniffed money.

Zack nodded pleasantly. "Mr. Usher. I've seen you and your sign many times on the traffic island at College and Albert. I pass by you on my way to the office. You're hoping to get home for Christmas – a commendable wish – and I think if we all act wisely, your wish may be granted. Now, please excuse us. Declan will refresh your drink while my wife and I chat with our hostess."

Declan knew how to pick up a cue, and long practice had taught him how to pour drinks.

Louise's step was unsteady as she led us down the hall, but she didn't spill a drop of her vodka. The overhead light was blazing in the study; Louise doused the light, turned on a floor lamp that cast a gentler glow, and lowered herself carefully onto a creamy leather chair by the window. I sat in the chair that faced it. Zack wheeled in close to Louise. "This must be a nightmare for you," he said.

Zack wasn't going to condemn her, and Louise's relief was palpable. She put her drink on the end table and clasped her hands on her lap like an obedient child. "There seems to be no end to my stupidity," she said.

Zack moved closer. "We all have nights we wish we could redo. Let's see what we can do to salvage this one. Now, tell me exactly what happened. Take your time, but I need to know everything."

"I spent the afternoon at my studio practising," Louise said. "Leland has promised to drop by Christmas morning, and I planned to surprise him by playing the Prelude in C from *The Well-Tempered Clavier*. Our first Christmas together I played him the entire work, and he was charmed. Of course, that was in another lifetime. I'll never be that good again, but the Prelude in C is so easy that it's a study piece for students. I thought there was a chance I could carry it off."

She raised her drink to her lips, hesitated, and then replaced the glass on the small inlaid table beside her. "I've been practising every day. It's been going well, but today I was having problems with my hands. They were shaking. I thought one drink would steady me." Louise looked longingly at the tumbler on the little table, but she didn't touch it. "The rule is no drinking in the studio."

"Is that your own rule?" Zack asked, and his voice, roughened by his cold, was oddly intimate.

Louise shook her head. "It was Noah's idea, as was the studio, but I agreed. He thought – we thought – I needed a place where I had to stay sober to do what mattered to me."

When Louise didn't continue, Zack touched her arm. "But today that didn't work," he said.

Louise's face contorted with self-loathing. "The first drink helped, but of course for me there's no such thing as one drink."

"It's a lonely battle, isn't it?" Zack said.

Louise had been skittish, waiting for the whip of opprobrium. When it didn't come, she relaxed. I remembered Noah commenting once on Zack's tenderness with his clients. "He's like the Horse Whisperer with them. It's fascinating to watch. No matter what they've done, he somehow convinces them he understands, that he's able to see the world through their eyes. They stop being afraid and they start trusting him. That's the first step to a successful defence."

By anyone's criteria, Louise Hunter's behaviour during the past ninety minutes had been lunacy, but her account was straightforward and unapologetic. She trusted Zack to get her through. "I was very drunk when I left the studio. Actually, I'm still drunk." She flexed her hands and stared at them. "Sadly, events are starting to come back to me. The old couple who live in the other apartment on my floor were getting off the elevator when I was getting on. They were carrying groceries and I bumped his arm, knocked the bag out of his hand. All these grapefruit rolled out. What would old people need with all those grapefruit? I started to get down on my knees to help, but the old man stopped me. He has Alzheimer's but he has moments of clarity. He said, 'You've been drinking. If you get down, you won't be able to get back up.' He was right, so I got in the elevator and went out back to the parking lot. I was driving very slowly and very carefully. I didn't want to do anything . . . " Louise narrowed her eyes, searching for the word. "Irretrievable," she said finally. "I didn't want to do anything *irretrievable.* I guess I was driving too slowly because I thought I saw a police car starting to follow me."

"But you do have your licence back, don't you?" Zack said. "You only lost it for six months and that was in the spring."

"The May long weekend," Louise said. "The Great Victoria Day DUI round-up. And I didn't – I don't – want to lose my licence again, so when I saw this man standing on the traffic island, I opened up my car door, jumped out, handed him the keys to the Mercedes, gave him my address, and told him to drive me home." She tried a laugh. "You have to admire that kind of thinking. The folly of what I had done hit me when he followed me into the house."

"Had you invited him in?" Zack asked. There was no censure in Zack's voice.

"Of course," she said. "I'd promised to pay him, but when I saw him standing in my living room I panicked. That's when I went into the bathroom and called Declan."

"And told him you'd been in an accident," Zack said.

Louise appeared beaten. "It was the simplest explanation. I don't remember hitting Mr. Usher, but he says I did, and I've been wrong before."

"Whatever happened, calling for assistance was the right thing to do." Zack's voice was raspy. "Why don't you go upstairs and relax. We'll take it from here."

Louise pushed herself to her feet. Her step was unsteady. She held out her arms. "What's the matter with me?"

Zack shot me a supplicating glance. "Could you help Louise, Joanne? I'm going to need Declan."

"Of course," I said. I linked my arm through Louise's and we headed for the front hall.

By the time we reached the bottom of their curved staircase, she was hanging on me. Louise Hunter was a small woman, but she was a dead weight, and the stairs were steep and slick. When we made it to the second floor, I stopped to catch my breath. Zack's coughing jag echoed up the stairwell and I felt a stab of anger. I didn't offer help as Louise wove her way down the shining parquet of her hallway. At the end of the hall, she turned and looked back at me. "I have to pee, and I don't want to fall in the bathroom. You'll have to help me."

I did. I also helped her remove her makeup, brush her teeth and hair, and don a silky nightgown the same shade of champagne as the silk sheets that matched the walls of her huge and lonely bedroom. She refused to let me remove the platinum cuff bracelet I'd noticed when I'd met her at the Wainbergs, saying that it was a gift from her ex-husband and she never took it off. I thought about my own husband downstairs getting sicker by the moment as he attempted to extricate Louise from a morass of her own making and felt my gorge rise again.

When finally she was safely in bed for the night, I started out of the room.

"Your husband is much kinder than you," she said.

"Agreed," I said, without turning.

"At least have the decency to look at me when we're talking," she said.

I walked back to the acre of bed in which Louise lay, her thin, pale arms resting on the duvet, the platinum cuff bracelet gleaming dully in the light from the lamp on her bedside table.

"Why do you hate me?" she asked.

"I don't hate you, Louise. I've just seen your act before – many, many times. My mother was an alcoholic. Now if there's nothing else . . . ?"

She waved me off. I turned and saw that Declan was standing in the doorway. When I walked past him, I squeezed his arm. "You heard that?" I asked.

He nodded. "Do you ever get over it?"

"No, but you do finally realize it's not your fault." I met his eyes. "Declan, call if you need me. I mean that."

"Thanks," he said. He shrugged. "Well, guess I'd better check on my mum."

Zack was in the hall zipping his jacket when I went downstairs. "Declan found you?"

"He did. Louise's needs have been met. Let's get out of here."

Zack took his gloves from his pocket. "I appreciate this, Jo."

I zipped my coat. "So how did it go with Paul Usher?"

"A happy ending for Mr. Usher. Declan took him to the bus station, bought him a ticket to Kamloops, and gave him $1,000 spending money."

"Kamloops seems like a pleasant place to recuperate from injuries," I said.

"Funny thing about those injuries," Zack said. "Declan tells me they disappeared the second Mr. Usher pocketed Louise's cash."

"You think he'll be back for a second instalment?"

Zack shrugged. "Probably, but not tonight, and that's all I care about. I'm bushed." He opened the door and rolled out into the darkness.

While Zack was showering, I turned on our electric blanket. I would turn it off again before we settled for the night, because Zack's paraplegia made him susceptible to unfelt injuries. Then I called Henry Chan. He had been Zack's doctor when we met, and when my MD retired, Henry took on Taylor and me. I liked him. His wife, Gina Brown, was a nurse-practitioner, and together they had created an office that was both welcoming and efficient. The magazines in the reception room were current, the walls were bright with photos and drawings from kids, and the wait times were acceptable. Henry and Gina were a good team: easy-going and knowledgeable. They also lived two blocks from us, and we'd been involved in enough neighbourhood activities together for me to call their home that night without feeling guilty. When I heard Henry's voice, I felt my pulse slow.

"I know you don't make house calls," I said, "but I was hoping you could drop by on your way to the office tomorrow. Zack has the flu. He has a temperature, his breathing is laboured, and he has a wicked cough. I'm doing the usual or trying to, but I'd like you to look at him."

"I'll stop by tomorrow morning but, Joanne, if he gets worse in the night, take him to Emergency. The paraplegia complicates things. Zack doesn't have the resistance an able-bodied person would have."

"I like to think of him as indestructible," I said.

Henry heard the fear in my voice, and he was reassuring. "Basically, Zack is very healthy, I just want you to take precautions because he's one of the few guys I can consistently beat in poker."

"That's not the way he tells it," I said.

Henry chuckled. "We're all the heroes of our own epics. But let's keep an eye on this. See you in the morning."

Zack's skin was pink from the shower when he came back into the bedroom. "You look better," I said.

"I just need some sleep," he said. "Who was that on the phone?"

"Henry Chan."

Zack wheeled towards the bed. "So what did Henry want?"

"To see you."

Zack cocked his head. "Professionally?"

"Yes," I said, "but his profession, not yours. He's coming over tomorrow morning to check you out."

Zack transferred his body from his chair to the bed. "Is that strictly necessary?"

"I guess we'll know tomorrow," I said. "Can I get you anything?"

He glanced at his nightstand. I'd assembled the usual arsenal people gather to fight the flu: Aspirin, a decongestant and antihistamine, a cough suppressant, a Thermos of water, a box of tissues – and something else – a tube of Polysporin. "Looks like you've anticipated my every need," he said.

"I aim to please," I said. I picked up the Polysporin. "You have a couple of pressure sores on your back. Let me rub a little of this on them. We don't want to take any chances."

When I was finished, I helped Zack get comfortable. "Wake me up in the night if you need anything."

"You coming to bed now?"

"I'd better let the dogs out one more time, but once that's done, I'm on my way. It's been a long day."

When I finally slid between the sheets, I moved close to kiss Zack good night. He turned his face away so that all I managed was a cheek peck. "You don't want to get this," he said.

"You're right, I don't," I said, "but as soon as you start feeling better, I want one of those kisses that Kevin Costner talked about in *Bull Durham* – a long, slow, deep, soft, wet one that lasts three days."

I'd just come back from my morning run with the dogs when Henry Chan arrived. He turned down my offer of coffee and went straight in to see Zack. He stayed with Zack long enough to make me fretful, and when he came out he seemed preoccupied. He went to the kitchen sink, washed his hands, then took a prescription pad from his briefcase, leaned against the counter, and began writing. "This one should help with the congestion," he said. He tore off the first prescription and handed it to me. "You must have noticed the pressure sores," he added.

"Last night I put Polysporin on them," I said.

Henry nodded. "We may need something a little more heavy-duty." He leaned over his pad and began writing again. "Every four hours for this one," he said. Then he wrote out a third prescription. "Zack's throat is inflamed and there's swelling in the lymph nodes, but this should do the trick. I'll check in on my way to the hospital tomorrow morning." He picked up the winter jacket he'd flung on the kitchen chair when he came in and began readying himself to leave. "Keep an eye on him. If you don't think this is moving in the right direction, call Gina. Apart from that, just keep on doing what you're doing." He zipped his jacket, pulled on his toque and gloves, and headed for the door.

"Henry . . . " My throat tightened. I couldn't say anything more. For the first time that morning he really looked at me, and he saw how frightened I was.

He stopped. "Gina always gives me hell for not paying enough attention to the spouses. I apologize, Joanne, I have a long day ahead, and my mind was on what I was going to do next. I know you love Zack, and barring something unforeseen, he'll get through this with flying colours. It's just that there are no small illnesses for paraplegics, and from what Zack said, he let this one get away from him. The trip to Ontario, and then going out again last night."

"I should have stopped him."

Henry's smile was gentle. "You think you could have?"

"No."

"If it's any consolation, being married to you has added years to Zack's life."

"How many years?" I said.

Henry met my gaze. "Nobody can answer that, but Zack is no longer living like an eighteen-year-old kid with a death wish. He's cut down on the booze and gambling, he's monogamous, and he tells me he no longer drives like a maniac."

"I wish he'd cut back on his workload," I said.

"So do I," Henry said. "And Gina wishes I'd cut back on mine. But leopards can't change their spots. We are as we are."

It was too early to take the prescriptions to be filled at our druggist in River Heights, so I poured a glass of orange juice and went into the bedroom.

Zack was lying on his back. His BlackBerry was within easy reach on his nightstand, but he wasn't thumbing it – not a good sign.

When he heard me come in, he turned his head towards me. "Did Henry tell you you're an alarmist?"

I sat on the bed beside him. "Do you think I'd tell you if he had?" I said. "He gave me some prescriptions to get filled and, on my own initiative, I've decided to make chicken soup – the real kind, with feet in it."

"Actually, that sounds pretty good."

"You're also confined to quarters for the foreseeable future."

Zack reached out and took my hand. "As long as you're here, I can live with that."

"I'm here," I said. "I'm going to have to call about a dozen people and tell them we can't make their Christmas parties this week. We had two parties tonight alone – and it's only Monday."

"Disappointed?"

"Are you kidding? I'm thanking my lucky stars. No pantyhose to struggle into; no crab dip with a dubious heritage; no eggnog that's been sitting out too long; no trotting out the conversational gambit I picked up forty years ago from *Growing Up and Liking It*."

"What's *Growing Up and Liking it*?"

"It's a booklet girls used to send away for when they got their first period. It was distributed by a company that produced sanitary napkins and it was filled with useful advice about menstruation and dating."

"Pretty much covered the gamut, huh?"

"Pretty much. I've forgotten most of the advice except that when a girl is on a date she should never tell a boy about her interests; she should always just ask him about his interests."

"Did it work?"

I held out my left hand and pointed to my wedding ring. "Worked for me." I kissed his forehead. "Go back to sleep."

When I went back to the kitchen, Taylor was leaning over the sink eating her new favourite breakfast: a crumpet dripping with butter.

"Eating over the sink gives you warts," I said.

She swallowed. "This is worth it." She wiped the glisten off her chin. "Hey, was somebody here earlier or was I dreaming?"

"You weren't dreaming," I said. "Henry Chan came over to check out your dad."

The fun went out of Taylor's face. "He's all right, isn't he?"

"It's just the flu," I said. "But being in a wheelchair complicates things, so I worry – you know me."

She nodded, finished her crumpet, and rinsed her hands. "Can I go see him?"

"Of course," I said. "Seeing you always makes him happy."

"I hate it when anybody in this family gets sick," Taylor said. "It scares me."

"Me too," I said. "Now you'd better get a move on. Only two more days of school before the holidays. You don't want to be late."

She glanced at her watch. "Whoops. Can I borrow $5.00 please? We're supposed to chip in for flowers for Ms. Perdue. She broke her foot doing her improv routine during chapel Friday." Taylor brightened. "But before she broke her foot, she raised $231 for the Christmas fund."

"There's always a silver lining," I said.

My purse was on the telephone table, and I found a five-dollar bill in my wallet. When Taylor came back from seeing Zack, I handed her the money. She gave me a quick hug, and I breathed in the scent of rosemary from the organic shampoo she favoured this month.

"I told Dad I love him," she said. "I love you, too, Jo."

For the hundredth time, I noticed – and was angry at myself for noticing – that Zack, who had been in Taylor's life for two years, was "Dad" and that I, who had been in her life for ten years, was still, except for an occasional slip, "Jo." I knew my daughter loved me as deeply as I loved her, but somewhere deep in Taylor's psyche, the word mother still meant Sally.

I took the Christmas card Alwyn had given me from my purse, and looked again at the picture inside the holiday frame. For her entire life Abby had enjoyed a close and loving relationship with the man and woman she believed were her biological parents. Discovering the truth, that her birth mother was a stranger and that her father was a question mark, would have been a shock, but no matter how I looked at it, I could not convince myself that the revelation would have caused Abby to give away her child.

I was still, as my grandmother would have said, "in a brown study," when Myra Brokaw called. I had problems of my own, but I sat down and prepared to hear her out. With luck and care, Zack would be his old self in a week or so; Myra's husband would never recover.

"I know it's early," she said. "But I wanted to plead my case one more time before you made a final decision about Theo's role in your program about the Supreme Court."

"Myra, it's not my program, and I don't make the decisions. NationTV decides whether or not a particular show is worth doing, and if they green-light the show, my friend Jill Oziowy produces it. My connection is tangential. The series, such as it is, came out of an idea I had about making some of the institutions that affect our lives more understandable to the general public. I've done some research and some writing, but that's the extent of my involvement. I suggested Justice Brokaw because he was from

Saskatchewan, and I'd read in the paper that he was retiring here. I thought explaining the workings of the Court to a lay audience might be an interesting project for both of us, but it was just an idea. Nothing was set in stone."

"But it's a fine idea," Myra said and her voice was fervent. "The challenge is how best to bring the idea to life. My suggestion that an actor read from Theo's judgments simply won't work. For television, you need to involve the eye. And we can do that, Joanne."

When I didn't ask how we could involve the eye, Myra sensed my interest waning and hurried on. "Whenever Theo was interviewed for television, I made certain we got a copy of the tape, so I have all his public utterances, neatly catalogued. And even better, I filmed him frequently myself. He had such a brilliant legal mind. I knew I was part of something significant that could not be lost. I had an obligation."

"Myra, I don't think . . . "

"Joanne, please just look at the films. They're family films, of course. They show the man himself, but they offer so much more. Theo sitting on the dock at our cottage talking about how knowledge of art and literature places the law into context. And footage of him wandering the corridors of the Court at night alone, pondering a judgment. And he did this lovely thing – every year, he and his students went skating on the Rideau Canal. He's a fine skater and I have film of that, and there's always an inspiring sequence at the end where Theo and his students sit on a bench by the canal drinking cocoa, and Theo explains how the law is like skating – push, glide, push, glide. A time for assertion, a time for reflection. Such a precise metaphor. I want people to remember him."

"People do remember him, Myra," I said. "When we were first contemplating this show, I talked to people in the legal community – not just here in Saskatchewan but throughout

Canada. They hold Theo in very high regard. They know he was a fine jurist and scholar."

"So they've already written his eulogy," Myra said, and her laugh was bitter. "Robert Frost was right. 'No memory of having starred/Atones for later disregard,/Or keeps the end from being hard.'"

Her pain was as palpable as her love for her husband.

CHAPTER

10

After I'd found my old friend Helen Freedman's handwritten recipe for "Harvey Calls It 'Jewish Penicillin' Chicken Soup" I made a list of the ingredients I'd need and called Mieka.

"How's everyone in your kingdom this morning?" I said.

"The girls are bouncing off the walls. I'm doing as well as can be expected this close to Christmas. How about you?"

"Zack has the flu."

"Bad?"

"Bad enough for me to call Henry Chan. He says to keep an eye on it."

"Anything I can do?"

"I'm in a soup-making mood," I said. "If you could pick up a stewing chicken and whatever vegetables look good and drop them by before you go to work, I'd be grateful."

"Done," she said. "You don't have to take the girls skate shopping after school, you know."

"I'd forgotten all about it," I said. "Age."

"You've had a few things on your mind," Mieka said.

"Thanks, but the girls have been talking about getting their new skates for a week. More significantly, the skates are from Pete and Angus, and they've already given me the money."

Mieka chortled. "Shrewd move to get Angus to pony up ahead of time. He still owes me for ten years of Mother's Day presents."

"Slip him the bill when he graduates. Anyway, let me talk to Zack about the skate shopping. My guess is that he won't be happy if he thinks the ladies missed out on something because of him. Besides, Taylor will be home from school by the time I have to leave. We can work it out."

I opened my appointment calendar by the kitchen phone. Sure enough, the girls were pencilled in for skate shopping at three-thirty. There was a luncheon at the university that had also slipped my mind, and Zack and I had a client's party at five and another, in the same hotel, at six. I called the university and the clients' offices and left regrets. I glanced at the rest of the week, and slumped. Each day seemed black with commitments. Too much. Then I thought of Theo Brokaw thanking me for visiting because "not many do" and felt a pang for complaining about the abundance of my life.

As penance, I got out the lemon oil and began to polish the sideboard above which we'd hung the pomegranate wreath Myra had crafted. Polishing was the kind of job I enjoyed – mindless and instantly gratifying. I'd just finished when Nadine Perrault called.

Her voice was strong and calm. "Alwyn and I had coffee today and she suggested I get in touch with you. She said you'd be pleased to know that I'm continuing to make progress."

"That is good news," I said.

"For me, too," she said, and with an openness that I found appealing. "For weeks now I've felt as if I was sitting in front of a jigsaw puzzle. The pieces were scattered all around me. I knew if I put them together I'd see the truth. But I was so afraid of what the final picture would be that I couldn't make myself pick up the pieces."

"Now you're not afraid."

"No. Because I know that Abby loved me, and that makes all the difference. I'm going to find out what happened to her, Joanne. I'm coming to Regina. Obviously, the explanation for Abby's actions is tied somehow to Delia Wainberg. I've hired a Regina lawyer. His name is Darryl Colby. Do you know him?"

"I don't think so," I said. "But I'm sure Zack will. Do you want Zack to get in touch with him?"

"Not until Mr. Colby and I have had a chance to talk. I've asked him to hire an investigator. I have to learn what convinced Abby that she could no longer survive our life together. No matter how painful the answers."

"Zack always says it's better to know than not know."

"The truth shall set me free?"

"Or at least make it easier for you to sleep nights," I said.

Nadine's laugh was shadowed with irony. "I'd settle for that."

When I placed the cordless phone back in its charger, I thought about Nadine and, oddly, about Myra. It was difficult to imagine two more different women, but they were embarking on parallel journeys: Nadine, coming to a distant prairie city to discover why the partner she loved had turned into a stranger; Myra, moving to a city where she was a stranger, to mine her husband's archives and recover the man she had revered for forty years. Seemingly, when it came to doling out hope and heartbreak, life was remarkably even-handed.

Zack was stirring when I went into our room to check on him. I sat on the bed beside him and felt his forehead.

"Well?" he said.

"Still warm."

"How come you don't use a thermometer?"

"I don't need one," I said. "Thermometers make you crazy. Touching works just as well, and it lets you feel things a thermometer can't measure."

"Such as?"

"Such as whether the patient is glad to have your hand on his forehead."

"I'm glad," Zack said. "I'd be glad if you just sat there all day."

"That's exactly what I'm planning to do except I promised Madeleine and Lena I'd take them skate shopping after school. Taylor will be home. Do you think you'd be okay for an hour?"

"Sure. The girls need skates and I never tire of Taylor's updates on Declan." Zack took my hand in his. "Anything happening in the big world?"

"Nadine Perrault called. She's coming to Regina."

"Not welcome news, but hardly surprising," Zack said. "Should I gird my loins?"

"I don't think so. Nadine's pretty open about what she wants. Ultimately, she wants Jacob, but she told me today her immediate need is to find out what made Abby believe she could no longer survive the life she and Nadine shared."

Zack winced. "That's a phrase that will stick."

"The phrase is Nadine's," I said. "And it will stay with me too. It's hard to fathom what could make a woman as gifted and strong as Abby turn her back on everything that mattered to her. And if it's hard for us to understand, can you imagine what it's like for Nadine? Anyway, logically enough, she thinks the answers must be here, and she's hired a Regina lawyer."

"Who'd she get?"

"His name is Darryl Colby."

Zack scowled. "Interesting choice."

"Do I know him?"

Zack shifted his position and groaned. "You met him at the Bar Association Christmas party."

"The one with the big booming bass who sang 'You're a Mean One, Mr. Grinch'? He seemed like a lot of fun."

"Don't let that big booming bass disarm you, Ms. Shreve. Darryl is, in the immortal words of Dr. Seuss, as cuddly as a cactus and as charming as an eel." He also appears to have misplaced his conscience somewhere along the line." Zack pushed himself so he was lying on his side.

"Better?" I asked.

"Nope. I still feel like homemade shit."

"Let me try something," I fluffed up the extra pillows on the bed, brought them over to Zack's side, and positioned them against his back. "How's that?"

"Good," he said.

I smoothed Zack's covers. "Darryl Colby doesn't seem like the kind of lawyer Nadine would choose."

"Putz Llewellyn probably recommended him. Guys like that have a network. They slither out of the same eels' nest." Zack heaved a mighty sigh. "I'm through talking, Jo. I'm dead." Within seconds, he was asleep.

I brought in the newspaper and sat in the chair by the window. It wasn't long before Zack half-opened his eyes. "That wasn't much of a nap," I said. "Can I get you anything?"

"Water?"

I poured some from the Thermos and helped him into a sitting position. Zack drank thirstily and then lay back on his pillow. "I was dreaming about eels," he said.

"That's because before you drifted off we were talking about Darryl Colby."

"Shit. I was hoping that was just part of the dream." Zack narrowed his eyes. "So Colby really is Nadine's lawyer."

"Yes, but you're tough," I said. "You can take him."

"Darryl's certainly waited long enough for a chance to take a shot at me."

"You two have a history?"

Zack nodded. "Darryl worked for Murray Jeffreys."

"The lawyer who died after he and Noah were fighting."

"Yeah. Darryl came to my apartment the morning after Murray died. He'd been to the morgue and noticed that for a guy who'd died of a heart attack, Murray had a lot of bruises. I told him to shove off, but he pushed my chair out of the way and strong-armed his way in."

"Was Delia still there?"

"Oh yeah, and wearing one of my T-shirts. Darryl asked Delia why she put out for everybody but Murray and him. At that point Noah showed up and threatened to kill Darryl. It was quite a morning."

"And you think Darryl's waited all these years to get even?"

Zack shrugged. "All I know is if I were advising Nadine, Darryl Colby is exactly the lawyer I would have suggested. He's a junkyard dog. Even when he's winning, he never misses a chance to snap at opposing counsel. People respect Delia. Most of the lawyers in town would have a tough time going full bore against her. Darryl will dig up the dirt, and lick his chops as he tears her reputation to shreds." Zack rolled over. "God, I feel awful."

"Too much talking," I said. "Go back to sleep. I'll go up to the drugstore and pick up your prescriptions, and then we'll get you into the shower and change your sheets. Okay?"

Zack just nodded and shut his eyes.

When I came back from the drugstore, Mieka was in the kitchen, unpacking groceries.

"You're a wonder," I said.

"Nope, just one of Lakeview Fine Foods' best customers. I called ahead and they had everything ready."

"Zack always says the more people you know the more people you know who can do something for you."

Mieka made a face. "Cynical, but true. Is he doing any better?"

"Not yet," I said. I held up the bag of medications. "I'm counting on these."

"And on Helen Freedman's chicken soup," Mieka said.

"That soup's been our standby since you were in kindergarten," I said. "And this time I'm really counting on it because life is not getting simpler." I took off my jacket. "Do you have time for a cup of coffee? I should get Zack started on his pills. But if you have a moment, I'd like to talk."

Mieka glanced at her watch. "I'm already over-caffeinated, but I'm okay for time."

I had to wake Zack up to take his pills. "Nurse Ratched here," I said. "Do you want this medication orally or should we arrange another way?"

Zack pushed himself to a semi-sitting position. "I never figured you for a mean woman," he muttered.

I kissed his shoulder. "Would you believe me if I said I would rather it was me going through this than you?"

"Hell, yes. I'd rather it was you, too." He gave me a weak smile. "You do realize that was a joke, don't you?"

"It better have been," I said. "I'm the one who controls the drugs."

When I got back to the kitchen, Mieka was washing the stewing chicken.

"Bucking for sainthood?"

"No, just for someone to babysit the girls New Year's Eve."

"Won't you be at the lake with us New Year's Eve?"

"Yes, and I was hoping I could bring a date."

"Anyone I know?"

"Yes, but it may fall through, so don't get your hopes up," Mieka said. "Anyway, just in case, could the girls stay with you and Zack New Year's Eve?"

"Absolutely. An excuse for me to have my perfect New Year's Eve. Everyone in bed by nine o'clock."

Mieka smiled. "Same old Mum."

"Same old Mum," I said.

Mieka opened the knife drawer, took out my heavy-duty knife, and waved it in the air. "Do you want to do the honours or shall I?"

"I'll do it," I said. I took out the cutting board and set to work.

"Okay, so what's going on?"

"Abby's partner, Nadine Perrault, called this morning. She's coming to Regina."

"So, this is bad news?"

"It's going to make life more complicated for Zack," I said.

"If Zack weren't involved, where would you think Jacob should be?"

"I don't know. Nadine would be a very good parent. She's warm and thoughtful. She doesn't put herself first, and she's capable of great love. But Abby Michaels wanted Jacob to be with Delia and she must have had her reasons. Certainly Delia's legal position seems solid."

"Why 'seems' rather than 'is'?"

The leg came free and I severed the thigh from the drumstick. "Zack's uneasy about this case," I said, "I guess it's rubbing off on me."

"So what's going to happen?"

"I think Jacob will end up with the Wainbergs. It's not going to be a fairy-tale ending, but if life unfolds as it should, it's possible that everyone involved will be reasonably content. Delia's prepared to offer Nadine access, and if Nadine's lawyer can prove that Abby's decision was based on something other than concern about Nadine's character, the access should be generous." I began cutting the other leg free.

Mieka shook her head. "You didn't spend much time with Nadine, Mum. She could have some skeletons rattling in her closet."

"The priest at Nadine's church in Port Hope didn't think so. He told Nadine that everything Abby did at the end grew out of her love for Nadine and her desire to protect her."

Mieka's eyes widened. "Are priests in Port Hope allowed to divulge the secrets of the confessional?"

I cut the joint between the drumstick and the thigh. "Apparently this priest had a generous heart, and the moral decision with which he was faced was clear-cut. He saw a good person suffering needlessly, and he was able to help. He was lucky."

"But you're not?" Mieka asked.

"Zack is Delia's lawyer, so I can hardly make overtures to Nadine."

Mieka frowned. "I understand why Zack can't, but I don't see why you can't do what you want to do."

I began removing the wings. "You may have a point. I like Nadine, and she is going to be so alone. Given the circumstances, there's no guarantee that Delia will even let her see Jacob. It might be perceived as a concession."

"Where's Noah in all this?"

"Where he always is – with his arms protectively around his wife."

"That sounds a little bitchy."

"When it comes to Delia, I'm a little sensitive these days. She has an amazing success rate as a litigator, but the men around her treat her as if she'd fall apart in a stiff breeze."

I turned the bird onto its breast and began cutting along each side of the spine to remove the backbone.

"So does your ire extend to Zack?"

"I'm probably overreacting to the Ontario trip but, yes, it does. He treated Nadine badly and he risked his health because he felt he had to protect Delia."

"Jealous?"

"Probably. There's this primal thing among the partners at Falconer Shreve. It goes way back. No matter how brilliantly Delia performs as a lawyer, Zack still sees her as the girl he had to hold all night because, the year they were articling, she was at the centre of a fight."

"And Delia felt responsible?"

"As Zack described it, it was more that she was in a state of shock. Anyway, there was no shortage of knights in armour prepared to defend her."

"And Zack was among them," Mieka said. "So, was there a romance?"

"I doubt it. Zack's had a lot of women, but Zack's and Delia's feelings for one another go deep. I can't see them risking their relationship for a one-night stand." I removed the stewing hen's backbone, cut through the breastplate to make two halves, and flourished my knife. "Done," I said. "This chicken is ready for the pot."

After Mieka left, I covered the chicken parts and gizzards with water, chopped onions, carrots, parsnips, and fresh thyme and added them to the pot, seasoned the broth, and turned on the heat. Chicken soup, the anodyne for all the ills of the world, was on its way.

Mieka and I had arranged that I would pick the girls up at school at three-thirty. The day ahead was clear. I took a biography I'd been waiting to read into the bedroom, sat by the window, and looked out at the day. It was bright, still, and cold enough to create sun dogs in the sky. I turned to the first page of my book. It opened in Tennessee. A young woman was driving through heat so blistering the plastic of her car seat was sticking to her legs. She was singing, "I'm Going to the Chapel and I'm Going to Get Married."

My husband stirred. I moved my chair closer and continued to read. It was a quiet morning. I awakened Zack when it was time to give him pills and liquids. At intervals, I skimmed the soup. Mid-morning, a courier arrived with three large and unwieldy packages. When I ripped off the paper, I discovered that I'd signed for three copper pots filled with poinsettias in Zack's favourite deep red. I brought the pots into our bedroom, placed them on a low table close to the window where he could see them, and went back to my book.

An hour before noon, I skimmed the soup and, following Helen Freedman's recipe, made and refrigerated matzo balls. When Zack awakened, I was ready. I kissed him. "Welcome back," I said.

Zack took my hand. "Always glad to be where you are, Ms. Shreve. So what's going on?"

"Someone sent you flowers," I said.

"Am I dead?"

"No, just worthy of spoiling." I handed him the unopened card. He slipped on his reading glasses. "From Louise," he said. "She sends her affection and apologies."

"As well she might," I said.

Zack gave me a sharp look. "I take it things didn't go well with you two last night."

"No. I was angry at what she was doing to Declan, and I was furious that she dragged you out of the house when you were sick to clean up the mess she'd made."

Zack shrugged. "I agree with you about Declan. But Leland Hunter pays the firm a sizable sum to keep his family out of trouble, so I was just doing my job."

"Has Leland ever considered doing that particular job himself?"

"Too busy earning money. Considering that Louise is his ex, he's very responsible. Over the years, he's paid a number of people to keep her from self-destructing. She used to have a kind of babysitter who went to restaurants with her and sat at the next table. The theory was the guy would keep Louise out of trouble, but half the time she gave him the slip. Finally, Leland realized that no matter how many people he hired to protect Louise, she'd always find a log with which to set herself on fire. Last spring when she was charged with DUI, she was weaving and driving so slowly that the cops ran her licence and were there waiting at her front door when she finally wended her way home."

"Do you think she wants to get caught?"

"I'm not a shrink, but my theory is that Louise's motivation is the same as Declan's – she wants Leland to pay attention to her."

"So Louise teaches her son that to get his father's attention, he just has to break the law," I said.

"You know I can't answer that," Zack said. "Anyway, aren't you being a little hard on her?" He started to cough and he couldn't seem to stop. I put my arm behind his back and pulled him upright. When the coughing finally ended I was scared and furious. I rested my forehead on his shoulder.

"To answer your question," I said, "I don't think I'm being too hard on Louise at all."

Zack slept deeply for the next three hours. He was feverish, and even when I wiped his head with a cool cloth, he didn't awaken. Concerned that he was becoming dehydrated, I took him a glass of ginger ale and roused him. He'd managed to drink half of it when the doorbell chimed. He made a gesture of dismissal and lay back on his pillow. "I'm good," he said. "Better see who that is."

The guest on the porch was Debbie Haczkewicz. Her cheeks were ruddy with health and cold, but her eyes were tired.

"I was in the neighbourhood, so I thought I'd stop by to see how Zack's doing," she said.

"He's been sleeping pretty much on and off all day," I said. "But I can see if he's awake."

"It's nothing important. Just tell him I came by."

Debbie looked as weary as I felt. "Would you like to come in?" I said. "I'm dragging, and I was about to make myself coffee."

"Dragging is my permanent state these days," Debbie said. "Caffeine helps, and I'd appreciate a cup of something that didn't taste like the floor sweepings we have at headquarters."

Our kitchen caught the afternoon sun. It was a cheerful place in which to sit, and Debbie and I had our coffee there. "So how's it going?" I said.

"Not well," Debbie said. "It's been nine days since Abby Michaels died, and all we have are questions. We know from the forensic pathology results that Abby Michaels didn't fight her attacker. Usually in these cases the victim's fingernails are a treasure trove for the M.E. – samples of the attacker's hair, skin, and blood – but Abby's nails were clean."

"Is it possible that she was drugged with something like Rohypnol?"

Debbie sugared her coffee. "Nope, Toxicology's still running tests, but so far no traces of any of the classic 'date rape' drugs, including alcohol. It seems that Abby didn't perceive the man who killed her as a threat."

"She was a stranger here. Whom would she trust that completely?"

"I have a theory," Debbie said. "Abby Michaels had just given away her child. She was traumatized. She went to someone whom she believed would help her deal with what she'd done. I think she put herself in his hands. The element of surprise was on his side. The autopsy results suggest that the man strangled her, raped her, dragged her down at least one flight of stairs, then pulled her through the snow to her car and drove her to the parking lot behind A-1."

I shuddered. "Do you ever get used to seeing that kind of viciousness?"

Debbie was measured. "No, but that degree of contempt for another human being is revealing. It suggests a psychosis, and nine times out of ten, that means we're dealing with a habitual offender. If we're lucky and can match the semen on the victim with semen in the VI-class data bank, we can start checking halfway houses and the location of inmates on mandatory release and sooner or later, we find our guy. But we've already established the semen found on Abby doesn't match any in the VI-class data bank."

The sun was pouring into our kitchen, but I felt a chill. "If he was able to take Abby by surprise, he must seem trustworthy," I said.

"Or he's in a profession that makes a woman feel it's safe to let down her guard," Debbie said tightly. "And, of course, that's why he poses such a threat to his potential victims and to the police force. There's a deadly mix here: We have a disarming psychotic, and we have a public desperate for action because Abby was educated, middle-class, and not known to indulge in risky behaviour."

"People identify with her," I said.

"And they feel vulnerable," Debbie said. "Abby could be their sister, their girlfriend, their wife, or their daughter. People are scared."

"And that puts pressure on you," I said.

"You bet it does," Debbie said. "Nobody likes to admit it, but when we get the call that a body's been found, there's an adrenalin rush. All the possibilities are open. We choose the members of the lead investigative team, let them know they're up to bat and meet them at the crime scene. By the time I get there, the uniforms are already ricocheting, bagging evidence, taking photographs, taking notes, making guesses. Everybody's charged up. But that's Day One. As the days go by and nothing pans out, the adrenalin seeps away. We all start getting antsy, and that's a dangerous time in an investigation because this is when we start getting seduced by false clues. It's as if we're all standing in the dark – waiting for a sound or a flash of light. When there's been nothing but silence, and one of us hears the snap of the twig, there's always the danger that we'll overreact – give that twig far more attention than it merits. That's where we are now, Joanne, and it's not a good place to be."

We walked to the front hall together. When Debbie was dressed to leave, she turned to me. "If there's anything I can do . . . "

"You're doing it," I said. "Arresting the man who killed Abby will bring Delia a measure of peace. Take my word for it – that will make Zack's job easier."

Debbie pulled on her gloves. "I hope so. Zack's a fine man. I wouldn't have Leo today if it hadn't been for him."

"Was it that bad for Leo?"

"My son tried to kill himself," Debbie said. "In my estimation, that's as bad as it gets. All his life people had admired Leo; suddenly, they pitied him. I'll never forget the deadness in his eyes the day he was told he'd be in a wheelchair for the rest of his life."

I thought of Abby. "Leo didn't see how he could survive his new life," I said.

"That's right," Debbie said. "But luckily, he had Zack."

In one of life's small cosmic jokes, Madeleine and Lena had found the skates they dreamed of, but the skates Madeleine coveted were available only in Lena's size, and the only pair left in the style for which Lena longed was in Madeleine's size. They accepted their fates with uncharacteristic equanimity. Christmas was growing closer, and our granddaughters were fervent believers in Santa's list.

We left the store with time enough to take the new skates to be sharpened by Eddy, the wizened gnome who had sharpened our family's skates since my children were little.

Eddy's tiny business, in the basement of a store that had once sold tobacco products but now sold vintage comic books, had been there for as long as I could remember, but this was the girls' first trip. They had been chatting nonstop since I picked them up at school, but as we walked to the back of the comic book store and stood on the threshold of the steps that led to the basement, they fell silent.

The steps were steep and poorly lit; the air from below was dank and smelled of tobacco. When the girls and I started down the steps, we were met by an odd and unsettling whirring sound that caused both girls to grab my coat from behind. We were, indeed, descending into the heart of darkness.

In every essential way, Eddy and his business were much the same as they had been when I met him thirty years before. I had never seen him without a cigarette. There was always a pack of Player's Plain in the pocket of his muscle shirt, and there was always a lit cigarette in his mouth. His skin was the colour of a cured tobacco leaf and his arms, now stringy with age, were heavily tattooed with images of anchors and calls to patriotism. Yellowing pictures of busty bathing beauties with come-hither smiles and upswept hair blanketed the shop's ceiling. Periodically, Eddy would tilt back his head, peer through the smoke from his cigarette, and wink at them.

Madeleine and Lena were mesmerized as Eddy went into action, clamping each skate so that the blade touched the grinding wheel, setting the wheel in motion, whirring away just long enough, taking the honing stone to the sharpened blade to remove the burr. Eddy never spoke a word until he was through and he muttered a price. I paid. He pocketed the cash and we left the stygian depths.

We were on the street before either of the girls spoke again. "That was weird," Madeleine said.

"But not too weird," Lena chirped. "Just weird enough." She looked across the road at the skating rink on Scarth Street Mall. The sun was out; the sky was blue. The sun dogs had disappeared. The day was warm enough to try out new skates. "Could we have just a little skate, Mimi?"

"Let me call your granddad and see how he's feeling," I said.

I dialled Zack's cell. He picked up on the first ring. He sounded terrible.

"How are you doing?" I said.

"I'm okay," he said.

"Is Taylor taking good care of you?"

"She was with me until a few minutes ago. She hovers, so I sent her packing."

"Are you feeling worse?"

"I'm fine. Did you get the skates?"

"We did and we had them sharpened. The temperature is reasonable, and we're standing here looking at the Scarth Street Mall rink. The girls are eager to try out their new skates. Would you be okay for another forty-five minutes?"

"Sure. Hey, take some pictures with your BlackBerry and send them to me."

"I'm not sure I remember how."

"Maddy can give you a hand."

"Stay tuned," I said.

Regina is a city with a population of 200,000, but over the years, I've displayed an uncanny knack for running into the one person whom I least wish to see. The girls were laced up and slip-sliding their way around the ice when Theo and Myra Brokaw approached and sat on the bench next to me. They were dressed for a winter walk: Sorel boots, stylish grey down jackets, and the red scarves they'd been wearing the night of the Wainbergs' party.

"How nice that you've found the time for an outing," Myra said.

"I promised our granddaughters I'd take them skate shopping," I said.

"And a promise is a promise," Myra said. The edge in her voice was unmistakable.

"That's Madeleine in the green jacket and Lena's the one in purple," I said, pointing them out.

Theo shook his head. "Daughters." As the girls moved around the rink, Theo's eyes followed them. "Push. Glide. Push. Glide. Push. Glide. Push. Glide," he said softly.

I looked at Theo Brokaw. He was still a handsome and virile man. Age had not blurred the classic lines of his profile; his skin was taut, and even in repose his body had the coiled-spring energy of a man who found pleasure in physical exercise. When Delia clerked for him, he would have been in his late forties. Attractive, learned, and revered by his colleagues, Theo Brokaw was exactly the kind of man to whom a young woman who lived for the law would have been drawn.

The possibility that Theo had fathered Delia's child had been at the edge of my consciousness from the morning Delia sat in our kitchen and told us about the baby she had given up for adoption. As Zack noted, nothing in Delia's history or character suggested that her romantic life would be conducted so casually that she would be unable to identify the father of her child. Logic pointed to a serious love affair. So did the spark that flew between Theo and Delia when she greeted him at the door the day of the party. There had been nothing tentative or confused about Theo's embrace; he had clung to Delia with the passion of a lover.

It occurred to me that the tapes Myra had mentioned might offer a glimpse into Theo and Delia's relationship that year in Ottawa. I turned to Myra. "This morning you mentioned that you had footage of Theo talking to his students. That might be good television."

Myra arched an eyebrow. "It *would* be good television," she said. "That's why I've already couriered the DVDs to your home."

"Thank you," I said. "Myra, I admire your determination. I wasn't trying to brush you off when you phoned. Zack is ill, but he was adamant about not disappointing the girls."

"I understand," she said. There was sly amusement in her smile. "I understand a great deal, Joanne. I am not a stupid woman."

When I got home, Willie greeted me at the door, his stump of a tail moving like a metronome marking the beats of his joy. The package from Myra Brokaw was on the hall table.

I unzipped my boots, hung up my coat, and went to my husband. There was a half-glass of ginger ale on the table beside him and Taylor's practice bells from Luther were on the nightstand within easy ringing distance. Louise's three poinsettias had been joined by six more – all large and all red. I kissed Zack's forehead. "So what's with all the flowers?"

"Taylor brought them in. The cards are there by the bells."

"I take it the bells are for summoning your nurse."

"That's right. I told you she hovered."

"She loves you," I said. "I love you." I gestured towards the poinsettias. "Everybody loves you."

"What the hell are we going to do with all those, anyway?"

"Save money. I was going to buy a poinsettia for Mieka, one for Pete's clinic, and one to put in Angus's room to welcome him home. Now I don't have to. You can spend the money we save on your heart's desire."

"You're my heart's desire," he said. "Did we save enough to buy you a Birkin bag?"

"I don't need a Birkin bag."

"Damn," he said. "In that case, let's just talk. Tell me about your afternoon. The pictures were very good, by the way."

"Maddy and Lena took them," I said.

"I kind of figured that when there weren't any pictures of the two of them together."

"The girls and I missed you," I said. "You're our team photographer, but you'll have plenty of chances. It isn't even officially winter yet. Besides, Maddy and Lena had an audience. Theo and Myra Brokaw were down at the rink, watching the skaters."

Zack frowned. "No one had a better legal mind than Theo Brokaw. It's sad to think of him spending his day watching other people's kids go round and round and round."

"Myra told me Theo used to take his law students down to the Rideau Canal in the winter to skate."

Zack chuckled. "And so he could deliver his famous push-glide-push-glide speech – Delia told me about it. Then, of course, I heard about it from other lawyers who'd clerked for Theo."

"What's the speech?"

"It's just a little gem Theo used to trot out for one of his 'teachable moments,'" Zack said. "Theo explained that the law is like skating. Push-glide-push-glide. Argue – allow the argument to sink in – argue – allow the argument to sink in. If Theo had been hosting your show about the Court that kind of crap would have been pure gold."

"Actually, I did ask Myra to send over some of her home movies. But she beat me to the punch. The DVDs are already on the table in the front hall."

"You're not still thinking of using Theo in that special, are you?" Zack's voice, already raspy, was a growl. "Because you can cut and paste all you want, but all the king's horses and all the king's men aren't going to put Mr. Justice Brokaw together again."

"I know that," I said. "My interest in the tapes isn't professional. I thought that with Nadine coming to Regina, it might be useful to narrow down the possibilities about the identity of Abby's father."

Zack gave me a sharp look. "So you think it's Theo, too?"

"It's logical," I said. "The way Theo behaved when he saw Delia at the Wainbergs' party was telling. These days, there must be a great deal that doesn't make sense to Theo, but Delia's perfume seemed to be a link to an old safe world when he was young."

"And a force to be reckoned with." Zack exhaled slowly. "Life really can be a bitch, can't it?"

I kissed his hand. "I guess that's why, all those years ago, Helen Freedman gave me the recipe for 'Harvey Calls It "Jewish Penicillin" Chicken Soup.' Think you'll be able to handle a bowlful?"

"Bring it on. I'm going to call Delia and ask her to come over tonight."

"Are we going to look at Myra's home movies?"

"Depends, but the very fact that they exist presents us with one of Theo's 'teachable moments.' A DVD of her skating days might remind Dee about the importance of full disclosure."

"She's kept that part of her life closed off for many years. You really think some old home movies will do the trick?"

Zack shrugged. "Who knows? But I'm tired of screwing around. I'm going to tell Dee that unless she opens up, I'm off the case. Until she tells me the truth, my hands are tied. And for a paraplegic, that's no option at all."

CHAPTER

11

Taylor was not a fan of chicken soup. After she and Declan left to go to our favourite neighbourhood restaurant, the Chimney, for pizza, I took a tray to the bedroom and Zack and I had dinner for two. He finished his soup – a good sign – but refused seconds, and I didn't push it.

I cleaned up our dishes and when I came back, Zack was on his BlackBerry. I went out in the hall and made a call of my own. Nadine was touchingly grateful when I offered to pick her up at the airport and introduce her to Mieka, who, as far as any of us knew, was the person who'd spent the most time with Abby in the days immediately before her death. I hung up feeling relieved that I'd made the effort. When I came into our bedroom and told Zack, he was less sanguine. "There are two sides to this case, Ms. Shreve," he said, "and you're stepping over the line."

"It's a very small step," I said. "I'm simply extending the same courtesy to Nadine that we'd extend to anyone coming to Regina."

"Maybe," Zack said, "but I'm guessing Darryl Colby isn't going to be any happier about this female bonding than I am."

"That's a problem for tomorrow," I said. "So let's leave it alone."

"Fair enough," Zack said, "because we have enough going on tonight. I called Dee. She's coming over to watch Myra's home movies."

"Zack, how much are you telling Delia about the police investigation?"

"The bare minimum," Zack said. "Dee doesn't need to hear the details. Why do you ask?"

"Debbie Haczkewicz came by this afternoon while you were sleeping. I thought you might want to hear what she told me before Delia arrived."

"That's probably best," he said. "So how's Debbie?"

"Tired. Frustrated. Worried."

"Unsolved homicide cases are tough on cops," Zack said. "The last time we talked, Debbie told me that all they've nailed down is the 'window' of time in which the attack took place. Abby's car was not in the parking lot at A-1 when the power went off, but it was there when the power was restored."

"That's a pretty small window," I said. "The power went off just before six and came back on at eight-thirty."

"Apparently, the power downtown wasn't restored till after eleven," Zack said, "and even when it came on, visibility was lousy because of the blizzard. Debbie assigned some poor rookie to go through the A-1 security tape frame by frame, and he spotted Abby's car in the first frame after the power came back on."

"So no pictures of the man who killed Abby leaving the scene?"

"Nope. Debbie has uniformed officers going door to door to see if anyone heard anything, but in that area houses are few and far between and the people who live in them are not overly fond of cops." Zack looked hard at me. "Your attention seems to have drifted," he said.

"Not at all," I said. "I'm just trying to figure out how everything that happened to Abby could have taken place within five hours."

Zack winced. "Is your back hurting?" I said.

He tried a smile but all he managed was a grimace. "Nothing a change in position won't fix," he said. "Could you give me a hand?" I put my arm around him and lowered him so he was lying on his side, facing me. I placed a pillow behind his back for support.

"Thanks," he said. "Does any of this make sense to you, Jo? A smart woman, who happens to be a lesbian, comes to a city where she's a stranger, gives away her child, and then goes off with a man whom she instantly trusts?"

"Debbie has a theory that Abby sought out a professional to help her through the trauma of giving up Jacob. She thinks it wasn't the man, himself, whom Abby trusted. She thinks it was his profession."

"So we know he wasn't a lawyer," Zack said.

I raised an eyebrow. "Nothing like a lawyer joke to ease tensions," I said.

"You almost laughed," Zack said. "Anyway, if lawyers are out, what's left?"

"Doctors and clergy, and Abby's Catholic, so I guess we can assume doctors and priests."

"There are bad apples in every profession," Zack said. "So Abby leaves Luther College, meets up with a doctor or a priest, goes somewhere with him, he attacks and kills her, pulls her down a flight of stairs, drags her through the snow to her car, drives to A-1, and gets away. All within five hours. You're right. It doesn't add up."

"Are you going to tell Delia?"

"Nope. I think movie night might be enough misery for my partner." Zack looked at his watch. "Dee won't be here for another three-quarters of an hour. She wanted to give Jacob his bath. Shall we have a preview?"

I fetched Myra's package and we watched the DVD she'd had made from the movies shot the year Delia clerked for Theo. Most of the footage was of Theo thinking aloud about decisions he was about to make. Dry stuff, but Myra knew how to bring her husband's legal ponderings to life by placing him in compelling settings: beside a rushing river on a soft green spring day; atop a ski slope in the Laurentians; strolling alone along a shadowy deserted corridor in the Supreme Court.

"Always alone," Zack intoned theatrically, "except, of course, for his ever-present wife with her ever-present camera. Boy, talk about ego. I can't imagine you taking pictures of me wrestling with my conscience."

"The temptation's there," I said. "A lot of lawyers in this town would pay serious money to see if you *had* a conscience."

Zack laughed, which of course set off another coughing attack. When it was through, he closed his eyes. "Watching this crap is getting us nowhere," he said. "Myra obviously didn't send over the X-rated version. Let's turn it off, and watch the rest when Delia comes."

"Wait," I said. "Here comes the skating."

There was an establishing shot of the frozen Rideau Canal. Then the camera zoomed in on a man and woman skating. He was tall and confident of his prowess; she was petite and moved tentatively. They weren't touching, but they moved in perfect harmony, and they turned and began to skate towards the camera at precisely the same moment. "Hold on," I said.

As the man and woman locked eyes, the person behind

the camera froze the shot. Even twenty-seven years later, the heat between the lovers was palpable.

We watched to the end of the sequence. As Theo delivered his familiar push-glide speech, Delia's eyes never left his face.

Zack clicked off the DVD. "So now we know," he said.

"It was a long time ago," I said. "By now, it's probably ancient history for both of them."

"I'm not sure it is for Dee," Zack said. "On that fated day when I had to decide between buying you a toothbrush or getting a new Jaguar, I went to Delia for advice. To be honest, the reason I chose her was because I was certain she'd tell me I should bid you sayonara, but she surprised me. She told me I should go back to you. She said that otherwise, I'd spend the rest of my life wondering."

"And you think that's what happened to Delia?"

"I do. She and Noah were married the week after she came back from Ottawa. The marriage came out of the blue. Everyone was shocked, and nobody was more shocked than Noah. I was best man at their wedding. Noah looked like a guy who'd won the big prize in a lottery he didn't know he'd bought a ticket for."

"And you think Delia's been wondering ever since?"

"I guess we're about to find that out."

Before Delia arrived, I gave Zack a sponge bath, helped him into fresh pyjamas, changed the sheets, tucked the prescription drugs out of sight, then began removing some of the flowers that had been delivered.

"You don't have to do that," Zack said.

"You said the place looked like Walmart."

"It was just an observation," he said. "Come sit next to me for a minute."

I went over, lay on the bed beside him, and slipped my hand under his pyjama top onto his chest.

"This is more than I asked for," Zack said.

"And it's only the beginning," I said.

For an evening designed to elicit a revelation, Delia's visit was surprisingly without fireworks. When I showed her into our room, she went straight to Zack and embraced him. "I'm so sorry," she said gently.

He patted her shoulder. "It's okay, Dee. It'll work out."

"I hope so," she said. She glanced around the room. I'd left the curtains open so we could see the night sky. The snow outside the window was blue-white, and on the low table in front of the window the three copper pots with their deep red poinsettias glowed. The room was very quiet. "It's so peaceful here," Delia said.

She was all in black, her face was pale and drawn, and as she pulled a chair close to the bed, she moved with her characteristic taut intensity. "Might as well get this over with," she said.

"You don't have to watch the movies, Dee," Zack said.

Delia picked up the remote. "I've ducked this long enough," she said, and she hit power.

I'd taken the DVD back to the beginning. As Theo came on screen looking as he had twenty-seven years ago, Delia's face grew soft.

Zack had been watching his partner, but he dropped his eyes at her show of emotion. Then his eyes shifted to the screen.

We watched in silence till the sequence on the canal was over.

"That's it," I said.

"I thought he was the sun and the moon and the stars," Delia said. "I was very young." Her husky voice broke in its strangely adolescent-boy way.

"Dee, the point of showing you the movie wasn't to

make you miserable," Zack said. "It was to find out everything we could about the circumstances surrounding Abby Michaels's birth."

Delia shrugged her slender shoulders. "It's the old sad story. I fell in love with Theo. He said he loved me. I thought he'd leave his wife. He said he wanted to be with me, but that Myra had invested everything in him, and I had my life ahead of me. Case closed."

"Did you tell him about the baby?" I asked.

Delia shook her head. "No. Eventually, of course, he must have realized I was pregnant, but he never mentioned it, and neither did I."

"He never asked if the baby was his?" I said. "I would have thought . . . "

"To be fair, by the time news of my pregnancy made the rounds in the Supreme Court Building, Theo had every reason to believe the baby wasn't his."

"What happened?" I said.

"Someone started a rumour that I'd been screwing pretty much everything that wasn't nailed down. A kind soul told me she'd been at a drinking party where they narrowed the list of potential fathers down to five and everybody voted."

"Jesus," Zack said.

"Welcome to the world of women," I said, and Delia shot me a grateful glance.

"Anyway," she said, "I appeared before the Court many times over the years, but, quite correctly, there was no acknowledgement from Theo that he knew me."

"He never made any attempt at a personal connection?" Zack asked.

"No, nor did I. Come on, Zack, you know the rules. Anything like that would have been highly unethical and it might have compromised a client, so Theo and I soldiered on, protected by the anonymity of our robes: just another justice; just another barrister. And it would have continued that way if it hadn't been for Abby's letter."

"But you did tell Theo that Abby was his daughter?" Zack said.

"I took the coward's way out," Delia said. "I wrote to him. I knew he'd retired suddenly and moved back here. He was no longer a judge, so that particular barrier to communication had been removed, but to be frank I didn't want to face him. I didn't know how he'd react. Anyway, I sent him a letter setting out the facts. I relayed Abby's request and told him that he could do as he wished, but that I thought it was fair to convey the medical information his biological daughter requested, and I believed her when she said she had no wish to have further contact with either of us."

"Did you get a response?" Zack said.

"I did. One line typed on monogrammed stationery. 'The matter has been taken care of,' and then Theo's initals, 'T.N.B.'"

"Were the initials typed or handwritten?" Zack asked.

"Handwritten," Delia said. "I should have just let it go, but the ambiguity was unsettling. I decided to arrange a face-to-face meeting. I wrote a note addressed to Theo and Myra. I said I understood they had moved back to Regina and that Noah and I were having a gathering on December 5. There would be people there whom they would find congenial, and we'd be delighted if they could join us. I gave them my contact information, and I received an e-mail accepting the invitation."

"Was the e-mail from Theo or Myra?" Zack asked.

"It was signed 'Theo and Myra,' which of course means nothing. Noah always signs both our names when he responds to invitations. The Brokaws' note was cordial but it was just the usual. There was certainly no mention of Theo's health problems." Delia stood and walked over to the window. "And here's something that puzzles me. Doesn't Alzheimer's take time to develop? After our party I had calls from lawyers who'd appeared before the Court last spring, and according to them, Theo was fine. Nobody, including me, had ever heard of a case where the disease moved that quickly."

"It isn't Alzheimer's," I said. "Theo had a fall. He was shingling their cottage roof last summer, and he fell. He suffered a traumatic brain injury that's left him in a state similar to advanced Alzheimer's."

Delia bit her lip. "Just one false step, and an entire life changes." Her eyes moved to me. "How do you know all this?"

"NationTV is considering a show about the Supreme Court. It would be part of a series they're doing explaining the institutions that affect our lives. When I heard Theo was retiring here, I thought he'd be a good fit, and I e-mailed him. Myra responded for him, but I didn't think anything of it. I just assumed he was busy and she handled his correspondence."

"I sent my letter towards the end of November," Delia said. "Myra would have handled it, too."

"Presumably," I said.

"And given Theo's state, she would have been the one to decide whether or not to get in touch with Abby."

I nodded.

"And we'll never know whether they did." Delia's eyes dropped. "There's so much we'll never know."

She went to Zack. "You look as if you've had enough," she said. "I know I have." She bent and kissed his forehead. "I'll call you in the morning."

I walked her to the door. She put on her boots and jacket and draped around her neck the scarf that she'd knit when she was trying to quit smoking. The scarf trailed to her knee on one side. "I feel so guilty about this, Joanne."

"Zack's flu was probably incubating before he went to Port Hope."

She tried a smile. "But you won't deny that the trip made a bad situation worse. I seem to have developed a reverse Midas touch. I'm losing confidence in my decisions, and that's always fatal."

"And futile to dwell on," I said. "There's no going back. Given the circumstances at the time, we do the best we can."

"I still believe that giving Abby up was best for her. She had a good life. I don't know why everything fell apart." Delia's eyes filled with tears. "The first time I saw my daughter's face was in that parking lot. The men who found her had left the door open. I got in. It was so cold. The key was in the ignition, so I turned on the heat. After she was born, I told them I didn't want to see her, and when I got in the car with her, I knew it was my last chance. It was like looking in a mirror. I held her hand and talked to her. I knew she was dead, but I kept on talking. I promised her I would make things right." Delia wiped her eyes with the back of her hand. "I usually can, you know."

Pale, tense, her slight body seemingly dragged to one side by the weight of her scarf, Delia was a forlorn figure. "I've always known how to cut my losses and move along, but I can't forget her," she said. "Suddenly, I can't forget anything."

I didn't relay any of Delia's conversation to Zack that night, but I slept fitfully, haunted by Delia's account of sitting with her dead daughter, concerned about my husband's laboured breathing and the appearance of his pressure wound, and wondering whether I'd made a grave error by offering to pick Nadine up at the airport. In the small hours I went down to my office, turned on my laptop, and checked out the appearance of pressure wounds that were non-threatening and those that were dangerous. I couldn't tell the difference.

The next morning, for one of the few times in my life, I had to drag myself out of bed. It was an effort to complete my morning run with the dogs. When I got back to the house, all I wanted to do was sleep, but real life had its demands, and its unsettling surprises.

Nadine called when I was making the porridge. The fact that she was calling on her cell while she waited in line at Pearson International in Toronto might have accounted for her curtness, but the chill in her voice was undeniable.

"I've just been speaking to my lawyer in Regina," she said. "He's going to pick me up at the airport. Thank you for your offer, but Mr. Colby feels it would be ill-advised for you and me to spend time together."

I tried to defuse the situation. "I understand," I said. "Mr. Shreve feels exactly the same way."

"Well, Mr. Shreve is certainly the master of the game," Nadine said, and she hung up.

Henry Chan came by just as the porridge was ready. "That looks good," he said.

"Would you like some?"

"Thanks, but I've got appointments starting in half an hour. I just thought I'd check on my poker partner. How's he doing?"

"No worse, but no better. He still has a fever. That pressure sore we were concerned about still looks angry. And he's dealing with a case that's really gnawing at him."

Henry shrugged off his coat and went to the sink to wash his hands. "I can't believe that a firm the size of Falconer Shreve doesn't have somebody who could at least assist Zack with his case."

"It's not that. The case involves one of the partners, and they want it kept confidential."

"I'll talk to Zack about priorities if you want."

"It wouldn't do any good," I said. "If he wasn't in charge of this case, he'd be fretting about it."

"If that's what you've both decided . . . "

"We didn't both decide," I said. "Zack did."

Henry looked at me closely. "And you're unhappy."

"I did a little Internet reading last night."

Henry's chuckle was dry. "That would make anybody unhappy," he said.

"The article I read was about the danger of pressure sores. The writers focused on Christopher Reeve's case. He had the best possible medical care, but he had a pressure sore that became infected; the infection became systemic; he had a heart attack, went into a coma, and died. There was nothing anyone could do. He was fifty-two years old."

"I won't lie to you," Henry said. "Pressure sores are always a concern."

"And I'm not competent to judge whether what I'm looking at on my husband's back is just an abrasion or something serious. I'm out of my depth here, Henry, and I'm scared."

"We could put Zack in the hospital till this clears up."

"That has to be the last resort," I said. "Zack hates hospitals. He spent so much time in them when he was a kid. He loves our home. I know he'll get well faster here."

"How would you feel about getting a private nurse to come in to check once a day – keep an eye on the wound and give you a hand getting Zack in and out of the shower?"

"I would feel immensely relieved," I said.

"I'll get Gina to call Nightingale Nursing. They're expensive but they're good."

"I don't care how much it costs," I said. "I just want to be sure that nothing slips by me." Willie leaned heavily against my leg. "Henry, can you make sure the nurse is comfortable with dogs? Pantera is very protective of Zack."

Henry finished drying his hands on a paper towel. "I've noticed," he said.

After Henry left, I brought Zack's breakfast in and sat down with him while he made a heroic effort to eat what he clearly didn't feel like eating.

Finally, I took away the tray. "Can I get you something else?" I said.

"Do you know what I'd really like?"

"Name it. Eggs Benedict with smoked salmon? Steak tartare? Crepes Suzette?"

Zack made a face. "All of the above, but not today. Today, what I'd like is for you to get into bed with me. I'm tired. You're tired. Let's get some sleep."

I took off my jeans and shirt and slipped in beside my husband. He was very hot, but I was cold. I curled into him. "Is this okay?" I said.

"God, yes," he said. "You are so soft and so cool . . . "

I moved closer. "Zack, how would you feel about – "

He began to snore.

I lay there feeling his heat, listening to the familiar and reassuring buzz of his breathing. At one point he moved and groaned. The pressure wound was sensitive, and if his position wasn't right, it was painful.

I adjusted the pillows behind his back and then put my arms around him. "You are the love of my life," I said. "Don't leave me." I waited for a response, and when none was forthcoming, I too fell asleep.

Two hours later, I awoke. Zack was staring down at me. "Do you have any idea how hard it is to suppress a cough?"

"Why did you suppress it?"

"You were so peaceful. I didn't want to interrupt."

I stretched my arms. "Well, thanks. Because I slept like the proverbial log, and I feel about a hundred times better than I did before Henry came. How about you?"

"I woke up after a while and watched you sleep – almost as good as the real thing. Till this bug goes away, let's do this every day."

"Fine with me," I said. "I'm not going anywhere."

My husband drew me closer. "Neither am I, Ms. Shreve," he said. "Count on it."

I made Zack tea, showered, ate a crumpet dripping with butter over the sink, and finally felt ready to start the day. There was a note from Taylor on the kitchen table. She was in her studio working if we needed her. I glimpsed out the window, saw the light, and smiled. I checked my messages. Most of them were from people concerned about Zack's health, but Myra Brokaw's concern was not for my husband's well-being but her husband's legacy. She asked me to call her as soon as I'd "reviewed" her films of Theo, so we could discuss our next step.

It wasn't exactly Paul on the road to Damascus, but it was insight enough for me. Somewhere amidst the *sturm und drang* of the past days, it seemed we had all forgotten that the shortest distance between two points was a straight line. Myra had the answers to questions that were plaguing us. Myra had invited me over. I would accept her invitation and ask the questions.

When I got back to our bedroom, Zack was lying on his side thumbing his BlackBerry.

"Anything spectacular going on?" I asked.

"Lots," he said. "I guess the most pressing item is that Darryl Colby wants to see me."

"He'll have to come here," I said.

"I hate the idea of that creep coming into our home."

"It's Christmas. We'll be hospitable. I'll make cocoa and sugar cookies, and you can play 'You're a Mean One, Mr. Grinch' on the piano and ask him to sing along."

Zack shuddered. "Jesus, there's an image that'll ruin my morning. But I do have to meet with Darryl. I don't like him skulking around in the shadows."

"Can you put it off till tomorrow? Give yourself a day to get better."

"No. I have to move on this."

"Tell Darryl it'll be a ten-minute meeting," I said. I sat on the bed. "I've decided to move on something too," I said. "Myra called. I think she's hoping against hope that her home movies will have sealed the deal with NationTV. I'm going to pay her a visit."

"You going to let her down easily?" As Zack shifted his body, the expression on his face was pained. I reached over and adjusted the pillows behind his back. "Better?"

He nodded.

"To answer your question, yes, I'm going to let Myra down easily. I'm also going to ask her if she read Delia's letter, if she got in touch with Abby, and if Abby got in touch with her. Then I'm going to ask her how much Theo understands about the situation and suggest that she and Theo support the Wainbergs' attempt to get custody of Jacob."

Zack rolled his eyes. "What have you been smoking? Even I wouldn't try to pull that one off."

"I'm tired of letting this dominate our lives," I said.

"So am I," he said. "But storming the Brokaws' bastion seems out of character for you."

"Blame osmosis," I said. "When we were in bed together, all that body heat you were generating moved into me and made me a warrior."

He gave me a weak smile. "Go get 'em, tiger."

"That's my plan. And one more thing. Henry's going to send over a nurse to give us a hand for about an hour a day. I could use help getting you in and out of the shower. You're a sexy guy, but you're not a little guy. More seriously, I worry that I'm looking at that pressure sore through the eyes of hope. We can't afford to have me misread the signs."

"No," Zack said. "We can't. When's the nurse starting?"

"Today, I hope." I stroked his cheek. "I thought you'd fight me tooth and nail on this."

"Nope. When you crawled into bed with me this morning, you said that I was the love of your life and you didn't want me to leave. That goes both ways, Ms. Shreve."

"If you heard me, why didn't you say anything?"

"Because your words unmanned me," he said. "Let's do whatever it takes."

I walked through the snow to Taylor's studio. When I knocked, she invited me in – a sign that her work was going well. She was wearing ripped jeans, an old sweatshirt, and a pair of paint-spattered heavy wool socks. Her face shone with joy – a sign that she'd broken through the wall separating her from the art she wanted to make.

She held out her hand. "Come look," she said, and stepped aside so I could see her canvas. It was a self-portrait of her making art. She was standing at an angle to her easel. As she gazed critically at the work in progress, her head was tilted to one side and her expression was rapt. She wasn't smiling, but there was a stillness in her features that suggested that she was content with what she saw. Everything about the portrait, from the curve of her body to the way she held her brush, reminded me of Sally, but it wasn't just the subject matter that moved me; in some way I couldn't articulate, I knew that this piece represented a leap in Taylor's development as an artist. I gazed at it silently for a while.

Taylor's eyes searched my face. "Well?"

"It's the best work you've done."

"Why didn't you say something?" Her voice was unsure. The painting on the canvas was bold and assured, the creation of a mature artist, but Taylor was still fourteen years old, and she needed my approval.

I put my arm around her shoulder. "I was just overwhelmed – with how far you've come in your work. And everything about the painting reminds me of your mother – the hair is different, of course, but the expression on your face, even the way you hold your body, is the same. She had a certain stance when she was assessing her work. There's no way you could know that." I pointed towards the canvas. "But there it is."

Taylor's body tensed and when she spoke her voice was small and furious. "Jo, I am not my mother."

"You've always liked talking about her. You told me once it was a way of not losing her."

Taylor turned and went back to her canvas. The silence in the studio hung between us, heavy as the odour of paint in the air. When, finally, she spoke, Taylor didn't face me. "You don't know what it's like. When I Google my mother, every article and blog talks about how dazzling and brave she was as a painter, and how she wasn't afraid to live her life fully. No matter how good I am, people are going to measure me against her, and I'm just this boring kid. Declan says maybe I should change my last name to Shreve, then everyone will just say that for a lawyer's daughter, I'm a pretty good visual artist."

"Declan's a good friend."

Taylor dabbed her brush in a pot of paint and stared at her canvas. "He's more than that," she said.

"In what way?" I tried to sound cool and objective. I didn't make it.

Taylor turned away from her canvas with such fury that the paint on her brush flew off and spattered on my hand. "I was going to say that he's the only person who understands what I'm going through. It isn't always about sex, Jo. I'm not a skank like my mother."

"Taylor, your mother wasn't a skank. She was a complex human being who was just beginning to discover her own worth when she died."

I had delivered the eulogy at Sally's funeral. The chapel was full, but I was the only one present whose relationship with Sally went beyond the romantic or the professional. The eulogy I wrote had been carefully crafted to say all the right things without acknowledging the terrible truths at the heart of Sally's life. Ten years later as I stood watching her daughter's body trembling, I knew that I had finally found the words I should have used on that grey February day. Sally's life wasn't complete. That was the tragedy. She had just begun to discover her worth when her life ended.

I walked over to Taylor's painting and looked at it carefully. "You've only just begun. You don't have to measure yourself against anyone. You're that good." When I put my arm around my daughter, the paint that had spattered from her brush onto my hand dripped onto her shirt. "Sorry," I said. "I wrecked your shirt."

The shirt was already covered in paint. "It's okay," she said. "I have ten other shirts just like this one."

We both laughed, and then we moved so we could look more closely at the self-portrait. There was violence in the lines and the colours suggested turbulence in the relationship between artist and medium. "You're not where you want to be yet, are you?" I said.

She sighed heavily. "No. Not even close."

"But closer," I said. "Taylor, this really is the strongest work you've ever done. And you have something your mother never had. Time. You have time to get where you need to go. Find out who you are, and I have a feeling the rest will come."

CHAPTER

12

It was close to eleven when I parked in the space reserved for tenants and guests of the condo on Scarth Street. Louise Hunter's Mercedes was already there, and when I got off the elevator, I could hear her practising. I revelled in the moment, letting the Bach wash over me and watching the mirrored reflection of the twinkling white lights wound around a ficus by a window in the corridor. The morning had been a trying one. Despite what I'd told Zack about my bold plan of attack, I knew I was more roar than tiger. As I approached the door that held the wreath that was the twin of mine, I remembered Zack's observation that the French word for grenade was pomegranate. I pressed the bell, wondering how the grenade I was about to throw would change the lives of the people waiting for me inside.

Myra was dressed handsomely in a grey sweater and skirt, grey tights, and Capezio flats that matched the fuchsia in her patterned silk scarf. She tilted her head at the sound of the music.

"That must be lovely to listen to," I said.

"It is when the pianist is sober," Myra said. "Sadly, that has become increasingly rare of late."

I listened for a moment. "She sounds in fine form now."

Myra raised an eyebrow. "Have you heard Angela Hewitt play the Bach?"

The penny dropped. "We're listening to a recording," I said.

"Yes. Sad, isn't it? Louise Hunter and I haven't spoken much, but when we moved in, she told me she used the Hewitt recording to inspire her; now it seems she uses it to punish herself."

"Louise told you that?"

"She didn't have to. The sequence speaks for itself. At the beginning, when Louise was working towards what seemed like a realizable goal, she would listen to Hewitt, and then play the Bach. Every day her performance got stronger; suddenly, she just seemed to lose her way. Her playing became sloppy and inaccurate. She would pound the piano. Finally, she'd stop and put on the recording."

"And you think she's punishing herself by listening to how the Bach should be played?"

"I do. That's why I never complain when she's making a hash of it," Myra said. "Who knows what burdens another person is carrying?"

To quote Zack, Myra's words "unmanned" me, but I followed her into the apartment. There was no turning back. The tough questions had to be asked, and I was positioned to ask them.

I steeled myself but was immediately granted a reprieve. After Myra had taken my things, she touched my arm. "Could I ask a favour? I have a gift I absolutely must get in the mail. Normally, Theo comes with me, but he's having a bad day. I don't like to leave him alone. He becomes confused and angry, and I'm afraid he might hurt himself or do something foolish. If I get you two settled, would you be all right alone with him for twenty minutes?"

"Take your time," I said. "We'll be fine."

As she had before, Myra set the tea tray on the table. She filled our cups, excused herself, and slipped away. As soon as the door closed behind her, Theo smiled, removed the nesting doll from his pocket, and began the game he'd played the day he found them in my purse. He balanced the mother doll on his palm, said "I have a secret" in a light feminine voice, then opened the doll and produced the identical but smaller doll inside her. He repeated the sequence, pronouncing the words "I have a secret" in an increasingly high-pitched voice until he came to the last doll, the baby doll that could not be opened. "I am the secret," he said in a tiny, squeaky, child's voice.

With great care, Theo placed the nesting dolls on the table in front of him, arranging them according to size; then he extended a slender forefinger and, smiling, stroked the shiny painted head of each doll in turn. He picked up the smallest doll, cradled it in his palm, and then raised his eyes to look at me. "This is the baby," he said. His brow furrowed and he regarded me with suspicion. "You have a baby," he said.

"No," I said. "But there was a baby at my house, the day you visited. You brought me a package. Remember? Then you sang to the baby."

His eyes met mine. They had seemed opaque, but suddenly they cleared. "Was it your baby?"

"No." I touched his hand. "Theo, it was your baby. Your grandson. That's what I came to tell you today."

He looked at the wooden doll in his hand. "This is the baby," he said. His finger moved back and forth across the nesting dolls. One of these is his mama," he said. "But which one?"

I took his hand in mine and moved it back to the doll the baby doll had been inside. "This is the mama," I said. Then I moved my finger to the larger doll next to it. "This is the grandmother. Think of this as Delia – Delia Margolis. She clerked for you many years ago. Do you remember Delia?"

Theo's brown eyes were confused. He moved his finger back to the smaller doll, the doll that contained the baby. "This is the mama."

"I have a picture of Delia's daughter," I said. "Would you like to see it?"

I took the Christmas card Alwyn had given me and handed it to Theo. I started to identify Abby, but he seemed to recognize her. "That's my girl," he said, and there was rapture in his voice.

I didn't understand, but I seized the moment. "That's right," I said. "That's your daughter."

He grabbed the photo and looked at me angrily. "Not my daughter. My girl. My clever girl." He turned his eyes back to the photograph.

"She looks very much like her mother," I said. "It's easy to make a mistake. But this is Delia's daughter. The daughter you and Delia had together."

He looked at me angrily. "No," he said. He stood abruptly and began pacing the room, the card still in his hand. Finally, he stopped at a magazine rack. He took out a magazine, slid the card between its pages, and replaced it in the rack. He sighed heavily, like a man who had completed a complex and onerous task; then his eyes lit on the nesting dolls, and he hurried to place them back inside one another again. When finally they were all safely inside the mother doll, he slid the doll into his pocket and patted it contentedly. "My girl," he said. "My clever girl."

When Myra returned, Theo and I had finished our tea and were sitting silently. He didn't look up when his wife entered the apartment. Myra took off her coat and scarf, then came over and handed Theo a paper bag from a coffee house. He tore it open with boyish impatience.

"Biscotti," Myra said. "Theo's mad for them. I think they taste like cardboard, but when we're out on a walk, his feet always lead us to a shop that sells them." Her husband dunked a biscotto greedily in his tea, and Myra smiled. "I try to indulge him in his small pleasures."

"He's lucky to have you," I said.

Myra's mouth curved in a half-smile. "Wisdom comes from loss," she said. "It takes a wise man to realize that when he's lost everything else, his wife may have to be enough."

I stood. "Myra, could I speak to you for a moment? Privately?"

Myra signalled her understanding with a nod and walked me to the door of her study. We both glanced at Theo. His attention was fixed on his snack, but we kept our voices low. "I take it this isn't about the project," Myra said.

"No," I said.

We stepped inside and closed the door behind us. I drew a breath and plunged in. "Theo knows that Delia Wainberg gave birth to his child," I said.

There was something flat and cynical in Myra's face. "My husband knows there was a child," she said. "No one knows for a certainty if it's his. I doubt if Delia Margolis knows herself."

I met Myra's gaze. "Delia knows that Theo was the father of her child, Myra. That's a fact. Here's another one. Three weeks ago when their daughter, Abby Michaels, wrote to her asking for genetic information, Delia gave her Theo's name. I think it's a safe assumption that Abby Michaels communicated with Theo. By then, you were handling Theo's correspondence. Did you answer her letter?"

"I ignored it."

"But Delia received a note saying the matter had been taken care of, and the note was signed with Theo's initials."

Myra's gaze was cool. "It seemed the easiest way of dealing with something that was no longer of consequence. Like many things in Theo's life, Ms. Michaels was part of the past. Anyway, I understand she's dead, so that really is the end of it."

I tried to keep my voice steady. "Her child is alive. He has a right to know his genetic history."

Myra's voice was a knife. "Joanne, I'm not going to discuss this – not now. Not ever." She walked out of the study and waited at the front door until I'd put on my coat. She stood over me as I pulled on my boots. Even after I pushed the button for the elevator, Myra watched warily from the threshold to her apartment. Clearly, she wanted to make certain I was going to pass through the elevator doors and vanish from her life, but fate was not on Myra's side.

When the elevator opened, Noah Wainberg stepped out, and he was holding Jacob in his car seat.

If he noticed Myra hovering, Noah ignored her. He came directly to me. "Jo, you have no idea how glad I am that you're here," he said. "When I saw your Volvo parked out back, I became a believer."

My heart was pounding. "Is it Zack?" I said.

"No, Zack's fine. I was talking to him twenty minutes ago."

"And he's all right?"

"Sounded okay. The new nurse you hired showed up."

"Does Zack like her?"

"I guess. They're both Colts fans. Anyway, I'm sorry I scared you. I'm here because Declan Hunter called. Louise didn't come home last night, and she's not answering her cell. I told him that she might have spent the night in her studio. Sometimes when she's practising, she doesn't hear the phone."

"Well, Louise is in her studio. At least, she was. I got here about half an hour ago, and she was playing a recording."

Noah sighed. "Well, that's something. It's hard to look for a needle in a haystack when you have a six-month-old side-kick." He bent to nuzzle Jacob, and then raised his eyes to me. "I have a key to Louise's studio, but if she's been drink-ing, I can't handle both her and Jacob. Could you take care of him for a minute while I see what's going on?"

Noah put the car seat on the floor. I unbuckled Jacob, zipped him out of his snowsuit, and picked him up. "My lucky day," I said.

When he saw a strange face, Jacob howled. I waved Noah off. "He'll be fine. Go ahead and do what you have to do. I'll wait here."

I turned so that Jacob couldn't see Noah opening the door to Louise's studio, but Jacob was not fooled, and his cries grew even lustier.

I glanced over my shoulder to make sure Noah had managed to get inside Louise's studio, before I took Jacob over to look at the lights on the ficus tree. I was in the clear, or almost. Myra was just shutting the door to their apart-ment when Theo burst past his wife and reached to take Jacob out of my arms. Myra's voice was commanding. "No," she said. She grabbed Theo's sweater, but his need to soothe the child was strong.

"It's all right," I said. "Theo, why don't you sit on that chair over by your door, and I'll hand Jacob to you."

Theo's dark eyes darted anxiously from the baby to his wife. "You can sing to Jacob," I said. "The way you did at my house. He liked your voice, remember?" I moved towards the chair. "Sing to Jacob again, Theo."

Myra was glaring at me, but I ignored her. Theo sat down and held out his arms, and I placed the baby in them. The lullaby Theo sang was the same one he'd sung at our house.

His voice was sweet and the baby soon stopped crying. Myra positioned herself on one side of the chair, and I stayed on the other. When Noah emerged from the studio and took in the triptych, he shot me a questioning look. "Theo's helping us out," I said.

"Thank you, Theo," Noah said. Oblivious to everything but Jacob, Theo didn't acknowledge the comment.

Noah's eyes came back to me. "Louise is in pretty rough shape. I'm going to drive her home." He took out his keys. "Can we trade cars? You'll need the base for the baby seat in our car."

I took Noah's keys, fished mine from my bag, and handed them to him.

"I won't be long," he said. "Just take Jacob home with you and I'll pick him up after I get Louise settled."

"Zack's got that flu," I said. "It might be wiser if I took him to UpSlideDown. You can pick him up there when you're ready."

"Okay. Good," Noah said. "Why don't you take off now? I'll help Louise get her coat and boots on. She'd be humiliated if you saw her drunk again." Noah went back into the studio and I bent to take Jacob from Theo's arms. "This little guy has to go home now," I said.

Theo's eyes found Myra. "No," he said. His look was beseeching; he was seeking support, but none was forthcoming.

Myra's took his arm. "It's time to go inside," she said firmly. Then her voice shifted to the wheedling tone of parents dealing with stubborn children. "We have biscotti and I'll make you that coffee you like."

"You always say that and then you . . . " He hung his head. He had lost the words with which to argue. He handed Jacob to me meekly. "Don't let her . . . " The sentence was unfinished. I didn't know whether the 'her' meant Myra or me.

I took the baby. "You'll see him again, I promise."

Theo released his hold on Jacob, and Myra took Theo's arm and led him inside. Through the closed door, I could hear Theo's sobs. Knowing I had been the source of his pain made me sick at heart. I longed to leave, but I found that I couldn't take a step until the cries ceased. When finally the corridor grew quiet, I snapped Jacob into his car seat and pressed the button for the elevator. I was still waiting for it to arrive when Myra Brokaw came out of her apartment. For the only time since I'd met her, she was dishevelled. She had lost one of the turquoise-studded silver combs with which she held back her thick hair, and her face was blotched with anger. "Delia Margolis needn't think she was the only one," Myra hissed. "She was simply the first of many. My husband was always drawn to the same type: clever, pale, and Semitic."

She slammed the door. The elevator arrived and I stepped in with Jacob's carrier on my arm. I looked down at him. "Granted Myra was under stress," I said. "But that was still a really shitty thing to say." Jacob gazed at me thoughtfully.

As soon as I got Jacob snapped into his car seat, I called Zack. "How's it going?"

"Pretty good," he said. "I've been bathed and shaved, and the sheets are clean, so I'm ready for action."

"Really?"

"No," he said, "But Kym – incidentally, that's Kym with a y – assures me the pressure sore is looking marginally better."

"Thank God," I said.

"Agreed, so when are you coming home? I miss you."

"One more stop," I said. "I'll explain when I get there. It's been a bizarre couple of hours, but as long as you're okay . . . "

"Do what you have to do. Darryl Colby is coming over at three. If the day is inching towards the bizarre, Darryl will push it over the edge."

"I'll be there long before that," I said.

As I drove over to UpSlideDown, I kept repeating the reassuring words of my yoga teacher. "All will be well," I said. "All will be well."

UpSlideDown was even livelier than usual. Volunteers were packing up the gifts that had been collected for the Holiday Blast at the Core Recreational Centre, and some of the young guests were reluctant to see the gifts that had been mounting under the tree with such promise suddenly disappear. There were tears and reassurances, and when Mieka passed by Jacob and me, her arms full of presents, she murmured, "Next year, remind me to do the transfer of gifts under cover of darkness."

"Will do," I said. "I'll also remind you that Clare Booth Luce said, 'No good deed goes unpunished.'"

Mieka exhaled loudly. "You can put that one on my grave."

"Did people donate enough gifts?"

"We'll know later. The organizers at Core Recreational are going to call if there's an age group that's missing out. My plan is to hit Zack up for a fat cheque to fill the holes, and you and I can do some quick shopping. Sound okay?"

"Sure. Zack's a generous guy."

"How's that flu of his?"

"We brought in a part-time nurse to help."

Mieka's face clouded. "Zack isn't getting worse, is he?"

"No. The nurse is only coming in for a couple of hours a day. I just needed a little backup."

My daughter narrowed her eyes. "You are looking a bit worn."

"I forgot to put on makeup."

"I have an emergency supply in the cloakroom. Let me unload these parcels; then Jacob can entertain me while you give L'Oréal a chance to work its magic."

Mieka and Jacob were playing peek-a-boo when I came back from the cloakroom. Mieka gave me an approving nod. "Much better," she said. "Why don't you pour yourself a cup of coffee and enjoy the moment."

Logic would have suggested that Nadine Perrault pay a visit to UpSlideDown as soon as she arrived in Regina. I'd given her Mieka's business and home addresses and told her that in the days before her death Abby had spent part of every day at UpSlideDown. Still, that snowy afternoon, when Nadine came through the door, I was taken by surprise.

Her blonde hair was tucked under a black cloche, and her black scarf was knotted with the casual flair that seems to be the birthright of French women. In her grey wool pea coat, closely fitted grey slacks, and knee-high leather boots, Nadine was a figure of elegance, but elegance doesn't cut it when the mercury is hovering at thirty below. As she gazed around UpSlideDown, she hugged herself. Clearly, she was chilled to the bone, but despite the tempting warmth of the room, when she spotted me, she turned as if to leave.

I stood. "Nadine, stay. Jacob's here."

Her eyes sought out the baby, and when she saw him in Mieka's arms, she moved past the bright Christmas tree and the playing children and went straight to him.

After three weeks, Nadine was inches away from the child she loved; yet her first words were for me. "Thank you for not being angry," she said. "I regretted my rudeness as soon as I broke the connection at the airport. Now I'm doubly sorry."

I gestured to an empty chair at our table. "This is a terrible situation," I said. "You and Delia have been living through the worst hours of your lives for days now. That kind of tension takes a toll."

Nadine looked at Jacob, her face filled with longing. Mieka's eyes found mine. I nodded, and Mieka handed the baby to Nadine. Jacob held his hands out to her and smiled.

"He likes to sit, don't you, Jacob?" Mieka said.

At the sound of his name, the baby turned towards Mieka.

Nadine adjusted his position, so he could sit on her lap and she could look into his face. "You're growing up," she said, and her voice was low and gentle.

"Three weeks is a long time in a baby's life."

Nadine's smile was wry. "A long time in my life too."

Jacob watched her attentively. "I don't know anything about child development," Nadine said, "but Jacob seems very advanced. I guess all mothers . . . " She corrected herself. "I guess everyone believes that their baby is special."

Mieka put three bright rubber blocks that looked like bugs on the table. Jacob reached over and tried repeatedly to place one of the blocks atop another. "Jacob really is advanced," my daughter said. "Not many children his age even attempt that."

"Abby wanted a clever child," Nadine said. "Her criteria in choosing a father for her baby were stringent, and high intelligence was at the top of the list."

"Do you know the father?" Mieka asked. The question grew out of the conversation so naturally that Nadine didn't appear to find it intrusive.

She shook her head. "No. Abby felt it would be difficult if I knew who he was. She was right. It would have been incredibly painful to think of her being intimate with someone I knew. Of course, even though I never knew who the man was, I spent hours imagining what he was like. I always thought it was someone who had already proven himself in the world. Abby wouldn't have risked going through a relationship with a man unless she was as certain as one could be that she'd give birth to the child she wanted."

After that, we were all silent. Jacob played with his three bright bug blocks, stacking them, knocking them over, and stacking them again.

"Why don't I get us a carafe of coffee," Mieka said finally.

"None for me, thanks," Nadine said. "I'm content just to watch Jacob."

I touched her arm. "Nadine, any time now Noah Wainberg is going to meet me here to pick up Jacob, so if you'd rather not see him . . . "

"I appreciate the warning," she said. "But I'll stay. Maybe we've been given a second chance."

Noah arrived almost immediately. I introduced him to Nadine. When Jacob saw Noah's familiar grin, he held out his arms and said, "Da."

"He is a clever boy," Nadine said.

"You should see him when he's on the move." Noah looked at Nadine. "If you have a few minutes, we could put Jacob down and let him show you his stuff."

"I have all the time in the world," Nadine said.

Noah shrugged off his coat, picked up one of the mats Mieka kept for babies learning to crawl, and unrolled it on the floor. Nadine put Jacob down and placed the bug blocks at the far end of the mat. When Jacob dug his fingers and toes into the mat to press himself towards the pile, Nadine clapped her hands in delight.

Mieka walked me to the door. "Score one for second chances," she said.

When I got home there was a shiny black Lincoln in our driveway. I walked through the front door and was met by air heavy with the scent of musk. Seemingly, Darryl Colby had arrived early. As I took off my boots and greeted Willie, a man, who I deduced was Darryl Colby, came down the hall towards me.

He was tall, heavy-set, and deeply tanned; his hair, black as a raven's wing, was freshly barbered. As he came nearer, it was clear Darryl Colby used aftershave as a weapon. He was scowling, and I didn't blame him. Pantera was behind him, his nose lodged between the man's legs, pushing him towards the door. Pantera rarely left Zack's side, so the situation must have been grave.

"Leave it," I said. Pantera stopped, withdrew his snout, and loped back down the hall to our room.

"Pantera's protective," I said.

"He's a menace," Darryl Colby said, wiping drool from his slacks. "He's ruined this suit."

"When you have it dry cleaned, please send us the bill," I said. "Shall I show you to the door or can you find your way?"

"I can find my way," he said. He jammed his feet into a pair of toe rubbers on the mat in the hall and stormed out.

I went down to our room. Zack was dressed and sitting in his wheelchair. "I take it your meeting didn't go well," I said.

Zack shrugged. "Could have been worse. Darryl could have kicked me in the nads."

"Actually, Pantera may have done some damage to Darryl's nads," I said. "Your dog had his muzzle shoved pretty firmly into Mr. Colby's private parts. Pantera's never done that before. What happened?"

Zack's smile was innocent. "Peter told me that the night Noah brought Jacob by, he taught Pantera to obey the command 'push.' So when Darryl stepped out of line, I gave the command."

I laughed. "You'd better watch it," I said. "Darryl Colby strikes me as a litigious kind of guy."

"My favourite kind," Zack said. "Now, could you help me get back into bed? Strategically, it was important for me to deal with Darryl from an upright position, but I'm beat."

Zack shifted his chair so he could transfer his body from the chair to the bed. I didn't comment when the move made him groan. I helped him ease his body into a lying position, unzipped his trousers, and pulled them off. "So the meeting did not go well?"

"Nah, just the usual shit. Darryl has lined up some people who are prepared to swear that Delia is, to put it kindly, an absent mother. I was prepared for that. I was also ready for his dark allusions to Noah's violent past. But Darryl always surprises me."

Zack pointed to some glossy black-and-white photos on the nightstand. "Check out the new additions to the Wainberg family photo album."

I flipped through the photos. In all of them Noah was holding Louise Hunter in his arms. They were both laughing. Louise's hair was tousled; her strapless gown had slipped on one side, revealing a nipple, and Noah's hand was cupping her small breast.

I studied the photograph. "Who says pictures never lie? This looks bad, but if there'd been a photographer around the night I was putting Louise to bed, he could have snapped equally provocative pictures of us."

"You know that, and I know that, but a family court judge wouldn't, and Darryl assures me there are plenty more where these came from. His investigators have also dug up watchful neighbours who will testify that Noah spent the night at Louise's on more than one occasion."

"That's disgusting," I said. "Not the fact that Noah stayed with Louise, just that an act of kindness can be deliberately distorted."

"We're doing it, too," Zack said. "When Nadine and Abby were estranged, Nadine took a group of students to France. There were rumours that she became involved with one of the girls."

I helped Zack into his pyjama bottoms. "There are always rumours like that."

"These rumours were serious enough to warrant investigation."

"And . . . ?"

"And nothing was proven."

"Nadine still has her job," I said. "She teaches at a fine school, and they've produced a lot of lawyers. Nadine wouldn't be teaching if there were any questions."

"You sound like Darryl Colby."

"I sound like a sensible person."

"Well, that makes you a rarity in this situation."

"Actually, it doesn't," I said. "Before I came home I was at UpSlideDown with Jacob. Noah had asked me to take care of the baby because Declan needed his help with Louise. Anyway, while I was at UpSlideDown, Nadine Perrault arrived. She must have come straight from the airport. She held Jacob and she and Mieka talked. When Noah showed up, he asked Nadine if she'd like to stay and play with Jacob for a while."

"Reassuring to know that there's some decency in the world," Zack said. "Every so often the Darryl Colbys and the Zack Shreves crowd out the good guys."

"You're a good guy," I said. "I'm not so sure about me any more."

My husband opened his arms, and I leaned in. "Did you get knocked around a bit today?" he asked.

"I did. My visit to the Brokaws was a disaster. When I left, Theo was sobbing and Myra was livid. On the bright side, my blundering did result in one interesting piece of information. Myra told me that Theo had had many women, and all his women were the same type as Delia: 'clever, pale, and Semitic.' That's a direct quote."

Zack shook his head. "You hear something like that and it really does make you wonder about the old chicken-and-egg question."

"You mean, which came first?"

"Right. Did Theo play around because Myra was a piece of work, or did Myra become a piece of work because Theo played around?"

CHAPTER

13

A phone call at midnight seldom brings good news, but since I'd married Zack, the shrill of a telephone in our sleep-quiet house had ceased to terrify me. Clients and enemies of trial lawyers tend to keep irregular hours, and so as I groped for the phone the night after my visit to the Brokaws', I was more resigned than alarmed. The voice on the other end of the line was low, breathy, and vicious.

"Do you have any idea what you've donc?" thc voice said. "Listen."

I kept the phone to my ear a beat too long before I started to hang up. My caller was obviously holding out the phone to pick up the noise in the room. The sound I heard was primal – a man keening a loss whose magnitude I could only imagine. I knew immediately that Myra Brokaw was on the other end of the line, and that I had somehow speeded Theo Brokaw's descent into the abyss.

Beside me, Zack stirred and mumbled. I slid out of bed and moved across the room. "All right," I said. "I'm listening, Myra. What's happened?"

She spit out the words. "I found that picture you gave

him – the picture of that 'clever girl,' as he calls her. I found it, and I made him watch as I ripped it up. There will be no more clever girls in his life and he knows it. Listen to him."

Theo's wails grew louder. Surprisingly, I was able to keep my voice steady. "Myra, Theo needs help. Take your husband to Emergency and get him admitted."

Her laugh was harsh. "Oh, that would be perfect, wouldn't it? Having Theo out of my control and medicated. Under those conditions, he would be capable of saying or doing anything. Believe me, I know. That would be the end of Mr. Justice Theodore Brokaw. That would be the end of the intellectual jewel of Canada's Supreme Court."

"Myra, if there's anything I can do to help, I will."

"Stay out of our lives," she said.

"I will," I said. "Good night." I hung up, turned off the ringer on the phone, and crawled back into bed.

"Who was that?" Zack mumbled.

"We'll talk about it in the morning," I said. I put my arms around him and hoped he couldn't feel the pounding of my heart.

In December in Saskatchewan, the sun doesn't rise until almost nine, but dogs have their own internal clocks, and by five-thirty the next morning Willie and Pantera were pacing.

When I started to slide out of bed, Zack caught my wrist. "So what was that phone call in the middle of the night about?"

"It was Myra Brokaw," I said. "I did something stupid, and she wanted to make sure I was aware of the consequences."

"Stay here where it's warm and tell me what happened," Zack said.

I lay back down and put my arms around him. "Yesterday when I went to the Brokaws', I had what seemed at the time to be a stroke of luck. Myra wanted to mail a gift, so she left me alone with Theo. As I'd planned to, I told him he had a daughter. He didn't seem to grasp what I was saying, so I took out the family photo the Michaelses used as their greeting card last Christmas. Alwyn gave me hers for Jacob. The resemblance between Abby and Delia is so striking, I thought Theo might make the connection. Anyway, I showed it to him."

Zack whistled. "That was a high-stakes move."

"It was a stupid move."

"Did Theo react?"

"He did," I said. "He thought it was a photo of Delia. He called her 'his girl,' 'his clever girl.' He hid the picture in a magazine. Apparently, Myra found it. When she called last night, she told me she made Theo watch as she ripped it up. Zack, as long as I live, I will never forget the sound of that man's anguish. It was terrible, and it was my fault."

"You weren't the one who ripped up the picture, Jo."

"But I was the one who took it to the Brokaws' home."

"You had no way of knowing . . . "

"The truth is I didn't care. I just wanted the whole mess to be over. You were sick. We were both exhausted, and I was scared."

"That's not a crime," Zack said quietly.

"Maybe not, but what I did to Theo was stupid, and now there are consequences."

"The consequences may not all be bad," Zack said. "What kind of professional help is Theo getting?"

"None that I know of. Myra anticipates Theo's every wish. I think she enjoys the role of caregiver. She told me yesterday that a wise man realizes that when he's lost everything else, his wife has to be enough."

"But Myra isn't enough. Theo's problems are complex. I'm no expert, but I imagine that there are medications and therapies that could help him."

"So you're saying I can stop feeling guilty because Theo had to hit bottom before he could get the care he needs."

"That's about it."

I kissed my husband. "Nice try," I said. "But I'm not buying."

When I got back from my run with the dogs, Zack was on the phone. "Ready for some good news?" he asked.

I peeled off my outer layers and flopped on the bed. "God, yes."

"That was Noah on the phone. He's coming over later. He wants us to stop investigating Nadine Perrault."

"Hallelujah," I said. "I take it Nadine's side will reciprocate."

"Nadine has already agreed. Darryl Colby will shit bricks when he sees his golden goose slip from his slimy fingers."

"Glad to see the flu hasn't robbed you of your way with words," I said. "So what happens now?"

"I guess that's what Noah's coming to discuss."

"Will Delia be with him?"

"He didn't say, but I can't imagine this is a unilateral decision. Anyway, Izzy's coming."

"Taylor will be happy to hear that." I looked at him carefully. "Are you sure you're up for this?"

"Yeah, I'm feeling better."

"Honestly?"

"Absolutely. I had an erotic dream last night. That has to be a good sign."

"The best," I said.

"Kym's coming over in a few minutes to give me a shower and shave."

"Really," I said. "So was the erotic dream about me or Kym?"

Zack smirked. "You know how erotic dreams are – everyone just kind of swims together."

I turned so I could see Zack's face. "What does Kym look like anyway?"

His expression was noncommittal. "Nice-looking, I guess – not as nice-looking as you."

"That was the right answer," I said.

He tapped his temple with his forefinger. "That's why I earn the big bucks."

The doorbell rang. "That must be Kym with a y," I said. "I should have put on makeup."

"Kym with a y doesn't wear makeup."

I groaned. "Now I really hate her."

I opened the door to a red-headed bodybuilder with a brush cut, rosy cheeks, and a killer handshake. "You must be Joanne," he said.

"And you're Kym," I said. "You have no idea how glad I am to meet you."

I stood aside to let him come in. After he'd taken off his boots and jacket, Kym rubbed his hands together. "This warmth feels good. I had a cold walk from home."

"Where do you live?"

"In the old nurses' residences down by the General."

"Nice digs," I said.

"They are," he agreed. "Hardwood floors, high ceilings. Big rooms. Neighbourhood's a little sketchy, but you can't have everything. How's Zack this morning?"

"Trying to do too much, but I don't say anything."

"Very wise," Kym said. "Why don't I go spiff him up? Give you a break."

On the way down the hall, I caught a glimpse of myself in the mirror and decided I could use a little spiffing up myself. Taylor was already in her studio so I showered in her bathroom, and helped myself to her copious supply of beauty products. The result was a decided improvement. I made coffee, tried to call Taylor, but her cell wasn't on, so the dogs and I walked through the snow to her studio. This time when I knocked, my daughter came to the door instead of inviting me in. "Troubles?" I said.

"No. I just want to work on it for a while before you see it again."

"Fair enough," I said. "Isobel's coming over."

"That's good. She can come out here and read while I work. She's interested in that poetry book you got me for my birthday."

"That's okay with Isobel?"

"Yeah," Taylor said. "She and I like doing separate things together."

"I underestimate you," I said.

Taylor frowned and turned back to her canvas. "It evens out."

"Meaning?"

She gave me the Sally smile. "Sometimes we underestimate you."

Kym met me by the hall linen closet when I came in. "I changed the sheets," he said.

"Our washing machine's getting a workout," I said. "I just changed those sheets last night."

"I know, but Zack still has a fever, and clean sheets feel good."

"I'm enjoying them too."

"Zack tells me you're still sharing a bed – despite the coughing and sweats and chills."

"That's part of the deal, isn't it?" I said.

Kym nodded. "So they tell me. I'd better check on Zack. He wanted to shave."

"Why don't I go in and keep him company with that," I said. "He must be the last man in the world to use a straight razor."

When I went in, Zack was wearing a robe and sitting in his wheelchair shaving.

Being a paraplegic is expensive. Zack's bathroom was, in the phrase of the day, "universal," which meant it could be used by pretty much anyone whatever their physical limitations. We had been adamant about not having the bathroom look like a hospital, so all the features Zack needed to function independently had been incorporated into an innovative design that was sleek and beautiful.

I sat down on the edge of the bathtub. "Need anything?" I asked.

"Just someone to talk to," he said. "What are you up to today?"

"I thought since Kym and the Wainbergs are going to be here for a couple of hours, I'd get all my errands out of the way. We're supposed to get more snow this afternoon, so I thought you and I could crawl into bed and watch Tim Burton's *The Nightmare Before Christmas*."

Zack rinsed the soap off his razor. "I thought we were living The Nightmare Before Christmas."

"This version has songs," I said. "And it's funny."

"Bring it on," Zack said. He placed his razor back in its case, and turned his chair towards the door.

"After you're settled, I'm going to pick up groceries," I said. "Anything strike your fancy?

"Do we have any more of that chicken soup?"

"No, but I can make some. No problem at all. And I have to hit the mall – briefly. Mieka called, and the Core Rec Centre has seven boys between ages of fourteen and seventeen on their list and not a single present for that age group. I thought I'd get some Sports Mart gift certificates."

"Wise choice. Sports Mart has neat stuff. Jo, I'd like to make a donation too. Falconer Shreve's had a good year, and when I was a kid, I spent a lot of hours in places like the

Core Rec Centre. The Christmas party was always a big deal. Give me a minute to find my chequebook."

When the Wainbergs arrived, I told Isobel that Taylor was in her studio and that Pablo Neruda's *Odes to Common Things* was somewhere on her desk. Isobel's face lit up. "I love Neruda," she said before dashing off to get the book.

Noah's complexion was usually ruddy with health, but that morning, he was grey and careworn. After Isobel wandered down the hall to Taylor's bedroom, I poured him a cup of coffee. "Are you okay?" I said.

"I'm fine. I guess none of us is getting any younger. How's the man in your life?"

"His nurse, Kym, whom I am delighted to discover is a strapping young man, is here to keep track of him and decide when he's ready to confront the world again."

Noah added cream and sugar to his coffee. "Delia will be relieved to know that Zack's being well taken care of."

"How about you?" I said.

"I have broad shoulders, and we seem to be moving in the right direction. Did Zack tell you that Nadine Perrault and I agreed to call off the private investigators?"

"He did, and it's good news. As the needlepoint pillow my grandmother gave me says, 'Least said, soonest mended.' I keep the pillow in my office at the university. It's been very helpful over the years."

Noah gave me a sidelong glance. "If they handed that pillow out to new lawyers, the litigation rate in this country would drop by 90 per cent."

"Would that be a bad thing?"

He smiled. "I don't get a vote. A lawyer who doesn't practise is a eunuch."

I sat down opposite him. "Well, I'm not a lawyer, and I think that as a husband and father you're handling this very well. One way or another, you and Delia are going to have a permanent relationship with Nadine. You don't want to start out under a cloud of accusations and counter-accusations."

"Agreed. There's been enough ugliness. It's time to turn the page. Nadine and I discussed something along the lines of an open adoption."

"But Jacob would live with you and Delia."

Noah's blue eyes flashed. "Absolutely. That issue was never on the table. Nadine's a realist. She knows that if this case came to court, she'd lose." The tension left his face. "The point is that there isn't going to be a court case. Nadine was remarkably open about her mental state. Mourning Abby is taking a heavy toll. Nadine says she's exhausted and is having difficulty concentrating. We agreed that Jacob deserves better."

"He does," I said, "and so does Nadine. Finding out the hard way that she isn't capable of giving Jacob what he needs would only be another blow for her. My children weren't as young as Jacob when their father died, but I still cringe when I remember how badly I failed them during those first months. It was all I could do to get out of bed in the morning."

Noah looked at me hard. "That doesn't sound like you."

"*I* wasn't like me,' I said. "I know what Nadine's going through because I've been through it. And it's more than just the loss of a partner you love, it's believing that the death was absolutely arbitrary – a case of being in the wrong place at the wrong time."

"I don't think I ever heard how your husband died."

"The newspapers called it 'The Good Samaritan Murder.' Ian was coming back to Regina from a funeral in Swift Current. There was a blizzard. The driver of a stranded car flagged him down and when Ian got out to help, the driver and her boyfriend beat him to death with a tire iron."

Noah stared at his coffee cup. "I'm sorry, Jo. I didn't know."

"For months, the authorities treated Ian's murder as a chance occurrence – a case of someone being in the wrong place at the wrong time."

"Like Abby."

"Exactly," I said. "And, Noah, you have no idea how terrible it was. I'd been so certain that I could build a cocoon around our family by cooking balanced meals, observing the speed limit, and making regular appointments for us all to get our medical and dental check-ups. Losing Ian to what seemed like an existential blowout made me question the underpinnings of my life."

"And you think that's what Nadine's going through?"

"I do. Abby was a woman who left nothing to chance; yet she was raped and murdered by a stranger in a strange city. When something like that happens, the old safe world disappears, and there's nothing to hold onto – at least that's the way it was for me."

"Nadine says she's dreading going back to the house she and Abby shared. I suggested she stay in Regina for a while. She could spend time with Jacob and get to know us a little better."

"How does Delia feel about that?"

"I haven't asked her," Noah said. "I'm hoping to enlist Zack's support."

As if on cue, Zack wheeled into the room, Pantera at his side.

"Enlist my support in what?" he asked.

"Noah thinks it's time to be conciliatory towards Nadine," I said. "I agree. A little kindness at this point will ease tensions, and we could all use that." I kissed his forehead. "I'd better get moving. The sooner I leave, the sooner I can come home."

"I'm for that," Zack said. "Hey, you forgot the cheque."

He handed me the envelope and I dropped it in my bag. Pantera looked anxious. I patted his head. "Take care of Zack," I said. "If anybody suspicious shows up, remember your command and *push*."

Since the evening of the Luther concert, our holidays had been short on comfort and joy, but the sheltered world of UpSlideDown offered both in abundance. Mieka and the girls had decorated the tree with children's mittens, scarves, and toques – all donated, all destined for good homes. The air smelled of brewing coffee and fresh baking; in the background, very softly, a CD of children's songs was playing one of my favourites, the lullaby from Humperdinck's *Hansel and Gretel*. No child was crying. No child was screaming. No child was having a tantrum. It was a fragile peace, but it was good enough for me.

Mieka was standing at the entrance to the kitchen talking to a young woman wearing a Saskatchewan Roughriders ski jacket and toque. When my daughter spotted me, she motioned me over.

"Mum, this is Lisa Wallace from the Core Rec Centre," she said. "Lisa, this is my mum, Joanne Shreve."

I reached into my bag. "Perfect timing," I said, handing her the gift certificates. "I was just dropping these off for the teenaged boys on your list."

"Thanks," Lisa said. "Adolescent boys like to swagger, but they're still just kids, and they look forward to the Core Rec party."

"And I have a cheque from my husband." I held it out to Lisa.

"This is a godsend," she said. "With the recession we've had a lot of corporate donors pull out."

"Zack's a trial lawyer," I said. "I think every year is a good year for them."

Lisa eyed the envelope. "Would it be rude if I peeked to see how good?"

"Be my guest," I said.

She ripped open the envelope and glanced at the cheque. "Wow," she said. "That's more than generous, Joanne. We'll send your husband a tax receipt, of course, but until I get it in the mail, please tell him we're very grateful."

"When Zack was growing up, he spent a lot of time in places like Core Rec. I guess it all comes around."

Lisa looked thoughtful. "It's surprising how often it does," she said. She zipped her jacket. "I'll see you at the party, Mieka. Nice meeting you, Joanne, and thanks again."

"My pleasure."

"Lisa has a tough job," I said.

"She does," Mieka said, "and she gets paid zip, but she believes in what she does. I believe in what she does, too. She and I have talked about opening an UpSlideDown in the Core. Minimal charge, but mums and dads would have to stay in the playroom with their kids, the way parents do here." Mieka took my arm. Her eyes shone, and her tone was fervent. "The idea is first for the kids to have fun and second for parents, who are often very young, to learn parenting skills. Nothing heavy-handed – just learning by observing and doing. The mums and dads who come to UpSlideDown are always telling me how watching other families helps them figure out how to handle problems or to realize that a behaviour that was worrying them is perfectly normal."

Mieka's excitement about the project was infectious. "So is this an idea you and Lisa are just kicking around or has it gone further?"

"We've drafted a business plan, and we've found the property we want. Remember that old school-supply shop on 4th Avenue?"

"Markesteyn's?"

"That's the one. It has a big warehouse area in the back, so it would be perfect for us. And Lisa's brother's an engineer. He's checked out the building. He says it's solid."

"Good buildings don't come cheap."

"We're working on that."

"Zack knows people with deep pockets. Maybe you should talk to him."

"He's been pretty sick. I don't want to rush him."

"Neither do I, but this is exactly the kind of project he'd enjoy. Just wait a couple of days till he's back to normal. Actually, it might be something he and I could work on together."

Mieka rubbed her hands together gleefully. "Let's talk about it. As you probably noticed, I'm pretty stoked about this."

"I noticed," I said. "And it makes me very happy. Now, why don't you buy a potential investor a cup of coffee?"

"My pleasure," Mieka said. "By the way, you just missed Nadine."

"She was here?" I said.

Mieka nodded. "She wasn't here long."

"How did she seem? Noah was at the house when I left. He was concerned about her state of mind."

The timer on the oven clock began to buzz. "The muffins are ready," Mieka said. "Give me three minutes to get them out on the counter, then we can really talk."

I poured myself a mug of coffee, stood by the counter and looked around the room. The demographic of UpSlideDown intrigued me. A disproportionate number of the women were pregnant; most appeared affluent, and all were young. The men wore jeans, carried computer notebooks, and, without exception, were writing novels or screenplays.

It wasn't long before Mieka rejoined me. "To answer your question," she said, "Nadine seemed sad, but calm. When she came in, she did what Abby always did: ordered a latte, sat where Abby always sat, and nibbled at a piece of pastry and watched the kids playing. When I asked if I could join her, she seemed happy to have company."

"I imagine she wanted to talk about Abby."

"She did," Mieka said. "And there wasn't much I could tell her. The only real conversational possibility I ever had with Abby was when she asked me how I could reconcile faith in God with the cruelties of the world. I blew it, and the next night she was dead."

"Did you tell Nadine about Abby's question?"

"No. Once in a while, I actually exercise good judgment. You told me that Nadine was finding comfort in her faith, so I thought it would be kinder not to tell her that the woman she loved had stopped believing." Mieka picked up a paper napkin and dabbed absently at a small spill on the counter. "The only safe topic I could think of was child development. Nadine was fascinated by how much Jacob has learned since she last saw him, so she asked about what babies his age can normally do. Of course, that's the one subject upon which I'm an expert."

"That's not true," I said. "You're one of the smartest women I know."

"When I'm in my own small garden," Mieka said sardonically. "Anyway, I was babbling about the varying rates at which children develop skills, when Lisa came in. At first everything was fine. I introduced Lisa and Nadine. Lisa, who knew nothing about Nadine's circumstances, started asking the usual questions we ask people on their first visit to Regina in winter.

"Nadine was cordial, but they didn't talk long. Lisa had errands to do, so she told Nadine she hoped she'd enjoy her time here, then gave me the package she'd dropped by to return. You'll be interested in this, Mum. People who brought gifts here for Core Rec were supposed to pencil in the age and gender of the child for whom the gift was intended. But one of the gifts had a tag with Delia Wainberg's name on it."

"I'm assuming it was from Abby."

"Yes," Mieka said. "After Lisa told us about the tag, Nadine asked if she could look at the gift. She recognized Abby's handwriting and said she'd like to be alone for a while. Lisa and I took off, and that's when you came in. When Lisa left, I looked over to see how Nadine was doing, but she was gone." Mieka pointed to the table. "The gift is still there."

We went over to the table where Nadine had been sitting. Nadine's latte was still half-full and the gift, a book in which a parent records the highlights of a baby's first year, lay beside it.

I picked up the baby book. Bound in navy leather, its design was clean and handsome. Except for Jacob's full name and his date of birth hand-lettered in copperplate, the cover was unadorned. The heavy vellum pages inside were equally chaste. The first page, in the same copperplate hand, recorded Jacob's time and date of birth, his birth weight and length, and the fact that he had been born at home, in the cabin that Abby shared with Nadine. I remembered the warmth of its living room, the quilts on the walls, the sound of the river flowing past. It would have been a gentle place for a child to enter the world.

I turned to the second page and felt a fist in my stomach. The name of the mother, Abby Margaret Michaels, had been written in the same careful calligraphy, but the name of the father had been entered in an angry scrawl of black ink that had torn the paper.

The name was Theodore Lazar Brokaw.

I gasped. My first thought was that in her agony at discovering she'd lost the parents she'd believed were her birth parents, Abby had transposed facts. I turned the page. More furious scrawls of black ink. These scrawls all but obliterated the lettering that identified Jacob's maternal grandparents as Hugh and Margaret Michaels. The new names angrily entered were Delia Margolis Wainberg and Theodore Lazar Brokaw.

Mieka had been looking over my shoulder. "My God. How could that happen?" she breathed.

Fragments of conversations floated to the surface of my consciousness. Myra's chilling observation. "He always went for the same type: clever, pale, Semitic." Nadine's whispered hypothesis when Mieka asked if she knew who fathered Abby's baby: "I always thought it was someone who had already proven himself in the world." Theo's confusion the night of the Wainbergs' party when he saw Delia: "You've gotten old." The way he'd buried his face in her neck, and his relief when he smelled her Chanel No. 5, the same perfume Abby wore. The photograph I'd shown him, where he had identified Abby not as his daughter but as "my girl, my clever girl." His sense that Jacob was somehow connected with him. The world had become a confusing place for Theo Brokaw, but his damaged brain had stubbornly held on to certain facts. He knew that it was the second-smallest of the nesting dolls that was the carrier of the secret. He knew that Abby Michaels was the mother of his baby.

CHAPTER

14

Mieka touched the mutilated name of Abby's father and lover with her forefinger, and then closed the baby book. "What are we going to do with this, Mum?"

"I don't know," I said. "Abby wanted Delia to know the truth about Theo Brokaw's relationship to Jacob, but telling Delia isn't going to change anything. It's just going to cause more grief." I picked up the book. "Do you have a shredder?"

Mieka shook her head. "No, but I have a match."

"This book is evidence in a murder case."

"That doesn't mean it won't burn," Mieka said.

"We're not the only ones who saw it," I said. "Nadine Perrault knows the truth."

"She must be feeling as sick as we are," Mieka said.

"Yes, but I'm sure she's also relieved. The book is proof that Nadine wasn't responsible for Abby's despair in the last weeks of her life."

"Do you think Nadine will use this to get custody of Jacob?"

"I don't know," I said. I picked up the book and dropped it back in the gift bag. "But now that you've raised that possibility, I know that we can't destroy this. Nadine has a right to use it."

"It's a powerful weapon," Mieka said.

"It is," I agreed. "And if Nadine uses it, there will be collateral damage. She might get custody of Jacob, but he'll have to live with some very painful knowledge. So will the Wainbergs."

"Do you think that's where Nadine went when she left here?"

I narrowed my eyes at my daughter. "You seem to have developed a knack for raising the worst possibilities. But as Zack says, 'It's better to know than not know.'" I took out my cell and thumbed my address book till I found Nadine's number.

The phone rang repeatedly without a response, and I was about to end the call when she answered.

"I'd just about given up," I said. "It's Joanne. Where are you?"

Her voice was mechanical. "On the corner, just down the street from UpSlideDown – waiting for a taxi to come by."

"There won't be one," I said, "it's a busy time of year. Come inside. I'll drive you wherever you want to go."

Nadine came back through the door a couple of minutes later. She was wearing the smart outfit she'd been wearing the day she arrived in Regina, but the pea jacket was unbuttoned; the black cloche was stuck carelessly in her pocket, and her scarf hung around her neck, unknotted and askew. She was pale and she was shaking either from cold or shock or both. The deadness in her eyes scared me. "Did you see Jacob's baby book?" she asked.

"I did," I said. "Nadine, I'm so sorry. I can only imagine what you're going through."

Mieka noticed Nadine's pallor. "Sit down," she said. "I'm going to bring you some tea with lots of sugar. That'll help."

We found a table near the door. A mother with three very young boys was sitting on a bench next to us, attempting to get her children into boots and snowsuits. The boys, determined to stay and play, kept running off on her. When one of the boys ran past me the mother shot me a beseeching look. "Could you . . . ?" I reached out and touched the boy's arm. "Who's that on your boot?"

"SpongeBob SquarePants," he said.

"Could you hold still so I could see him?" I said.

The boy held up his foot. "Is he your favourite?" I asked. While the boy told me about SpongeBob, his mother zipped his brothers into their snowsuits and readied them for the trip home. When she took her son from me, she smiled at Nadine and me. "Thanks," she said. "I hope you both have a very merry Christmas."

"I'm sure you will," Nadine said. We watched as the mother shepherded her boys through the door and turned to give us a final wave. Mieka came back with the tea, and as Nadine drank it, the colour returned to her cheeks. When she was finished, she stood, buttoned her jacket, tied her scarf, and pulled on her hat. She was calm again; she was also very determined.

My mind raced as we walked to the car. I was certain that Nadine would ask me to drive her to the Wainbergs'. I couldn't refuse, but if I could convince her to wait until the morning to talk to Delia, there was a chance she'd arrive at the same conclusion I had: the price of revealing the identity of Jacob's father was simply too high.

When we had snapped on our seat belts, I turned the key in the ignition, but I didn't pull into traffic. I turned to Nadine, prepared to present my argument, but she beat me to the punch. "I'd like you to take me to Theo Brokaw," she said. "If you don't know the address, I'm sure Delia Wainberg will have it."

I was reeling. "I know the address," I said. "But taking you there is pointless. Theo had a serious fall on the Labour Day weekend. He suffered a brain injury that's resulted in something like advanced Alzheimer's. You won't be able to make him understand what's happened."

"I'll make him understand," Nadine said fiercely. "I'll make him understand that he's a monster."

"No one can justify what Theo did," I said. "But Delia says that he didn't know Abby was his child, and I believe her. Delia was in love with Theo, but he was married and their relationship ended." I took a breath. "His wife says that there were many other women over the years and all of them bore a marked resemblance to Delia."

"So he was drawn to Abby because she was his *type.*" Nadine spat out the word. "He must have been thrilled to prove his virility with the reincarnation of another young woman he seduced."

I touched her arm. "Nadine, don't speculate about what went on between Abby and Theo. It will tear you apart."

"I'm already torn apart. I've never believed I was capable of hating another human being. But I would kill Theo Brokaw without a second's hesitation."

"Given his present state, that would be a kindness," I said.

Nadine's laugh was bitter. "In that case, he gets to live. I still want to see him, Joanne. He committed incest. He destroyed the life of the woman I loved. Even if he doesn't understand my words, I need to make him feel the horror of what he's done."

"All right," I said. "I'll take you to him."

I'd just started to pull out of my parking spot when my cell rang. The ringtone was a new one but it was instantly recognizable: Marvin Gaye's "Sexual Healing." Zack had been playing with the ringtone that morning. His intent had been to make me smile, but his timing could not have been worse.

When Zack heard my voice, he was playful. "Like the new ringtone? It carries a message."

"I picked up on that," I said. "You must be feeling better."

"I am. When are you going to be home, Ms. Shreve?"

"Half an hour at the outside," I said.

"Would a martini be in order?"

"God, yes."

"I love you," he said.

"I love you, too." I rang off. When I turned to Nadine, I saw that she had tears in her eyes. "I'm sorry," I said.

"No need to apologize for loving and being loved," she said, and then turned away.

We didn't speak again until I turned into the parking space behind the Brokaws' condo. Louise's Mercedes was there. When I pulled the key from the ignition, Nadine seemed surprised. "You're not coming in with me, are you?"

"I don't like the idea of you being alone with the Brokaws."

Nadine gave me a quarter-smile. "Neither do I," she said.

Myra answered my buzz from the lobby, but when I announced myself she was curt. "We're not receiving visitors."

"If you want to keep Theo's incestuous relationship with Abby from becoming public knowledge, you'd be wise to let me come up. I'm not alone, Myra. Abby Michaels's partner is with me."

The entrance door clicked open. Nadine and I rode up in the tiny elevator. When we stepped out, we could hear Louise playing Bach. She was hitting the right notes in the right order. Once, when she stumbled, she went back and began the phrase again. We were hearing Louise, not a recording. She was still sober. One small candle in the darkness.

Nadine stood for a moment with her eyes closed, listening intently. "There's still beauty in the world, isn't there?" she said softly. The she squared her shoulders and breathed deeply. "I have to do this, Joanne. Thank you for understanding."

Myra opened her door as soon as I knocked, but she didn't invite us in, so I stepped past her. Nadine followed. "We won't stay long, Myra," I said. "This is Nadine Perrault. She was Abby's partner."

Myra's laugh was forced and unpleasant. "That's a new wrinkle. The last of my husband's clever girls preferred other clever girls."

Nadine tensed. I touched her arm. "Nadine wants to see Jacob's father," I said. "It's important to her, and it won't matter to Theo."

"You don't know a damn thing about what matters to Theo," Myra hissed. Then she slapped my cheek in a movement as vicious as it was sudden. "Get out," she said.

My face was stinging, but I stood my ground. When people behave badly, they want the encounter to end quickly, and I wasn't about to cede that advantage to Myra Brokaw. The quarrel with her was too significant to lose. My voice was surprisingly even. "Myra, you can't continue to care for Theo alone," I said. "It's hurting you both. You need respite, and he needs professional help."

Her tone was withering. "And where exactly do you think I could find a caregiver with the stomach to clean up the kind of messes that Theo makes?"

Nadine spoke for the first time. "Competent professionals know how to clean up a man who soils himself. That's part of their job, Ms. Brokaw. If your biggest problem is your husband's hygiene, you're blessed."

Myra's eyes were icy. "There are other ways in which a man can soil himself, Ms. Perrault. The night of the blizzard I walked into this room and found my husband having sex with your lover. At one point, she had been his all-too-willing partner."

Nadine's intake of breath was audible. "You knew," she said.

Myra's voice was thick with rage. "I've been spared nothing. After Theo's accident, I found their e-mails to one another. They were sickening. Theo and that woman believed their relationship was a fair exchange. She wanted a brilliant child and she got one; Theo wanted his youth, and for a few weeks he recaptured it. As it turns out, they paid in hard coin for their choices." Myra's smile was a rictus. "Apparently, when your lover found out the truth about her relationship with Theo, she came here to confront him. I was at the Medical Centre being treated for an injury."

"The wrist you sprained when you slipped on the ice," I said.

Myra corrected me. "The wrist Theo sprained when I kept him from going back to the Wainbergs' party to see 'his clever girl.' My point is that I left Theo alone, and that was a mistake. The scene I walked in on when I returned was stomach-turning. My husband was clutching his new clever girl around the neck, uttering endearments. From the angle of her head, I was certain she was already dead."

Beside me Nadine recoiled as if she'd been punched. Myra was oblivious. "I waited until Theo ejaculated because I knew that would calm him. Incidentally, he doesn't know your lover died. He thought she was simply distressed."

"You didn't tell him," I said.

"I try not to upset him."

Nadine stifled a sob, and I pressed on. "If Abby Michaels died here, how did her body end up in her car?"

"Theo has a wife who loves him," Myra said. "And a loving wife has a price beyond rubies." Her attention shifted to Nadine. "That's something you'll never understand, clever girl. A loving wife will perform actions that a 'competent professional' would never consider. After I'd cleaned Theo, I searched

Abby Michaels's purse and found her Ontario driver's licence and a receipt from a local gas station. I went downstairs, checked our parking lot, and saw a car with Ontario plates. The keys in Abby Michaels's purse fit the lock."

"You put Abby's body in her car and drove it to the parking lot," I said.

Myra's eyes met mine. "The pain in my wrist was excruciating, but we do what we must do, and Theo certainly wasn't capable of handling the situation. Despite my injured wrist, I dragged the body to Abby Michaels's car. I drove until I found an appropriately remote parking lot, pulled in, shut the car door, and walked home. Ten blocks, through a blizzard. Again, Ms. Perrault, not something your 'competent professional' would do."

"You left Abby alone," Nadine said bleakly. Her face crumpled at the image. This time, she made no attempt to control her weeping. The sound drew Theo out of his bedroom. As always, he was immaculately dressed. He went to Nadine and reached out to her as if to comfort her. She stared at him in disbelief, and then she began to scream. Theo looked blankly at his wife. "Did I make this one cry, too?" he asked.

"Don't give her a second thought, darling. She's just a whore, like all the others." Myra took her husband's arm. "Come sit by the window where you can enjoy the skaters," she said silkily. "In a little while, I'll bring your tea and some of those biscuits you like." She turned to us. "Get out," she said and slammed the door.

Nadine's eyes were wide with horror. "How can she do this?" she asked.

"I don't know," I said. I took the cell from my bag and called 911. After I'd described the situation to the police, I called Zack and told him that Theo Brokaw was about to be arrested for murder and he'd need a lawyer. I explained that Myra would be charged as an accomplice and she would need a lawyer too. As I knew he would, Zack said he'd be right there. When I rang off, I dropped the cell back in my bag, and Nadine and I walked out into the corridor to watch the twinkling lights on the ficus, listen to the piano, and wait. At one point, Louise Hunter opened her door a crack and saw us. "Is there anything I can do to help?" she asked.

Pain ravaged Nadine's delicate features. "Keep playing Bach," she said.

Louise's music was the only sound we heard as we waited for the police. The Brokaw apartment was silent. At one point, Nadine's eyes travelled to the Brokaws' door. "What do you think Myra's doing in there?" she asked.

"There's no way she can prepare Theo for what's to come," I said. "I imagine she's just making him comfortable."

"Being a good wife," Nadine said. She shook her head sadly. "Myra had the quotation wrong, you know. It isn't a wife whose price is beyond rubies. It's a virtuous woman."

After the police arrived, everything happened quickly. Nadine and I were escorted back into the Brokaws' apartment in time to witness what, under other circumstances, would have been a poignant scene. Uniformed officers separated Myra and Theo, so they could be interviewed. Theo appeared dazed and frightened, and as he passed her, Myra took one of the martini glasses of candy from the counter and shook some jellybeans into his hand. Theo gobbled them and gave her a winningly boyish smile.

A male officer stayed with Nadine in the corridor and Debbie Haczkewicz ushered me into Myra's sitting room. I sat on the cranberry-coloured reading chair. Debbie's eyes met mine. "I am so relieved that this is over," she said.

As I answered Debbie's questions I faced the photographs Myra Brokaw had taken to create the self-portrait of the aging fragmented woman she believed herself to be. I remembered the sympathy I'd felt for her as she'd talked about the "little death" she'd experienced in leaving everything of her old life behind in Ottawa. Then I remembered her cold disposal of the woman Theo had raped and murdered, and averted my eyes.

Zack came. He'd brought another lawyer with him, a man named Tyler Maltman. I recognized him, as we'd been seated across the table from one another at a fund-raising dinner a few weeks before. I remembered Zack had told me that, of all the smart young defence lawyers in town, Tyler Maltman's name was the one most frequently written on the walls of the cells. According to Zack, a positive jailhouse rating was the equivalent of a starred consumer report. As I watched Tyler stride into the room where Myra was being held, I knew he had his work cut out for him.

After Zack embraced me and assured himself that Nadine and I were both all right, he told me that, given the complexity of this case, he might be a while. His excitement was palpable. He wheeled his chair with real vigour towards the room where his new client was waiting. For him, the good times were back.

Nadine and I left together. When we stepped outside, Nadine's eyes swept the pedestrian mall. People were shopping and skating, and the man who looked like a sumo wrestler was ringing his bell for donations. "Ordinary life," Nadine said. "All this was going on when we were in there with Myra. How can that be?"

"I don't know," I said. "All I know is that you and I have to become part of ordinary life again, and the sooner the better. How would you feel about going back to my place and taking our dogs for a run?"

Nadine's smile was faint. "You're the driver."

Except for Willie and Pantera, the house was deserted. There was a note from Taylor on the kitchen table reminding me that it was our turn to feed the feral cats, and Declan had volunteered to help out because she knew I'd been delayed. I called and told our daughter that all was well and that Declan was on my hero list.

There'd been many times in my life when I'd found physical activity to be the perfect antidote for overheated emotions. That day as Nadine, warm in one of Taylor's jackets and a pair of her snow pants, ran beside me along the levee, I knew that while the horror of the last few weeks would never leave her, Nadine had not been broken by it.

Later, sitting at the kitchen table waiting for the milk to heat for cocoa, Nadine leaned back in her chair. Our run had drained the tension from her body, and she was ready to talk. "I was aware of Theo Brokaw," she said. "Not that he was the one; just that Abby and he were acquainted. When she was finishing her dissertation, Abby needed a summer without distractions, and she rented a cottage at Stony Lake. Theo Brokaw was her neighbour. He was working on a book, and he, too, required solitude."

"Myra wasn't there?"

"Abby never mentioned her, but she did speak highly of Theo. She said he'd read her dissertation and asked all the right questions."

"A mentor," I said. "Someone she could trust."

"What's going to happen to him?" Nadine asked.

"Zack should be home in a while, he can give you a general idea, but Theo's his client, now, so . . . "

"I understand." Nadine stood. "Joanne, is there a church near here where I could go to mass tonight? One within walking distance?"

"Holy Rosary," I said. "But it's a long walk."

"I need a long walk," she said. "My mind is crowded with thoughts that have no place in a church."

When she was leaving for mass, Nadine started to put on

her pea jacket. "You'll freeze in that," I said. "Wear Taylor's jacket and snow pants. I can drop your clothes off at the Chelton tomorrow morning."

"Thank you," Nadine said. "But please don't bring the clothes to the hotel. I'd welcome an excuse to come back for a visit."

When Zack came through the front door, he looked like himself again. "I think I could handle a martini," he said.

"Nothing like a red-meat case to bring a guy back from the brink," I said.

Zack grinned. "And this case is going to be a doozy."

"What's going to happen to Theo?"

"Well, the only way out, if the facts can be proved – and they will be proved – is to show that Theo had no capacity to form intent. There are differing intents for murder and manslaughter. I'm going to be straddling a fine line. I need to prove Theo had no capacity to form intent when he killed Abby, but that will be difficult if the Crown can prove that despite Theo's brain damage, there were moments when he did remember his relationship with her."

"And there were those moments," I said. "There were also e-mails revealing the nature of his relationship with Abby. Myra found them."

Zack tensed. "Do the e-mails still exist?"

"My guess is that Myra printed them out and filed them. She has an archivist's zeal to preserve every scrap of information about her husband."

"Even his e-mails to another woman? Boy, Myra really is something else. When I left to go to the police station with Theo, she advised me not to try to separate Theo's interests from hers. She said that she and Theo cast a single shadow and that there was no way I could destroy her without destroying my client."

"Consider yourself warned," I said.

My husband shuddered. "Warned and spooked," he said. "Myra makes the hair on the back of my neck stand up. Fortunately, while the Brokaws may cast a single shadow, the law makes it impossible for them to share a single defence. I'll call Debbie and tell her about the e-mails, but between thee and me, I hope the cops don't find them. If anything in those e-mails suggests Theo was capable of remembering his relationship with Abby, it'll be tougher to prove his capacity was diminished when he put his hands around her neck."

"What if he thought the woman who'd come to him was Delia? You saw how time shifts for him. He and Delia were lovers, and for Theo, twenty-seven years ago and yesterday appear to be pretty much the same thing."

Zack raised his glass to me. "Glad you're on my side, Jo. Jesus, what a mess, eh?"

"So what's going to happen to Theo?"

Zack sighed. "He murdered a woman and then raped her, so he won't be sentenced to a day at the beach. If we're lucky and he's found not criminally responsible because of mental disorder, he'll be held in a suitable secure facility until a review panel finds him 'recovered.'"

"Which will be never."

"Barring a miracle – and I'm not counting on one – Theo will be in a closed medical facility for the rest of his life. The court will have to determine the appropriate place. My guess is he'll end up in the regional psych centre in Saskatoon.

"Anyway, that's the best-case scenario. At the moment, my job is to find a psychiatrist to show insanity or diminished capacity. How it plays with the jury depends on testimony about Theo's conduct before and mostly after the fatal encounter with Abby. Of course, the Crown will be calling its own psychiatrist."

"What about Myra?"

"She'll be charged as accessory unless Tyler can cut a deal with the Crown on a lesser charge – something like obstructing justice or fabricating evidence. In any case, chances are high she'll be convicted. She may even plead guilty in return for a lighter sentence."

"And then what?"

"If Tyler gets the Crown to agree to a lesser charge, Myra will serve nominal time, then she'll be let out on probation. She'll have to perform a whack of community service, but she will walk among us."

"Do you think Tyler will be able to get the Crown to agree to a lesser charge?"

Zack raised his eyebrows. "His chances would have been better if the police hadn't found a loaded revolver when they searched the Brokaws' condo. Myra said that the gun was her insurance policy in case Theo grew worse."

"She was planning on a murder-suicide?"

"That's what the lady claims. But I'm sure the Crown will point out that more than one loaded gun has been used for a purpose other than the one for which the gun was purchased. This is not going to be a slam-dunk for Tyler, but he's sharp and he has a good ear for what resonates with a jury. He'll pull out all the stops. Myra was the loyal wife who subsumed herself in her husband's career. She devoted herself to Theo, enduring his repeated infidelities with grace, and then, when he committed an act of unspeakable horror, risked everything to preserve his reputation."

"It sounds as if Myra has the right lawyer."

"She does," Zack said. "And this case won't do Tyler any harm. It's going to be high-profile – plenty of media, plenty of focus on the principal players. By the time the case comes to trial, Theo and Myra will be legends."

"Yet another example of being careful what you wish for," I said.

"How so?"

"Myra was afraid people would forget her husband. Now it appears that both she and Theo are going to be remembered for a long time to come."

That night as I made my final pass through the house, making certain that doors were locked and that everything that should be turned off was turned off, I stopped in front of the pomegranate wreath Myra had crafted. I was already in my pyjamas, but I didn't hesitate. I found a jacket and boots in the front closet and, dressed for outdoors, came back to the living room, took down the wreath, and walked out on our deck, then across our yard to the gate that opened onto our back alley. After I put the wreath in the dumpster, the lid slammed down with a satisfying finality.

The Brokaws were not so easily disposed of. Despite his bravado, Zack was still recuperating, and another pressure sore had developed. At my urging, Henry Chan ordered Zack to conduct as much business as possible from home at least until the New Year. So from the beginning I had an insider's view of how Zack was handling Theo Brokaw's case.

In the late afternoon on the day after Theo and Myra were arrested, Theo's sisters arrived on our doorstep. The Brokaw women were sturdy, handsome, and sensibly dressed for a Saskatchewan winter. They were also clearly at a loss about how to deal with this situation.

I ushered them into our office where Zack would have the cruel task of explaining how their adored baby brother had come to be arrested for rape and murder. There was one bright spot. That afternoon we had received information that made Zack's task easier and, though they would never know it, lightened the burden the sisters would carry for the rest of their lives.

The DNA test results had come in, and as Abby's mother

and Jacob's grandmother, Delia was told the results. Noah delivered the information to us in person. Characteristically, he was direct and matter-of-fact. "Theo is Jacob's biological father," he said. "But he didn't father Abby."

"Whoa," Zack said. "So if it wasn't Theo, who was it?"

Noah's crooked smile was infinitely sad. "Me," he said. "And there's no doubt. When the police took the DNA sample from Delia, I asked them to take one from me. It wasn't likely, but it was possible. Delia and I had sex when I took her home with me the day after the fight at the restaurant."

"Why didn't she mention this earlier?" Zack said.

"She didn't remember," Noah said. "I guess our love-making was of so little consequence to Dee that it just slipped her mind."

Zack and I exchanged glances and lowered our eyes.

"I'm okay with this," Noah said softly. "Actually, more than okay. It hurts to know that Abby died before we had a chance to meet. But I'm grateful that Delia and Jacob don't have to carry that ugliness with them." He stood. "I thought you should know about the DNA before Theo's sisters arrive. No need to make the situation worse for them than it already is."

I wasn't present when Zack talked to Theo's sisters. When they filed out of the office, they had obviously been crying, but they held their heads high.

The final sister to leave seemed to have been appointed spokesperson. Her words were oddly formal, as if she'd written them out and memorized them. "It wasn't Theo who did that terrible thing," she said. "It was the shell of the man he was. Deprived of humanity and faith, we're all vulnerable to evil." She raised her dark eyes, so like her brother's, to meet mine. "Do you understand what I'm saying?"

I remembered the baptisms of my children and grand-children. And the old question: *Do you renounce the evil powers of this world, which corrupt and destroy the creatures of God?*

"Yes," I said, "I understand what you're saying."

Zack threw himself into Theo Brokaw's case with the fervour of a first-year law student. The legal arguments were complex and engrossing, but it was the medical aspect of Theo's case that intrigued Zack. He had never had reason to delve into the science of traumatic brain injury, and he was greedy for knowledge. His desk was heaped with printouts of articles that dealt with the symptoms and consequences of injury to the frontal lobe of the brain, and every morning someone from Falconer Shreve would arrive with new information. Zack devoured it all.

I had my own preoccupation. For over a year, I'd been weighing the possibility of taking early retirement from the university. I liked my work, but I was no longer passionate about it, and there were many other things I wanted to do. The idea of helping Mieka and Lisa Wallace bring their project for inner-city kids to fruition appealed to me, and it appealed to Zack, who had been an inner-city kid himself. When I expressed interest, Mieka was quick to take me on a tour of Markestyn's, the empty school-supply shop on 4th Avenue. To my untutored eye, it was the perfect site for UpSlideDownToo. Centrally located in a residential neighbourhood whose best days were long past, two blocks from a community school, the new UpslideDown could become a magnet for young children and those who cared for them.

On our next visit to the building, Mieka and I had company. Zack and his partner Blake Falconer, whose specialty was real estate, came along. They were both impressed. Blake said he'd get a structural engineer to check out the building, but it was a nice piece of real estate. "A good investment for your old age," he said.

When he heard Blake's words, a shadow crossed Zack's face.

I met his eyes. "Zack and I pretty much focus on the here and now," I said.

"Fair enough," Blake said, and that was the end of the discussion. But for me, that shadow was the tipping point. The deadline for requesting early retirement was December 31. Our wedding anniversary was January 1. I went home and wrote my letter.

I wasn't the only one with plans to change her work life. Delia was honouring her promise to practise law part-time. The adjustment wasn't easy for her, but she had committed herself to caring for Jacob, and she was doing a fine job.

Noah finished the woodcarving of the small bear that represented Jacob, and on the longest night of the year, the Wainbergs had an informal ceremony on their lawn to put the new carving in place. Nadine stayed in town for the event, and at her suggestion, Noah ordered wood for a final bear – a female who would represent Abby.

Kym continued to come over for a couple of hours every day until the morning of Christmas Eve. He and Zack had hit it off, and so when Kym left me his contact information, I filed it carefully, even though I hoped it would be years – or at least months – until I had to use it.

Christmas was the usual blur, but there were some fine moments. Zack managed to score two extra tickets to the Pats' game, so he and I had our first of what we assumed would be many double dates with Declan and Taylor. Angus and Leah, both beaming, and with their cheeks burnished from hours on the ski slopes, arrived back from Whistler on Christmas Eve. I didn't need to hear the announcement to know that they were once again a couple. I had always believed that Leah Drache was the right woman for Angus and knowing that she was in our lives again was the first gift of our holiday.

There were other memorable gifts. Taylor finished her self-portrait in time to give it to Zack on Christmas morning. Zack was not an easy man to thrill with a gift, but he was so touched by the painting that he called a halt to the present opening until he could see how the self-portrait looked in our family room. My gift from Taylor was a pair of fuzzy socks and two rectangular canvases. On one canvas, she had copied out Pablo Neruda's "Ode to a Sock" in English; on the other, she had written out the poem in Spanish. The margins of both canvases were decorated with fanciful drawings of socks.

When I'd given her Neruda's *Odes to Common Things* for her birthday, she'd been polite, but she hadn't been exactly bowled over. "I didn't know you even opened that book," I said.

"That day Isobel came over, she read some of the poems out loud while I painted," Taylor said. "You and I had had that talk about the kind of life experiences I needed to make art, so when Isobel was reading, I really listened. Then I read the poems myself, and I started to think about what Pablo Neruda was saying. You've read the poems, haven't you?"

"Many times," I said.

"Then you know what they're about," Taylor said. "They're about how amazing ordinary things are: tables, chairs, yellow flowers, oranges, French fries . . . "

"Cats," I said.

Taylor grinned. "And dogs. And socks." She frowned. "Is that what you were trying to tell me by giving me the book?"

"No," I said. "I just wanted my socks back."

We drove up to the lake on Boxing Day. I hadn't yet seen the skating rink that was my Christmas gift from Zack, but the minute our children and grandchildren spied the smooth expanse of ice, we knew it was a hit. The kids skated, with occasional ski and toboggan breaks, all day, and after dinner, they turned on the fairy lights strung across the branches of the trees circling the rink, and went back at it.

Zack and I stayed indoors watching, our hands touching. We were at peace and grateful for it. When Lena and Maddy spotted us watching them from the window and turned to wave, Zack and I exchanged glances. "Who has more fun than us?" he said.

"Nobody," I said. "Nobody has more fun than us." The shadow I'd seen on Zack's face the day Blake Falconer talked about our old age appeared again. This time I was ready for it. I stood. "Do you remember promising that when you were better, we'd have a Kevin Costner kiss – one of those long, slow, deep, soft kisses that last three days?" I said.

Zack nodded. "I remember," he said.

"It happens that I'm free for the next three days," I said.

Zack pointed his chair towards the hall that led to our bedroom. "That's lucky," he said. "Because so am I."

As long, slow, deep, soft kisses frequently do, Zack's and mine developed into something more stirring than a kiss. It had been a while since we made love, and for both of us the joining of our bodies was a homecoming. Finally, sated and grateful, we lay hand in hand, listening to the kids playing on the ice, convinced that we might be immortal after all.

ACKNOWLEDGEMENTS

Thanks to Janette Seibel for suggesting the possibilities of the articling year; to Rick Mitchell, retired Staff Sergeant in charge of Major Crimes Section, Regina Police Service; to my editor, Dinah Forbes, for her intelligent and sensitive editing and her friendship; to Lynn Schellenberg, for bringing a fresh and perceptive eye to the manuscript; to Ashley Dunn, who is as determined as she is lovely, and – as always – to Ted, who makes everything possible.